THE STONE IN THE SKULL

THE
STONE
IN THE
SKULL

ELIZABETH BEAR

TOR

A TOM DOHERTY ASSOCIATES BOOK
NEW YORK

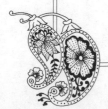

THE STONE IN THE SKULL

Copyright © 2017 by Sarah Wishnevsky Lynch

A Tor Book
Published by Tom Doherty Associates
175 Fifth Avenue
New York, NY 10010

www.tor-forge.com

Tor® is a registered trademark of Macmillan Publishing Group, LLC.

The Library of Congress Cataloging-in-Publication Data is available upon request.

ISBN 978-0-7653-8013-5 (hardcover)
ISBN 978-1-4668-7207-3 (ebook)

Our books may be purchased in bulk for promotional, educational, or business use. Please contact your local bookseller or the Macmillan Corporate and Premium Sales Department at 1-800-221-7945, extension 5442, or by email at MacmillanSpecialMarkets@macmillan.com.

First Edition: October 2017

Printed in the United States of America

0 9 8 7 6 5 4 3 2 1

*This book is for Gretchen Albright,
my oldest friend.*

Love and empires end together
where continuence[1] sliceth.
In the cage of thy ribs
the cold blade's finger
gropeth at the heart.

> —The poetess Ümmühan,
>   fragment, circa 1700 A.F.
>   (After the Frost)

[1]In the original Asitaneh, the word the poet selected means something like "time" and something like "the enduring influence of past choices" and something like "history and the impact of history."

Dragon Lake

Eighteen
River Crossing

Wretched Mountain

Singing Towers

THE SONG
PRINCIPALITIES

Dragon Roads
10,000 Mile Tomb

BITTER SEA

Stone Lily

Amoy

D O M

Guran

SEA
of
STORMS

Banner Isles

RHYS DAVIES

THE STONE IN THE SKULL

1

THE MOUNTAIN WORE A MIRRORED MASK. ICE SHEATHED THE SHEER
face rising above both a steep river valley and the melancholy man in
the red coat below. That ice reflected a pale sun that blazed light
without heat. The glacier shimmered against a sky like glass, so lim-
pid and still that it seemed each of the encircling peaks held its
breaths against some whispered promise.

The ice-gilt mountains were themselves reflected, and bent toward
a vanishing point in the polished egg-shape of another mirrored mask,
this one much smaller. This mirror made up the face—the entire
head—of a brass man who toiled mechanically up the slope of the
notch below and between the snow-bright peaks. A wrap of cowl had
fallen back from his featureless metal skull. His heavy hands gleamed
as if they wore brass gauntlets. His brass feet were strapped into iron-
thorned crampons without benefit of boots.

He climbed without urgency.

The crampon spikes bit into the ice of a river made into stone by
the cold. A hawser thick as a woman's wrist draped over the brass
man's shoulder. It stretched behind him on a weighty arc, reaching
back to the curved prow of a strange ship: square-rigged, boasting a

lofty reptilian figurehead gallantly painted in red and gold—but resting on two curved, ice-encased runners that bore it over the surface of the stone-hard river as if glass slid oiled on glass. A pilot stood on the little platform at the back of the bowsprit, peering up at the slopes above through a glass. Though it was early in the winter for avalanches, it was never too early for care.

Behind that ship was another, its dragon head limned in azure with copper gilt, drawn by four of the shaggy nimble oxen common to the region, as well as seven people with their own iron cleats strapped over their fleece-and-fur-lined boots. Behind that was a third, in shades of orange and crimson, likewise being dragged by its erstwhile passengers and a pair of the hairy yaks. And at the back of the line was the fourth and final ice-ship, painted wood mimicking carven jade and beryl, with its complement of laborers and cattle, and behind *that* walked several people considered unsuited to heavy hauling by dint of size, rank, age, status as paying customers, or infirmity.

The man in the red coat followed them all. He was last in line because he chose to be last in line. And because he was watching behind and below, as befitted a caravan guard—which was what he was. At least, it was what he was today, though the caution of the guardian was not the only anxiety gnawing in his breast.

He was a Dead Man, or he had been, and he wore the name of his former profession still. He and the other walkers stayed to the edge of the river for two reasons. First, they did not have cleats—those were reserved for the people hauling the becalmed ice-ships—and so they sensibly kept to the rougher ice and better traction along the bank. Second, the four ice-ships dragged and groaned in their heavy traces.

The pilots made a profession of bringing people safely through the mountains called the Steles of the Sky, it was true. And it was true also that it was mere superstition to cling to the riverbanks, when if by some mishap the ice-ships were to break loose they were unlikely to meekly follow the course of the river back down again.

Even knowing this, the Dead Man still edged off to the left whenever he could. It made him feel a tiny bit safer, even if they were walking from a place where he had never belonged to another one where he expected to feel restless and alone once more.

He had learned young that it was fruitless to worry about things he could not control. And there was very little here that he could have any effect on, but he could not seem to find his calm, or—as his long-lost beloved Zillah would have said with a smile, his resigned soldier's center—and let events take what course they would.

It wasn't the caravan duty that still had him so agitated, when they had left Asmaracanda months before, and unless you counted the Lizard-Folk brigands and the wildfire in the grasslands, those months had been mostly uneventful. No, what he was worrying about—still—was that it had *been* months.

He and the Gage carried a message, and that duty was the real motivation for their travel. Because they had been entrusted with it by the so-called Eyeless One: the most powerful Wizard in the world's greatest city, which was the teeming market center called Messaline.

The mere existence of that message, and his charge to deliver it, left the Dead Man jittering. Wizards generally had terrible, selfish reasons for what they did, but the Eyeless One was different. This duty came from a being who had preserved Messaline in its time against plague and invasion. And while the Dead Man had no idea what catastrophe might result from a failure, he was confident that it would be far worse than a mere destroyed caravan and a few dozen souls perished in the snow.

As if to give the lie to his thoughts, the wreckage of other caravans were heaped here and there, abandoned under a halfhearted cover of drifted snow, providing no additional reassurance. Since breaking camp that morning, the caravan had passed at least a half-dozen shattered wagons and staved ice-ships, eyeless and picked-over as scavenged carcasses. In summer, there was the danger of avalanche. In winter, there was . . . well, there was the winter.

Like the brass-fitted Gage at the top of the column, the Dead Man

had no public name in particular. Unlike the Gage, he hadn't ne-
glected his cowl, and wore a veil drawn up to conceal (and warm) his
face, leaving revealed only a set of eyes that few dared meet. He wore
the red, felted, skirted coat that marked him as a Dead Man, one of
the elite royal guards of a caliphate that no longer exactly existed.
He had not set the livery of his fallen empire aside, even though it
was tattered, much-patched, and faded to a turmeric color in places,
and though he wore another and bulkier overcoat on top. And although there were, per se, no Dead Men anymore. Not the proper
sort, with capital letters, in any case, though the Dead Man assumed
that the other, improper sort would always be leaving the world.

He was cold in the felted coat, despite the layers of other garments
beneath and over it. And he was anxious to the bone. Anxious because
the caravan was a fortnight behind schedule. Anxious because he had
promised someone to complete a task he was given to understand was
critical, and critically timed. And that anxiety, that need to be moving, would not leave him alone.

He knew it helped nothing when he invented scenarios of disaster and cast himself, his partner, and their cargo of dire importance in
the leading roles. When he wrote tragedies that began with the loss
of a note and ended with the loss of a kingdom. And yet, the worm
of urgency gnawed behind his breastbone anyway, spoiling his
frozen and dried and rewarmed-with-boiled-tea dinners, making even
exhausted sleep ragged. If he didn't know better, if he didn't trust
the Eyeless One nearly as he trusted his own Scholar-God, he'd swear
he had been cast under a geis.

Every inevitable and perfectly routine delay along the way—
storms, and illness, and difficulties in obtaining supplies—added to
his burden of anxiety. He wanted the job done, his boots off, and a
well-earned cup of wine. And yet there were still the mountains to
get past, and beyond them a half-dozen warring princedoms.

And yet, *this* mail must go through.

He sweated from the steepness of the pass, and feared the sweat
freezing in his clothing. He was lean as sinew, and that was part of

his misery of chill. The mountains were another element: it was colder here than he had ever known it could be, and even the yak-felt stuffing his boots and his heavy mittens could not keep him from feeling it, though the good clothes kept his fingers and toes from freezing solid.

The Dead Man acknowledged that these factors had some bearing on the shiver in his aching joints and rising up his spine. But as he scanned the sky above and the slopes to either side, he could not help but slide a mittened hand under the flap of his overcoat and touch the hilt of his curved sword. This chill he felt was no mere artifact of the mountain winter, but something inner, and he knew that because it was also no novelty. He'd felt the like before, and knew it for a premonition.

His lips moved in silent prayer to the Scholar-God: *Count on Your beaded necklaces blessings and forgivenesses for this unfortunate one, Most Holy. Dip Your sacred nibs in ink of jewel colors and scribe in the book of Luck good fortune for this unworthy.* Then he wondered what she could do for him, so far from his home and her power, here under the strange sky of strange gods whose names he did not know.

The Dead Man paused for a moment, huffing as he watched the caravan creep incrementally away. Far ahead, the Gage trudged up, implacably. Technically, they were guards—well, they'd signed on as guards because they were traveling to the Lotus Kingdoms with that private message anyway, and they might as well get paid twice for the same trip if they were going—and not draft animals, but the Dead Man had never known the Gage to turn down any task that needed doing.

Maybe invulnerable immortality got boring. The Dead Man, being neither, could not have said.

He pulled into place the slitted wooden mask that protected his eyes, somewhat, from glare, trying to seat it where its inadequate padding would gouge neither chilblains nor pressure sores. He'd catch up in a moment. That feeling of anxiety, of looming threat, was not subsiding. Was worsening into an apprehension of immediate danger, and the Dead Man trusted his instincts too much to shrug it off. Especially now, especially here. He let his attention wander from the Gage and the ice-ships and the teamsters to the passengers who trudged on ahead. Perhaps the threat would come from one of them?

The majority of the gaggle of fur-swaddled, brightly dressed walkers seemed to make less of the slope than the Dead Man did. He supposed that was because they were mostly rather a lot younger, but there was also the matter of the circus.

The Dead Man was an accomplished swordsman—raised to it, and trained in dealing death since he was old enough to pull himself upright with the assistance of a sword and babble at his nursemaids. That was what it meant to be a Dead Man. And he had thought himself fit.

That was before he'd spent two months with three dozen or so youthful acrobats from Song. They were tireless, limber, and prone to breaking into uphill sprints through the snow just for high spirits, like so many colts. *Then* they inevitably had the energy for an hour or two of vaulting, juggling practice, and choreography in camp each night, when all the Dead Man wanted to do was shovel in a bowl of food—the hotter and richer the better—and tumble into sleep while the Gage took the night watch.

The mountains were glorious under the stars. The Dead Man was well and thoroughly sick of them. He wanted a hot bath and a warm bed and a cup of tea that hadn't been brewed off the same stewed leaves two or three times. Or a pot of coffee, sweet and rich with cream. Even better.

There were some additional travelers beyond the circus, and by and large the Dead Man noticed them less because they didn't annoy him. He'd been raised immune to the peculiarities of nobility and the wealthy, and the rest of his charges comprised two merchants, a man who claimed to be a merchant and was probably a smuggler, a minor Song prince and his entourage, a minor Uthman bey and *his* entourage, and a noblewoman from Ctesifon traveling to be married in the Lotus Kingdoms—or, as the locals called them,

Sarath-Sahal or Sahal-Sarat, depending on which of the two major local dialects you were dealing with.

The noblewoman had only a maid and two guards and largely kept to herself, as was proper. The bey was walking; the Song prince was being carried, for the nonce, in a small collapsible sedan chair. It looked less comfortable than walking, given how his attendants lurched and struggled with the ice and snow.

Well, these people were the Dead Man's responsibility, all. No matter how he felt about them.

He would get them to the Lotus Kingdoms hale and hearty, as was proper. He'd only failed a charge of protection once in all his life, so he allowed himself a brief moment of acknowledgment as to how he might be good at it. Then he commenced again to climb.

He wasn't alone in that chain of thought. Above, roustabouts called encouragement to the trudging passengers, and what passed for rough reassurances: "We've climbed this pass every year since the Rasan revolution! We haven't killed a whole caravan yet!"

They were having a little fun at the passengers' expense. The Dead Man was sure that that was all.

The Dead Man turned his head once more, scanning the bright peaks and the knife-cut, shadowed canyons. Earning his pay, even though he didn't expect to be needed. There was that prickly premonition, sure. But it didn't always mean anything. And it didn't always come when it could be useful, either.

There was nothing in this life that you could count on. Not even the intervention of the devoutly worshipped divine.

The Dead Man didn't expect bandits. This would be a damned fine place to starve in the winter, if you were a bandit. Once snow closed the pass, nothing would be getting through for months. No caravans to rob would mean no source of food, with predictable results. But there were other dangers.

He saw the plume of snow burst into the air from the slope above before anyone else except for possibly—*possibly*—the Gage. He saw the sinuous shape slide into flight from the cover of the drifts above and he saw the frozen veils thrown wide as wings snapped out, particles turning, turning, glittering in the painful light. His eye took in the long neck, the fluted tail stretched rigid to counterbalance as the ice-wyrm took wing.

As a swordsman of decades of experience, his professional opinion rapidly concluded that a saber wasn't worth a damned thing under these circumstances.

The Dead Man reached for his gun.

Bright sun shining through translucent wings picked out the colors of snow, silver, ivory, palest dove in twining patterns like intermingled veins, like the reaching branches of bare trees. Light glazed the swift form, stark against a transparent welkin. Then the shadow fell over the caravan, and the sound reached them—not the roar or shriek the Dead Man had anticipated, but just an echoing hiss.

Heads turned. People and livestock froze as if they were mice in the shadow of a hawk. The Dead Man heard one teamster curse, low and fluently, just loud enough to carry in the still air, over the echoing ice.

The wyrm turned, an impossible writhing, a flick of its wings and a reversal within its own length as eloquent as any darting trout within its stream. The wyrm passed over them, low and contemplative, so close the Dead Man felt the wind of its wings and saw the glacial, crystalline eye. The thing was as long from nose to tail as a seagoing vessel, though not as big as a dragon. Its perusal minded him of a sultan idly considering a banquet, wondering with which sweetmeat he should begin.

Because the Dead Man was looking, he saw the moment when the Gage resettled the hawser over his shoulder and dug in—hauling harder, and unbelievably, *speeding up* as he approached the crest of the notch. It wasn't a bad idea: they were pathetically exposed where they were, and the Gage couldn't exactly let go of the rope.

But—below the Gage and above the Dead Man—cattle lowed and struggled, their hooves thrashing on the ice as they fought against

their yokes to run. People pushed and shouted, scattering in singles
and small clumps, skidding and falling in ice and snow.

The wyrm reversed itself once more, making a sweeping pass
over the valley behind them and coming in on a sharp, swooping
glide. This, the Dead Man thought. This was a strike, a raptor's stoop
to the prey. The predator's trajectory was designed, he realized, to
herd them higher in the pass, where the crest would offer them up to
the wyrm's talons with a minimum of risk to the beast.

The Dead Man stood between the wyrm and the caravan.

He pulled the ivory pin from the smaller nozzle in his copper-
chased powder horn between his teeth. The wyrm came on, pale
wings sculling with deceptive languor. With a practiced twist, the
Dead Man primed the snaplock's pan, then replaced the pin. Sparks
near an open powder horn stood a good chance of simply managing
the wyrm's dirty work for it. He dropped the horn on its strap, cocked
the pistol with a grunt of effort, and in a matter of moments had it
leveled.

The wyrm was nearly on him. He raised the pistol as the wyrm
swept over, and when the scales of its belly were in sight—seemingly
so close he could just reach up and stroke them—he squeezed the
trigger.

The pistol slammed his palm. He held on to it, turning to see if
the wyrm was hit. He didn't imagine he could have missed. Not so
close, at something so large. How hard were those scales, anyway?
The thing looked clinker-built, with its overlapping rows of them;
could they turn a pistol ball?

If he had hurt it, it did not seem to have been badly. It struck like
a seabird fishing, reaching down with hooked talons on its powerful
hindlimbs and backwinging to attempt to pluck the more flashily
jeweled of the two noblemen (the one in the sedan chair) from the ice.

It would have succeeded, too, if one of the prince's loyal retainers
hadn't thrown himself under the talons, overturning the Song prince
and his chair.

The bearers staggered under the dual blow. The foremost went to his knees; the rearmost was knocked sprawling. The loyal retainer shrieked once as a fish-hook talon long and curved as a scimitar emerged from his chest, showering red on his lord's silks and jewels and all the snow surrounding. The retainer clutched at the talon with both hands. Another shriek was cut off as the wyrm lofted on the updraft out of the notch, its great wing membranes bellying taut.

If there were any blood from a—strictly hypothetical—bullet wound, it was lost in the crimson spray.

The prince leapt to his feet and shrieked after the wyrm. Or after the retainer, the Dead Man realized, when a few words of the shrieking carried. He was promising retribution on the poor retainer's family, for the sin of having laid hands on the prince.

Fortunately for him, the retainer was too dead by now to regret his self-sacrifice. The prince hopped in the snow, shaking his jeweled fist so facets flashed in the sun. Probably, the Dead Man considered, a poor idea given the existing body of evidence on what provoked ice-wyrm attacks.

Blood rained down on the caravan as the wyrm ascended, banked, and turned its head to snap the now-limp retainer in two. It spiraled up, dining, shedding horrible bits as it rose.

Now the cattle shrilled in panic, surging and falling, as blood and shreds of meat drenched them. "Set the brakes," someone yelled from the nearest ice-ship, but it didn't carry.

The unfortunate retainer's robes fluttered empty from the wan, white sky, trailing like a defeated banner.

"Clear the ice," someone else cried—a woman's voice, clarion-carrying. "Climb, you idiots! Climb!"

That seemed like good advice. The Dead Man floundered uphill, toward the steep slope along the side of the notch. He tried to keep facing the wyrm as he struggled through unpacked, waist-deep drifts, and with his teeth he yanked the larger, bone pin from his horn. In a lack of foresight, his premeasured loads were inside their usual pocket, on the inside hem of his once-red coat, tucked safely away and far out of reach. He would not make that mistake again, if he lived long enough to amend it.

He had to stop climbing to measure the powder. His ammunition case was on the same baldric, and he dragged it out of his open coat-front, not even really feeling the chill. He'd dropped his mittens somewhere and his fingers were numb and clumsy, but he got the case open. The balls were already wadded in oiled patches, and he shook one loose.

A huge voice boomed, resonating as if through a speaking horn. "SET THE BRAKES!"

It was the voice of the Gage, might the Scholar-God bless him, infidel though he was.

The Dead Man fell on ice then, and dropped the ball. But he managed to hold the pistol up, and the pan stayed dry, and the barrel too. He hoped, he hoped. He didn't stand, but balanced on one knee and fumbled for another ball.

Oiled flannel left its grease on his fingers, and the ball slid down the barrel. He pressed the flint back against its spring and primed the pan, not daring to look up until the pistol was loaded and cocked, despite the echoes of screams.

Profoundly, the Dead Man hoped the tales of avalanches provoked by careless whispers were oversold. He did not merely hope; being a religious man he also prayed.

Banks of snow blocked his view on every side around where he crouched. In cold so sharp, the snow was light, powdery. He forced himself to lift his head. He lifted, also, the pistol. His hand shook.

The rearmost ice-ship was in trouble. The laborers had deserted their lines, which tangled the hooves of the yaks. The oxen fought the yoke and one another, and whether the spring-loaded spikes that served the ships as brakes were set or not, it had begun a ponderous, inexorable diagonal slide. Acrobats hustled less-agile nobles and retainers out of the way as the thing skidded and began to grind downward, dragging the bawling cattle with it. The spikes *had* fired. He could tell by the plumes of ice they scraped up on either side of the bow and stern as the thing's plunge accelerated.

Despite the slitted goggles, he'd lost the wyrm in the glare of the sky.

Seasoned warrior, he thought. *Misplacing a whole God-forsaken ice-wyrm.*

He shaded his eyes with cold-blued fingers and searched again. He hoped he lived long enough to continue missing his mittens. It would serve him right to die here, in the snow and the mountains, miserable and cold—

There! A shimmer off scales like sun off ice, a thousand shades of gray and white and ivory all rimmed with silver at the edge. It had circled the peak, and now it fanned like a waiting hawk and hovered on still wings, having found some sufficient updraft. He lifted his pistol as it hung in the sky as if magicked there.

The sharp tang of powder brushed past him as an eddy of wind swept the primer from the pan.

The Dead Man didn't curse. He was not a blasphemer. But he grabbed and released one deep breath between his teeth as he fumbled, again, for the horn.

The skidding ice-boat crashed to a halt in a drift just below the Dead Man. It stuck there, canted among rocks, cargo spilling from the staved hull. The oxen cried piteously, battling the snow to a pinkened mire.

The wyrm's head turned from side to side as it considered its next target. One plump retainer wasn't much of a snack for a creature forty cubits long. Though he pitied the struggling cattle, the Dead Man hoped its attention would be drawn by them rather than the running people, though that idiot prince deserved whatever evil might befall.

The cattle were closer to the Dead Man and tethered to the wrecked ice-ship. Too big to carry off, he hoped. And he had the snaplock loaded and primed again, finally. If the damned wyrm would just settle down and take a few bites, he might be able to get off a shot from close enough range to make a difference. He'd glimpsed the vast, blue, faceted eyes.

They'd make a good target.

The wyrm swooped past again, the herding, flushing behavior rather than the stoop to kill. The Dead Man crouched, head barely above the level of his snowdrift, and tracked the beast with his pistol sight. Too fast, too high. He could take another shot, see the bullet deflected, and spend another long minute fumbling his reload with ever-colder fingers.

But he thought the wyrm was focused on the broken ice-ship, and somebody had gotten the Song prince to put his head down and start moving again. Now he was largely anonymous among the figures floundering upward through the snow.

If the thing settles down on the wrecked ship, the Dead Man thought, *maybe we can get everybody else moving and escape up the pass while it eats. Two yaks ought to be a big enough supper. . . .*

Since he wasn't sure he could kill it with one shot, maybe he ought to hold his fire if it settled in to dine. Rather than getting it riled up again.

It circled back, and the shadow of its wings fell over him. Terror welled inside the Dead Man like water from an icy spring. He flinched, huddling lower in the snow, though in his time he'd faced down wild beasts, murderous necromancers, and the odd cavalry charge. He saw the great wyrm tip side to side between the steady cantilever of its wings, then furl them slightly and begin to settle.

The hairy oxen cried out in fear and outrage as their death descended. The Dead Man wished he had a bullet for each of them, to end their terror and pain. There was nothing else he could have done from this distance, under these circumstances.

He braced his pistol in both hands, consciously relaxing the muscles of his arms and fingers to still his shaking. It worked, somewhat.

He drew a bead on the ice-wyrm's nearer eye. The angle was still bad, as it was above him and the eye was protected by the bony shelf of cheek below. The best shot would come when it descended past him, into the bottom of the valley. After that, he'd be aiming at the top of its head.

He forced himself to breathe as smoothly as possible, though the cold made his lungs wheeze and whistle. He rested a finger on the trigger. Another moment, while the ice-wyrm cupped air and calculated its descent. Hard sunlight shattered off its back as if the thing were faceted from crystal.

He was sure it hadn't seen him. He prayed to the Scholar-God and all her mercies that it hadn't seen him.

Now, he thought—as a glittering figure, brilliant as the wyrm but warmer-colored, launched itself into the air on a long, improbable arc and struck the ice-wyrm hard.

The Dead Man managed not to yank the trigger as the Gage wrapped both arms around the ice-wyrm's long neck and began to squeeze. The ball probably wouldn't have *hurt* his old friend—in fact, he was morally certain that it wouldn't do more than dent the Gage's hide—but he'd hate to miss a second shot. And now the Gage's enormous weight was dragging the wyrm's head down, pulling it off course as the wyrm beat its wings frantically to try to reclaim flight.

It flapped and staggered in the air, tail and head thrashing, flurrying out of control. The wyrm screamed; the cattle screamed; the Gage was deathly silent except for the clashing of strained gears.

The wyrm and the Gage crashed into the slope below in a tumble of wings and metal. The next the Dead Man knew, he was running—or sliding—or plowing—through the drifts, trying to keep the snaplock upright so the primer didn't spill from the pan *again,* trying not to simply catapult head over heels the length of the slope and wind up sprawled under the hooves of the panicked, injured cattle. Or, better yet, slide right down into reach of the ice-wyrm.

The beast had shaken the Gage from its neck, though the Dead Man could see long smears of blood where escaping had cost it tissue and scales. Now it reared back, wings beating, as if it had thought better of its dinner and wished only to escape. Predators generally were willing to risk less than their prey in any confrontation—representing the difference between a meal, and a life.

But the Gage had the thing by the ankle, as if he were a heavy brass shackle binding it to earth, and had hunched over to bend its talon up and back. The wyrm's head whipped around and it blunted its teeth on the Gage's glinting armor with a hair-raising scrape.

The ice-wyrm beat heavily against the thin, cold air. It lifted, a little, and suddenly the Dead Man's inner eye filled with the image of the Gage tumbling, sparkling, from a tremendous height.

The Dead Man's breath hurt him. The Gage could not get crushed by a dragon. If everyone else got eaten up here, the brass man still had to get his package to the queen.

The eye. The eye. It shimmered like a watery aquamarine as the Dead Man sighted along his barrel. He braced himself and—just as there was a tremendous snapping sound—he squeezed the trigger. The incense of powder smoke, whipped back on the strong wind up the valley, stung.

The thing didn't shriek, but it exhaled explosively with a hiss like a punctured lung. It kicked out, hard, and the Gage was thrown loose and thumped into snow just a handful of cubits downslope from the Dead Man. The earth shook with the impact, but he kept his footing and offered a quick prayer of thanks that the Gage hadn't landed a little higher, where the Dead Man would have been crushed.

The Dead Man snatched up his powder horn and began to reload.

The wyrm's head snaked around. It took a hopping, hobbling step upslope, one of its killing talons flopping broken. It made a horrible, breathy hiss and spread its wings, raising them for a downstroke. Its eyes, both unharmed, fastened on the sprawled Gage and the huddled Dead Man.

The Dead Man dropped the pistol into his overcoat pocket, grasped the hilt of his saber, and drew it out without ever lowering his eyes from the wyrm. A white-edged gouge furrowed the tendriled, toothy face just below the eye he'd been aiming for, streaming red blood like a weeping queen's kohl. A bad wound, but as the beast lunged upward, patently not an incapacitating one.

The Gage was creaking slowly to his feet. The Dead Man saw dents and scrapes, the marks of impact and enormous teeth, in the hard brass shell. He took two hops downward through the snow to stand beside his friend.

"You ought to run," the Gage said conversationally. "I'll hold it as long as I can."

"Ehn," the Dead Man replied. "For what other reason do I live?"

He couldn't leave. The Gage had the message. He raised his saber as the thing's head darted forward, teeth snapping a cubit or two shy. One more wing-bating hop would do it, though, and as the creature launched itself he extended his saber in a crude stop-thrust unsuited to the curve of the blade and stood ready to at least stab it up the nose while it swallowed him.

The shock on his extended saber never came. He hadn't flinched, but he was focused. So he found himself whipping his head up in surprise as someone cried out behind him and the Gage.

The wyrm twisted in midair, made its pounce a leap into flight, and skimmed over them with terrible clawed wing-tips brushing the snow to either side. The Dead Man turned in his tracks. The Gage, who had no eyes, didn't bother. Pillars of snow swirled in the breeze and settled over them. The Dead Man stared up the slope, lifting his eyes from the blue shadows that lay in the furrowed drifts as the wyrm passed hard and low. The Gage stood expectantly beside him.

A human figure stood above them. The tattered sleeves of black woolen robes belled from upraised wrists in the wind of the ice-wyrm's passage. The hair was a wiry twist of curls and the skin as black as any Aezin noble's, but with an olive tone underlying the darkness rather than burnished red. The figure was a slash of midnight on the burning snow, a pen-stroke authoritative on bleached paper. Something metallic glittered in the socket of the left eye.

There was a whistle of mighty wings, and a spatter of red melted into the snow as the wyrm made another low pass. The Dead Man ducked away, raising his saber to fend, but the figure in black stood unmoving. It held its hands higher, and cried out in that Lotus tongue called Saratahi: "In the name of the Good Daughter, reaver, leave us in peace and be gone with thee!"

The voice was deep and, despite the figure's Southern complexion, carried the inflections of the northern Lotus Kingdoms. Despite the frailness of the robed outline, the wyrm sheered off again, shaking blood from its muzzle. It climbed, wings thundering, and vanished up the slope toward the peak from whence it had first fallen on them.

The Sarathai priest—if that was what the figure was—watched it go, and then for long moments watched also the place where it had vanished to. Satisfied at last, the figure sighed, lowered bare hands, and dusted them together.

The priest stepped forward. Feet rested barefoot on the waist-deep snow, barely denting it, so the figure towered over the floundering Gage and Dead Man.

"That damned thing," the priest said. Gaunt features arranged themselves in a smile. They were elegant, and on another day the Dead Man might have paused to appreciate them, and the priest's thin tall frame like a willow swaying. But what he noticed now was not the high ledges of cheekbones under drawn skin, but the smooth, burnished, golden orb that rested in what should have been the socket of the left eye.

Still, that deep voice was warm as their rescuer continued, "How badly are your people hurt?"

"I don't know yet," said the Gage. "One dead at least."

The priest might have nodded, or perhaps a slight incline of the head simply caused light to flash off the gilded eye.

The Dead Man caught his breath. His cold fingers numb on the hilt of his sword, he fumbled for the scabbard with his other hand. He couldn't feel it. He needed his mittens.

He turned to the Gage and gasped, "Is it safe? Do you have it?"

Lightly, the Gage touched his chest where scratched brass showed under torn rough-spun.

Other travelers were stepping out, calling to one another. "Is it gone?" "Roiieh, where are you?" Some approached the stricken yaks. Some approached the three figures on the hill.

"I'm Nizhvashiti," the enigma said. One bare hand indicated the Dead Man's. "You're going to have frostbite if you don't get warm."

"I know it," he replied.

Nizhvashiti cupped the Dead Man's hands, crouching and stooping to do so. Warmth flooded him, and well-being. All the little aches and pains and stiffnesses of his hard life on the road seemed to lift away, as they might with the first soothing flush of wine. He gasped, and with a little laugh the priest let his fingers drop.

"That should take care of you until you find your mittens."

People had come up the hillside. The Dead Man heard the whispers behind him over the creaks of the Gage shifting his weight in the cold: *Saint. Godmade.*

No saint of his, he decided, looking at the scarred, hard, elegant visage. No sainted follower of the Scholar-God. Instead, some heathen creature. Absently, he rubbed his hands together. They tingled. Nizhvashiti could talk to the wyrm. Make it follow commands. What if the priest could do *more?*

What if the priest had *sent* it?

The caravan master, a small sturdy Sarathai by the name of Druja, came up, stomping his feet in his boots for warmth. "Prince Mi Ren is furious," he said to the Dead Man, in the sort of tone that indicated he thought it was the Dead Man's job to do something about it.

It was the Gage who answered. "At least he's alive to *be* furious."

"Who's this?" the caravan master said.

"Priest," the Gage answered.

Nizhvashiti stepped forward and again made an introduction. Having determined that the person speaking was, in fact, the caravan master, Nizhvashiti added, "I've been waiting for a caravan. I made a nest in one of the old wrecked ice-ships and have been meditating to conserve my resources. I've only three days of food left. I'm so glad you came when you did. I need to get to Sarathai-tia, to the kingdom of Mrithuri Rajni."

Eyelashes lowered over that expressionless gilded orb, and the Dead Man shuddered behind his trained, impassive exterior as every speculation that this might be a coincidence deserted him.

Usually, making people shudder was his job.

He glanced at the Gage, who was not—of course—glancing back. Still, the Dead Man felt he was understood: this priest was bound where they were bound. On a similar errand, or a contrary one?

"We won't turn you out to die," the caravan master said. "But this is a business, your divinity."

"Oh." The tall figure's lips curved to reveal teeth ranked as white as the peaks surrounding. "I have plenty of *gold*."

THEY COLLECTED THE CARAVAN AND THEIR SCATTERED PEOPLE, AND redistributed what they could salvage from the shattered ice-ship among the other three, which meant that more passengers were left to shank's mare for their transportation. There was some grumbling at that, though the much-cloistered noblewoman seemed actually happy to get out and walk.

She wasn't fast, but she didn't complain.

One of the injured yaks had to be sacrificed. The other was limping, but the Godmade declared that it could be helped, and so it was given into Nizhvashiti's charge. The Dead Man concealed his misgivings.

For certain, the Godmade's appearance was convenient. But that didn't *absolutely* mean the whole thing had been planned. He tried to be charitable: if it *hadn't* been planned, Nizhvashiti had saved his life and the Gage's shiny hide. And if it had been planned, the priest might represent an allied power. Or even be another friend of the Eyeless One.

You never knew, with Wizards, what they might be plotting. And what information they might choose to withhold, for purposes of their own. The profession attracted people of such a temperament as to treat knowledge as a precious thing, and they would either bore your head sore showing off how much they had hoarded, or they would lock it away and hide it from everyone.

What the Dead Man couldn't determine was what staging the whole thing could have accomplished better than just showing up with a bag of gold and purchasing passage.

You're too suspicious, the Dead Man told himself. *You've been a sell-sword too long, and you were never cut out for it. You're much too old for this.*

He wondered if there was a noble family somewhere in the Lotus Kingdoms who might hire a retainer of impeccable loyalty and training. He'd be willing to pledge both to the nearest reasonable liege that didn't demand baby-strangling or kitten-stomping, and who was also willing to make all the complicated decisions without too much input from his or her minions.

They did not stop that night at the edge of the spring atop the pass that sourced their river, as they had intended. They pushed on several more miles, finding less comfortable shelter in the lee of a sharp overhang that might discourage nighttime predators.

At least there was a good meal of fresh, roasted yak to look forward to. For everybody except the Gage, who didn't eat. Though he did do something mysterious with red wine on a fairly regular basis.

2

MRITHURI AWAKENED IN SOGGY SILKS AND KNEW THE RAINS WERE coming. Her bedclothes dragged at her skin as she arose from the softness of her pallet. The impression of her narrow body remained in damp cotton and wool batting beneath its tufted cover.

Her mouth was dry and her limbs aching. She felt heavy, cramped, wool-witted, as she could not afford to be. She drifted through the predawn dimness in her nakedness. Knotted rugs of strong-hued wool and tiles of gold-veined indigo lapis lazuli warmed and cooled her soles by turns as she crossed to the window. The draperies were near-transparent layers of silk crepe in blue and violet and tangerine hues like dawn. They stirred over the pierced stone lattice. Mrithuri drew them aside with a hand still naked, soft-fingered, and merely human for now—decorated as it was only with elaborate stained patterns of henna.

There were no guards within Mrithuri's chamber. Her bhaluu-kutta, Syama, lay before the door, as tall at the shoulder as a big man's chest, and twice as heavy as that same man would have been. The bear-dog's eyes were open, but her head lay on her paws. Syama was better than any human guard. She could not be blackmailed, and she could not be bribed.

Mrithuri's servants slept lightly. Yavashuri, her clever middle-aged maid of honor, and Chaeri, a hypochondriac maid of the bedchamber, had already rolled from their thinner and less sumptuous pallets along the wall by the time Mrithuri reached the window. She ignored their movements as she leaned forward, veiled in her unbound hair. She wished to cherish the self-deception of privacy for a few moments longer.

Her chamber overlooked the gardens. The white lattice and the rail of the balcony beyond framed a view like a Song silk-scroll watercolor. Whorls of mist caressed the gnarled boles of ancient cassia and almond trees, lay thick across planting beds. The trees would soon drip with blooms—pink or gold for the cassia, delicately blushed white for the almonds. The beds would surge with helleborine and lilies between their banks of rhododendron and laurel. But all were naked to the summer heat for now.

And for now the sky above was transparent, and the killing drought of summer had continued unabated for so long that Mrithuri had to remind herself that other weather was possible. She took another breath of moister air. She turned her attention to the northern horizon, which showed a bright fine demarcation as the Good Daughter, Sahar, whisked her spangled drape off the face of the sky, leaving the brilliance of her Heavenly Mother, the sacred river, unveiled in the sky as on the earth.

There were no clouds to the east, yet. The sea lay west, and the winds came from the west, and weather came from the west. But the storms that made a thriving city and agriculture possible, here in the heart of the arid lands—those came every year without fail from the east, and Mrithuri as rajni and priestess could feel their herald in her bones.

Mrithuri stood in silence and watched the day brighten toward nightfall and the mist burn off. The edge of the veil slid higher, revealing indigo sapphire lit by a hundred thousand million stars as fat and sparkling as the diamond band restraining a rajni's hair. If it weren't for the mist cloaking the gardens below, Mrithuri could have looked down and glimpsed the broad expanse of the earthly manifestation of the sacred Mother River Sarathai from the edge of the garden-hung roof above. But as she raised her eyes to the heavens, the black disk of the Cauled Sun set in the south amid its nest of transparent silver flames and the celestial manifestation of the river's full glory was revealed overhead. The sky and the gardens brightened and the evening blazed.

Only the brightest stars could shine through the dark of day, dimmed as they were then by the Good Daughter's shawl and the silver corona of the Cauled Sun. By night, however, the whole vast twisted arch of the river of light across the sky's meridian lay revealed. Its brilliance glowed down from the vertex of the sky, wreathed in gleaming mist as befitted the heavenly extension of the river called Imperishable, called Daughter of Mountains, called White-Limbed, called Faithful, called Unmanifest, called Plaited, called Gilded by the Moon, called Peerless, called Mother of Bread.

"Your Abundance?" the lovely girl Chaeri said, calling Mrithuri from her reverie. The title of courtesy amused Mrithuri, though she hid her smile: it was a silly title for a virgin rajni. Even when that rajni was also a priestess, and the personification of the great Mother River on earth, as the Good Mother was her personification in heaven.

Mrithuri turned from the window before the mist was fully lifted, aware belatedly of the chill that had prickled her skin. The first cool evening of the season. Yavashuri held out a heavy robe of embroidered charmeuse. Mrithuri slipped into it gratefully, stretched her shoulders until the spine between them cracked.

Chaeri limped over as if her joints hurt her. She lifted Mrithuri's sandalwood box, large enough that the girl needed both hands to hold it. She raised it up despite Yavashuri's frown of displeasure, and something heavy slid inside. The ache in Mrithuri's joints itched for the solace within, but it must wait.

"Not this morning," Mrithuri said, and was proud of her self-discipline.

No one will know, Chaeri's eyes said, as she lifted the lid. But Mrithuri turned briskly away, despite her aching heaviness. A good mother saw to her children first, as a good daughter saw to the needs of her mother. As the earthly avatar of both Good Mother and Good Daughter, Mrithuri could not betray that trust on a night when she felt the requirement to fast in her blood.

Mrithuri spoke the words, then—the words that would begin her yearly silence, except for the necessary song and prayers. "Tonight will come the rains," Mrithuri said, her bones ripe with the knowledge imparted upon a true sister of the sacred river, a true daughter of a true raj. Even the discomfort of a fasting morning could not entirely dull the sense of the Mother River's constrained excitement surging through her. The river was hungry, after the long dryness. And today she anticipated the feast.

Mrithuri's women shared a glance. It was early in the year—very early!—and so many things would not yet be ready for the rains. But the sky did as it willed, and Mrithuri was only the messenger. They bowed, accepting what she said.

Mrithuri heard the faint whispering, a susurrus of voices from within the pierced interior walls. The voices rose to song, an unaccompanied chant that rang through the rajni's apartments as the cloistered nuns who moved through passages within the walls sang out their morning prayers. It was a sweet, powerful sound—so many clear women's voices intertwining—but today, without the solace of the box, Mrithuri winced in headache.

She hid it, as befitted a rajni. She closed her eyes and bowed her own head over her folded hands and—with her maids of the chamber—sang to them in answer her praises of the day, and of the rainy season come again.

AFTER THE MORNING PLAINSONG, MRITHURI SUFFERED HERSELF TO BE bathed and coiffed and robed quite elegantly, in honor of the changing season. She wished she'd had the wit to realize how soon the rains would be coming, and eat something substantial before bed. But it was too late now. She would fast until after the ceremony.

Chaeri and Yavashuri closed Mrithuri's snake-collar about her throat, and slid into place the serpent's head, attached to the flexible blade that curved within and locked the jewel in place. Her narrow hands vanished into the armatures of her fingerstalls, their long curving oval nails glittering with patterns of ruby, orange sapphire, and diamond. Her wrists shimmered with slender glass bangles that clattered and chimed. Her brown arms, seeming even more slender above the heavy drape of bracelets, were left bare to show the elegant intertwined outlines of sacred bull, tiger, elephant, dolphin, peacock, and bearded vulture that had been inked on her skin as she progressed through her training in the priestess mysteries.

That had been five years before, on her nineteenth name-day, and Mrithuri had managed—so far—to remain unmarried. Someday, she knew, the lines would feather. Her courses would cease, and the skin of her limbs would slacken and lose its tautness. Perhaps on that day her counselors would finally cease their importunings that she marry and get an heir.

She allowed Yavashuri to smooth the weight of her patterned vermilion drape over her shoulder and fasten it to her cropped silken blouse with a heavy jewel. Her belly would be chilly, but the dress would flaunt the red-gold glow of the Queenly Tiger in her navel. Perhaps the radiance of the jewel would remind her counselors and sycophants, after all, of who truly was rajni. Even if, being a woman, she could not sit upon the Peacock Throne of her grandfather—and of his grandfather before him, who had been the legendary Alchemical Emperor and unified the kingdoms of both Sarathai and Sahalai into the Lotus Empire, which had endured not a dozen years after his death at the age of one hundred and eleven.

She rubbed her aching hands together and thought again of her scented sandalwood box, and the relief it contained.

The servants of her chamber seated her upon a stool, then powdered Mrithuri's feet with gold dust and decorated her bare toes with rings and jewels. They helped her to rise again and she stood under the weight of all that cloth, all that gold.

The falling scarf of her drape demanded she hold her shoulders back, and high. The headdress demanded the same of her neck and skull. She took a breath and settled into herself; the posture of a ruler.

She stepped from her chambers accoutered and constrained, every inch a rajni. Syama levered herself up with agile strength and followed, light rippling on the black and gold brindle of her coat as she passed before the windows. This was still Mrithuri's private wing of the palace, where the rajni and the cloistered nuns lived. Only her household, and certain very specially honored guests, were allowed to tread here. Only the servants of her body would ever see her other than in her mask of majesty.

Unless she deigned to marry after all, she mused, with a faint secretive smile.

Her people paused and bowed as she passed, eyes downcast. As always, it struck Mrithuri as a tremendous waste, to spend so much time and money on making her resplendent when no one was allowed to look at her directly. Maybe she *should* take a husband. Just so somebody would be able to appreciate properly the results of all this fuss. The rest of her court spent all their time staring at her gilded toes.

She walked sedately, in deference as much to her headache and the heavy dress as to her rank, and restricted herself to the gliding steps that would keep all her finery balanced. The scarf of her drape flowed out behind her on the slight breeze of her passage, while Syama padded silently at her heels, ever-watchful. Stout, dour Yavashuri and voluptuous, round-hipped little Chaeri followed her at a respectful distance. Their eyes would be downcast too, but they were mistresses of watching for any slipped hair or trailing hem through their own lowered lashes. The nuns in their cloister within the walls followed also; Mrithuri glimpsed their silver-threaded white cotton gauze veils and heard their slippered footsteps through the latticed stone.

She hated shoes quite passionately. She would have never made a nun.

Courtiers and the rest of her entourage—the people who fancied themselves important—awaited her beyond the golden gates that guarded the entrance to the rajni's household. They fell in on all sides: counselors and sycophants, priestesses and courtiers, ambassadors and—for all she knew—assassins. Some were her favorites; some only thought they should be. She kept her measured pace and did not speak to any.

Nor did they speak to her. Word had passed with the morning plainsong that today was a day of ritual. To distract her now would be to disturb her meditation. Which she probably should be paying attention to, though it was hard to do so as they passed the turning to the throne room and its storied, unoccupied chair. No one had sat in it since Mrithuri's grandfather's death. No one had dared.

She squinted against the glare as her centipede chain followed her out into the bright morning sun. Instantly, a silken shade was raised over her—a blessing, as she couldn't shade her eyes with her heavily decorated hand without risking putting one of them out on a finger-stall, and it would have been a break in decorum to do so anyway. She walked across smooth cobbles still cool with morning, down the narrow path bordered with jasmine and the imported, coddled ylang-ylang, neither of which were yet in bloom. It didn't matter that they were still scentless. The spice and incense of the court atmosphere followed her into the fresh air of morning, carried on her clothes and the clothes of her entourage.

She wished she could put on a tunic and trousers, shed all these bridal fripperies (elaborate enough to weigh down any flighty fian-cée), and go skipping down the path at a run. It amused her to think of all the courtiers rushing after her, out of shape and out of breath. She bit her lip against the giggle.

Mrithuri made herself instead stop decorously at the edge of the constructed rise her palace sat upon. The man-made hill elevated Mrithuri's home safely above the yearly deluge while allowing the rajni to remain within sight of the sacred river. No dike had ever been raised that could hold back the Sarathai when the floods began, fed as they were by the monsoon and by the meltwater flowing down from the Steles of the Sky, where spring began much later than in the hot lowland countries.

Mrithuri turned her gaze up to the stunning vaulted sky above, the vast cool shining of the Heavenly River with its curving bands, the coppery rim of a full moon rising heavily to the north. No clouds yet, and the depths of the sky were as deep and transparent as the eye of a dragon.

Her entourage held its breath around her. She turned thoughtfully, and was gratified to catch the eye of Ata Akhimah, the Aezin-born Wizard who was Mrithuri's doctor, the court astronomer, and her closest adviser and friend. *She* wore flowing black trousers and a loose, white tunic, sleeveless to show off her velvety complexion and her muscled arms. *She* didn't avoid looking Mrithuri in the eye. Silver bangles chimed and ivory bangles clicked as Ata Akhimah raised her hands. "Open the gates!"

Three footmen sprinted down the hill toward the tall wrought gates that dominated the gap in the white stone wall. Watching them left Mrithuri envious again. They wore their long, full, white cotton skirts wrapped up between their legs into a sort of blousy trouser and ran without impediment, and their heads probably didn't hurt. Unless they'd been drinking a little rice beer the night before.

She thought longingly of the ivory-and-jet inlay of her sandalwood box. Chaeri would have it for her when this was done. She just had to get through the fast and the ritual, and she could have her breakfast and her tea and her bite as soon as the rain came down.

The runners reached the gates. They were about to raise the bars and turn the keys when a loud male voice cried out, "Your Abundance, Your Abundance, I must speak with you immediately!"

That the shocked intakes of breath on every side were the only answering sound was a testament to the self-discipline—or perhaps the devoutness—of Mrithuri's court. They all turned, except Mrithuri. She kept her eyes on the water gate, and tried to keep her mind on the ritual. She'd been so successful so far, after all. Besides, she could see who was coming out of the corner of her eye, and she wouldn't give him the satisfaction of responding.

She didn't need to. Yavashuri had already detached herself from the procession. Without speaking a word, she had touched two burly men on the elbows and led them over to intercept the blasphemer.

The man who swept toward the royal procession was tall and broad. His tidy beard and thick dark hair were streaked with gray. The neck that protruded from the open collar of his long linen blouse was broad and thick. Over the blouse and his trousers he wore a saffron-colored tunic heavy with embroidery and goldwork along the open plackets. He was not quite moving at a trot—that would be beneath his dignity and authority—but his stride betokened no little impatience.

It was Ambassador Mahadijia, scion of the household of her troublesome cousin Anuraja, who was the son of Mrithuri's grandfather's sister, the king of the rich port city of Sarathai-lae, and a constant irritation.

Syama took two long steps to come up beside Mrithuri. The bear-dog curled her lip over her long, yellowing canine. She did not moan her threat, as was the habit of her kind. Her lopsided snarl was utterly silent, and utterly convincing—from the flash of her fang to the furrow of her brow.

Mrithuri put a jeweled hand on the bear-dog's shoulder to restrain her.

"Your Abundance!" Ambassador Mahadijia called again. "It is imperative that I speak with you at once!"

He stopped, mirrored sandals flashing, as Yavashuri and her enforcers stepped before him. Yavashuri had been Mrithuri's nurse. Mrithuri did not need to turn to know that Yavashuri was raising a finger to her lips, a stout little tiger facing down a much, much larger bear.

There was a flurry of movement—the enforcers closing ranks— and over his protests Mahadijia was bundled away. They would not lay a hand on him, Mrithuri knew. The ambassador's person was sacred.

They would just present an immobile and rather nimble wall, and keep edging him back until he got the idea that he was not currently welcome here.

Weren't ambassadors supposed to have some sort of skills involving tact and diplomacy? Mrithuri stifled a sigh. Anxiously, she wondered what could possibly have been so damned important that it was worth risking the displeasure of the Good Daughter. Or possibly Mahadijia was just too daft to realize what had been happening.

"Your royal cousin," he yelled from beyond her line of sight, "will hear of this outrage!"

Mrithuri still never turned. She gestured with one glittering hand for the opening of the gates to continue.

It was done, in silence except for the faint rubbing of heavy, well-oiled metal. The ambassador's voice faded away. And there, at the bottom of the path, flowed the mighty river, Thousand-Named, Ship-Bosomed, Gilt With Lotuses.

She was certainly gilt with lotuses now. Great mats of vegetation like floating islands clothed her silt-pale flanks. The earthly river was as white as the heavenly one, though less shining, the water as opaque as the milk of the sacred cattle it so resembled.

The lotuses were new this morning. They, too, were a sign of the rain returning—independent of the rajni's infallible premonitions. They bloomed for the first time each year on the eve of monsoon, and were the first flowers to return to soften the breast of the Mother River, and the land she watered, after the summer's heat baked all the winter's petals dry.

Mrithuri strained her eyes through the last swirls of mist slowly burning off the water. The Broad-Bosomed was thick with boats, but they stayed respectfully far from the sacred sweep of the lotuses. The rajni could make out the colors of augury splashed in the unfolding petals—pinks and whites and ivories, yellows and blues, the rarer greens and oranges and lavenders. And there, like a prick of blood among the paler colors, she glimpsed what she had been afraid to see: one single lotus, bobbing with the others, red as a beating heart.

Was there a black one? Was she that unfortunate? Not near the red, at least. Mrithuri resisted the urge to stand up on tiptoe, which did not befit the dignity of a rajni. By the Good Daughter's lost lover, the light reflecting off the water was no friend of her headache.

There. Off by itself, like an ink spot on paper. One splash of black on the creamy surface of the river. Unless it was a violet so dark as to seem black, which was nearly as unsettling.

Well. At least the mere possibility of a dangerous augury did not mean that the fates would, perforce, supply its completion. Mrithuri looked over and saw Ata Akhimah glancing at her worriedly again. Their gazes brushed. The Wizard nodded and turned away.

She had not been raised or educated in Sarathai-tia. But she had lived here all of Mrithuri's life, and then some. She knew her duty, and she knew her adopted religion very well indeed.

Mrithuri took a breath to settle herself and tried not to think of the heavy sliding inside her box. She tried not to think of red lotuses, or black. She focused her eyes a little closer, instead, and smiled. At least, there at the bottom of the path, was the gilded stair. And beyond the stair, her old friend Hathi waited for her, hung as Mrithuri herself was in tangles of silk and ropes of gold.

That was where the resemblance ended. Hathi's great chinless mouth was at the level of Mrithuri's crown. Her pale, tan-spotted ears fanned wide as she caught sight of her friend, and her trunk raised high. She shifted her weight impatiently, causing the belled chains on her ankles to chime.

No one had ever been able to convince the white elephant that she was a sacred symbol of the Mother River, and that she ought to comport herself with dignity. And she had never quite figured out why her friend, the young princess who used to run to her after meals with smuggled sweets leaf-wrapped and tucked into the pockets of her tunic, had become so stiff and formal in public as they aged.

Or maybe she did know, and just didn't care what people thought of dignity. Hathi was old, after all; she'd been born around the same time as Mrithuri's grandfather, and had been a naming-gift to the young prince then. And the old, Mrithuri thought, often had little use for the sorts of time-wasting pomp and ceremonies indulged by the young.

With a hand gesture, Mrithuri bade Syama wait with Chaeri. The bear-dog flicked her ears in disagreement, but did not otherwise protest, and settled in beside the maid-of-the-bedchamber with a show of forbearing.

Mrithuri mounted the little stair, balancing herself with her palm against the rail. She couldn't close her hand on it, not with the fingerstalls on. Fortunately, she was well-schooled in achieving her old friend's back even with all their clutter hung on them—and Hathi's rig was designed to be climbed by someone even more encumbered than Mrithuri was.

She settled herself sideways on the shoulders, stroked the elephant's warm, dry hide, and concealed a sigh. What they called a white elephant wasn't, really. Even scrubbed and exfoliated, Hathi's hide was a dull pewtery color, though much lighter than those of most of her kin. Her dressers made up for this by whitewashing the beast—quite literally—in baths of limestone water. (The whitewash also helped to protect her from sunburn—a real consideration, given the paleness of her hide.)

Hathi bore Mrithuri down to the river with a gentle, swaying stride.

Elephants only appear ponderous to the uninitiated. From her perch on Hathi's back, what Mrithuri felt was a light-footed, rolling gait that reminded her of a ship. The elephant's bells jangled pleasantly, and she reached her delicate trunk-tip up to inspect her rider carefully. Their escort followed behind as the white elephant bore her rajni down to the sacred river's muddy bank. There, they paused.

Mrithuri knew it was because Hathi had sensed the shift of Mrithuri's weight, and so known at what place to hesitate. But she also knew that to the crowd gathered on the bank, it seemed as if the elephant had come to some decision, or was following an invisible sign. Well, perhaps that was accurate.

The Mother River, the lady with all her names, stretched before them as broad and placid as could be imagined. She was narrowed with the dry season, and still Mrithuri could barely glimpse her farther bank. Slow-moving, knotted islands of green vegetation floated on the gentle current. She was clotted with long, low boats, on this auspicious evening, and the boats were loaded with women robed in their finest, and with men in loincloths poling gently to hold position. They had all come out to see Mrithuri, and Hathi, on the eve of the rains—and to witness with their own eyes the augury of the coming year.

A snout like a toothy longsword broke the water several body-lengths out, followed by an almost-eyeless head and the muscular curve of body and a sharp, upright pectoral fin. A *bhulan*: one of the Mother's blind dolphins, swimming on its side as they did so commonly.

A good sign. A sign of the Mother's pleasure, that the sacred swimmer—twin to the one marked on Mrithuri's forearm, and twined with a tiger there—would come in among the boats of so many observers, gathered to mark the auspiciousness of the day. And there were any number of boats—from the daily fishing vessels, to the longer, lower scows with their equally low cabins and their free-board so slight that they looked like nothing so much as roofs floating independently along the water. Those were houses, and the people who fished from them lived on them, entire families in one tight little floating room, mostly underwater.

All the river's people, summoned by the blooming lotus, had gathered to watch the ritual and witness the augury.

Mrithuri unpinned her drape at the shoulder, willing herself not to fumble despite the awkwardness of her fingerstalls. She rose up on Hathi's shoulders and balanced on her gold-dusted feet as she unwound the ells of cloth from around her waist until she stood up only in her blouse and petticoat and so many sparkling heaps of jewels. She handed down the drape and the brooch to Chaeri just as Yavashuri returned, looking even more cross than usual for this hour of the day and no breakfast. Syama sat back on her haunches and laughed up at Mrithuri and Hathi.

Hathi reached her long nose over, and fondled the bear-dog's ear. The bear-dog ducked good-naturedly.

More boats swept along the river, assembling nearby. These were more of the fishing craft, poled by men already stripped down to loincloths and headdresses, though the heat of the day was already cooling. Though the Cauled Sun gave but little light, it produced heat in abundance.

Mrithuri watched them come, and found the silence of everyone a little eerie. A babe cried, and no one hushed it. She pressed the jeweled nail-tips of her fingerstalls against her thighs to seat the damned things more firmly on her digits and rocked her weight forward, onto the balls of her bare feet.

Hathi knew what that meant. With an amused flick of her pink, spotted ears, the elephant moved forward, just exactly as if she had decided—spontaneously—on her own to do so. She crouched slightly going down the bank, flexing her hind legs to keep her back level. Mrithuri, bejeweled hands upraised in a spectacle of benediction, reflected that she'd known a lot of human beings less considerate of their fellows than this elephant.

Hathi slipped into the water without so much as a splash. The only ripple she raised was where the sacred river's current parted around her thighs, and then her chest, and then her mouth, which grinned with amusement at the trick she and her old friend Mrithuri were playing on all these gullible ones. She slid into the river like a fine lady into her milk bath, and the parts of her body below the boundary of air and river vanished as completely as if she has somehow stepped into a flat surface of mother-of-pearl. Except for their own ripples, the river had gone mirror-still in a breath-held absence of wind.

Mrithuri could feel through her soles the moment when Hathi's feet lost contact with the rich white river silt, and she was swimming. There was a strange buoyancy, as if Mrithuri stood on the deck of a barge. A large, warm barge, with a play of muscle beneath a hair-bristled hide.

Mrithuri pressed down with her toes. Hathi, with every appearance of independent decision, raised her trunk, exhaled, and submerged completely. The elephant's silken trappings billowed around her, nearly lost from view in the milky river. But Mrithuri could still feel Hathi laughing silently through the soles of her feet as the sacred water lapped over the elephant's back, and as the sacred river washed the gold dust off Mrithuri's feet. A small sacrifice, that, and vanished in no more than a swirl of glitter.

The river was warm at the surface, and she—she, Mrithuri, rajni of Sarathai-tia, was gliding across it as if on oiled wheels. Like a bird across the sky, borne on an unseen wind.

Hathi exhaled again, further lifting her trunk, and the waters rose higher. They swirled around Mrithuri's calves, then her knees, whipping the wet silk of her petticoat between her thighs. That it stayed on at all was a testament to the weavers of the laces.

The water was colder as she descended. Warmth could not penetrate far below the surface, and the deeper currents reminded her that the Sarathai had its source high in the snows near the Rasan summer capital of Tsarepheth, where the Rasani Wizards kept their famous Citadel.

Mrithuri fought the urge to hunch against the chill. It was all about keeping up appearances, this annoying business of being a rajni. At least the cold eased the ache of fasting in her head and joints.

Something tickled and tingled her skin. She thought she knew what. She crouched down, plunged her hands under the water, and—awkwardness of the fingerstalls and all—hooked hold of the raised handle at the neck of Hathi's harness. Now the water broke against Mrithuri's chest. The elephant's gentle forward momentum was enough to swirl a muddy ripple around the rajni. She held on, carefully—to fall now would be a terrible omen—and just as carefully kept her face impassive and her coifed head above the current.

Her whole heart and lungs seemed to vibrate with a throbbing unheard cry. The blind dolphin's song was a thrill reverberating in all the empty spaces of her body. She had seen one; she could feel dozens. Their voices shivered in the nerves of her teeth, the minuscule bones anatomists like Ata Akhimah said lay deep inside her ear.

Along the margins of the Mother, where the current slowed and the banks sloped down, that was where the sacred lotuses grew—in their profusion, in their sweep of many colors. In their grace and fineness.

Hathi responded to the shift of Mrithuri's weight, the curl of her toes. She swept back toward the bank, high up from the landing, where the sacred lotuses bobbed and swayed in the gentle flow of a river too broad and deep to hurry on her way. The boats had left a path for her and she kept to it, trunk uplifted as if she were as conscious of the need to put on a good show as ever was Mrithuri.

Hathi bore her away from the black lotus, segregated as it was from the others. That was a small relief at least. That single splash of crimson among all the pale pastels and sunny yellows and oranges was less avoidable. The red lotus had grown in the sacred bank with the others, which had not happened in Mrithuri's memory, though she knew its varied meanings. Mrithuri could still see it, even from here. The color stood out starkly against the blues and peaches and ivories and whites.

She heard the stir as those of her people who had not already spotted the bloody splash noticed it, the petals as broad as a serving plate lifting and falling on each of the river's slow swells. They did not speak, but they shifted and sighed. They might as well have shouted, when even the wind held its breath like this. *Red. A red lotus!*

Its mere blossoming was a warning, and a portent. If Hathi chose it . . .

Mrithuri shifted her weight to urge Hathi away from the single scarlet bloom. Theoretically, the sacred elephant was supposed to make her choice without the rajni's command. But if she was honest with herself—herself at least, if not her people—Mrithuri had been performing this role since she was her grandfather's granddaughter and not rajni in her own right at all, and she suspected that the bond between herself and Hathi was such that she *couldn't* have kept her opinions from the elephant.

For the first time in their association, the elephant did not seem to understand Mrithuri's unspoken hints. Hathi kept swimming into the bank of lotuses, and as Mrithuri watched with a settling helpless chill, the elephant reached out, unhesitating, and pulled the stem of the single scarlet flower dripping from the mud.

The pit of Mrithuri's stomach dropped, and a cry went up from the boats and from the shore as hours of pent-up, sacred silence was given vent. The people did not even know yet if they cried out with joy or sorrow; the emotion they felt would not be defined for them until the court astronomer had considered the augury. They cried out largely because they could not stay silent an instant longer. They cried out in the relief of crying out. That was all.

Mrithuri settled back on her heels, unconsciously, and this time Hathi sensed her movement and acknowledged it. The elephant ceased her progress and floated, moving gently to stay in one place. She waved the scarlet flower to and fro at the end of her trunk, playfully, the long trailing stem flicking water and mud into the crowd.

The rajni must have sat still too long, because Hathi turned back to shore of her own volition and, having swum the little distance to the cobbled ramp, began gently to climb. The motion startled Mrithuri into thought, at least.

You're a rajni, Mrithuri. Act like it.

She gathered herself, and as Hathi emerged from the river, streaming muddy water and all her whitewash dripping down, Mrithuri stood and spread her arms wide. She had schooled the shock from her face, and managed—she hoped—a mask of queenly impassiveness as Hathi gained the bank, still waving her scarlet lotus cheerfully.

The royal astronomer stood forward, reaching out to accept the lotus. Hathi teased her with it, holding it high. Ata Akhimah was no fool, and turned her gesture into one of arms reached upward in benediction.

Give it to her, you great goof, Mrithuri thought fiercely. Hathi relented, and placed it in Ata Akhimah's hands.

"The red lotus!" she said, buying time. "My rajni, a potent portent indeed! For its color presages blood."

A murmur swept through the crowd. Mrithuri lowered her own arms and kept her attention on Ata Akhimah. The Wizard bent her head to study the lotus, picking through the petals with care, examining the stamens and pistils. Mrithuri clenched her jaw to keep her teeth from rattling as gooseflesh prickled across her wet skin. The light of the Heavenly River was brilliant, but the evening was still chill.

Their eyes met, queen-priestess and Wizard-doctor. Neither dared frown.

Work your magic, Akhimah, Mrithuri thought. *The last thing we need right now is a terrible augury for the year to come. On top of Mahadijia interrupting the ceremony, that's not consolidating to my reign.*

But despite her foreign name—so masculine in its sound!—and despite her foreign schooling, Ata Akhimah had been long in Mrithuri's land. She knew a thing or two, and Mrithuri trusted her.

Akhimah winked and turned so that her back was to Hathi, and she faced the assembled crowd. "The lotus that grows by the palace of Sarathai-tia is the reason that palace is here," she said. "This lotus bloomed here before the Alchemical Emperor united the kingdoms of the Sarathai and the kingdoms of the Sahalai into one Empire. This very lotus, this plant from which we pluck our auguries. Upon whose sacred roots and stems and nuts we sup. From whose sacred stamens we brew our tea. For the lotus is eternal, undying.

"This blossom bloomed white, they say, in those days. It bloomed when all lotuses bloom. But the Alchemical Emperor came here, and sat upon his bank, and saw it—blooming white in its purity, having lifted itself from the mud. We are told that this courage touched the Alchemical Emperor, and so he touched in turn the lotus. And it was the stroke of the hand of the Alchemical Emperor himself that caused it to bloom each year and offer a prophecy."

She brandished it again, red as hearts-blood, dripping silt water across her ebony fingers.

"This sacred blossom budded in the mud. It rose out of the mud. It grew tall and beautiful from the mud, until it floated on the water and emerged on the bosom of the earthly river, in the light of the Heavenly River, for all to see. This sacred blossom on the bosom of the Mother River reflects the sacred stars that bloom on the bosom of the Heavenly River, and light our nights below.

"And it offers us a glimpse of a happy future now!

"Blood can come from birth as well as death," Ata Akhimah intoned, with admirable projection. "Here, in the depths of the blossom, there are traces of gold. That presages richness rather than conflict. The Mother has spoken! In the coming year, the auguries predict for our beloved rajni a marriage, and an heir!"

Oh, Mrithuri thought. *Well, thanks for that, old pal.*

Ata Akhimah lifted the blossom, cupped on both palms, as if she were offering it to the starry river above. Hathi rumbled, as if to say *don't mind if I do.* She reached out, plucked the portent from the priestess' upraised hands, and popped it into her giant mouth, where it disappeared in a couple of casual chews.

Mrithuri kept her face impassive as the elephant began to walk idly up the path. *Faster,* she urged silently.

The contents of the pierced sandalwood box awaited her attentions. *And vice versa,* she thought, and hid a smile.

AFTER HATHI WAS LED AWAY FOR HER BATH AND BREAKFAST, THE NUNS within the piercework walls sang Mrithuri back into her chambers. She was shaking with the cold by the time her handmaids pulled her sodden petticoats and blouse off her, dripping sacred, silty river water all over the tiled portion of the floor. The water in the rajni's private bathhouse was hot—Ata Akhimah had long ago overseen the installation of modern plumbing, with a hypocaust and boilers kept stoked and bubbling. It was a great luxury, and the rajni's women would have bathed her immediately to get her warm.

Normally, she would have permitted it, too. But the clouds had slid across the heavens as she climbed the steps, and by the time she was back in her own rooms and her women were pulling the stalls from her fingers, a gentle patter of rain had begun to fall. The echoes of thunder rolled distantly, growing louder. The river's fast, and the rajni's, were both ended.

Yavashuri was before her at once with a pierced ivory plate loaded with tiny morsels. And Mrithuri's stomach rumbled in answer to the distant thunder at the smells of cardamom, turmeric, saffron, and cumin. But Mrithuri was impatient, agitated with the augury of the red lotus, shivering with gooseflesh and nevertheless still standing naked except for a rug wrapped across her breasts and then draped around her shoulders. Her fast was doing nothing for her temper, either, as she waved Yavashuri away with ardent hands.

"Bring me my damned box," she said, and Chaeri scampered off to get it, forgetting in the excitement to limp.

Yavashuri set the food aside and lifted a bowl of lotus-scented tea to her with both hands, ceremoniously. Steam coiled up, but Mrithuri waved it away as well. "I don't want that," she said. "You know what I need now."

Irritably, she rubbed at the likeness of the sacred snake tattooed on her arm.

"It will be a moment, Your Abundance," Yavashuri said tiredly. "And you are cold and have eaten nothing. The tea will warm you, Your Abundance."

Mrithuri glanced away, ashamed of herself a little. The craving in her was stronger than cold, stronger than hunger. But Yavashuri, her old nurse, never used her title except as a reproach. And it was traditional to break the sacred fast with this tea, flavored with the stamens harvested from those selfsame sacred lotuses.

She sighed and accepted the cup, glancing anxiously after Chaeri. Relief for her headache and aching joints would come faster on an empty stomach. But the tea was plain, unsweetened and without milk, and should not lessen the effect.

"My pardon, Yavashuri," the rajni said. "It has been a trying evening."

While they quarreled, the tea had cooled enough for drinking, and she sipped it. It would do for now.

She drained the cup, but irritably waved away the platter of dainties Yavashuri lifted to her again. She did not want sweets soaked in rosewater syrup, or delicate folded pastries, or dumplings so tiny and crisp they would melt like butter on her tongue. She did not want tidbits of snail sautéed in butter and allium, then skewered and returned to their shells. She did not wish tiny balls of saffron rice and meltingly tender slivers of meat.

She would eat the lotus stems and the sliced and fried rhizomes, as tradition demanded. But first . . . yes, first.

Here was Chaeri now, the big sandalwood box in her hands. The woman handled it carefully, remembering—Mrithuri hoped—that Mrithuri had rebuked her for carelessness not too long ago. Mrithuri would not care to rebuke her again unless she must; that one incident had led to a week of enduring suffering sighs and sidelong, sulky glances.

She reminded herself that Chaeri had a difficult history, and that tolerance was a benediction of the Mother. Chaeri set the box down on a low table and backed away. Mrithuri sank gratefully into the inlaid, square-armed chair beside it. Lacquer and gilt everywhere, the brightness doing nothing for the increasing throb of her headache.

She reached out and stroked the carved fretwork of the surface of the case as her women backed away. Chaeri smiled. Yavashuri frowned. The others were carefully neutral, and the nuns sang on.

The rajni had no secret from the nuns. But the nuns were nothing but secrets. They never left their cloister, and they never spoke to anyone outside the residence of the rajni.

Mrithuri slid the lid aside, very gently. That which dwelt within was not overfond of sudden movements, sudden lights, or vibration.

A faint hiss answered her motion nonetheless.

She waited, then gently reached inside. Now her motions were steady, her gaze calm. If a chill still prickled the flesh of her arms and made her grit her teeth to keep them from clicking, she did not let it affect the dexterity of her hands.

She felt a curve of firm muscle, a cool leathery body. A flicker of questing tongue. Gently, she eased her fingers around the denizen until it was encircled. She slid her fingertips up scales the wrong way, feeling their raspy, feathery edges and careful to touch lightly. There were the heavy muscles of the skull, the softness of the cheeks.

She glided the lid aside the rest of the way and firmed her grip on the serpent within. As she lifted it from its comfortable burrow, her ladies turned away. Except for Chaeri.

The snake was perhaps as long as her arm, though thicker through the body. It was a moss green in color, rich and soft, and upon its long back were delicate, definitive patterns that resembled the figures of brush calligraphy in some complex, unreadable tongue. Its lidless eyes gleamed like jade, and its black tongue flickered, tasting.

"Hello, precious," Mrithuri cooed to it, holding it behind its heavy jowls quite firmly. It tested her grip, but she managed it. The bulky body was unbelievably strong, and very heavy. The skin felt like the finest leather.

The door to her private chamber slid aside in its runners.

She didn't drop the snake. She pulled its face away from her own, and raised her chin to look at Ata Akhimah.

The Aezin Wizard slid the door shut behind her without turning back to look at it. She had traded her earlier clothes for a halter of white linen and white linen trousers, worn under an open black robe that swept the floor behind her red knotted hemp sandals. She sighed, and crossed her arms over her chest in the wide sleeves. Her bangles clattered, some glittering, some the yellow-white of bone.

The Wizard said, "It would not do to become too reliant on that Eremite venom, Your Abundance."

The serpent seemed to be growing heavier. Mrithuri allowed the mass of its body to rest upon her lap, keeping control of the head only.

"She is as dependent on me as I am on her," Mrithuri replied.

She pushed aside the bath rug, and applied the serpent's fangs to the left side of her chest, just above the small swell of her bosom, next to a ragged row of a dozen pinprick scabs surmounting layers of tiny white scars. The snake, discomfited by the noise and argument or perhaps by the chill of her hands, was all too content to oblige her. It bit hard and bit deep, a sharp pricking pain followed by the deep, spreading feeling of burning. Mrithuri felt the jaw muscles work against her fingers. When it stopped, she pulled the snake away.

A bubble of blood formed on the snake's mouth as its jaw closed. Warmth moved through its cool flesh. It had fed, and would be sluggish now. She cradled it close against her, still controlling the heavy, triangular head.

She leaned back in the square, uncomfortable chair and released herself to the burning. It crawled through her from the site of the wound, a slow painful warmth that pulled the chill from her flesh far more effectively than the tea had done. A trickle of blood wound down her breast as she relaxed. The aches in her joints extinguished themselves. The pounding in her head began to recede. She closed her eyes and enjoyed clarity, energy, the feeling of well-being that followed.

When it had settled in, Mrithuri opened her eyes again. Gently, she replaced the satiated serpent in her den, beside her sisters. She closed the lid, making sure the air flow would be unimpeded, and waved Chaeri to her with a negligent but much more relaxed gesture than previously. When the girl had taken the serpent away, her long brown-black curls swaying with her walk, Mrithuri looked around with a sigh. What had Yavashuri done with the damned breakfast?

Oh, there she was with it. She had set it on a slightly larger table across the drawing room, with the remains of the tea, and was pulling up a second chair.

Mrithuri stood, her limbs light and full of energy. Yes, she thought she could face breakfast now. "Did you find out what that damned Mahadijia wanted?"

"No. But it's nothing good, I'm sure of it," Ata Akhimah replied, studiously turning her eyes to the barren gardens beyond the windows. "Your cousin Anuraja is a weasel."

Mrithuri looked down, and tugged her bath rug back into something resembling modesty. "Weasels are useful. They keep the rats and cobras in check."

Akhimah snorted. It was as close as she came to a laugh. Mrithuri had not known enough Aezin to guess if that was a cultural trait or a particular one. It was true, though—tensions between cousin Anuraja, to the south in his kingdom of Sarathai-lae, and cousin Himadra, to the north in *his* kingdom of Chandranath, helped to keep Mrithuri and her own little speck of land safe. And as long as she could keep juggling both of them and marrying neither, she stood a good chance of maintaining the independence of her corner of this crumbling empire.

"Sit and eat with me." The Wizard's bangles chimed as she gestured. "Every discussion is better over breakfast."

Mrithuri sat. All the thought about balancing terrors reminded her of something. "No word from your old master yet?"

The Wizard, ladling mango puree over a dish of rice, looked up and frowned. "'Mentor,' I would say, not 'master.' She and I were of different schools, and I got my training at the University."

"Someday you'll explain to me what the difference between Aezin and Messaline Wizardry is."

"It would be faster to explain the commonalities." Ata Akhimah smiled. "We—my school—are healers, architects, geomancers. We build and repair. The Wizards of Messaline also build things, some of them, but what they build are automatons. Or they raise the dead, or see the future . . . it's really not the same thing at all." She waved a wrist dismissively, chiming. "Were you hoping she would come herself?"

"I was hoping she would at least send help," Mrithuri admitted. "Or some kind of a message. Something to aid us. Her reputation, after all, wraps the world. She might know something that would give us an advantage over the neighbors. I don't expect her to come *herself*. I know the Wizards of Messaline do not like to *leave* Messaline."

Mrithuri looked down and pushed a morsel of baked fish across her plate. Nothing appeared appetizing.

"Be patient," Ata Akhimah advised. "I foresee that you will still have a kingdom and still be a rajni when her messenger arrives. Red lotus or no red lotus. Your Abundance."

Mrithuri rested her forehead on the palm of her hand. "From your lips to the Mother's ears, Akhimah."

3

THERE WAS A WORD FOR A MARK THAT REMAINED AFTER THAT WHICH
made it had moved on—a path worn in earth, ink on a page, a bruise
on skin, a dry riverbed, a scar. Or, well, not precisely a word for the
thing. But a word for the act of so marking. A word that by extension
meant the thing that acted to cause the mark, and the thing that was
acted upon and so became a thing that was marked, and also the
mark itself, and precisely and significantly the action of marking that
forever linked those things and joined them into a continuum, even
long after they had moved apart again.

It was not a word in any human language, and it could not be
pronounced well by any human tongue. It didn't fit—quite—into
the human categories of nouns and verbs as discrete and different
things . . . but the Gage knew it. Having been constructed by a Wizard
was good for one's vocabulary.

The word was *rlmyrranndl*, or close to it. He'd shared it with the
Dead Man once: the Dead Man had made an observation that even
ancient races had a primitive concept of the Scholar-God's pen.

The Gage had withheld comment, as good friends sometimes
learned.

The thing the Gage was observing now was just such a mark. Which in itself was not unusual: the whole world was constructed of the remainders and reminders of processes past. But *this* mark was special. It demanded consideration.

The caravan were coming down out of the mountains, having crossed the watershed's divide and found the smoothest of the tributaries of the Sarathai. The winter had given way to spring and then to weather almost summery as they descended. The overloaded ice-boats now wallowed down the swift current with the cradles that held the runners unbolted from the hulls and balanced on the decks in disassembled pieces. The surviving yaks had been left at a Rasani way station by the river's headwaters; Druja would retrieve them on his return trip. From here, the ice-boats floated. And floated quickly, too.

This frustrated the Gage, who would have liked to have studied the mark more closely. He would have leaped from the deck of the ice-boat to the shore and trusted in his ability to catch up later, but he was confident that would capsize the ice-boat, or at least swamp it. And since he was on the lead boat, that would be a disastrous misadventure for all of them, as the others would inevitably be swept into the first.

So the Gage walked swiftly the starboard length of the ice-boat. His weight shifted the boat's trim, and he heard the rudderman curse, but all he could do was try to step lightly. Which he would have done anyway, because as compelling as it was to keep the mark in sight as long as possible in order to study it, it was more compelling not to put a foot through the deck planks.

He met the Dead Man coming the other way, though they were old enough comrades that the Dead Man stepped out of his way without asking any questions. Without asking any questions *first*, anyway. He certainly asked enough, through his indigo veil, after he fell into step with the Gage.

"What are you looking at?"

"Spoor," the Gage replied. He pointed with a finger that glittered where it caught the sun. Trees carpeted the surrounding slopes now, and the snow protected by evergreen branches had not yet melted. But nor was it unruffled and unperturbed. A packed trail ran alongside the nameless river. "What do you suppose made that?"

The Dead Man frowned, leaning out—though not so far out that a reaching branch might snag him. The Gage kept an eye out anyway, just in case. "Hard to tell. We're moving fast. Looks like pugmarks rather than hooves, though."

"Tiger?"

"Big for a wolf. Don't they have those bear-dog hybrids south of the mountains?"

"They're not hybrids," the Gage said. He could have spoken on, and told the Dead Man that bhaluukutta were an animal as distinct in every way from both bears and dogs as the tiger is from the fox—and more distinct, at that, than tiger from lion or than fox from wolf. But the Dead Man would then have drawn the Gage into an argument on whether—since bear-dogs did not exist within the sight of the Scholar-God's sun, and thus could not have been created by the Scholar-God—they were an abomination, of demonic origin, or simply one of nature's small mistakes.

Instead he paused for a moment before continuing, "Big even for a bhaluukutta, I'd say."

The Dead Man might have pursed his lips. Who could tell, behind the veil? But he definitely considered, and having done so nodded thoughtfully. "I'll let the lookouts know we're in something's territory."

The Gage could not frown, so he simply nodded. For the time being, it would have to serve.

THEY MADE SWIFT PROGRESS THROUGH THE DAY, AND THE PUGMARKS were eventually left behind. But as twilight dyed the backdrop to the peaks its particular shade of lavender, it would have been too dangerous to continue down the river into the dark. They tied up the boats and made themselves as comfortable as possible, posting a double watch. A double watch in addition to the Gage, who did not crave rest as did mere flesh and blood. He merely imbibed a cup of wine, and that was enough to sustain him.

The Dead Man slept like his namesake, for a change. The Gage patrolled the bank, brass feet sinking deep in the soft, sucking mud. He moved a little farther up the slope, where there were pine needles under the snow and he was less prone to bog down. He *could* haul himself out using trees, if they were of sufficient size, but his metal hands tended to gouge and scar the bark, damaging the tree, and he preferred to avoid killing or wounding living things where he could.

This was not the best environment for him.

Eventually, the Dead Man must have awakened—or been awakened—and come to take a turn at watch. The Gage noticed his partner coming up behind him and paused, but didn't turn. As he had no eyes—no ears, no nose—the Gage's senses were less directionally focused than a human's. He sensed what he sensed and saw what he saw, and his direction of travel had little to do with it.

The Dead Man moved smoothly, all-but-silently. He was surefooted through the dark. The Gage tried to remember how well humans saw by starlight, with a reflective cover of snow under dark boughs. But it had been too long. The Dead Man had traded his thick snow boots for a softer pair with less room for wadding up wool around the toes. They barely dented the loam that the Gage's feet were sinking down in as if he stood in a particularly sluggish patch of quicksand.

The Dead Man paused fifteen feet away. "Gage?"

"I saw you," the Gage answered.

"You are the last person I should care to startle." There was a smile in the words, under a friendly layer of acid. The Gage and the Dead Man understood one another.

"I'm not a person," the Gage said.

The Dead Man flipped his hand in that dismissive gesture he liked so well. "Nor are you merely an automaton. And as you've no wings to speak of, you cannot be a dragon."

"How would you know?"

"You *look* like no dragon."

The Gage made an amused noise. "When have you ever seen a dragon?"

"Near enough a dragon by my lights, not a month since in the mountain pass."

"That?" The Gage dismissed it with an oiled metal shrug. "That was just a wyrm."

The Dead Man seemed to consider. At the very least, he paused and chewed over his next words. "There is some difference more significant than size?"

"Wyrms aren't smart. Dragons are. Dragons are much bigger. And wyrms don't carry the serpent-sickness."

The Dead Man had one of the little cheroots rolled from hemp leaves that he smoked occasionally. He lifted his veil to slide it between his lips, then lit it against a magicked heatstone he kept in a case strapped to his wrist. He puffed aromatically. The ember glowed red in the dark. "I had heard the serpent-sickness was a legend. A tale to scare children."

The Gage tipped his head. "That is not what is written in the medical texts."

"Would that be aught you learned from your Wizard too?"

"I'm a Gage," said the Gage. "All I know is what a Wizard told me."

The Dead Man was silent. The Gage knew that the Dead Man knew it wasn't entirely true. But he also knew that the Dead Man wasn't going to bring up the ancient past, because that was a door the Gage could open just as easily.

"Have you ever seen a dragon?" The Dead Man paused. He drew a breath and qualified. "A real dragon."

"No," the Gage said.

"Then how do you know they exist?"

It was a good point. The Gage had seen the blasted wastelands purportedly left by their deaths. He'd seen teeth, kept well behind leaded glass to prevent their sickness from spreading. He'd never met a Wizard who did not accept the existence of dragons and of the serpent-sickness as a proven, objective, scientific fact.

He said, "I don't know. But it seems more reasonable than the alternatives. Gages exist; gods exist—"

"*God* exists."

The Gage ignored him. "Why not dragons?"

The Dead Man puffed his cheroot, then let his veil drop back while holding a deep breath in for several seconds. He released it with a satisfied sigh that made his veil fluff.

"Because dragons make me nervous," he said. His hand described the arcing flight of the ice-wyrm. "I should not care to contemplate . . . a creature bigger and smarter and meaner than *that* monstrosity?"

"Well," the Gage said. "Maybe not meaner. Maybe not that." He stroked the bark of a tree with unfeeling fingertips and made a guess about the source of the Dead Man's distress. "The message is safe."

"This is still too lengthy a journey. Anything could be happening while we are delayed."

Fair, though they were now traveling as fast as humanly possible. And moving through the mountain passes was always chancy. They were lucky to have gotten off as lightly as they had. On the other hand, their lack of intelligence from Messaline *or* Sarathai-tia was anxiety inducing. The Gage could choose not to experience such inconvenient emotions, but the Dead Man could not.

And the Gage could remember that urgency through a veil, as if thinking back to childhood. The burning need to be doing something, anything, even if it was futile. The chafing, the craving for action.

The Dead Man stood sideways to him, picking at a fingernail with the opposite thumbnail. With a start, the Gage realized that all the cuticles and the edges of the nail beds were bloody. Surely, the mountain air had caused hangnails and frostnip. But the Dead Man's fidgeting had kept the wounds from healing.

The Gage laid a hand on his own chest. "It's here, Serhan."

The Dead Man looked up at him with worry-wide eyes.

"It will go through."

"It *must* go through," the Dead Man said. "And in time to prevent some tragedy. I know it with the writing on my bones."

"I think that son of a bitch laid a geis on you, partner," the Gage said.

"The Eyeless One?" The Dead Man shook his head, slowly side to side. But what he said was, "I think you're right."

He wished to sigh, and knuckled the sockets of his eyes. "Well, if she did that, I guess she must have had a pretty good reason."

The Gage was immune to geasa, having the one imbued at his construction firmly and always in place. He was not so confident in their patron as the Dead Man was. But his was a constitution refined for constant loyalty with decades of training.

The Gage had been built to be loyal. But everything he had ever owed allegiance to was dead.

THE NIGHT DRIFTED ON UNEVENTFULLY, AND EVENTUALLY THE DEAD Man pinched out the remainder of his cheroot, tucked it into his pocket, and took himself back to what passed for his bed aboard the third of the three remaining ice-boats. Whether he slept or not, slung in his hammock crowded among those of almost a dozen acrobats and sword-jugglers, the Gage could not have said.

When the sun began to paint the sky—revealing by its color and position that they had not yet left the boundaries, however loosely determined, of the Rasan Empire—the Gage was still standing on the bank, considering the amplifying light. Watchers on the boats began to wake the sleeping crew and lie down in vacated hammocks for their own rest. At the mounting bustle, the Gage splashed through the shallows of the river and climbed the reinforced boarding plank the crew lowered for him. The rest of the passengers and crew were clambering up and down ladders as they saw to nature's morning necessities. The Gage would have shattered *those* in a beat of the heart he did not have.

The first boat rocked in its trim as he climbed aboard, anyway.

Then the humans were breakfasting on hard tack and dried fruit and fish—all at once, which the Gage would have found unappetizing even if he were a creature with the possibility to develop an appetite— and the ropes were being untied and cast off from the shore, and the hands were scrambling up the ladders at stem and stern to board as fast as they could while oarsmen pulled against the current to hold the ice-boats back.

Everyone made it aboard without incident. The boats sailed on merrily, swept down by a current through rapids that were most likely considered less-than-slight by local standards, but which the Gage found more than sufficient for concern. He would be unlikely to suffer injury under most circumstances, but very few of his frail, fleshly human companions could say the same. The Gage sat quietly over the keel of the ice-boat with the hood of his robe drawn up and tried not to look too closely at where they might be going. The shores were very interesting, anyway, with their foreign vegetation and strange landscapes.

So it happened that he was taken completely by surprise when they came around a sharp bend and one of the bowmen put up a great cry of alarm. A moment later, before the Gage could stand without capsizing the ice-boat, its prow struck something that gave with a splintering crash. The current pushed the boat sideways. There were more splinterings, great and small, and the contrasting snapping sounds of dead wood and green as the stern began to swing around.

The Gage had managed to stand without putting fist or foot through the deck, or hull. He did not turn—being featureless had its advantages—but simply raised his voice to its full preternatural volume and bellowed. *"HOLD HARD!"*

If the gods were kind, the trailing ice-boats would hear him in time to keep from slamming into the lead ship with all the force of the current behind them. The Gage acknowledged grimly that kindness was not the sort of thing experienced people generally expected from their deities. He braced for impact.

It came, but not from astern. As the ice-boat's pivot brought it perpendicular to the bank amid more snapping sounds, the starboard side collided heavily with something. The Gage glimpsed evergreen branches and massive trunks as the boat wallowed. It reminded the Gage of an enormous beaver dam.

It did not look in the least accidental.

Someone screamed—one of the crew—but before the Gage could look for him, a sound neither shriek nor roar resounded through the narrow confines of the valley, rising even over the tumult of the rushing river. It would have curdled the Gage's blood, he supposed, if he had such a thing as blood to curdle.

A blur of black and russet swept through the lifted branches of the toppled and heaped-up trees. It moved from shore to the center of the dam in a single leap—an astounding distance even by the Gage's standards.

The cries of the men on the trailing boats carried across the water. The Gage did not need to turn his head to see that the crews were hauling backward hard on oars usually reserved for steering. If their plan was to run the ice-boats aground, well. It was likely to be marginally better than all three boats piling up against the massive blockade, and each other.

Steering ice-boats was somebody else's business. The Gage had more immediate problems.

The individual drawing itself up atop the barricade was an adult male Cho-tse—a creature at once humanoid and tigerish, taller and broader than the Gage and with his tattered ears slicked back against his massive skull. His lip curled up in a hideous snarl, revealing yellowed, furrowed canines like ivory tent-pegs. His fingers were flexed, and heavy, curved claws protruded from the fingertips.

The gunwales of the narrow ice-boat dipped on the side away from the trap. The force of the current was shoving against the hull, and soon the ice-boat would be swamped. The Gage balanced himself. The best thing he could do for the trapped ship was to get off it, lightening its load.

"Heave to and prepare to be boarded!" the tiger cried. His Rasani was barely intelligible, with a heavy Cho-tse accent—the *ps* and *bs* blurring into softer, burring, whistling sounds.

The Dead Man hauled himself dripping over the railing behind the Gage, and drew his sword. He must have thrown himself overboard from the trailing vessel and let the current sweep him toward the trapped one. Courageous, and more than a little mad. The Gage could hear the Dead Man's teeth chattering as he stepped forward.

The Cho-tse eyed them both, but didn't flinch.

"Just what this expedition was in need of," the Dead Man said conversationally. "A pirate tiger."

The Gage replied, "When did you learn to swim?"

He dropped his robe on the deck. Light struck curved reflections from his body, speckling wooden objects on all sides. The Cho-tse's eyes narrowed, and perhaps there was a little less certainty in his snarl. He might never have seen a Gage—many hadn't—and perhaps he hadn't even heard stories, so far east as this. The Gage was intimidating whether you had any idea what you were getting into or not. He'd been built for it.

The Dead Man slung his saber from side to side with a loose wrist, warming up quite casually. His wet coat draggled from his frame and his shirt was plastered to his wiry chest, but he didn't fuss with either. He reached up with his left hand and ceremoniously drew his faded indigo veil down from his face, letting the sodden cotton gauze hang below his chin.

It was the greatest threat a Dead Man could make, to look upon one of the living as an equal. It said, *You too will be my brother soon.* The Gage wondered if the Cho-tse brigand had the education to appreciate it for what it was.

Well, he thought. *It won't matter for long.*

He felt—mostly—tired. Tired, and concerned with the boat swamping and for what had happened to the crewman who screamed. Not in particular concerned with this rag-eared exile tiger, whose expression was beginning to resemble that of a kitten who had scaled too large a tree. The Cho-tse had expected easy pickings and quick capitulation, and his scorn for the hairless monkey-men had left him at a serious disadvantage.

He was obviously considering whether to spring. The Gage wondered if this particular Cho-tse had access to the strange innate magics some of them were said to possess, or if it might be the sort of thing that was stripped from an exile with shredded ears. Perhaps there was a way to let the tiger off with some face intact?

If so, the Gage couldn't think of it. But quick thinking under pressure had never exactly been his strong suit.

The Cho-tse never had to decide. There came a swoop and a rush of air as if through vast black wings. The Godmade—Nizhvashiti—settled beside them, at the Gage's left hand as the Dead Man was on his right. The narrow booted foot came down on the deck of the tilting ice-boat, and the deck that had been in danger of swamping settled and leveled. The Godmade folded long fingers at chest height, over the knob of an ebony staff, and sighed with an expression that said clearly, *You picked the wrong caravan, friend.*

The Cho-tse looked like he knew it, too.

"Look," the Godmade said. "How about you help us get these trees out of the river, and we can all part friends? It's the path of least resistance."

The Cho-tse brigand had crouched back, anticipating an attack. Now, though his lip curled, he straightened up and even leaned a little forward. His accent was so thick it took the Gage several moments to understand his next words. "What's in it for me?"

He had balls. Large, furry ones, as a point of fact.

The Gage said, "We'll pay your labor, of course."

Slowly, the Cho-tse nodded. "All right."

The Dead Man sighed, much put-upon. And reluctantly pulled his soaking veil back up again.

IT WAS HARD, DIRTY WORK. BUT IT WAS JUST WORK, AND AT LEAST IT wasn't killing. Druja the caravan master came out to supervise, and seemed irritated that the Gage had offered to pay off the brigand rather than just slaughtering him. But he forked over some gold that the Gage also knew perfectly well had been set aside for bribing border officials, and was this really all that different?

Perhaps some people thought so.

The Cho-tse, honestly, didn't do that much work, and slunk off as soon as nobody was looking at him. He was probably irritated too, since he'd have to put his barrier back up again before he could stop the next caravan. The Gage wasn't bad at heavy lifting, though, and once they all hauled the ice-boat out to get it free of the barricade and to inspect the hull, the felled trees were swiftly dealt with.

It would have been faster to portage *one* boat. But not all three.

It turned out that the Godmade, with the intercession of the Good Daughter, had summoned up a favorable current to push the trailing ice-boats out of the trap, and that was what had prevented a massive collision. Druja was more impressed with that—even when the Godmade explained that it had only been possible because the water of *this* river was in some metaphysical sense also the water of the Sarathai—but he didn't offer to refund Nizhvashiti's price of passage.

At last the ice-boats were afloat again, but it was nearly dark, and Druja made the decision to tie up and wait out the night, despite the Dead Man's fretting over lost time. The Cho-tse was judged likely to stay cowed, and it seemed reasonable that there would be no other brigands or large predators in his territory.

"And where am I supposed to find another crewman between here and Sarathai-lae?" Druja complained. One man had been tossed overboard in the collision, and crushed between ice-boat and trap.

The Gage didn't even bother shrugging. Logistics, thank the gods, were not his department.

"Examine the benefits," said the Dead Man with intentional fatuousness. "Didn't it work out well that you invested in a pair of caravan guards after all?"

"Well," said Druja. "I'd hate to have wanted you and not had you. I'll go that far."

He turned his back and went to reboard the second boat. Nizh-vashiti looked after him, looked at the Dead Man, and shrugged. "You're getting paid for this?"

"Nobody," the Dead Man replied, "said anything about dragons."

"Ice-drake," the Gage corrected.

The Dead Man ignored him.

"I'll take the last boat," Nizhvashiti said. "You two stick together for now."

THE RIVER EVENTUALLY VANISHED INTO AN UNNAVIGABLE GULLY while the road rose up the flank of the mountain above it, so they had to pull the ice-boats out again, affix axles and wheels in place of the runners, and replace the oxen with teams from another tiny supply depot, this one no more than a cluster of tents and corrals and a tax official or two. They also managed to replace the ruined ice-boat with a somewhat rickety wagon, and the caravan continued on toward the border with the first of the Lotus Kingdoms.

They toiled until they crested the pass, and the Gage could set aside the harness with which he had been assisting the oxen. The Dead Man had come up beside him, leaving the Godmade to the back of the caravan. A shoulder of the mountain, sheer rock above and not much more than that below, divided them from the forward view.

They came around the bend.

The Dead Man stopped short as if struck. The Gage caught him by the elbow and kept them moving, so they were not trampled by the cattle hauling the ice-boat just behind. But if he had not been a machine, the Gage would have been pausing too, in wonder.

They had stepped from daylight into a starry, brilliant night, with the sharp demarcation of a border crossing. But their journey from Messaline had been full of starry, brilliant nights. What the Dead Man now craned his head back to see was a thin pale braided slant of light across the indigo heavens, like an arch viewed from below—and against it, the stark circular silhouette of a blackness so utter it might have been a hole in the sky. It was ringed in a corona of whispery, transparent tongues of flame that shimmered like mother-of-pearl. These, and the stars, and the bright arch, all cast a phantasmal light across the snowy peaks behind, and the sloping valley before. It was as bright as a dim, overcast day—and like such a day, it cast no shadows. Or perhaps it would be more accurate to say that it cast myriad shadows, each pale and overlapping, so the effect was still of a light quite directionless.

"The Cauled Sun," said the Dead Man, his words ruffling his veil. "And the Heavenly River. Well, we're here."

The Gage knew the Dead Man's deadpan sarcasm shrouded embarrassment at having been overcome. He had recovered himself enough to keep walking without the Gage leading him.

The Gage's voice rang even-toned, as if spoke a bell. "We've got a fair number of Lotus Kingdoms to get through before we take our boots off. But at least we're under the right sky."

They walked a while longer, while the ice-boats and the wagon rattled and clattered behind them. The way grew steeper. The edge of the darkness lifted above the shoulders of the mountains behind them, revealing a brilliant edge of blue and vermilion to the north—at the edge of the world, a bright Lotus evening dawned. It was less like a sunrise as the Gage knew them and more like a beautiful woman lifting the gauzy edge of her veil, showing a soft and gold expanse of skin. The Cauled Sun set before them, dropping in the south, and the arch of stars overhead became a braided star-river of such brilliance that though no nightsun rose and the temperature dropped with evening, the light was several times brighter than it had been during the day.

This was the Heavenly River, the glorious twist of light that made the peoples of the Lotus Kingdoms wake by night, in general, and sleep in the dimmer, warmer day.

The caravan halted when the teamsters called a pause to hitch the draft animals behind the ice-boats, where they could brake them, and the Gage—who was impervious to the cold—watched the Dead Man stomp and blow and pace up and down, chilled again due to altitude and nightfall.

He gestured to the sky. "This is bright enough to see by. To *read* by! We could be moving!"

"We'll be traveling through the Boneless's territory," the Gage observed. "There'll be bandits there."

"Privateers, you mean." The Lotus prince known as the Boneless was more of a bandit lord, when it came right down to it. He was notorious for encouraging rogues and reavers and outlaws, so long as they paid him tribute and didn't hunt his own property or anyone who owed him fealty. And his kingdom's position right on the border of the Rasan Empire and the Lotus Kingdoms, along one of the major trade routes, meant that he did better on that than he would have done on "legitimate" taxes and bribes—and that caravans coming from the west were hard-pressed to avoid his lands.

The Dead Man turned his head and spat. "I have heard it said that he got his name as the Boneless because he's cunning as a snake. I've heard it argued also that it's because he's impotent."

"They call him the Boneless because he's Boneless, you daft twat." The Gage would have been smiling when he said it, if he had the means to smile.

"How could it be that a person was actually boneless—without bones—and live? Does he bear a curse? Did he anger a god?" The Dead Man shuddered. He took gods much more seriously than the Gage reckoned they deserved.

"I heard he was born that way." And wasn't that horrid to think about? It seemed a good time for a change of subject.

There was always the future. Both the Gage and the Dead Man had good reasons to prefer the prospect of the future to the prospect of the past. There was only one more pass between them and the descent into the flatlands of the western Lotus Kingdoms, the lands along the Sarathai. Maybe it was a good time to start planning.

"Once we drop the package off," the Gage asked, "have you given some thought to what we might do next?"

The Dead Man scuffed his hands together in their mittens, then stuffed them back in the pockets of his coat. "Would you consider my answer?"

"I assume we're not settling down and digging a farm."

The Dead Man shrugged. A seam on the shoulder of his dull red coat was going. "I await the word of God to guide my choices. She will send a sign, perhaps. In some fashion."

The mountain wind whipped the Gage's hood back from the smooth mirror of his mask. "Having any luck with that?"

The Dead Man turned at the creak of traces, but the ice-boats were still being rehitched. He turned back and shook his head behind the veils. "Alas, not yet. My god is a stern god, and perhaps it is Her belief that I ought to be old enough to look it up by now."

PERHAPS GOD WAS IN THE AIR, THE GAGE THOUGHT, FOR IN THE DARK of night—or perhaps it should be the dark of day, when the Cauled Sun floated in the starry sky above, and the brilliance of the Heavenly River that so strikingly illuminated the sunless hours was dimmed— when all the others should have been asleep, he followed a thin chiming strand of music through the camp and into the scant, piney forest clinging up the walls of steep-sided canyon. Frozen pine needles cracked and sank under the Gage's mass, until his cleated brass feet rested on the bark of the hardscrabble roots clutching the slopes beneath them. The pines made their own soil, and held the mountainside together through force of will as much as anything.

The snow was wind-scraped thin—frosted across the surface like sanding sugar, caught in the little rough chevrons made by the pine needles—so at least the Gage did not have to wade through that.

He climbed, thinking of a time when the sensation would have come with the welcome stretch and pull of working muscle. There was no effort in the activity now, and so, no joy. But the thread of music still tugged him, and as he raised himself tirelessly step by heavy step up the slope, it resolved itself into the peal of tiny silver bells.

He made enough noise for a battalion, and so did not expect to surprise anyone. The chiming continued, though, and as the Gage paused at the edge of a clearing he was surprised in his own right to find that all his racket apparently had done nothing to disturb the musician.

The Godmade sat cross-legged on the cold ground in the shadows of the sparse pines, narrow body robed only in a thin sheath of black-dyed linen, eye lowered to the floss stretched between spread and upraised fingers. The strand would have been crimson in better light, the Gage judged. Minuscule bells—silver, and seemingly tissue-walled—were knotted onto the silk at regular intervals, and they chimed with each calculated motion of Nizhvashiti's hands.

A low murmur of prayer rose and fell like the rhythmic babble of a brook. The Gage had found the Godmade at devotions.

He waited politely, observing, certain that he could not have arrived unnoticed and therefore could not be eavesdropping. His kind were not built to pass unobserved. If Nizhvashiti wished privacy, the Godmade had only to turn and stare at him.

Since no glare was forthcoming, the Gage assumed he was not unwelcome, and settled in to watch.

It was a simple ritual, a counting and ringing of bells while the prayers were chanted. Some time passed, and Nizhvashiti at last bowed to the earth, raised the floss and the bells overhead, and then touched forehead once more to the earth. The Godmade seemed untroubled by the cold despite bare hands and feet, but as Nizhvashiti reached forward and raised a small brass cup from its place nested among the needles, the Gage's senses prickled and he stepped forward.

Nizhvashiti was about to press cup to lips when the Gage very gently insinuated a hand over the opening.

Nizhvashiti frowned up at him. "Why do you interrupt the ritual?"

"Godmade—"

"I am no more so than you."

"Oh, I was made by a Wizard's hand, not that of any deity." The Gage shook his featureless mask. "You must not drink that. It is a deadly poison."

"I know," Nizhvashiti said. "I brewed it."

The Gage kept his regard on the priest's face. It was calm, and Nizhvashiti did not seem like somebody contemplating suicide. Why would you fight off an ice-drake and negotiate with a brigand if all you craved was death? Unless it was death in one's own homeland, the Gage supposed: they had just gained the borders of the Lotus Kingdoms.

Slowly, the Gage pulled back his hand. Just as slowly, Nizhvashiti finished the arc of the little figured cup, and drank—first the poison, and then what seemed to be pure water, poured from a little flask. The priest winced at the taste, and then grimaced as if in mild pain, but made no other sign of discomfiture.

The Gage watched with renewed interest. It occurred to him that he had never seen the Godmade take nourishment—not even his own diet of mystically imbibed wine. When Nizhvashiti had taken a final mouthful of water, rinsed and spat into the snow, the Gage asked, "Are you like the Wizards of the Citadel, then, to transmute the poison in your veins into nutriment?"

"Oh no." Nizhvashiti settled back in a far more relaxed pose. The string of bells vanished up a dark sleeve and was silenced there. "It is poison. But I am . . . accustomed to it. And in its fashion it sustains me."

"Do you eat and drink nothing else?"

A smile on the skull-spare face, squinting the good brown eye and leaving untouched the staring blank of the gilded one. "A bit here and there. I require very little. I learned the discipline in the Banner Islands, and I have pursued it for years now. It would be a pity to let all that practice and discomfort go to waste."

"Discomfort?"

The Godmade winced again. "It *is* poison."

"But it serves a purpose."

The Godmade closed the seeing eye. The blind one gazed at nothing as Nizhvashiti reclined carefully on the frozen needles, moving as if burdened with limbs of some fragile substance like spun glass. "What do you know of the Good Daughter, metal man?"

The Gage thought on it. She was one of the Lotus goddesses. He had seen icons of her. She seemed to him as if she might not be dissimilar to Kaalha, the Messaline goddess of death and mercy whose face was the half-scarred, half-pristine face of the moon. He had always been very fond of gentle Kaalha, in whose house there was an end to pain.

But that was something he wondered, he decided, not something he knew.

"Nothing," he murmured.

Nizhvashiti's long body shuddered. "Awareness is the foundation of duty."

"Is that what the Good Daughter celebrates?"

The priest smiled—a strained smile. "Duty. Filial devotion to the deserving parent, the Good Mother. Absolute honor and obedience to just commands. Faith to ideals and principles. She is a good and loving child."

The Gage thought about that. "She sounds terrifying."

"She is the most frightful god under any sun, metal man. Because how can absolute devotion be met other than by absolute devotion? She is ruthless in her dutifulness and even more ruthless in her compassion. She will see what must be done, and then she will *do* what must be done."

They were silent for a little while. Then the Gage said, "And this is how your people worship her?"

Nizhvashiti laughed, a painful sound that bubbled. A little seizure shook the pine needles all around. "This is how I worship her. With a foreign rite, but one that celebrates the ruthlessness of my own duty to her. I borrowed it, and now it is mine. It *does* lead me to strength such as is not usually known in my order."

"Oh," the Gage said.

Slow coils of mist fingered between the black tree trunks. They were not thick enough to block the view of what scraps of starry sky could be seen between the boughs.

"I was a foundling," the Godmade said. "Left on the convent steps. I was raised to the Good Daughter's service. But I was not meant to be immured in a cloister, you understand. So I chose to become a mendicant. There is an aspect of my goddess that reflects deception for the greater good, you understand. A trickster has a duty, too."

"Why are you telling me this?"

The Godmade's good eye opened. "Metal man. Do you think you are the only one who has wandered the world in search of a purpose? In search of answers? You think you have outlived your usefulness—"

"I outlived my creator," the Gage interrupted. "And I outlived my revenge."

Such a skin-lipped smile the drawn dry flesh almost seemed ready to crack over the bones. One corner of the thin mouth split, and the red blood that trickled free seemed thicker than it should have been, and stank heavily of metal. "There are always duties. We simply choose which ones we take up, when the ones we were born to are ended."

"You're trying to convert me."

"I am," the Godmade gasped, "a priest."

Then the jaw clicked shut on a moan, the body jerked, and Nizhvashiti's eyes rolled back, showing a rim of white above dark lids. The priest thrashed hard, stiffened, then went completely and suddenly slack.

The Gage bent over the stricken form, fearing this most violent convulsion had been the death throes, had done the worst. For a moment, the dimly starlit woods were silent. Some night bird (day bird?) piped and shrilled. The fog flowed down the forested slope like chilly, insubstantial water.

A bubble rose and broke on Nizhvashiti's lips, too desultory to have breath behind it.

The Gage leaned closer and stroked the priest's chill flesh with a chillier finger. Stillness, for a moment. Utter calm.

And then a warm breath fogged the Gage's cold mirror as Nizhvashiti coughed out a rattling, stentorian exhalation and gasped back to life.

One more shudder, another twitching spasm, and it seemed the worst had passed. Nizhvashiti lay quietly for a moment, panting. Breath slowed soon, and the priest raised one hand. "Help me up, metal man."

"Call me Gage," the Gage said, and did as he was instructed.

4

THE WIDOWED SAYEH RAJNI OF ANSH-SAHAL PREPARED HERSELF TO
leave the shady, hanging gardens of her Orchid Court. It was the
advent of the rains, and at dawn, she was to go out and watch the
water-divers perform their annual propitiations. It was far from their
only task over the course of the year, but it was the most ritually significant, and so the rajni must attend.

Sayeh had been awakened long before nightfall by an earth
tremor—the most recent of several—and so she was ready early and
restless as she waited for the appointed time. She actually quite enjoyed the pomp, the circumstance, and the break from routine.
She enjoyed the draping robes of fine white linen worked with silver
bullion, and she enjoyed the jeweled silver sandals with their cords
laced up her slender calves. She enjoyed the cosmetics and adorn-
ments and the fussing with her hair. The best thing about being
rajni was the clothes.

The second best thing was that somebody *else* had bathed and dia-
pered and fed her young son Drupada, and now that Sayeh was
ready to depart, the wet nurse Jagati brought him up and handed him

to her, garbed in his own snow-white miniature tunic and trousers and sandals.

"He tried to piss up my nose today," the nurse said. "Watch it if he reaches into his nappies."

"He's discovered he can aim," Sayeh said, shaking her head. "Nothing's safe now."

Sayeh balanced the toddler on her hip in the approved style, though he was getting heavy and he squirmed to get down. She bent down and pressed her nose into the crown of his head, amazed for the moment that something so big and fine had come out of her own body.

"Hush, my little king," she said. "We're going to have an exciting day today."

That got his attention. He blinked up at her with brown eyes as lush and fringed as those of any sacred cow. "What are we doing, Mama?"

It was the blurred, lisping voice of a small child. And yet, as always, she could not help thinking how clever he was, how smart, how special. How advanced. Surely, all parents felt this. Their own children must always be the cleverest, the smartest, the most special. The most advanced for whatever tender age they had attained. She felt the tiger's desire to kill anything that threatened him, and did not so much conceal that desire behind a camellia-petal smile as . . . incorporate it. "Do you remember last year, when we went down to see the water-divers and their ceremony?"

He didn't. She didn't really expect him to. But she watched him bite his lip in concentration and then nod, as if he was certain that he was *supposed* to remember, even if he didn't, exactly. She looked at him with pretend sternness. "Do you really remember, Drupada?"

He shook his head. She laughed, and turned to his wet nurse and the door attendants. "I shall carry him out to the litter," she said.

It wouldn't hurt anyone to see her in a maternal guise. The fact that she did, in fact, dearly love her only child and heir didn't change the fact that Sayeh was also keenly aware of politics and appearances.

"Now sit still, princelet," she told him. "We're going out where our people can see."

AND SO THEY DID. SAYEH CARRIED HER SON DOWN THE CARPETED stone path between waist-high stone planter walls filled with the pregnant-bellied stems of a heavy-blossomed flower called desert rose. The thick, knobby stalks were rich now with blossoms of velvet red, silken white, and a black shot through with threads of burgundy. They had lost their narrow leaves in the aridity of the dry season. Bees buzzed heavily around them, powdered with the golden pollen that hung fat in hairy caches on their hind legs, but soon the rains would shred the delicate flowers, and coax the waxy leaves to bud again. Seeds would scatter, and the seedlings would be well-drenched and well-warmed for their eventual debut.

Sayeh reached out and let her free hand trail over the still-dry, still-perfect petals as she passed.

Beyond the planter wall stood a rank of liveried servants, their tunics and trousers clean and new with the beginning of the year, as was fitting. They held up slender white poles, and between those poles was stretched a translucent canopy of silk, to shade the rajni and the prince as they stepped out of the palace doors into the brilliant starlight.

Beyond them were some of the Orchid Court's gardens and orchards, tier upon tier of the mandara tree, the aromatic myrtle, and the fig and pomegranate huddled up dormant and waiting for the rain. There were citrus, too, their waxy leaves and bright green thorns dusty and dulled for a few hours more. There was no water to irrigate them, until the rains came. And there were wisteria, their bare gnarled canes woven over arbors that would—one day soon—drip with white and periwinkle flower clusters.

Under those trees and arbors, silent and watchful, her people stood.

Sayeh settled Drupada on her hip again, regretting her decision to carry him. He wasn't getting any lighter, and his little fists knotted hard and dragged at her white robes as he steadied himself. But she was committed now. She stopped at the bottom of the path and turned back to her palace, hanging on to Drupada as she shifted her weight and bowed to the place that gave her shelter, the place that symbolized her kingdom of Ansh-Sahal.

The Green Palace of the Orchid Court was white as weathered bone. At least at this time of year. A sort of tiered pyramid or ziggurat, it rose up in a succession of levels, each one bordered by a row of bare, thirsty, sunburnt trees. At their bases, a faint frizz of green could be glimpsed even now: the barbed garland of a plant called thorny spurge, which kept its leaves even in the driest times. She was too far away to see its tiny, two-petaled red or yellow flowers. After the rains came, the whole palace would drip with greenery and blossoms as if they fountained from it, the white bones cloaked in a verdant flesh.

"Mama," Drupada asked, "what you do?"

"Shh," she told him. Obviously, she wasn't getting him out of the palace often enough if this came as a novelty. Her lips moved in a prayer, and when she straightened and turned back, she told him, "I am thanking our house for keeping us safe."

He giggled and hid his face against her robes, obviously taken with the idea.

She carried him down the steps and out from under the translucent silken shade to where their palanquin waited. It was gilded and enameled, sparkling with sapphires, hung with pale drapes. She made a point of showing no strain from his weight or his lack of skill as she helped him into the sedan chair. He insisted on climbing up "himself," and succeeded with only a little assistance, though it took slightly longer than he had apparently expected. Sayeh was relieved to have somebody else hauling her rapidly growing child for a while, and settled onto the bench beside him with a relieved, if silent, sigh.

The heavy ivory charmeuse curtains fell closed around them, filtering the light of the Heavenly River into a pleasant glow.

Her bearers were well-trained. They lifted her so smoothly that she felt only the slightest shift, and their steps were perfectly timed.

As they began to carry the tiny royal family of Ansh-Sahal down to the Bitter Sea, a cheer went up from the people gathered around the palace.

Sayeh knew it was as much for the imminent rains as it was for her son and herself. She allowed herself to enjoy it anyway.

"WHY ARE THEY CHEERING?" DRUPADA ASKED.

They were well on their way, not that the sea was far. Sayeh glanced over at him, taken with his small studious face. Had he been thinking about that all this time?

Maybe. "Because we are the rajni and the prince," she said. "And because we are going down to the sea to call the rains to Ansh-Sahal, and bring an end to the dry season."

"NO!" His face screwed up. She was answering the wrong question.

She both looked forward to and dreaded his increasing command of language. She wondered if maybe he could not remember what were the rains, yet, and what their difference was from the season of dust. Sayeh missed the moments of her own childhood, when the Kingdoms had been united under her grandfather's reign, and she and her mother had gone west to the wetter, more moderate climates closer to the ocean for the dry season.

Though the capital city of Ansh-Sahal was built on the shore of what was by courtesy the inland Bitter Sea of Sahal, and it was certainly *salty* enough to be a sea—saltier than the ocean, at least at the surface—that sea was not large enough to soothe the air-spirits as the ocean did. Ansh-Sahal was also at a higher elevation.

The dry season here was drier, and hotter; the rainy season colder and more wet.

That was probably not what Drupada wanted to know, so Sayeh said mildly, "That is not how we ask politely, my princelet."

He sighed in exasperation. She was old to have such a young son;

the Mother had not seen fit to bless her until her fortieth year, and she had been forty-one before Drupada was born. She doubted she would ever have another. But distant as her own childhood was, she remembered dimly from it that, in general, adults were exceedingly obtuse.

"Politely?" she reminded.

He sighed, much put-upon. "Why am I prince?"

Why am I a prince? Oh. Well. That was a much easier question than she had been afraid of. "You are a prince," she said, organizing her thoughts, "because I am a rajni and you are my son. It is my duty to oversee my people, and make sure they are fed and safe from strangers, and that the gods are attended as the gods desire. Someday, that will be your duty, too. When I am gone."

He clutched at her, eyes suddenly wide.

She stroked his hair. "That won't be for a very long time," she reassured. "You'll be as old as Old Parrah before I go away."

"But who take care me?" he squeaked.

"You'll still have people to advise you, little otter. But everybody's turn comes to be the one who takes care of other people someday. And you'll have had plenty of practice by then. You'll be a daddy yourself, like I'm your mommy now."

That stopped him, and got him thinking. And it was just as well, because the smell of the sea was growing stronger, and Sayeh could hear the ceaseless private whisper of the waves. The filtered light outside grew dimmer: the veil rising with the Cauled Sun, hiding the river of stars.

She could also hear the voices of her people gathered already, and the footsteps of the hundreds following her little palanquin with its bearers and squads of buffering soldiers down the road. Her father had been prone to traveling with a small army, and keeping the populace at a distance. Sayeh thought it a better practice in the long run to keep fewer guards about her, and make of her people friends.

The bearers placed her sedan chair in a set of mounts. She could tell the difference, because they did not lower her as far as the ground, and because she felt the click as the carrying poles went into the brackets. That was better; less sand in the rugs and cushions, and easier to climb out gracefully.

There was a clatter as the steps were brought. Sayeh gathered her son into her lap—he only squirmed a little—and waited for the chief of her personal guard to draw the curtains back. Her guard captain Vidhya smiled through his gray-streaked beard. He reached down and lifted Drupada from her grasp. Vidhya balanced the boy on his shoulder—much manlier than the hip trick, Sayeh thought, concealing a grin—and extended a hand for her to use to lever herself upright with as much dignity as could be managed.

She stood, and surveyed her domain.

Her palanquin had been set down at the base of a long bight overlooking the glittering curve of the sea where the rocky and occasionally precipitous coast swept up toward the north. The water lay dark beneath the silvery glints reflecting from the Heavenly Sahal that brightened the veiled daytime sky behind the Cauled Sun. Snowcapped mountains, the southernmost reaches of the Steles of the Sky, lofted themselves above the haze of horizon to the west, to shimmer in the light of so many cascading stars.

Sayeh looked down and glimpsed the sea so many lengths below. A rocky pier stretched out to sea before her. It was built out from the cliff edge, seemingly unsupported except by its own span, a feat of Wizardly engineering. It was of black stone flecked with plates of mica that glittered as bright as the facets of the waves below. It was no more than Sayeh's height in width, but over two hundred fathoms long. There were no rails.

Sayeh did not step too close to the edge. It would not do for the rajni to collapse mid-blessing from unchecked vertigo.

Along the clifftop behind her, her people stood ranked many dozens deep. They too wore white and silver, or as close as they could come with their limited resources. Keeping white clothing white required a certain expenditure of money and time, and in practicality many were garbed in the soft duns of undyed homespun. They murmured among themselves, their voices soft but lifted and carried to her by the wind blowing out to sea.

Sayeh wished she could not hear a lack of confidence in those murmurs, even now. The auguries that had attended the beginning of her regency—and the beginning of the dry season—had not been favorable. She needed good omens now.

Along each side of the pier stood the water-divers. They too wore white—a scanty brief twisted around their loins, and nothing else besides their water-belt—a wide band of waxed canvas folded and wrapped tight about each waist, secured with a steel toggle pushed through a loop of hemp. They were women all, and all were slender, almost bony. Their hair was shaved or cropped short. They wore no jewelry.

Upon them, in the dry season, the life of Ansh-Sahal, and her rajni, and all her people, depended.

Sayeh fought the urge to glance back over her shoulder, at her people arrayed in judgment along the edge of the cliff. Their judgment was for her, she knew: a rajni alone, a widow, and *shandha* to boot. They wanted a raja, as they had wanted a raja when, in her fifteenth year, she had married Ashar, the beautiful third son of the raja of Sarathai-lae, to give them one.

They might celebrate her beauty—even now, with four decades behind her, Sayeh knew they did. Modesty had never been expected of a princess, thank the Good Mother, because she didn't know how she would have managed it when day in, day out, everyone she met had been praising her graceful feet and the shining part of her hair since she was old enough to paint her eyelids and blush. But they were not ready, yet, to accept that she might be a fitting regent for their raja-yet-to-be.

Drupada squirmed in the grip of the guard captain. Vidhya held on to the boy, murmuring to him to settle down, that what he was doing was dangerous. He set the prince up higher on his shoulder, and Sayeh tried not to watch. This only heir, this only child of her body—squirming and tickling a hundred fathoms above the sea.

She could not ward him from everything, especially not from his own curiosity. Not and expect him to grow into a capable king in his own time.

"Mama!" he called.

Sayeh squared her shoulders and stepped away from him, out into the center of the long stone pier. She extended her hands, her arms held wide like wings at shoulder level. The fanned, pleated sleeves of her robe flared like pinions. The front of the robe, unfastened except for a silver clasp between her breasts, whipped out and back in the sea breeze, fanning like a tail because bands of silver embroidery weighted the hem. Her gauzy trousers smoothed themselves to her legs, and only the heaviness of more bullion held the bottoms at her ankles.

The water-divers turned to watch her come.

As she passed each pair, Sayeh reached out right and left in a benediction. She touched their naked shoulders and murmured a blessing meant for their ears alone. She had learned it at her father's knee, and it was meant that no one ever heard it pronounced except the water-divers, and the ruler. Certainly the sea wind roaring up the cliff ripped the holy words from her lips and threw them skyward. She could not even be sure the water-divers heard what she said.

It didn't matter. They knew the words by heart.

Some of the women were old, with slack bellies and breasts like stray flaps of flesh and bony scapulae like dull blades stretching skin as soft and thin as gauze. Some of them were very young, their eyebrows black and their limbs rounded and firm. Almost all of them smiled to see their rajni. On one or two, the smile seemed forced. Sayeh tried not to hold it against them.

She remembered who these women were, and what they did.

Behind her, she felt the movement, heard the whoosh of lifting wind as, pair by pair, the women dove off the sides of the pier. She did not turn to watch them: she just blessed the next pair, time after time, as she came to each.

The sea below was too far down for her to hear the splashes about the waves and the wind. But when she turned back, they were all gone. All but one, one of the youngest, who Sayeh could not remember ever having blessed before. She must be new, elevated from an apprentice since the last year's blessing to take the place of a water-diver who had retired. Or who had been crippled. Or killed.

The girl gave Sayeh a seething glance, one of heady resentment. It shivered along Sayeh's nerves until she could practically taste it: bitter, electrical. Sayeh could not hear the people on the shore above the sound of the wind, but she could see them shifting, pointing. Captain Vidhya almost started forward, but then remembered that he had the prince on his shoulder. And before he could hand Drupada away—

—the girl turned her back on Rajni Sayeh, composed herself, lifted her arms, pointed her toes, and stepped calmly off the pier.

FORGETTING HERSELF, SAYEH RUSHED TO THE EDGE, THEN CLUTCHED herself back at the last instant, her head reeling. She still saw. It was a long enough dive that there was plenty of time to watch the last instants of it.

The girl parted water like a knife, vanishing beneath the sea with almost no splash at all. A perfect entry, for all her insolence. And then there was nothing, the long silence, the wait. At least the Sea of Sahal was small enough that the waves knocking the base of the cliffs were not towering, and not powerful enough to throw a woman against them and dash her to death on the rocks.

Not unless there should be a storm.

The first bobbing head broke the black sea close to the cliffs, where the earliest divers had gone in. Sayeh saw her rise, struggling in the water as if dragged down by a tremendous weight. She was a strong swimmer, but what dragged at her unseen was both enormous and heavy.

The tender boats had begun their rush in from the perimeter as soon as the final diver committed herself, and now Sayeh saw them turning to meet the surfacing swimmer. Someone in the boat extended a pole to her, one with a blunt hook at the end and a long rope drooping from the boat-edge to a ring just beside the hook. Sayeh saw the diver thrust something through the loop—a big metal toggle, which caught and held. Then the hook was around her body, under her arms, towing her back to the boat.

The other tenders were circling, and now and then one rowed frantically toward an exhausted, reappearing head.

Once the first water-diver was on board and wrapped in a blanket—the deep water was spring-fed down from the roots of the mountains and it was icy cold, compared to the temperatures at the surface—the men in the tender threw the line over a winch and began hauling the bulk at its end in. Each heave rocked the boat, as if something heavy indeed dragged at it.

Before too much longer, they had surfaced a great waxed canvas bag that—swollen and sausagelike—was larger and obviously much heavier than the body of the woman who had worn it into the deeps wrapped as a belt, then opened and filled it. The boatmen hauled it up into the tender, and one of the men gingerly opened the tight-knotted top, just a little. He dipped a cup inside and handed the result to the resting diver with a little, formal bow.

It was a pretty gesture, and she returned it. She sipped at the cup, and Sayeh saw with relief that she then tossed her head back and drained the rest of what was contained there.

The harvest was sweet.

The water at the top of the Bitter Sea of Sahal-Sarat was saline, warm, stagnant. Wizards said it had been trapped there for ages of the world, and as the sea shrank and shrank, the water became more salty and sterile. But the water at the deeper layers, rising from underground springs, was cold and sweet and pure. The water-divers were how Sayeh's people got to that water, and between the rains, it was what sustained them—along with what they drew from cisterns holding saved rain, and such deep wells as they could manage to chisel into the unforgiving rock.

Sayeh threw her hands up in victory. A good omen. A great omen, if *all* the water-divers came back safe today, this last dive of the season, before the rains came.

As she began to walk back to the clifftop and her son, the sea wind freshened and shifted, becoming a cold, landward breeze. A lowering cloud that she had not noticed while watching the divers had slid across the face of the Heavenly Sahal, racing from the east, a blessing from the Sea of Storms.

The first drops of rain spattered on the shoulders of her robe, and she smiled. Another dry season survived; her first as a widow. Perhaps she would hold her throne as regent long enough to see her son come of age and be crowned.

BEFORE SHE COULD HOLD HER THRONE, THOUGH, SAYEH WOULD HAVE to hold her position on this rain-swept, windswept stone so dizzyingly outreached above an increasingly violent sea. The storm did not slip up gently, after those first tentative drops. Instead, the rain came down like a thundering chain of glass beads hurled from a height, pounding on her head with stinging force. The air tugged at her white robes as if they were sails; the falling water blinded her. The footing grew increasingly slick and treacherous. She could not leave, however, until all the water-divers had surfaced and been hauled into the tenders. Every single one. Including that final, insolent girl.

The tenders could not go back in until they had recovered the divers. So neither could the rajni. Especially not a widowed rajni, whose power needed the support of every grain of respect she could eke from her people.

Sayeh glimpsed black fluttering through the driving veils of rain. She turned her head to center the motion, blinking droplets from her lashes like stinging tears. That shadowy darkness was the coat of her Citadel-educated Rasan Wizard, the estimable Tsering-la. The petaled skirts of his close-seamed black coat were sodden, but the wind was so violent that they streamed out straight as planks. He was a small, round man, with angled Rasan features, and the tight-seamed coat did not flatter him. He seemed more like a plump little blackbird hopping along the pier than a carrion crow on the wings of the storm.

Still, he came toward her, seemingly much more anchored to the pier than she, and when he touched her arm she felt as if her feet sank through the slick of treacherous water and founded themselves strongly to the stone. Wizardry, of course.

That was what she kept him around for.

She turned and felt her hair stream out on the rising wind. It whipped across her face. "The divers!" she called.

Tsering-la shook his head. "The waves are rising!"

Sayeh bit back a curse. No: not fair. It had been a good omen! That the storms should come in a little too early and turn that into a portent of doom . . .

She drew herself up, shivering in the cold rain. She was a rajni; there was no place in her vocabulary for fair or not-fair. There was only what was true, and what must be done.

"You will aid them," Sayeh commanded, and never knew if Tsering-la nodded his agreement because she was rajni, or because he would have done so anyway.

A narrow, rail-less stair led down the stony cliff face from near the base of the pier. Tsering-la brought her to it, her guard surrounding them as they stepped off the stone pier so far above the angry water. Someone tried to hand Sayeh her son, who was screaming for her and wailing. She glared and snapped, "Take him back to the palanquin," angry that it had not been done already.

Vidhya stepped in and Sayeh gripped his arm. "Take him home. Keep him safe."

The guard captain did not argue. He regarded her, nodded, and took four of his men aside to briefly issue them orders. She watched her son carried away, over his violent protests, and hoped it would not be her last sight of him. She thought of her earlier promise to be with him until he was old, and hoped even more fervently that it would not be his last sight of her.

One of the guards tried to argue her away from her course, but she simply pushed past him. He didn't have the moral fortitude to lay hands on his rajni.

Then somehow she and Tsering-la were on the stairs, led and followed by her men. The wind whipped past them, curled by the cliff edge, howling and trying to pluck her feet from the rain-slick stones. She hugged the wall, one hand on it, as if she could clutch the vertical rocks and somehow hold herself in place against all the savage weather could do to her.

This, she thought, would be a wonderful time for one of the earthtremors to which Ansh-Sahal was so disposed.

Another step or two, though, and she realized she could see. The water in her eyes was that which dripped from her headdress and hair; the wetness on her body was from her robes plastered close to her skin. The air around them was warm and dry, the cloth of her sleeves faintly steaming. She turned her head to glance back at Tsering-la, and saw a frown of concentration and a faraway expression. He was using his Wizard's will to bend the raging elements around them, keep them in a bubble of relative safety and comfort.

It might have saved her life. It might have saved the lives of her guardsmen.

Sayeh, Tsering-la, and the four guards stopped abruptly roughly twice a man's height above the sea. The waves shattered against the stone below them so violently that Sayeh felt the impact through the stone under her soles. They could descend no farther. She turned her head; the storm still raged no more than an arm's length away. She could put out her hand and drench her fingertips in the pummeling rain. Superstitiously, she clutched her fingers in the cloth of her robe to keep from doing so, as if her touch could somehow shatter the witchery of peace that Tsering had laid around them.

"There's a walkway," Tsering-la said, gesturing. "It leads over to the dock. It's still above the water."

Sayeh squinted through the falling rain. It was like trying to see through a hail of jewels; the heavy fall of water obliterated and ob-

scured. The dock was where the tending-boats were launched from.
It was accessible by a steep road cut through the cliff from above. It
was long, and stone, and protected by breakwaters. And Sayeh could
see that it still stood above the raging waves. Indeed, some of the tenders had tied up to it, sheltered by the breakwaters, and women and
bags of water were being unloaded from them, though it was hard to
tell one huddled shape from another in the rain.

"If the waves rise, though," the Wizard continued, "I and all the
Six Thousand cannot promise to keep us from being swept off."

"Then we will go quickly," Sayeh said, and urged her vanguard
forward.

The walkway was better than the stairs. As narrow, but the level
surface made a world of difference. They achieved the end of the dock
without trouble.

There they found a bustle of evacuation and activity. People were
hauling the tenders out of the sea, tipping them on their sides and
covering them, and more people were leading protesting draft animals up the steep road, which had become the next best thing to a
river. They dragged carts laden with the water sacks, and with water-
divers huddled under blankets and oiled hide roofs that were doing
little to keep off the rain.

Sayeh's guardsmen found one of the foremen of the dock. Even
in the driving rain, he was identifiable by his orange hood. She pushed
her way forward, Tsering-la at her flank, and demanded, "Are all my
divers safe?"

"That's the last tender being hauled out now," the foreman said.
"We've found all but one of the divers."

"Where's the last? Why are you hauling the boat out if one's still
out there?" Outraged, she waved a hand at the bucking sea.

He shook his head. "The sea's too rough, Your Abundance. Even
if we found her, the tender couldn't come up to her. She'd be dashed
against the side!"

Sayeh pushed past him, waving her Wizard along as she stalked the length of the dock. The guardsmen rushed after. Sailors and water-divers ineffectually tried to prevent her march into what they must have perceived as increasing danger.

When she reached the end of the dock, the howl of the wind and the crash of the waves was deafening even within her Wizard's battered bubble of calm. "Tsering-la," she shouted. "Make a light! If she's still swimming she needs to know which way to go!"

He raised one hand in a familiar gesture. She expected the baroque-styled, warm yellow crescents of his witch-lamps to flock and spiral above them, but instead what went up was a tower of light, a great hissing flare of lemon-white that speared up level with the clifftop and cast shadows stark as chasms before Sayeh and everyone.

And there—sliding down the slope of a wave towering beyond the breakwater—gleamed a little pale face, visible for a bare moment in the spear of light.

"There!" Sayeh shouted, but Tsering-la had already seen her. The gasps and cries from the onlookers had not faded when the Wizard reached out, grunting with effort, and made a gesture with his hand as if he were pressing down hard on something that struggled against him.

Warm monsoon rains thundered on Sayeh's head once again. They stung her eyes and plastered her lashes. She squinted under a raised hand to see; the shelter barely helped at all.

The sea did not calm, exactly. But a patch around the valiantly swimming girl smoothed a bit, and she struggled less and stroked more easily. Tsering-la crooked his fingers and scooped, drawing toward him, and a golden glow seemed to seep and settle into the water's surface around the diver, pulling her and the patch of smoother water in.

She kicked forward, angling to pass behind the breakwater a good distance from its tip, in order to keep from being dashed against it. She reached the calmer waters near the dock, and now Tsering-la seemed able to assist her. She drew close fast, faster than she should have been able to swim by herself, and when she clutched the ladder up to the dock and hauled herself over the edge, Sayeh's guards were there to help her.

Sayeh saw that the water belt was still fastened at her waist, the long lines behind it taut with the weight of the bag she had been dragging.

Good Daughter, Sayeh thought in awe. *Here is one of your own children.*

Then the girl raised her face, and Sayeh saw it was the insolent girl, the one who had challenged her and dove last. She must have gone deep, too, to be so long returning.

She collapsed to her hands and knees as the guards went to haul her water to the surface. Sayeh wanted to tell them to slash the damn lines, cut the silly thing loose—but the girl had almost died for her duty to return it. Sayeh would not abrogate that sacrifice.

The wind whistled around their eerie bubble of calm as Tsering-la resumed his local protection. He bent over the girl, working her belt free, checking her for injuries. The Rasan Wizarding tradition, like the Aezin one, trained its practitioners as physicians.

Her spine, Sayeh could not help but see, was a bony string of beads along her back. The rajni stepped forward as Tsering-la guided her into a sitting position and wrapped her in a woolen blanket some sailor had handed over.

The girl looked up and frowned at Sayeh. She opened her mouth, then closed it, swallowed, and seemed about to speak again. Whatever she might have said, though, was interrupted by one of the guardsmen gasping "Phaugh!" as they got the water bag open and a mighty stench rolled through the little isle of calm.

It reeked of rotten eggs, sulfur and sourness. Sayeh involuntarily took a step back herself and covered her nose with her hand. The girl turned, too, but she didn't seem startled—and Sayeh thought there was a tiny smirk of self-satisfaction flickering about the corners of her mouth for a moment before she smoothed it into neutrality.

Sayeh strode toward the guards and the water bag, her feet slapping on wet stone. The stench increased as she drew closer. She paused, then closed the final distance in two quick paces. Holding her breath, she plunged her hands into the sacred water and lifted it up to her lips.

It was too rank. Like rotten soup. And warm, when the water from the deep springs should be cold and sweet. She gagged, and could not force herself to drink, or even touch it to her lips. She straightened her arms abruptly, throwing the tainted palmful away, and held her hands out far from her body to let the rain wash her fingers clean.

When she brought them back into Tsering-la's bubble of dryness, she saw that the skin was red and rough where the water had touched them, even from such scanting contact.

"What is this?" she asked the water-diver, who huddled in her damp blanket and shook.

The girl raised bottomless brown eyes. "An omen, my rajni."

5

THE PLUNGE DOWNRIVER BECAME TOO STEEP FOR THE ICE-BOATS EVEN-
tually, and in any case to follow the meandering path of the Sarathai
would have taken them very far out of their way: back into the
Empire and eventually all the way to Rasa itself, on the great rippled
plateau where the major tributaries of the Tsarethi—as the river was
called to the north, and farther east—converged. Instead, they turned
right, and headed overland and through passes deeper into the Lotus
Kingdoms.

As the caravan wended south, the roads became wider and far
more heavily traveled. They entered the territory of Himadra the
Boneless, prince of Chandranath, with little fanfare. There was a
border, and there were guards. The Dead Man lurked genially in the
background while Druja the caravan master was interrogated by them.

"Where are you going?" the one with the most gold on his uniform asked Druja.

"Through the Lotus Kingdoms down to Sarathai-lae," Druja
answered.

"Not to Ansh-Sahal?"

Druja shook his head. "We've no cargo nor passengers for the east."

"Just as well," the man said. "You wouldn't want to get too close to that creature Sayeh's territory. You might get buggered. Or worse." He made a leering gesture.

Druja scowled but spoke gently as he moved the conversation along.

A tariff was extracted from Druja, and the various passengers were shaken down in their turns and according to their means—or slightly beyond them. The caravan's guards weren't particularly hassled—perhaps out of professional fellowship, perhaps because they seemed perfectly content not to start anything with these ostensibly legal highway robbers—and the Gage was hassled least of all. The Dead Man came in for a little provocation, but he had been raised to be a stone-faced, elite imperial guard with no personality and even less in the way of opinions. He was only subject to being visibly provoked when he so chose. So he simply answered the sallies about his religion, his ethnicity, his fallen nation, and his presumed sexuality with pleasantries, and he did his seething internally and imperceptibly.

It was hot, and it was sticky, and it was boring as hell. After a half-day of overly elaborate paperwork-checking and unpredictably accruing fees and subfees, the border guards seemed to decide that they had squeezed this stone dry. Or perhaps the larger and potentially richer caravan appearing on the horizon had something to do with it. It would be sad to have all one's berths filled when a better candidate for extortion rolled through.

As this radical change of heart swept through the border guards, they shifted from impeding the caravan's progress to chivvying Druja and his people to move on as quickly as possible. As the caravan swung out again, the Dead Man took advantage of the safer roads—at least, safer from politically nonconnected brigands—to move up to the front of the column and walk beside the Gage. There were plenty of guards at the rear, and he found his old friend's presence calming. Even when they argued.

Perhaps especially when they argued.

"You know," the Gage said, not disappointing the Dead Man, "you cause a lot of your own trouble."

Beside him, the Gage stank of heated brass. The Dead Man's veil gave welcome shade. Clouds were piling on the eastern horizon, sliding up across the vivid Lotus sky. The Dead Man leaned his head back and gazed up at it. It was very interesting to be able to look to the east and watch the new season coming.

"It appears the monsoon is upon us," he said to no one in particular.

The Gage didn't need to turn his head to see, so the Dead Man couldn't be sure if he'd registered the Dead Man's comments. Or if he'd noticed long before the Dead Man did, and hadn't troubled himself to say anything.

But at last he said, "Have you noticed that the wind is from the west, and yet the weather is coming from the east?"

"Does it portend magic?" asked the Dead Man.

The Gage shrugged. "They do call that big gulf there the Sea of Storms. And the one to the west they call Arid, though it is to all appearances full of water."

The Dead Man sighed meditatively. "I am no Wizard nor yet a sailor, to understand the nuances of meteorology. Do you require grease in your joints when we stop tonight?"

The Gage gestured to his coat. "If you'd take off that ragged old thing, and your veil, you'd find yourself in a lot less trouble than otherwise."

"If I removed my veil, however, I should have to murder everyone I met," the Dead Man said mildly.

"You wear that thing around like a child flaunting a scraped knee."

That stung. But it probably stung because it was fair.

The Dead Man shrugged. "Will you not tend your own fire, Gage? You carry your own hurts close to the surface." The Dead Man's finger hovered just before its mirrored reflection in the Gage's head. "You've collected your vengeance. Your service is ended. Why don't *you* lie down?"

"I'm not suggesting you die."

The Dead Man pressed a raveling thread of embroidery back against his cuff. "Aren't you?"

That brought the Gage up. He didn't stop walking, though, so neither did the Dead Man, stretching his legs to keep up. "Well," he said. "After a fashion, we're both dead."

"We have so much in common," the Dead Man agreed placidly, belying his internal urgency. "My death is merely symbolic. So far."

The Gage shrugged. "My heart has stopped. And before it stopped, it was drawn beating from my chest and replaced with a thing of pistons and gears."

"I suppose that counts for something on the death front," the Dead Man agreed. "Though I feel we're getting distracted by technicalities. But only inspect the situation from my perspective."

The Gage crouched down a little lower, gazed around ostentatiously, eyelessly, and unnecessarily before straightening up again with a shake of his head. Despite himself, the Dead Man laughed. The Gage's shoulders straightened in that posture that the Dead Man thought of as a smirk.

"Your perspective," the Gage urged.

The Dead Man plucked up a pinch of his threadbare wool sleeve. "You have metal. I have this. You are a Gage, and I am what I am. What you were before doesn't matter, as you have been at pains to demonstrate to me." He didn't actually believe that—the Dead Man knew perfectly well that what had driven the Gage to become a Gage was still driving him. Was a wound unhealed. But he was certainly willing to use the other's self-delusion to win an argument. What otherwise was the intimate knowledge of friends for? "And I have never been anything but a Dead Man. So I don't even have a past self to fall back on. You want me to move forward from the thing that creates me. And I'm not sure I want to. Or that it would be good for me, frankly."

The Gage thought about it quietly for so long that thunder crackled eerily, and it began to rain. "There are things in the past you don't care to give up."

"I suppose that's one way to look at it. Another is that the thing I was created for still gives me purpose, after a fashion."

"To defend a dead, deposed caliph?"

The Dead Man's tone held a sorrowful simplicity. "To serve the Scholar-God. Whatever land She takes me to."

THE RAIN, ONCE IT STARTED, CONTINUED HARD AND LONG AND UN-abated. The oxen went from clopping along packed dirt to splashing through liquid, sucking mud in a matter of an hour. The ice-boats and the wagons bogged down by turns and had to be levered out of each other's ruts, and—fairly soon—also out of the ruts left by earlier travelers.

Breathing through the wet veil plastered against his face, hair escaping his queue as he leaned on a lever, the Dead Man bit back on a curse that would have scandalized his one-time spiritual mentors and wondered if maybe the Gage didn't have a point. They *had* greased up the Gage's joints with handfuls of rendered fat, and now the Gage, laboring beside him, gave off the aroma of a slightly rancid barbecue.

The stink of sun-heated brass had been, the Dead Man admitted—though only to himself—preferable.

They struggled on.

The planned route took them through a range of what were technically mountains, but after the heart of the Steles of the Sky seemed no more than foothills. Though the pass was low, by the Dead Man's new standards, he felt the buzz of relief when Druja came to him and said that the rains had come earlier than anticipated, and they would be diverting through the lowlands. It was a longer route, but the roads there were paved. They would lose less time—and entail less risk—than they would struggling up the sliding, saturated roads on the flanks of the hills.

Druja did not look relieved at his decision, however. He looked concerned, and not with the usual concern for timetables and schedules that always creased his brow.

"What is it?" asked the Gage, his booming voice lowered to something like a murmur.

Druja shook his head. "The low road takes us through the Boneless's capital. Which is where the bey is headed anyway, so it means we can deliver him precisely to his destination—"

"He's leaving the caravan in Chandranath?" the Dead Man asked.

"Business interests," said the caravan master.

"Pity it's not that damned Mi Ren instead."

Druja didn't speak, just turned his head and spat. It vanished in the rain as if it had never been.

"More tariffs on the low road?" the Dead Man asked.

"If we're lucky. Maybe we can claim we're pilgrims." Druja gestured ahead, to where the Godmade walked along the edge of the road some fifty paces ahead, the long staff a pendulum whisking in time with every second stride.

The Dead Man asked, "What is it your people mean when they say Godmade, Druja? A priest, obviously. I have never encountered one such before—"

"Not just a priest. There are priests and priestesses, cloistered nuns and sacred royalty, some of whom can beg the direct favor of the Mother or the Good Daughter and be heard, on occasion, in accordance with their duties. A Godmade is different . . ." Druja searched for the words. "A saint, of sorts, I suppose. A prophet. Like your Ysmat."

Not like Ysmat, the Dead Man thought, but he had dwelt among heathens long enough to bite his tongue. "Godmade are not common?"

Druja seemed uncomfortable. "I saw one preaching once, when I was young. Not since."

"Does each of them win favor with your Mother through self-denial?"

The caravan master thought it over. Thin, cloying mud splashed at every step. "I do not think so. But Nizhvashiti's sacrifice may be for some private purpose. Or perhaps in payment to the gods, who are said to respect such devotions."

The Dead Man thought of something. It almost made him trip as he considered the implications. "If a Good Daughter serves your Mother River, Druja, does that mean there is also a Bad Daughter?"

Druja was silent for a long time: five steps, ten. Then he kissed his teeth and said, "We do not speak of her."

That chill was surely only the rain running down the Dead Man's back under coat and shirt. He would never be warm again. His eyes tracked the black-cowled shadow of the Godmade walking before them, far down the caravan line. There was a flash, a glimpse of gold, almost-imagined as Nizhvashiti turned toward them and winked, just as if they were clearly audible despite the distance and the falling rain.

The Dead Man was not new to the ways of preachers. Still, he was impressed.

AFTER TWO NIGHTS IN THE RAIN, THE DEAD MAN WOULD HAVE BEEN willing to wrestle Himadra the Boneless personally, just for the privilege of a dry place to sleep. (Although, if he really were literally boneless, that raised the interesting question of how good a wrestler he could possibly be, and what wrestling him might be like.)

The liquid mud flowed like slimy water. It got into everything—boots, eyes, ears, hair, the interior spaces of the ice-boats—and it dried (when you could get it to dry) into a heavy, stiff, cumbersome suit of coagulated dirt that weighed one down and flaked off into dust at the slightest provocation. The mud came in many interesting colors—pale gray and dull red, in particular, and occasional patches of a dusky blue-purple—and it was as slick as that rancid axle grease. More slick, in fact: the axle grease was a lot thicker.

"I have come to believe," the Dead Man deadpanned, digging his heels in while a rope abraded his palms and his boots slid in a patch of slick purple, "that the local soil must be unusually rich in clay."

"Yes," the Gage said from a few knots up the rope. They were skidding one of the ice-boats down a steep patch. "I believe the region is known for its pottery."

One of the major drawbacks of spending time with the Gage was the impossibility of determining if or when he was making a joke based on facial expression or modulation of his tone. The area probably *was* known for pottery. On the other hand, the Gage also probably thought it was extremely funny to point that out when they were both glazed with slip to the armpits.

The Dead Man decided to laugh. Chuckle, at least, while blinking stinging rain from his lashes. Around him, the shadowy shapes of the caravan's passengers straggled, spread out dangerously in the rain. If he were a brigand, the Dead Man would wait for days like this, and attack caravans struggling through the monsoon by preference. There was absolutely no way they could run, if they were beset now. They were strung out all over the landscape, and it was all but impossible to keep a lookout with the weather drumming on their heads.

Brigands were not in general known for their devotion to hard and uncomfortable work. It was just as likely under these conditions that they would choose to stay home. Still, he kept an eye peeled, as well as he could under the circumstances.

At least the rain was warm. That probably meant all these mud puddles were full of cholera. The Dead Man passed himself a mental note to try not to swallow any of it.

He glanced down at his mud-encrusted hands. He'd just avoid eating or drinking or wiping his face for the next month and a half.

"Only another hour or so to the paved road," the Gage said cheerfully.

"And no hope of a hot supper," the Dead Man replied.

Then the rope slipped again, and he cursed, and got on with the problem of controlling it and with it, the ice-boat. If they made it to a paved road, he swore, he was going to get down on his knees and kiss the flagstones in the name of the Scholar-God, who had invented civil engineering, and also architecture.

Oh, right. Except for the cholera.

*   *   *

THEY DID GET STONES UNDER THEIR WHEELS, AND THE DEAD MAN, true to his prayers, got down and kissed them, though dryly, and he wiped his mouth after—much to the amusement of caravaneers and passengers. At least the draft animals seemed to have no opinions. The rain didn't let up, but by God's mercy they were out of the mud, and the body-warm water washed the clay from their skins and clothes after a day or two. Those passengers who cared to even got to go back below and get dry—dryish, as dry as anything could be in the soggy cloying humidity—though the quarters inside the ice-boats were so cramped the Dead Man hated to imagine being stuck in there for days due to weather.

The marriageable noblewoman was still walking. And so were the acrobats, who actually seemed to enjoy the water falling from the sky. They were stripped down more or less to their underclothes, which probably helped with their comfort. The Dead Man could hear the spoiled Song princeling excoriating his people even through the heavy curve of the scaled hull every time he wandered too close to the second ice-boat.

On the evening of their third day in Himadra's lands, the roads grew less deserted; more miserable travelers began to edge around them in both directions, gawking. On the morning of the fourth day, city walls hove into sight. It was their first glimpse of Chandranath, the throne city of Himadra the Boneless, Warrior-Lord of the North. Or the South, if you happened to be coming from the direction of the Steles, the Dead Man supposed. The rain and mist broke briefly as they crested the pass, giving a fine view of the valley below.

By the Dead Man's Caliphate-honed standards, it wasn't much of a city. The citadel was impressive—it hulked amid the granite roots of mountains a thousand feet above, accessible only by a road so steeply switchbacked that from here the stacked lanes looked like steps carved for a giant's foot. Chandranath itself huddled at the foot of the peaks, and seemed to be built chiefly of mud brick, straw, wood, and daubed wattle walls. The buildings were one story—two at the most, and those few—with heavy roofs of thatch overhanging the earthen walls to keep them dry in the rainy season and cool in the rainless one. A wooden stockade atop an earthwork dike surrounded it, but the Dead Man could see over those quite plainly into the town itself as they descended the pass.

The city could not have held more than five thousand, the Dead Man thought. If they slept stacked up like cordwood, perhaps double that.

Cleared fields surrounded the city on all sides. Terraced rice paddies even crept up the base of the mountains behind it, though they did not reach to the citadel—and were currently deserted to the driving rain. Only here and there could the Dead Man pick out the silhouette of a draft animal—some sort of black ox that waded through the muddy water stolidly, heavy horns draping the skull from a center part like pigtails.

Beyond the city, the road continued through more fields. But at the edge of the fields, a dark forest loomed, and the road dipped into it, vanishing into the tree shadows.

"Pity we didn't push on a little farther last night," said one of the acrobats—Ritu, by name. She was a woman in middle age, mother to most of the aerialists. She was barefoot in the slimy mud, and wore only a pair of pantaloons that were plastered to her muscled thighs, and a halter that revealed a strong midriff under skin puckered from childbearing. The circus seemed to be made up of one or two large, extended, intermarried families. Ritu was one of the ones who had chosen to get out and walk alongside the caravan guards, rain or no rain, and she wasn't bad company. "We could have slept warm in beds."

The Dead Man sighed. "Were I not a religious man, I would place a wager that Druja will not care to stop now, either, with so much light ahead of us. Rain or no rain."

He realized later that he had been speaking out of his own desires rather than observed facts. It was a bet he would have lost. And so did the Scholar-God protect her faithful.

Druja, like most successful caravan masters, was not known for his spendthrift ways. But even that parsimonious bastard realized that if he marched his sodden, filthy, miserable staff and passengers past a perfectly functional coaching inn and caravanserai, he was likely to have an armed revolution on his hands. They would rest there a day, he decreed, and move on in the morning.

The Dead Man would rather have been on duty. If he could not have progress, his restlessness required distraction. But he drew the red stone for the first shift of liberty.

He drew also such partial wages as the caravan master was willing to allow him—Druja wouldn't pay them off for the trip still short of their destination, even if he could afford to without collecting the value of his cargo—and went to find a bathhouse and a laundry and some food that didn't taste of months in barrels on the road. He'd never seen a Sarathai city before; this seemed too fine an opportunity to miss. It wasn't home—what could ever be home again, without Zillah, without a sacred charge?—but at least it might be interesting.

Sadly, he had to leave the Gage behind, as the Gage had drawn a green stone. But the Dead Man thought he was likely to be able to keep himself *mostly* out of trouble. The boring kind of trouble, anyway. He would have welcomed a little of the other kind, at this juncture.

Whistling, he asked directions to the nearest bathhouse in his fragmented but improving dialect. The woman he asked looked at him quizzically from under the shelter of a banana leaf held over her head—the rain had recommenced after all too brief a pause—and pointed. "There is only one," she said.

I hope there's more civilization where we're going, the Dead Man thought, regretting that the Gage was not there to share the thought with. The Gage wasn't much for bathhouses anyway, being made entirely of metal, but he did enjoy a cosmopolitan environment.

Chandranath wasn't big enough to get lost in, and the bathhouse was no more than ten minutes' walk from the caravanserai. It was identifiable by a red clay tile roof and the clouds of steam rising up from it in the damp, warm air—a striking sight, even though it was physically incapable of adding to the humidity. A wall surrounded it, mortared stone broken by a wrought gate. It was the most permanent-looking structure he'd seen here, other than the wooden coaching inn.

The rain made every area without stones laid on top into a sucking morass. At least the streets were paved in the city as well as along the routes leading to and from it. Glancing up at the gray stone citadel looming above, the Dead Man suspected that had as much to do with defense and putting down peasant rebellions as it might with encouraging trade and keeping the pubs open.

He shrugged, and went through the garden gate into the courtyard. If he could not get closer to Sarathai-tia, at least he would distract and soothe himself.

His appearance in the dooryard of the bathhouse occasioned some comedy at first, as the attendants were utterly at a loss with what to do with him. The language barrier didn't help. At last, he determined that the problem was one of social rank, which apparently the good citizens of Chandranath took exceedingly seriously. As a foreigner, he was considered outside the system—but as somebody who wanted to wash himself in a public bath, he needed to be slotted into it somewhere.

He imagined it had to do with how dirty the water would be when it reached him, and shuddered.

Finally, inspecting the color of his money and the hilt of his saber, the attendants appeared to arrive at the conclusion that he was warrior-caste. They accepted his purse and his blade for safekeeping, gave him a glazed tile on a string to hang about his neck as a token for reclaiming them, agreed to launder his clothing while he bathed, and showed him in through the second of six doors on what he assumed was the men's side of the baths. There, he found a changing room, longer than it was wide, with a series of cubbies along each wall. The empty cubby he selected was constructed of woven mats hung on wooden stakes, and did not quite reach either ceiling or the clay tile floor. But it was replete with hooks and shelves, and he skinned out of his mud-stiff clothing with relief, leaving only his veil in place.

He followed the sound of splashing and the clouds of steam to the edge of the bathing pool. It was probably not done to jump into the baths themselves while still filthy, he suspected, so—ah, there. A big iron cauldron with a wooden dipper beside it rested over a bed of coals, and cold water dripped from a wooden pipe over it. A tray of clean, damp white sand rested beside. That seemed self-explanatory. He dipped up hot water, diluted it with the cold until the temperature was bearable, and proceeded to sluice and to scrub, sighing in pleasure as road-filth and rain-filth peeled off him like rinds.

The other men were watching him, he knew. Here was a stranger, and one with a blue scarf twisted bizarrely across his face in a *baths*, of all the places. They were too polite to murmur much, at least, and all but the young boys and the old men dropped their eyes when he turned back. The young boys were too curious and inexperienced for him to take offense, and the old men were old men: their survival had earned them the right to not give a damn if they stared. He washed out his veil, too, taking care to keep a wrap across his face for modesty.

He rinsed off the last of the sand and walked to the edge of the tub. It too was tile—red tiles, painted with intricate black glaze— making the Dead Man smile in memory of the Gage's dry humor. More woven rush screen hung between sections of the pool, separating the classes. The Dead Man could hear voices beyond them in each direction. He sized up the bathers he *could* see, relying on the overhang of his veil to conceal the direction of his gaze from anyone who was not staring directly at him.

So. These men were the warriors of Himadra the Boneless.

They looked a worthy lot. Some were lean and some were stout, but all were muscled. They all had scars—even the boys—of a sort the Dead Man recognized: ether the scars of combat, or of a lifetime of training for combat. He saw them recognizing the same on his own body, and a ripple passed through the room. It was too soon to tell, he thought, if that marked acceptance or if it represented an increase in tension.

He stepped onto the sloping ramp that led down into the pool as if he had not a care in the world. *Let's see how desperate they are to start trouble.*

Not, apparently, very. Scrubbed and rinsed and rinsed again, the Dead Man walked down the curved ramp from the lip into the pool. The water was hot enough that he gritted his teeth and took it by stages, but once he was in, he acclimated and a great ease stole over him. He let out a great, cascading sigh, and one of the men near him chuckled. But it was a friendly chuckle, or at least a knowing one, and anyway they'd all stopped staring at him when he was halfway down the ramp. A disciplined force, then, or one kept busy enough that they hadn't the time or energy for brawling with someone who gave no offense.

The chatter resumed by stages, as the Boneless's men either got bored with him or decided to dissemble in their interest. It was too rapid-fire and slurred for him to understand anyway, given his flawed Saratahi. The Dead Man let the water float him to his toetips, feeling the delicious stretch of muscles abused with walking, hauling, fighting, cold, damp, and bumping around in the bellies of the ice-boats for far, far too long. Everything eased, and it was a good sensation. He let his eyes drift closed.

He wondered if there was an easy way for a mercenary to make enough money to retire to the sort of manor house that might offer baths with a hypocaust. Maybe he could go back to Messaline, the Mother of Markets. Maybe there were such houses in fabled Tsarepheth. That mountain fastness—the Rasan summer capital—lay in the shadow of a famous volcano, and was reputed to be rich in hot springs. Though volcanoes had the unsavory habit of exploding every once in a while. And the city was supposed to be overrun by Wizards.

Hmm, maybe not that, then.

A voice spoke up beside him, in stilted but perfectly comprehensible Uthman. "Not getting any younger, are we?"

The Dead Man didn't startle. He didn't even open his eyes. He'd heard the whisper of water on skin, and felt the currents as the other man came up beside him. "Not so many make it to our age in this game," he replied in his own stilted Saratahi. "I'll take it over the options."

That got a laugh. "A good answer." The man lapsed back into Saratahi, but did the Dead Man the courtesy of speaking slowly and with care. "You come from the caravan."

It wasn't a question, but the Dead Man nodded. Water tugged at the drifting ends of his veil.

"Where to?"

"Want a job?"

The man laughed again. "I'm a sword for the Boneless," he boasted, but lightly. "I should be offering you a position. If you think you're good enough."

At that, the Dead Man cracked an eye. He lifted his head a little so water didn't sting it, though his neck protested the resumption of his skull's weight. "Himadra hires mercenaries?"

"*Lord* Himadra," the man said. He stood somewhat up the ramp, half out of the water, with his arms folded over a small solid belly. He had the stance and stolidity of a sergeant, and the no-nonsense attitude, too.

The Dead Man felt a pang of homesickness. Loneliness, too, for the simple company of brother soldiers. Maybe *he* should look into becoming a warlord. There were probably heated baths up at that castle on the cliff. . . .

But a deeper pang broke his longing. It was stupid to dream. He was rootless, unmastered. Making a connection, looking for a home, just meant something else to be abandoned when the time came to move on. He belonged nowhere. He fooled himself to think he ever would again.

"He doesn't take just any mercenary, no. But word has gotten around that there's an Uthman with old Druja's boats who wears an old red coat, and I thought you might be him." He shrugged and held out a hand. "Even here, the red coat comes with a certain reputation. He might like to meet you. I'm Navin."

The Dead Man took the hand. "Serhan," he said. Because there weren't Dead Men anymore, and it was as good a name as any, and one he'd used before. He wondered if Himadra offered a finder's fee for the recruitment of competent cannon fodder. "Alas, I'm contracted," he said. "The caravan goes through to Sarathai-lae."

He and the Gage did not go with the caravan that whole distance: their contract ran out in Sarathai-tia, with the delivery of a package there. But nothing he'd said was a lie, and he thought perhaps it would be best not to give too much information away. He had heard rumors that there were tensions between Chandranath and Sarathai-tia. As it would be strange if there were not, honestly: a mountainous land with unforgiving soil would no doubt have an interest in raiding away produce of the rich bottomlands of an agricultural neighbor such as Sarathai-tia was reputed to be. The Dead Man, desert-bred as he was, was quite curious to see this fabled land where spice trees supposedly bloomed in all seasons, and you could pluck juicy exotic fruits merely by putting out a hand whenever hunger threatened, or thirst.

"Well," Navin said. "Your loyalty to your contract does you credit."

The Dead Man laughed. "Druja hasn't paid me off yet."

Navin shrugged and lowered himself into the water so he, too, could float. "Take a shorter contract on the way back, maybe. It's not a bad life for a fighting man."

THE DEAD MAN HAULED HIMSELF OUT OF THE WATER AT LAST ONLY when his heart pounded from the heat, and his head spun slightly. He crossed to the cold water and poured it over his arms and neck to cool himself somewhat, but he could not, quite, bring himself to sluice it over his whole body as he'd seen the others doing. Instead he toweled himself roughly dry and stepped out into the antechamber to dress, letting the cooler air there restore his alertness without sacrificing the delicious sensation of being *warm* for the first time in . . . he couldn't remember when. His clothes, as promised by the attendant and paid for when he entered, had been laundered, and were crisp and dry. He wondered how they managed that, but it couldn't be just magic: the wool coat hadn't been returned yet. It was given back to him, still very slightly damp, when he asked at the desk—along with his sword and purse.

He'd left most of his coin with the Gage as a sensible precaution, but the purse didn't even seem to have been rifled. Seeing as he somehow still had some money—these country towns were cheap, at least—he paused at a market on the way back and bought an oil-cloak with a hood, and two bottles of what passed for a decent wine out here in the hinterlands. He'd share one with the Gage as a thanks for keeping his coin.

The Gage might not eat or sleep or drink of necessity, but he did have some inscrutable system for . . . imbibing . . . when the mood took him, and he seemed to enjoy it.

The rain had not ceased, but the Dead Man re-entered it better accoutered and thus far more comfortable. He picked his way between puddles, trying to keep his boots from soaking through again. It was a losing battle, but it kept him occupied.

So occupied, in fact, that he was within a few houses of the main street leading to the caravanserai before he noticed the crowd gathered ahead of him. The town had been as deserted on the way out as in, and now he paused, feeling as if he had unexpectedly stumbled upon a secret. A fanfare of horns suggested it wasn't as secret as all that, however, and the people gathered along the sides of the street seemed to be waiting or watching rather than traveling. So he tugged the oiled cloak a little higher to hide his foreignness and stepped up to the back of the crowd.

The Dead Man had been a soldier long enough to know that all *sorts* of tidbits of information had the potential to be useful. Or interesting.

He wasn't disappointed.

From the direction of the stockade came a short procession. Triangular banners draggled in the wet, but though he could not make out the devices he could see they were of two different colors. There were several ranks of horses, with armored men upon their backs in differentiated rows, like courses of colored bricks. First, those that wore dark red, gold, and brown livery. Then those that wore saffron-orange and a blue like sapphires, before the brief pattern repeated itself. The effect was a little like the stripes of a particularly gaudy tiger.

After the ranks of armed men came eight more soldiers on horseback, these holding a shelter resembling a light, portable roof aloft on long wooden poles. Among them rode two men on horses almost as fine as any the Dead Man had seen, whether of the lines of Asitaneh, or of the Qersnyk tribes. Or—

Well, one was a man, in any case. He had a heavy, gray beard—unusual in the Lotus Kingdoms, from what the Dead Man understood—and was both tall and built like a wine-tun: not so much barrel-bodied as well-nigh spherical. His carriage was erect nonetheless, and he held his chin with a haughty poise.

The creature that rode beside him . . .

Don't be cruel, the Dead Man told himself, remembering that the Scholar-God counseled always to compassion. *He cannot help it that he is cursed.*

And cursed he obviously was.

Any man could be crippled in an instant. But not any man could be crippled like this.

The Gage had been right. Himadra the Boneless was a dwarfed and misshapen lump in the saddle of his fine mare. Despite his disadvantages, he obviously knew his horse and his horsemanship. She was one of the gaited western breeds—the Dead Man was not enough of an equestrian to name which one—with a silvery-gray coat and a fine-boned head. She moved with a strange gliding stride that managed to be both elegant and dramatic, as if she skated on air where merely mortal horses might be accused of walking.

Her rider was a dark-complected man with a proud nose and fine high brow, despite his stature. He wore his hair dressed in ringlets down over a fine red wool robe, which was belted open-chested over a black leather breastplate chased with silver. A mace swung from the saddle by his knee. That particular red made the Dead Man violently, momentarily homesick. He plucked at his own sleeve; the moth-eaten wool had long since faded from that shade.

His terrible illness aside, this Himadra looked like a man who could command warriors. His eye was keen; his gaze intent.

That gray-bearded, whole man he rode beside could not have been more of a contrast.

He was a king, that much was plain. He was garbed in the same saffron-orange and sapphire as some of the troops were, but being trimmed with fur and bullion in his case it was obvious that this represented a mark of office and not mere livery. But even at this distance, and even through the rain, the Dead Man could see the drinker's network of split veins thickening his nose. He could see that this princeling in his soft boots had nevertheless kicked his feet free of the stirrups, and seemed to hold them away from the irritated horse's sides gingerly.

Gout, probably. Or the foot pain that came with the pissing evil that also resulted from too much rich food and too much drink.

The Dead Man caught himself sneering at this petty potentate, this little king who traveled with the army of his little kingdom like a boy playing soldiers with his toys. He found himself comparing these men and their troops to the glittering caliph and his glittering legions . . . and he stifled a laugh at his own arrogance. You forgot how far in the world you had fallen, and you started judging others by the standards of a world that had been lost, now, for more of your life than it had existed. And the rheumatism got into your bones, and the cataracts got into your eyes, and pretty soon you were thumping your cane and sneering about how the world had been in your day.

No. The world was a dune. It wore on, and things and places and people you had loved or hated or had your heart broken by vanished beneath it and the only mark they left was on your soul. And that was that. Whatever words there might be in long-dead languages for the traces left behind, those languages were dead too. And erased. Only the pen of the Scholar-God wrote real and lasting truth. All other marks wore out, despite what the Gage sometimes said about his ancient abstract concept of the mark, visible or invisible, that remained behind when any piece of the world touched on or interacted with any other.

He was here now, in this muddy little bandit kingdom in this impoverished corner of a crumbled empire. And he was seriously thinking about taking a mercenary post with this hardscrabble little lord when his current messenger duty was done.

He had no palace to sneer from. That empire was dust. The Caliph was dust. And these little potentates remained.

These little potentates—and the woman who followed them.

She rode a horse that hated her, and her saddle blanket was a tiger skin. As soon as the Dead Man saw her, he forgot the little kings she apparently served, and forgot that it was blasphemy to stare at women, and he gaped unreservedly.

She was tall and broad with muscle, and her black hair piled high and stuck with glittering combs made her seem taller. She dressed in red leather boots and green-blue silks and brocade that somehow remained unspotted by the rain, trousers and a blouse and a jeweled jerkin resplendent in pointed epaulets constructed to make her seem even bigger. Her gelding suffered her weight ungracefully, sidling and snapping his jet-colored tail as he snatched at the bit and spattered bloody froth with every irritated toss of his head. He was a leggy blood-bay with tiger-striped legs and an iridescent coat that proclaimed steppe-horse ancestry, though he was far too tall and heavy-necked to be of the pure line. The tiger skin under her tooled saddle covered his entire back and flanks, the snarling head resting just above his tail, the eyes winking orange as if with glittering, malevolent life.

The Dead Man started, feeling as if the dead thing stared at him, but they were only padparadscha stones. "Only" pink-orange sapphires, faceted and as big as a hen's egg.

As if the movement attracted her attention, the lady herself turned and looked at him. He met her gaze in startled blasphemy.

For a moment, he thought her eyes flashed as orange as the tiger's cold stone ones, but it was just the reflection of the rainy light filtered through the canopy above. She tilted her head and awarded him with a faint smile, and he saw the real color of her irises—a clear shade of brown.

She was not pretty, this woman, with her short nose and heavy upper lip. But she had a presence—a charisma—that made the Dead Man want to step forward and fall in line behind her. He reined himself back at the edge of the watching crowd. Somehow, he'd slipped between watchers to come right up to the verge, though he couldn't remember having done so. Even with his soldier's discipline, he thought he might have followed her, if it weren't for the pressing itch of the message he and the Gage were charged with.

She turned away, and the desire faded. He gasped into his veil.

"Ravani," the man next to the Dead Man whispered, as if he had asked aloud. "The foreign princess."

"From where?"

The man shrugged, grinned with weather-split lips. "Foreign."

Geography was obviously this one's strong point.

"Has she troops?" the Dead Man collected himself enough to ask.

The man shook his head. "She needs no troops. She is a sorceress."

THE DEAD MAN WAITED UNTIL THE WARLORDS AND THEIR ATTENDANT sorceress had gone on their way, so he could turn his back without any risk of giving offense to two kinglets and a few hundred armed, damp, irritable men. As soon as it was politic, he hustled back to the caravanserai.

Unease seethed in his belly, though the cause was not immediately identifiable. It wasn't just the reminder of how far in the world he had fallen, how little he could afford snobbery or pride. It wasn't just the shame of having forgot himself so far as to stare at a woman's face, like an uncultured dog. It was something he couldn't name, but it prickled nonetheless.

So he did what he always did, these days, when the world didn't make the sort of sense he wished it would. He went to fight about it with the brass man.

The Gage stood easily on the stern deck of the blue-painted iceship, his back to the stockade wall. He was at rest, as motionless as a statue, and from the ground he could have seemed a thick, sodden homespun robe draped over a ragged stump. When the Dead Man got closer, though, he smelled the greasing of suet in the Gage's joints.

He gave a little sigh of homecoming as he stepped into the shelter of the helmsman's roof, close beside the Gage's post. It was ridiculous what you could get used to.

"How were the baths?" the Gage asked.

"Salutary," the Dead Man answered. "One of Himadra's sergeants tried to hire me on as a soldier."

"It probably wasn't anything personal," the Gage commented. "They give recruiting bonuses."

And just like that, the thing that had been niggling at the Dead Man slid into focus before his inner eye. This was, indeed, a poor, hardscrabble little mountain town. The fields surrounding it were poor, the agriculture barely enough to support its people. It existed here only because the trade routes through the mountains unavoidably crossed. And it was in a principality whose major industry was the taxation of trade, either legally or through banditry.

How in the coldest corner of the Scholar-God's most benighted hell was Himadra going to support not just a visiting dignitary, but two standing armies? And why was he so eagerly recruiting to increase the size of that army, when he would only have to feed and house those men?

"Because he has no intention of quartering them for any longer than necessary," the Dead Man said out loud, to clarify the situation to himself more than to impart any information to the Gage.

"Pardon?" the Gage said, absently.

The Dead Man thought of the message sewn up in oilcloth, dangling ribbons and lead seals, hidden within the Gage's secret compartments. A message from a Wizard, to a queen. His heart beat faster. His belly seemed to drop right out of him.

Would Himadra march them in the rainy season? Did these foreigners campaign in winter? It seemed to the Dead Man so very unwise, but he had to admit there was a great deal he did not know about the Lotus Kingdoms. Perhaps the summers were worse.

Perhaps.

He said, "We're riding into a war."

THAT NIGHT, THE STORMS BROKE OVER THEM IN BRAND-NEW EARNEST. If the Dead Man had thought he'd seen rain before—well, now he saw rain, and thunder, and lightning. He sat beside the Gage in the darkness of the wheelhouse, aware that he should sleep but unwilling to give up the serenity of a stormy night so easily. He even drew out his rarely used pipe and his hoarded tobacco, and managed to strike a light into the aromatic shag despite the damp.

He was still there, seated leaning against the helm and smoking slowly, when Nizhvashiti climbed up the railing.

Some light from the kingdom's spectacular night filtered through the roiling clouds, making them seem like smoke lit with an inner fire. The Godmade hesitated atop the railing, robes flapping black against a darkly glowing sky like some inquisitive raven.

"Gage? Would you mind company?"

The Dead Man felt an irrational surge of jealousy. *He has company.* But he bit his tongue: Nizhvashiti had been brilliantly useful, though the Dead Man's earlier suspicions about the convenience of it all had not waned. And the caravan had problems that perhaps the Godmade could help find the solutions for.

"We're up here," the Dead Man said.

Nizhvashiti hopped the railing, robes swinging soddenly, and joined them in the dark. Just as the wheelhouse was becoming all the more crowded, lightning flashed violently overhead. It gleamed off the Godmade's golden false eye, and the thunder crackled almost immediately with the flash. The Dead Man jumped, on his feet before he knew it.

The Gage put out a hand to steady him. "Keep your powder dry, Serhan."

Nizhvashiti . . . laughed. Not a cruel laugh, but a chiming, merry one. The Dead Man blinked: he wouldn't have imagined it. But then, he was a Dead Man, and he supposed most people would be startled to hear him laugh, also.

"Hello," the Godmade said.

"Hello, Nizhvashiti," the Gage answered.

The Dead Man nodded—it was not so dark that the gesture was useless—and asked, "Can't you end this damned storm?"

The Godmade laughed again, gentler this time. Almost a womanly chuckle. "It is not my place to control what the Good Mother makes. Or the Good Daughter, either. They know the world and its needs better than I. So I merely ask, and they answer."

The Dead Man bit back the acid reply he would have leveled at the Gage—*you do not know this strange priest well*—and reminded himself that he had a similar relationship with his own god. Except She never answered. Not in so many words. The Scholar-God was above other deities, which were minor demons and angels and demigods, all. They might intervene. She chose to act only through intermediaries, saints and prophets, so as not to upset the terrible, trembling balance of the fragile world She had written into being so very long ago.

He grasped after a philosophical mood and eventually found enough shreds of one to cloak himself in even if the cold wind still bit through. "Well," he said, "I suppose watching it gives us something to do."

He scooched over before he sat back down. The Godmade sat with him, shoulder to shoulder, companionable. The Gage stood beside them, so stolid and silent it was easy to pretend he didn't exist. Together, they watched the storm.

Spray dashed up from the deck with each heavy raindrop, wetting the edges of the Dead Man closest to the lip of the overhang. His and Nizhvashiti's rears were out of the wet, at least—the helmsman's shelter had an elevated deck. The Dead Man wondered if ascetics minded sitting in puddles, or considered it simply a just element of their self-mortification.

It seemed rude to ask.

The Dead Man leaned back and folded his hands behind his head, trying to imagine himself on a grassy hillside in spring. He heard the Godmade breathing beside him, but stared instead up at the storm-dimmed sky.

The Godmade said, "Tell me about your god, then, Dead Man. As I have told you something about mine."

Was he being called upon to witness? To witness to a foreign cleric, and one of such manifest power?

It seemed a strange reason for his god to have brought him here, the Dead Man mused. But then, the Scholar-God moved in mysterious ways.

He realized, shocked and ashamed, that it had been days since he had remembered his meditations. One was meant to read the words and study them daily, to consider them and contemplate them until the meaning began to open to one's knowledge like the unfurling petals of a rose. That was the beginning of wisdom, and the root of holiness. Without a proper sun to remind him of the stations of prayer, he was becoming an apostate.

The Dead Man closed his eyes—the storm still lit the lids red with every flash—and opened his mind to a verse from the sacred texts, allowing whatever the Scholar-God would will to come. He was nevertheless surprised by the lines that rose to the forefront of his mind. They were not lines for catechizing an unbeliever, but rather words of questioning, of love of the world, of doubt.

He tried to feel the meaning of the words, speak them with passion nonetheless. If this was what he was inspired to, then he would not believe he had been inspired wrong. And it was wrong to simply intone the Scholar-God's arguments. They must be . . . internalized. Considered. Spoken as if they lived and breathed and were each day argued anew, not as if they lay dead and dusty in some tomb.

The Dead Man quoted, " 'There is day and there is night, brothers. Those are both sweet things. There is food in the belly; there are the stars afire above; there is water in the river. There is the sun hot on your back and the pulse of blood hot in your heart. These are *all* sweet things. Likewise there is the smell of your children's hair, the feel of a pen in your fingers, the song of the poetess. Life is always sweet, sisters. So who then would choose to die?' "

After what seemed a reverent pause, the Godmade said, "Are those the words of your god, Dead Man?"

"They are the words of Her Prophet, Ysmat of the Beads. They are Her words, as Her Prophet recorded them."

"Your god seems to argue there in favor of the secular world. Does not She offer a promise of an afterlife? Is not yours an ascetic religion?"

"Not so ascetic as yours." The Dead Man glanced down at the priest's skeletal fingers, which rested splayed upon the robe above the folded, sticklike knee.

The Godmade's head shook thoughtfully. "I practice a meditation of the Banner Isles, better to serve my Mother, as a good daughter must."

" 'Who then would choose to die?' " The Gage quoted, in his bass rumble. "And yet, there are those who do choose it."

The Godmade exhaled long and thoughtfully. "Perhaps we are meant to realize then that if the life that God has given us is sweet, then God being kind, death must be sweet as well. Perhaps the verse is meant to comfort us with that realization, when we come to it."

"Perhaps." The Dead Man glanced over. The priest's face was relaxed, the gold eye gleaming faintly in the shadowy daylight. "So few have returned with a report."

"Those words could be words in my own tradition," Nizhvashiti continued, as if the Dead Man had not spoken. "'There is food in the belly; there are the stars afire above; there is water in the river.'"

The Dead Man could not think of an answer. They rested in silence and watched the storm until, near the end of the bright night that served these strangers as day, the rain thinned and the clouds tore. A great rift opened above the eastern peaks, revealing the starry void beyond in all its brilliance.

Light spilled through. It washed over the bare brown mountains rising around them, illuminating folds and valleys from a low angle that made them stand out glowing against their own shadows. The sky behind was a tower of twisted cloud, gray and black like silk, tangled like warring banners. The light danced up that tower as it danced up the mountainsides, picking out tiny details, undulations and rills. These were not the flat, dull clouds of a stone-lid overcast. They were fantasias, pinnacles.

The Dead Man was weary, sleepless, cold. He caught his breath to look at this vision: the tiny wood-walled city huddled in the belly of all this vast implacable terrain.

"What a God-forsaken place."

He almost slipped out of his skin in startlement when chill, bony fingers crept into his own.

Nizhvashiti leaned on his shoulder for a better view and whispered, "God-forsaken is also beautiful."

6

THE SNAKEBITE MADE EVERYTHING MORE BEARABLE. MRITHURI'S
mind was clearer. Her body felt strong. She even felt up to dealing
with her grandfather's sister's river-rejected son. Or his emissary,
which amounted to the same thing.

In too short a time, Mrithuri was going to have to sit in the throne
room next to the Alchemical Emperor's empty chair and listen to
old men argue, ostensibly to improve or protect the lot of Sarathai-
tia and Mrithuri's people but in all reality to show off their rank and
importance to themselves and one another. For now, at least, she could
enjoy the peace and quiet with the snakebite fresh in her veins, making her thoughts as chilly, swift, and crystalline as the water from
the mountain springs that fed her own Sarathai.

After she and Ata Akhimah had spoken, they consumed a sparing
breakfast of lotus root and shoot, served with lentils and last season's
preserved fruit wrapped with rice in fluffy, delicate pancakes. Mrithuri
ate with one hand while reading reports with the other. She didn't have
an appetite for it after the snakebite, but she'd long since learned
that her own appetites had very little bearing indeed on her duties as
rajni.

Ata Akhimah broke the silence sooner than Mrithuri would have liked. Unsurprisingly, the Wizard wanted to talk about her duties as a rajni as well.

"About the lotus—" the Wizard said.

Mrithuri pinned her on a stare. Her body thrummed with energy; her mind burned clear. "You may be about to lose your reputation as a soothsayer, old friend."

"It was that or a war," Ata Akhimah replied. "And the lotus really was white at its heart."

"Conveniently, no one can check your work, as the lotus in question now resides inside an elephant."

"A marriage might serve your aims, my rajni."

Mrithuri sighed. She wanted to snap, but she knew that was only the nervous tension engendered by the snakebite talking. "We've been over this. I'm not marrying someone who will want to rule me. This is my kingdom, and I will hold it in my own right."

The Wizard smiled wickedly. "Well, you haven't spoken with Mahadijia yet. He might surprise you. There's a stepson from the third wife's previous marriage, isn't there?"

Mrithuri flicked rice at her. "Anuraja's not going to hand me over to a stepson. You know what he most likely wants. And how fast word of that lotus is going back to Sarathai-lae. There's not enough political advantage in the world to get me to lie down for Anuraja. Even if he wasn't in the habit of executing his wives to excuse his own impotence."

"I thought he was after your cousin Sayeh. He never was pleased that she married his half brother rather than him."

"She's already got an heir of her own. And is freshly widowed. Do you think she's going to want that gouty old monster when she didn't before?"

"You think Anuraja would make his ambassador interrupt the ritual of the returning rains to press suit for *another* marriage proposal? It was a theatrical ploy, and meant to force your hand."

Mrithuri set her pancake down, still without appetite. Grains of rice, golden with saffron, spilled onto the gilded plate. She concentrated for a moment on the music of the lyre drifting from within the cloister walls. The question didn't really rate an answer: "My cousin has buried five wives. Would you have me be the sixth, at least until he finds an excuse to execute me?"

"None of them was a rajni in her own right."

"So I have more lands for him to claim. The old bastard's stick is rotten with the black drip and his feet are festering from the pissing evil. Not all his wives and mistresses can give him a brat that lives longer than a few days, and he still insists it must be their fault. I'll pass, I thank you."

Ata Akhimah could not keep her lips from curving. "Pity your cousin Sayeh's son isn't a little older."

"If by a little, you mean twenty years." The boy was still in his swaddling wraps. Mrithuri picked up the pancake again and bit into it vindictively. The nuns were singing softly along with their lutes, an ethereal and almost wordless tune. She chose to let it soothe her. "I'm more worried about the Boneless than my entirely hypothetical marriage."

Himadra—to use his given name—was the raja of Chandranath, which lay in the mountains north and very slightly west of Mrithuri's kingdom of Sarathai-tia. Mrithuri considered him little better than a bandit lord.

"Your entirely hypothetical marriage might put you in a stronger position where Himadra is concerned."

"You mean troops."

Ata Akhimah nodded.

Mrithuri sighed. "Who could bring me troops? Or riches to buy mercenaries? I don't want some Song prince, or a second son from Rasa. Besides, all the older sons of Namri are married off already, so even if I was willing to take the—what, twelve-year-old?"

"Fifteen," Akhimah said tolerantly. "Samrukan, if I recall correctly."

Mrithuri waved the disregarded reports in her left hand as if fanning smoke aside. "Anyway, they have that bizarre custom where if you marry one brother you marry them all. As a reigning rajni, that sort of thing becomes very awkward very fast. And don't get me started on the Song princes. They'll want far more for their families than they'll bring to me."

"How about a nice barbarian?" Akhimah's voice was glossily cheerful. "Those Qersnyk tribes make babies like they're farming them."

"You help like puppies," Mrithuri answered, with a fond glance at Syama. The bear-dog's massive paws quivered faintly in her sleep, and she issued a low, snoring whine.

Mrithuri held up her hand for a napkin. One of the maids deposited the thick cotton cloth, well-drenched in warm water and lemon juice, in her palm. She wiped carefully and then dried her hands on the cloth that followed. She worked the elegant, encumbering fingerstalls back over her nails and sighed. "Well, I suppose it's time to go face the Dharasaaba."

The Dharasaaba was a parliament—a tiered assembly of nobles, clerics, and guildsmen with advisory and some fiscal authority over the ruler. Presiding at their councils was Mrithuri's daily chore—as if playing at priestess weren't a sufficient consumer of her hours. Well, that was the price she paid for being rajni and raja both. And a husband would not help with that. As much of a bore as she found it, she wasn't about to turn over the task of governing her beloved nation to some stranger—and a husband *couldn't* serve her role as the soul of the Mother River made flesh.

Mrithuri's maids offered again to bathe her—they would have used the sacred water of the river, but filtered to clear it of silt—and she again refused. Ata Akhimah averted her eyes again while Mrithuri's maids re-robed her. You wouldn't think a doctor would be so fastidious of sensibility. You would be wrong.

In clean petticoats, her skin freshly oiled to seal the sacred river's moisture into her pores, Mrithuri stepped again into the tray of gold dust and closed her eyes while her women painted her cosmetics into place. The thrum of the venom in her veins soothed her still.

Once the paint was done, they escorted her to the throne room for her early audiences with the Dharasaaba. It was hard to believe that the Heavenly River had made no more than a fifth of its progress across the sky. The night had been a lifetime long already.

"What do I expect today?" she asked Hnarisha. He was her secretary and castellan, the heart of her councils, and her chief annoyance on the topic of marriage. A man of delicate frame, he had a tendency to put on flesh that he was constantly at pains against. He also bore an incongruous Cho-tse name. How, exactly, a man from the south, not far from the Banner Isles, had wound up bearing a name that should have belonged to a five-hundred-pound bipedal tiger was a little beyond Mrithuri's comprehension. But he was a very good secretary, no matter what his mother might or might not have gotten up to.

He consulted his notes. "Mahadijia has requested a hearing in his role as emissary from your royal cousin Anuraja, my rajni. I'm afraid."

His lifted eyebrow told her that he'd heard about the interruption this morning.

Mrithuri sighed. She wondered what he'd wanted that could be so important as to break the sacred silence. Or perhaps the interruption itself had been the point. Discomfiting others was one way to show your power, and disrespecting ritual was another. It could not simply have been ignorance; the man was an ambassador, after all, and the customs of Sarathai-lae were not so very different from those of Sarathai-tia.

Perhaps it was as simple as Anuraja, and by extension Mahadijia, having no respect for a woman, whether in her role as priestess or as rajni. How could such a one honor the Good Mother when he had no honor for her Daughters?

Mrithuri thought of Anuraja's record of wives abandoned and executed. Could such a one honor the Good Mother at all? It seemed to her the rankest sort of hypocrisy.

She wondered if she had won or lost a point by refusing to acknowl-edge Mahadijia this morning. "He didn't want a private audience?"

"He may ask for that once he's presented."

She glanced about casually. No one was immediately close except her maid, who could be suffered to hear a few generalities. "Any mes-sages from the north today?"

"No news you have not heard already."

Her stomach twisted despite the sharp confidence imparted by the venom in her veins. Hnarisha was as much spymaster as secretary. His sources of information were second to none, and in Mrithuri's court, only Yavashuri could rival them. And what he was telling her was that nothing had happened to contravene the previous reports that her northern neighbor Himadra was building armies. Nor was there any reply to the request for aid and counsel she'd sent to her great-aunt, who had long ago left the Kingdoms and her imperial heritage to become a Wizard in Messaline, supposed to be the great-est city west of the seacoast of Song.

Mrithuri was one of the very few remaining who knew that the so-called Eyeless One's given name was Jharni. It was Jharni, as the Eyeless One, who had recommended Ata Akhimah into the family's service, so many decades ago. Mrithuri only hoped the old Wizard was still inclined to be kindly disposed toward a granddaughter of her brother when a son of her sister was the problem at hand.

"All right." She had long since lost the habit of nodding when she was accoutered as a rajni. It just sent chains and diadems sliding everywhere, no matter how many hairpins her maids stuck in. Very well then. Her grandfather would have urged her to have a plan, an understanding. And indeed, she would speak with Hnarisha, Yavashuri, and Ata Akhimah in a more private setting than this, and discover what information in detail their networks of informants could provide.

But that would have to wait until after she dealt with Mahadijia. And she was *not* sure what she was going to do about him.

She sighed and screwed her face into a caricature mask. "Maybe he could be induced to discuss the new taxes on salt and fish exports his lord is levying. And the tariffs on everything our Tian merchants would like to sell through or ship through the Laeish ports."

Hnarisha made a face the equal of her own.

Mrithuri laughed—he could always make her giggle, rajni or no—and uncrossed her own eyes. "What else, then?"

"They've plans to debate taxes on rice, and the schedule of tariffs on imported water chestnuts and cinnabar. There is a murder inquest that requires your judiciary, though the counsels have more or less worked through the case and wish only to present it for your consideration. And the lord of South Pashirad has informed the clerk that he plans to introduce a motion—"

Mrithuri held up a languid hand, as if the weight of politics had rendered her debilitated. "Mother help us all. Let me be surprised. It might add some excitement to the day."

Hnarisha subsided, but not without a censorious glance. Mrithuri was certain she'd regret the decision later, but right now silence seemed like the only option that would not drive her to insanity.

She accepted a richly decorated mask from Yavashuri. The maid of honor waited outside the throne-hall drapes. Today's mask was a fantasia of orange and red stones set in a red gold filigree that covered her face from the eyes down with an animalistic sort of snout. It matched the stones in her long, glittering fingerstalls, and in addition to her nose and mouth it concealed several layers of fine-woven linen filters.

The maid helped her settle it, and thus, half-defaced, Mrithuri entered the Hall of the Empty Throne.

The throne was the only thing about the hall that could be considered *empty*. Her private entrance led her into an alcove behind the dais. She paused there a moment, gathering herself. She could not see her people from here—but she could hear them. Their murmurings and shufflings, both on the floor of the hall and in its many galleries. The rustle of cloth and the patter of bare feet.

Mrithuri raised her eyes and her masked face to the light that streamed from the lanterns raised high overhead. Beyond the skylights and the high windows, the grayness of a stormy night loomed. Within, though, the air swirled with countless tiny, sparkling motes, as if small breezes themselves glistened in the presence of the Empty Throne. Gold dust, scattered on the floors and so light and fine that any passage stirred it, left it hanging shimmering in air.

She checked the pleats of her new drape out of nerves more than need, laughing at herself as she realized only now that the clean one was midnight-blue patterned in stars and edged with gold, making today's red and orange jewels stand out even more. It also spoke of the sacred river, and so recalled her power without making an obvious show. That would reassure her people.

It would reassure them more if you announced plans to marry.

Ata Akhimah had strong-armed her; that was no mistake. It had been perhaps the most positive interpretation of a bloody portent, and they had needed in that moment to put a beneficial spin on things. And the priestess had been encouraging Mrithuri to marry for the better part of a decade now. In part because until Mrithuri got an heir, her cousin Sayeh was next in line to the kingdom—though not the throne. Sayeh's nation of Ansh-Sahal was small and poor; if she were stretched out across two nations, even the richer Tian landscape would not provide enough resources to defend both kingdoms from Anuraja in the south and Himadra in the north. Especially as a rajni could never truly rule any kingdom of Sarath-Sahal in the eyes of its people—and especially as Sayeh was shandha, a soul returned to a body that did not suit it.

The wisdom that Mrithuri had learned as a girl destined to become a priestess and the embodiment of a goddess held that most souls were not strongly gendered, any more than they were strongly associated with a particular physical form—bird, or person, or horse. That creatures served their lives and duties in the roles and bodies assigned to them, returned in the fullness of time to the Heavenly Mother, and eventually served in another role when they were recalled to the world.

But some souls were fiercely attached to an image of themselves, and in finding themselves returned to the world in a form that did not suit them, must seek and struggle until they made some accommodation. Less educated people were not always understanding of the shandha, thinking that their souls were too proud, insufficiently willing to serve the will of the gods. People *would* look for excuses to choose sides. The nuns who had trained Mrithuri in her priesteshood had differed on the issue, but most argued that the Mother did not make mistakes, and so the shandha served a purpose in her design.

So it was with cousin Sayeh, or so Mrithuri had been told. The rajni of Ansh-Sahal had been thought a prince when born, but demanded eventually to be recognized as princess, and had married and even—through the miraculous intercession of the Mother River—conceived and borne a healthy son. That she had survived the birth of the child, without the means a woman normally used in bearing, was due to the services of her foreign Wizard and his skills at surgery.

But being rajni and not raja meant Sayeh could not take their grandfather's place any more than Mrithuri could. Only a rightful raja, by blood, could sit on the Peacock Throne of the Alchemical Emperor, on pain of death. A death enforced by the divine wrath of the over-elaborate chair—or perhaps more honestly, a curse left upon it by Mrithuri's semi-divine ancestor—and not any fallible human law.

As long as there was only a rajni, and a rajni with no sons, Mrithuri's claim was insecure. And Anuraja badly wanted the place, considering himself the rational heir, although his mother was the old emperor's sister and the old emperor was Mrithuri's father's father.

Ata Akhimah wasn't any more eager for the job to pass to Mrithuri's middle-aged, heirless, gouty cousin than was Mrithuri. Not that Mrithuri had really wanted to rule or even reign in the first place. She hadn't even known *what* she wanted, precisely. She still didn't; she had been nineteen then, and in the time since she had been busy with the business of governing her small, beleaguered nation. Not trying to decide what she wanted to be when she grew up.

She had to admit that as much as she disliked the job, she was growing into it. And she had Hathi still. And she was morally certain that word of the augury was flying in all eight directions even now, and that she would be rewarded for Ata Akhimah's machinations with a renewed stream of suitors, despite the rain.

Just when she'd gotten them thinned out a bit. She'd meant everything she'd told Akhimah about the undesirability of every last one of them who had been deemed an appropriate match by her advisers and the Dharasaaba.

Mrithuri smoothed her indigo pleats once more, still needlessly—though if she kept poking at them, that would change—and shook out her hem without ducking her head, raising a cloud of gold dust that swirled around her but disarraying neither her headdress nor her hair. Behind her, the draperies moved aside as Syama edged through them. She came up beside her mistress as Mrithuri began walking, so that side by side, heads high, they stepped into view around the dais.

The babble of conversation fell away, leaving behind only the chiming of the rain on the dragoncrystal panels set into the spaces of the tree-branched stone vaults overhead. Mrithuri's court needed no musicians when it rained.

The vault was old, and even impervious dragoncrystal had cracked or fallen in a few places. It had been replaced by rock crystal, or leaded crystal panes: those were easy to spot in the dimness because they did not shed the same faint glow of tourmaline light as the dragoncrystal. Some ancient artisan had arranged the small panes so that green-shining and violet-shining diamonds seemed to make the leaves and weeping blossoms on the great stone trees. The effect was as of fine, transparent grass-colored and lavender jade windows with a bright sky behind.

Mrithuri's people made their courtesies as one, a smooth ripple of motion that revealed shining black hair and stirred drapes and wide-legged trousers like curtains riffling in the breeze. One voice—a woman's—carried in the silence—". . . the new butterfly fabrics from Song . . ."—and then trailed off in embarrassment.

Oh, Chaeri. Mrithuri held in a sigh, and managed not to roll her eyes. But Chaeri, at least, supplied Mrithuri's needs and did not judge her. And for a rajni, not being judged for being human was a thing to be grateful for indeed.

"Rise," she said.

Her maids came forward to help her up the steps to her chair of estate. It was a classic Sarathai style, large and square with turned rungs and a ladder back, wider than it was deep, with a rectangular red velvet cushion that alleviated only some of its discomforts. It stood on a smaller platform, before and to the left of the dais, and was carved of gilt mahogany inlaid with many precious things. There were few other places in the world where this chair would seem the moderate and unpretentious choice.

But in this place, the Peacock Throne of the Alchemical Emperor towered on the dais behind it like a sulky bird of prey with wet wings slumped to either side. Mrithuri's legendary ancestor had earned his sobriquet, and he had made his throne of stones brought from every corner of his empire, melted together until they flowed like wax dripping down a massive candle's stump, and converted to massy gold with a rainbow of hues—greeny-gold, red-gold, white-gold, violet-gold—all streaking its surface. The base resembled the corrugated footing of an old tree as much as it did the draping tail of the peacock it was named for. It was paved with tiny diamonds that glittered softly with every shift of the light. Despite its slumped, squatting appearance, it was so tall it could only be mounted by means of the broad, red-velvet carpeted stairs that climbed its base. That way was blocked with a rope of jet-black silk hung with tiny silver bells.

The throne was too heavy to be moved. So heavy, in fact, that if the dais beneath it had not been comprised of a pillar of black volcanic basalt witched up from the depths of the earth—and still rooted down there—by some ancient Wizard for the Alchemical Emperor, it would no doubt have cracked the very foundations of Mrithuri's palace.

Alongside her own simpler chair stood a heavy branch mounted on a stand and wrapped with tooled red leather: a perch for the sacred bearded vulture. The great crested buzzard was black-winged, and the feathers of its body were a creamy white when the bird was clean, but now appeared to have soaked up the clotted red of old blood. Bearded vultures groomed red clay into their feathers, like some wild Qersnyk shaman anointing his barbarian features with ochre. The bird was unhooded, being accustomed to the fuss of the Dharasaaba, and it turned gleaming eyes on Mrithuri as she lowered herself into the chair it guarded.

She reached into a little basket of cracked, meaty bones beside her chair, picked one up between her fingerstalls, and offered it up to the bird. It accepted the morsel delicately, then—far less delicately— turned the bone in its beak, threw its head back, and choked the thing down whole and entire.

She handed him another, this one split to expose the marrow. He cheeped at her engagingly, fluffing his feathers. She stroked his crest with a fingertip encased in gold filigree. You could not touch the great birds often with a naked hand, or you would strip the oil from their feathers, rendering them ragged, unkempt, and unable to fly.

Mrithuri wiped her hand on the napkin provided by her maids. Again, the scent of lemon peel. The hooked tips of her fingerstalls snagged on the fabric and she carefully worked them free. The bearded vulture scraped his beak along the length of the split bone. He threw his head back and gulped, swallowing the knobby thing end first. Mrithuri wondered what furnace burned inside him, that could reduce even bone to greasy residue. Perhaps Ata Akhimah knew, or perhaps they could together devise an experiment to find out.

But she had to get through the rest of the day's duties, first. And that meant this court, and those within it.

"Pray," she said to those assembled, who had ceased their conversation and now all turned to watch her. "Let us begin."

Hnarisha and his various heralds and functionaries organized and subdivided the courtiers and the petitioners. Mrithuri caught a glimpse of Mahadijia, who had traded his saffron coat for a long one in somber black, as if he fancied himself a Wizard or a priest. The ambassador glowered at the back of one group.

The drifting glimmer of the gold dust stirred up by Mahadijia's feet gave the scene an otherworldly air. She watched it shine in the lanternlight, as if minute sparks drifted on the currents of the air. *I am rajni here*, she thought. *I sit in the shadow of the Peacock Throne.*

She did. Not Anuraja, and for damned sure not Mahadijia.

She lifted her face in the mask, careful for the sake of the hair ornaments not to move too abruptly. She did not look at Mahadijia, but rather off to the left, catching the eye of Hnarisha. The man's eyes widened as Mrithuri made a slight, definite gesture with her left hand—a flicking-away.

Her secretary was not a big man, or one prone to strenuous activity. He wore round little spectacles balanced on his nose and he limped on a foot twisted since birth. But he hesitated only an instant before stepping into the ambassador's path and bodily blocking his route to Mrithuri's chair. "Your Grace has not been summoned."

Mahadijia must have considered just plowing through the man like the bull he so resembled. Mrithuri would have sworn she even saw him lower his head and lift one sandal-clad foot as if to paw— or swing it forward to begin his charge. But he put the foot down again, sidestepped to the right, and would have slipped past Hnarisha except that the bear-dog Syama was suddenly beside the little clerk, her shoulders nearly on a level with his own, her rose-petal ears plastered back against her massive skull as she curled her lip in a snarl.

"Your Grace," Hnarisha said, stepping to his left to bring his hip in contact with the bear-dog's ribcage, "has *not* been summoned."

Forcing the ambassador to back down was forcing him to lose

face, and in front of the entire court. Would he? *Could* he, in his pride and dignity? Or would he actually come to blows with Mrithuri's people, and either be humiliated further or worse, be killed where he stood? *That* was a recipe for war. A war for which she and her people were woefully unprepared, and which would probably make Anuraja just as happy in the long run as if she came to him, begging for succor, of her own volition.

Worse, from Mrithuri's high seat, she could see Mahadijia reaching for something under his coat. A concealed knife, perhaps, the possession of which was most assuredly illegal in the royal presence. If he drew it, and plunged it into her gallant, silly little secretary, then she would have to execute him. And that too would eventually mean war, no matter how she prosecuted her right to enforce the law for her own protection. And the only way she'd be able to protect her own moral high ground is by assembling and moving an army before Anuraja assembled and moved his own.

And it would cost her Hnarisha, which was a sacrifice she was ill-prepared to make. Her courtiers were drawing back from the face-off between the two men and the bear-dog, sweeping their robes up and shuffling aside as if she had parted the sea with a gesture. A sergeant at arms was hurrying forward with four men in a sharp-tipped wedge formation, but the press of the crowd impeded him.

Mrithuri was unique in her elevated position and unimpeded view of the situation. She would have to do something to at least buy him the moments he needed to close the gap.

She rose from her chair quite suddenly, casting her arms wide to make her jewelry jangle and flash. Beside her, the sacred bearded vulture bated upward on its perch, startled by her movement, flapping wildly against the tethers that held it in place.

Mrithuri boomed through her mask: "Gentlemen!"

They did not turn to her—another mortal affront to her court from the foreigner, and what exactly were Mahadijia and Anuraja playing at?—but both froze in place. Not so much like startled rabbits as like dogs eying one another before the fight. Syama turned slightly, to catch Mrithuri from the corner of her eye, and Mrithuri gave her a slight gesture.

The bear-dog reached out her brindled head and closed her teeth around the wrist that Mahadijia reached beneath his coat, as delicately as if she had meant to pick up an egg.

Now he looked away from Hnarisha, first glancing at Syama and then, wide-eyed, up at Mrithuri on her dais.

Mrithuri took a slow, deep breath and lowered her arms. She waited in silence for a few moments while the bearded vulture continued its hopeless quest for freedom, the sweeps of its red-stained wings sending gold powder swirling around her like a glittering storm. It returned to its perch and settled, flipping long pinions closed across its back, but its beak opened and it uttered a raucous, croaking complaint that echoed loudly beneath the amplifying vault.

As for Mrithuri, she kept her peace for a few moments, until the captain and his men had closed the distance to the secretary and the ambassador. Then she spoke mildly. "Unless you wish to discuss tariffs, my lord ambassador, I'm afraid you will have to wait your turn. There is a murder inquest before us, and such matters of life and death must take precedence."

Mahadijia stared at her. Mrithuri stared back, glad for once of the heavy kohl and jeweled lashes that made her eyes seem huge and inscrutable. She breathed calmly—the crystalline blaze of the snakebite in her veins helped steady her, though it was ebbing already—and imagined the gaze of the Good Mother, with her beautiful heifer eyes.

Beneath the chiming of the rain, like a distant drumbeat, thunder purred. Syama must have growled—very softly—or squeezed with her jaws, because Mahadijia broke the connection first, glancing down sharply at the bear-dog who held his wrist in her jaws.

"Madam," he said. "If you would call off your hound."

"Syama," Mrithuri said. "Release the man."

Slowly, Syama opened her jaws. She stepped back—just a single pace—and did not sit down, but regarded her new enemy with a chary eye.

Just as slowly, Mahadijia drew an empty hand from beneath his coat and let it fall open to his side.

Mrithuri thought she could see Hnarisha's held breath sigh out in relief from halfway across the audience hall. She kept her face stern, her gaze steady: he could show emotions that she could not. Thank the Good Daughter for the venom in her veins that kept her hands from shaking.

"Sergeant," she said to the man. "I believe this gentleman could use some refreshment. Would you see him to an antechamber? Secretary Hnarisha, please summon the petitioners in the untimely death? The night is burning."

Mahadijia bowed low enough for it to seem mocking. "Your Abundance," he said. "I bear important messages from my raja, whose ports your ships must trade through. Surely you can spare me one small moment of your night?"

She considered, calming herself with the peal of the rain, the mumble of thunder. "Perhaps . . . later."

Mahadijia's expression as he was led away promised retribution. But some flicker of his mouth made Mrithuri think it likely that he was the sort of man who covered with his anger for fear.

Mrithuri swallowed an uneasy sensation that she hadn't won this round and turned her attention to the problem she actually could do something about tonight. She hoped that his continued interruptions were a manifestation of self-importance and disdain for her, some little foreign queen—and not a manifestation of some important news he wished to impart. She hoped her refusal to be hurried was a thwart to Anuraja's plan, whatever that might be, and not a service to it.

She shifted beneath her imperial gaud, uneasy. But no, surely, if it were anything but a power play, a device to make her seem weak, he could have found more appropriate ways to approach her?

Perhaps.

She waited until the ambassador was out of the room before she raised her voice again. "I am ready for the trial."

THE SISTER OF THE POISONED BOOKBINDER WAS ACCUSING HIS WIDOW of murder by arsenic, though he was a wastrel and a drunk and neither wife nor sister had liked him. With a doctor's evidence that the wife, too, showed signs of being poisoned—and the wife's undisputed testimony that the bookbinder's art made liberal use of antimony, lead, prussic acid, arsenic, and other horrors—Mrithuri managed to convince the two women to join forces, have the family well tested, and work together to provide for the dead man's elderly parents and young children alike. It was a pretty night's work, she thought, as she retired to the robing room and stood for Yavashuri while her maid of honor removed her mask and baubles.

The burn of snakebite was long gone. She shook with hunger and thirst, for of course no sustenance could enter her body while she wore the mask. She wondered irritably where Chaeri was: the maid of the bedchamber should have been in attendance with some refreshment—tea and sweets, at least, to give her strength until the morning meal that ended her time of duty.

Outside, the sky had dimmed as dawn overtook them. Though the rain still fell heavily, the day brought warmth, and the result was a steamy tropic heat that saturated and clung. The pleats in Mrithuri's drape were long sagged now, the back of it stuck to her seat with sweat and humidity. She was delighted to shed the thing for a cotton tunic and trousers in a subtle print of brown on bone.

Yavashuri was growing visibly more irritated with every moment that Chaeri did not arrive, which also soothed Mrithuri. If someone else was angry on her behalf, she did not feel so much need to be angry for herself. She actually found herself inhabiting a spirit of quiet peacefulness, despite her growling belly and the itch in her veins.

It lasted until the door burst open, and Chaeri rushed in, disheveled and shrieking. Her drapes were torn, her hair down in frayed braids. A knife protruded from her fist like a bloody tongue, and red dripped and sprayed all down her.

She doubled over, panting, both hands fisted around the knife hilt and the pommel pressed into her belly. As her knees struck the floor, she gasped, "I killed Mahadijia."

THE LAEISH AMBASSADOR LAY FACEDOWN IN THE HALL, HIS COURT robes spread around him like dark wings. One hand reached outward, fingers folded under, a bloody drag-mark where the nails had clawed at marble tile and failed to score the stone. The other arm was under him. An overturned tray lay beside him, tea and shattered crockery contributing to the mess.

Mrithuri, Yavashuri, Ata Akhimah, Hnarisha, and a selection of castle guards stood around the body. Syama leaned forward to sup great huffs of air through flaring nostrils. Mrithuri restrained her with a hand upon her shoulders.

Chaeri was there as well, though she did not so much stand as recline against the chest of a guardsman, her face buried in his neck, his hair stirred by quiet sobs. The hall had been cleared of others, and guardsmen held the doors leading into the Hall of the Empty Throne and out to other areas of the palace.

Ata Akhimah had relieved Chaeri of the knife, and held it wrapped in a length of silk to protect it from stray influences. Hnarisha turned to Chaeri, laid a hand against her shoulder, and said quietly, "Can you tell us what happened?"

Chaeri's sobs quieted a little. She struggled with her breath, got control, and said, "I tried to stop him. I tried to stop him. But he grabbed me and I spilled the rajni's tea."

Ata Akhimah looked at Hnarisha. Hnarisha looked back.

Yavashuri said, "Turn him over," in a voice of quiet command.

Two guardsmen moved forward. One took the dead ambassador by the shoulders. The other grabbed the cloth at his hips—a far less appetizing prospect, as Mahadijia had suffered the usual indignities of death—and on a count of four they heaved and turned. Blood-wet fabric left soak-marks on the tile as his jacket fell open.

He was thoroughly dead. A knife sheath under his left arm lay empty, and Mrithuri could see at a glance that it would neatly accommodate the dagger Ata Akhimah had confiscated from Chaeri. She touched the head of the serpent-sheathed dagger coiled around her throat. She turned and stepped over to Chaeri, intentionally turning her back on Ata Akhimah as the Wizard crouched down to examine the corpse. She heard the chiming of bangles, and laid a hand gently on Chaeri's shoulder. There was blood on her back as well as her front.

Chaeri looked up, face streaked and eyes swollen. "I took his knife. He had it in his hand." She picked ineffectually at the dried blood on her fingers. Her voice was thick, but less hysterical. She seemed to be mastering herself. "He grabbed me by the neck and swung the hilt at me. I bit him and got the knife away and then I stabbed him with it because he wouldn't. He wouldn't . . . he wouldn't let me go."

She crumpled again, against the guardsman's neck. Mrithuri sighed. Of all her household, it *would* have to be Chaeri.

And yet, Chaeri had done well. Mrithuri would not have thought she would have it in her, to foil an assassin, if assassin he had been.

"Put her to bed," Mrithuri told the guardsman. "Give her a little poppy." She held her hands a half-rod apart to indicate what she meant by *a little*.

She watched as the guard led Chaeri away, then turned back to where Ata Akhimah and Hnarisha crouched beside the body. Yavashuri had somehow miraculously produced a fresh platter of tea and food. Mrithuri did not think she could tackle the latter while standing over a fresh corpse, but the tea was sweet, with milk, and she took the cup Yavashuri put in her hand. It had cloves and nutmeg in it, which helped to mask the reek.

It also helped to steady the trembling of her hands. She cupped it before her as she watched the Wizard and the supposed-secretary work.

"There's the bite mark," Ata Akhimah said, clinically. "And there's green wax under his nails."

"Green?" Hnarisha said. "The colors of the Laeish seal are those of precious sapphires: blue and orange."

Those sapphires, which eroded from the rocks along the coast of the Arid Sea and sold for untold riches inland and overseas, were a chief source of Sarathai-lae's wealth and influence.

Yavashuri looked up from her teapot. "His personal color was green."

"Papercuts and ink on the hands," Ata Akhimah said. "Nothing unexpected there."

"So," Mrithuri mused aloud, "to whom was he writing personal letters?"

"I won't know until I open him, but from the angle of the wound I would say that Chaeri stabbed him under the ribcage and severed the great artery in the abdomen. Sheer bad luck for us: he would have died in moments, and no chance of questioning him."

"Wait," said Hnarisha. "What's this?" He held up a spindle of paper, folded several times. "Code."

"Diplomatic orders," said Yavashuri, who had crossed to peer over his shoulder. "I've seen the hand and a similar code before."

A servant won past the guards at the end of the hall and approached her. She stepped aside for a whispered conversation, then turned back to Mrithuri. "The ambassador's room has been searched, Rajni. There are papers freshly burned in the brazier, and either the Mahadijia or someone else has smoothed all the wax tablets that he might have been drafting letters on."

"Did they find a code key?" Hnarisha asked distractedly. Yavashuri generally handled intrigues within the house. Hnarisha generally handled those that stretched beyond. They were, however, accustomed to sharing duties and working in close support of one another.

"They are still searching." She shook her head. "I wouldn't have thought Chaeri had it in her."

Hnarisha stood, holding his befouled hands out. Yavashuri unobtrusively handed him a towel soaked in vinegar and rose oil. As he wiped, he said, "This cannot be anything except a pretext for war."

Mrithuri sighed. She took the spindle of paper that Hnarisha handed her and frowned over it. Strings of nonsense filled the page.

She sighed. "Find the code book. And find that missing letter, if you can."

7

THE GAGE WATCHED THE VEIL COVER THE SKY, DARKENING THE NIGHT. The storm ebbed, leading to no net change in brightness. It didn't matter to Druja, who bustled around waking people and animals in the thin rain and readying the caravan to move. The Dead Man had awakened him with news of the army's arrival as soon as they finished their conversation in the wheelhouse. Druja had taken the news silently, scowling, before giving the Dead Man a brisk piece of his mind for not alerting him even sooner. Then Druja had cursed his own self for a soft-minded fool for deciding the caravan could rest here for a day, and immediately started rousing all and sundry and putting them to work packing up and harnessing.

No one was spared the caravan master's attentions: not even the murderously arrogant prince, who the Gage himself had been sent to roust and set to packing his considerable sprawl of creature comforts.

Fortunately, the man was drunk in his hammock, and his servants were far more reasonable. So there would be no conflict there. At least not until he sobered up and found himself unexpectedly miles from where he had passed out. Then, the Gage expected, there might be a reckoning.

The Gage flexed his metal fingers. With any luck, such a reckoning might result in the Song prince parting company with the caravan. That prospect, the Gage could actually look forward to a little.

Before turning away for a hurried, worried consultation with a freshly arrived local youth whom the Gage did not know, Druja had also asked the Gage to alert the bride and her servants. Because he was made of metal, and presumably uninterested in the joys of the flesh, he was by custom considered the equivalent of a eunuch, and there was no social taboo to prevent him from entering even a noble lady's boudoir. Even when that boudoir was constructed of no more than a few sheets of cloth strung on cords across the bow of an ice-ship's hold. The noblewoman, unlike the prince, came and spoke to him herself, a veil across the lower part of her face, her dark eyes narrow with concern.

The Gage had never paid much attention to the noblewoman before. Now he found himself studying the features not concealed by her veil. Her brows were dark and of medium width: her eyes wide, and a kind of chipped ambery hazel. Her forehead was youthful, un-lined. The Gage thought she was probably pretty, unless the veil hid some terrible deformity. And she was certainly intelligent. She took in everything he had to tell her, unspeaking, staring into the mirror of his visage as if she were inspecting her own reflection.

When he was done, she asked only one question. "Do you think they're going to try to make us stay?"

"Yes," he said.

She nodded, slow and considering. He wished he could read her expression, but they both wore their own kinds of mask.

She said, "Thank you."

RAINDROPS PINGED OFF THE GAGE'S POLISHED DOME AS HE CROSSED THE caravanserai yard once more. His weight pressed the cobbles deeper into the mud underfoot. Men—not in livery, but with the unmis-takable bearing of soldiers—skulked around the edges of the yard.

The Gage counted them, as he had no doubt they were counting the caravan.

He made his way to the lee of the lead ship, to a tent where Druja, Nizhvashiti, and the Dead Man were huddled over a map, and stood by the flaps so he would not drip on it. "Have they contacted us yet?"

"No," said Druja. His sun-spotted forefinger traced a line on the vellum. "But they will."

Nizhvashiti whistled through teeth. "The path of least conflict would be to remain, and do as we are instructed." The Godmade's tone made it plain that this was not to be interpreted as a serious suggestion.

Without looking up, the Dead Man said, "It has always been my fate to die as a conscript in some lord's war. But I would as soon it were not this lord nor this battle." He looked up, and the Gage read his need to be moving toward their destination in the narrow gap below his head scarf and above his veil.

Druja snorted. "He'll press us all into service if he can. But I hired you lot on to guard this caravan and protect it from brigands. Even if those brigands are the whole gods-damned government, I expect that contract to be honored."

"We'd just as soon avoid impression as troops to the Boneless, now that you mention it." The Gage shook his head at the Dead Man. "And after all, we do have a package to deliver."

The Dead Man had schooled his expression, and now his face was as inscrutable behind his veil as had been the noblewoman's. His voice, though, had a bantering tone. "Have you considered just walking through the stockade dragging all three boats behind you? It's not like they could stop you. And if they rained down fire arrows, well. There's all this cursed wet."

"If you can't make a serious suggestion," Druja said, "do me the small favor of holding your tongue. We can try to fight our way out if we have to. But I'd prefer some subtlety. Some subterfuge."

Someone was coming up behind the Gage. The bride-to-be, under an umbrella held by her maidservant, both of them picking their way across the cobbles in high wooden pattens. The Gage pretended not to notice her until she cleared her throat behind him.

He stepped aside. She leaned around him to glance into the tent. She leaned back, then, and whispered for the Gage alone: "I might have an idea."

THE GAGE RETURNED FROM WALKING WITH THE NOBLEWOMAN TO FIND Druja slapping that same local youth on the shoulder in a friendly but definitive send-off. The boy jogged off through splashing mud, spatters flying up his bare legs and dabbing the Gage's once-shining hide. The Gage wished to sigh; the rain would soon enough wash it off again. And there was plenty more mud where that had come from.

The caravan master wasn't fond of the plan. Even less so when he heard it had come from a woman. But he seemed too distracted and concerned to fuss much, and he kept squinting at the sky as if the passage of time had suddenly become very important to him.

"It will never work." Druja turned away.

"Do you have a better solution?"

"I have very little." Druja's mouth twisted. He wiped rain from the tip of his nose. "Go and fetch the city guard."

". . . TWO OF MY PASSENGERS HAVE TAKEN VERY ILL," DRUJA PLEADED to the sergeant at arms. "Please, if you will allow us to stay in the city for only a few more days. They cannot travel as they are."

The Gage loomed behind the caravan master, just in case something went wrong. But it didn't look as if the sergeant was likely to take one single step past the hatchway. Behind it, in a room lit by oil lamps, the noblewoman and the Godmade each lay on pallets sour with sweat. Their faces were shiny with droplets, their eyes sunken, their cheeks slack as they labored to breathe. The Dead Man crouched beside the noblewoman's pallet, murmuring, "Oh, my bright Golbahar. My intended, my beloved. Your flesh is so hot. . . ."

The Godmade turned a fevered face to the door. The single eye blinked blindly, and a racking cough shook the skeletal form.

"Absolutely not," the sergeant said. "You'll have to move on. If you'd said at the gate that you were carrying sickness we never would have let you in."

"It's the lung-sickness!" the noblewoman cried in a thready tone. "I know it is. The Spawning Sickness! Do not lie to me, my love. You must leave me here and flee!"

The Gage thought she might be overacting slightly, but the sergeant took a hasty step away from the door. The Godmade began to cough, a monotonous hacking that the Gage found extremely convincing. The noblewoman hacked too, covering her mouth with a trembling hand. When she drew it away, her fingers were smeared with lumpy crimson.

"You cannot stay here!" the sergeant said. "You must move on at once! All of you!"

"You son of a bitch," the Dead Man snarled. He lurched to his feet, though the noblewoman clawed at his arm weakly and tried to drag him back. "Can't you see this girl is sick? You'll put us out in the rain?!"

He shook the noblewoman's hand free of his arm and charged the door. The Gage stepped forward to "intercept" him, catching the Dead Man as gently as he could so as not to bruise. The Godmade coughed louder—a deep, rending hack with a bubble in it, the sort of thing the Gage would have sworn could not be faked. Red seeped down a dark cheek. The Gage tried to recall the frailties of the flesh, and hoped they weren't overselling it.

He shouldn't have worried so much. The sergeant gasped, "Good Mother, it *is* the Black Spawning." Then hasty footsteps echoed down the corridor at a brisk stagger. The man paused halfway up the ladder to the deck and shouted down. "If you're not gone by the tolling of the midnight bell, I'll have every one of you put to the sword!"

The Gage listened until he was sure the sergeant was gone, then released the Dead Man's arm. From long practice, he could tell that the Dead Man was grinning at him behind the veil.

"Lady Golbahar," the Dead Man said, "yours was truly a most excellent plan!"

Sitting up, she drew her veil across her face once more. "It wasn't so bad."

The Gage wished he felt as confident. "That's one," he said. "There's still any number of toll points and closed borders between us and Sarathai-tia."

"Oh, celebrate a little, you old turd in the sand," the Dead Man answered. "How bad can the rest of it be?"

UNDER THE STARRY SKIES OF SARATH-SAHAL, THERE WAS NO COVER OF darkness: there was only the twilight day and the brighter night. So the caravan rolled out the gates of Chandranath in shadowless light, under red-slashed gray plague flags that ruffled listlessly from the standards. They had strung the rails with atonal rattles made of bits of tin strung on knotted leather. The procession moved in a clattering disharmony that etched even the Gage's nerves of bronze.

Wariness etched his nerves as well. He moved at the head of the column, bearing a plague flag as a banner, ready to shoo aside such as did not give way of their own volition and confront anyone who would not be shooed. These were few: not many were abroad in these unsettled times, and for those unlucky or stubborn travelers they did encounter, the plague tokens were a powerful argument.

The Cauled Sun cast braided strands of light over the Gage and the surroundings, like the bright refracted bands cast through ripples moving across a sandy pool. They made the road ahead all the more treacherous, because what seemed merely imagination might instead be a dangerous edge, and what seemed a rut might be only some trick of the light. The Gage found himself using the butt of his pennant as a guide, probing ahead, not trusting the mountain road until the solid thump of the stick told him what was real and what was shadow.

The Dead Man walked at the back, as had become his wont,

and the Gage found he missed him. The Lotus day with its black-ened sun and Heavenly River was spooky; the calls of birds through the changeable twilight too like the signals of bandits; the stars above strange and attenuated. A brass automaton might be imper-vious to most physical threats, but even a brass automaton could get the creeps.

The sensation wasn't eased when Druja climbed down from the forecastle of the leading ice-ship to poke along beside the Gage. In part because he did it without haranguing the Gage to move faster, which the Gage had been braced for. He just picked up a pole of his own and peered and poked and inspected the opposite side of the trail—which did a better job of moving them incrementally faster than a dressing down would have—and grumbled under his breath while intermittently glaring at the horizon as if searching for some landmark or a sign.

Wheels creaked in the thick mud, and the oxen slipped and struggled. Men used shovels and levers to keep the heavy ice-boats moving, their wheels turning, when they wanted to bog down in the road. The Cauled Sun ground its weary path against the Heavenly River. No pursuit materialized, though Druja kept glancing skep-tically back over his shoulder. The road began to drop off again, and they finally found themselves gaining some momentum when Druja glanced around, peered again at the sky, and seemed to mea-sure the distance between the Cauled Sun and the top of a striking upthrust tower of rock on the horizon against the width of his hand.

"Call a halt here," Druja said to the Gage.

The Gage would have stared at Druja, if the Gage had eyes. He tilted his featureless head to one side and said, "We just got the wheels running freely."

"Call a halt here," Druja repeated, with a slightly edged tone.

The Gage would have sighed if that were an option open to him. Since it wasn't, he said, "You pay the bills," and turned back toward the others to irritate the oxen and their drovers. The longer they sat in the mud, the deeper the wheels would mire. At least the road was somewhat stony here—that gave them a better chance of succeeding in getting moving again.

Other than that, though, this was a bad place for a halt. A good-sized cliff bracketed the left side of the road, and anyone could sneak up on them along the top of it, to push rocks down or hurl fire. On the right side, there was less dropoff and less mud than there had been—granite crumbled from the cliff overhead and pushed aside to clear the road scattered a steep slope. Below the boulder field, an open forest of conifers bent wet branches heavy under the weight of the rain.

Druja walked away, vanishing between wagons. The Dead Man came up to meet the Gage, his red coat so thicked with red mud that it resembled wet leather. He walked beside the ice-boats on the narrow verge, one hand stretched out to steady himself against their sides in case his foot slipped. Despite his caution, his stride seemed confident, secure.

His hood was up, the whites of his eyes in its shadows showing red and irritated from the rain. "This would be a most providential place for an ambush."

"You noticed," said the Gage.

"Does Druja want to wait for better light?" The Dead Man stood on tiptoe and craned forward and down, contemplating the road below. It didn't look any worse than what they'd come over already, the Gage thought. Or, for that matter, a whole hell of a lot better.

The Gage grunted softly, the low verbal equivalent of a shrug. "He didn't say. But I can hear pots clattering: we obviously mean to stay here long enough to heat up some soup. You should get some."

The Dead Man chafed his shoulders to warm himself, stopped when his gloves came back freshly muddied from the clay-caked coat. "May happen I will," he agreed cheerfully. "No telling when there'll be hot food again."

UNFORTUNATELY, THE DEAD MAN HAD TO COME BACK RUNNING through the muck from the soup line with his tin mug unfilled when the Gage bellowed for him. The snotty Song princeling had awakened with a nasty hangover, and was determined to take the lapse in his drunken stupor out on everyone around him.

The prince had staggered out the hatch of the crimson ice-boat and promptly tripped and fallen over the railing into the sloppy mud below. Somehow, he'd managed to land more or less upright, and now he was sitting on his jeweled ass in the mud haranguing the Gage and anybody else who would come close enough to listen.

"What the hell is this? Why have we stopped here? Why aren't we in the town?" The prince scooped up a slimy handful of mud and yak dung and flung it sidearmed. His aim was better than the Gage had anticipated. Filth spattered his wet brass carapace, clung and slid down. He sighed inwardly: the rain would wash it away soon enough.

The Gage considered going over to the prince and picking him up by the wrists, but the odds seemed pretty good that he would slide and fall over on the little bastard, crushing him to death. There wasn't a real downside there, except that the family would probably want some kind of revenge on Druja, and Druja wasn't awful enough to deserve that.

Fortunately, that was when the Dead Man arrived. He glanced around, assessed the situation with a sigh, and hooked his mug onto his belt. "Are you all right, sir?" he said to the Song prince. "You seem to have suffered a fall."

The prince was drawing breath to give the Dead Man a piece of his mind when he happened to turn his head and spot the plague flags. His upbraidment turned into a shriek and he scrambled to his feet, not even wincing. "What in the thirty-seven orthodox hells is that?"

"A plague flag," the Dead Man observed mildly. "Maybe you couldn't tell because it's pretty wet."

The Gage stepped forward to cover the Dead Man's flank. He knew this mood; his partner was angry enough to have started baiting the prince. This could now come to drawn blades very quickly.

"There's plague in the caravan? I can't be here! I'm the heir; I can't be exposed to plague!"

"You haven't been," the Dead Man said in his reasonable voice. "And if you'll return to your cabin, you won't be. The caravan is under quarantine, Prince Mi Ren. You'll be safest inside."

"I'm leaving," said the prince. Wincing a bit—perhaps the fall had affected him slightly—he turned and bellowed over his shoulder. "Footman! Pack up our things. We're leaving the caravan."

"You can't leave the caravan." The Gage stepped forward, letting his size be his argument. It was a facet of his automaton self that he had never quite gotten over taking joy in, even when he knew it was petty to do so.

The prince's jeweled slippers squelched in the mud. One of his tall wooden pattens dangled on its laces through the railing above him. Perhaps trying to walk in them on the rain-slimy deck had contributed to his slip and fall.

He bellowed again. Above the dangling patten, the face of a young Song man appeared, dressed in a tremulous frown. "Lord?"

"Pack!" the prince bellowed. "We're leaving the caravan."

The Dead Man sighed heavily. "You're not leaving the caravan," he called up to the worried servant. "The caravan is under interdict. Nobody leaves. We're *quarantined*."

The prince drew himself up to his full, squelching height. "Is that the case?"

The Dead Man set his hand on the hilt of his sword.

The prince sniffed haughtily. He wasn't wearing a blade. He didn't seem to think he needed one, because he stepped forward with his chin high. "And you and what army are going to try and stop me, Dead Man?"

THE SONG PRINCE DID NOT GIVE THEM ANY MORE TROUBLE AFTER that, because the Gage nailed him into a cabin. He didn't use a hammer, just the heavy tap of a bent forefinger. And he only used four nails, carefully placed so as not to damage the woodwork. They were really just there for reinforcement: Druja had locked the door and then pocketed the palm-long iron key.

"How are you planning on feeding him?" the Dead Man asked, as the two guards and the caravan master were walking away. Muffled yelps of outrage faded behind them.

"There's a porthole," Druja said carelessly. "I'm sure his servants can stuff sausages through it if they care to."

The Gage said, "I'm not carrying the corpse out if they don't."

He thought that Druja's forced casualness was an overlay on continued anxiety. Still, he checked the sky, and looked around anxiously as they walked along the rutted road. At the horizon, at that finger of sky-pointing stone, at the cliff above.

The day was lightening as night brightened the horizon, the dark line of the veil sliding up to reveal the true, scintillating glory of the Heavenly River in all its threads and washes of stars. The clouds must be retreating.

As they passed the lead ice-boat, the Gage heard a scrabbling rustle. He started to turn, to go and investigate, but Druja lay a restraining hand on his arm. The rain was increasing, tiny hard cold pellets falling fast and striking the Gage's mirrored skull with sharp musical pings.

"Rats," Druja said. "I'll put out traps for them."

It wasn't rats, but the Gage wasn't paid to argue with the caravan master. "What now?"

Druja glanced once more at the finger of rock, at the leavening sky. "Let's get these wheels out of the mud and these oxen moving before another caravan comes along and somebody has to back down a mountain to a cutout, shall we? Maybe we can make the border before the night's out."

The Gage decided that it would be completely pointless to ask why they had paused here for half a day after scrambling out of town as fast as possible, and now it was so important that they leave at once. So he went to fetch a lever, and a rope.

*　　*　　*

THE FINAL CURTAINS OF RAIN FELL SPARKLING THROUGH THE BRILLIANCE
of sunset, the gleam of the Heavenly River revealed as the veil swept
away and the clouds thinned and tore into wisps, then blew scudding
toward the east. At last, they rolled. The caravan, creaking and wallowing, proceeded down the mountain road and toward the borders of
Himadra's stony country.

They made better time now. Once they reached the bottom of the
slope, the road was in better repair, the ruts less deep. No one had
passed this way recently—they were the only refugees foolish enough
to brave the rains, apparently—and the mud was only a thin slick
layer over packed clay. The mud dried on the wheels and cracked off
in long, curved chunks with interiors polished smooth as bowls.

By morning, when the first glimpse of the veil was dimming the
horizon, they had found their way to the toll booth at the boundary.

The caravan drew up before a row of sawhorses dragged across the
road. There might have been a gate here once: now there were a pair of
stone gatehouses with crumbling mortar, smeared with orange rust
stains to mark where steel hinges and pins had melted away.

It was guarded, of course. Four men stood in front of it, and there
were wagons to either side, under whose tarpaulin roofs more rested.
There had been a barracks built here at some point. The stones of
its toppled walls were in the process of being cleaned of mortar,
sorted, and stacked.

What was intact, however, were the twinned ballistae atop the
gatehouses, pointing down at the road below and between. That was
a weapon that even the Gage thought worth treating with respect.

The Gage estimated that there were another twenty men divided
between the two wagons. He couldn't guess how many might be
inside the gatehouses. He stayed back beside the blue-and-copper ice-
boat, the hood of his robe pulled up, his arms folded inside the loose
sleeves of his rough-spun robe. It swung wetly from his chassis, steaming faintly in the rising warmth.

Some ranking guard came forward, flanked by two colleagues, and
Druja walked up to deal with him. He had a cargo manifest in his

hand, and his wet boots slapped against the paving stones that had re-emerged from the sucking mud as the caravan approached the border. He stopped well away from the guards, and with the rolled manifest he pointed up to the plague flags still snapping overhead.

He called out, "I'd recommend you not come any closer, sirs! Pardon me for the inconvenience!"

The guards did stop. The officer looked at his men, then shrugged. "We still need to see your paperwork. Hold it up, so I can examine it."

The man came forward a little more but still stopped arm's length from Druja. His guards followed restively, looking from side to side as if the threat of plague were an ambush.

The Gage tried to be unobtrusive. It would be counterproductive to intimidate the border guards: they would then feel the need to prove their manhood, and that sort of thing had a tendency to end very badly.

Along the far side of the ice-boats, the Godmade's robe swished softly as Nizhvashiti paced forward, moving as if idly wandering. The Gage would have scowled if he'd had a face to do it with. He'd learned to trust the priest; now he worried that the priest might be having a premonition of violence—or be about to provoke it.

The Gage studied the undercarriage of the red-gold ice-boat just ahead of the one he stood beside. He couldn't shut his eyes to what was happening between Druja and the guards, not having any eyes. But he could at least turn his attention away, and perhaps that would serve to make his presence seem less threatening.

The struts that currently held the wheels—and which had previously held the sled runners—were attached to a sort of cradle in which the curved hull could be slung. He'd never really examined the structure of it before. Now he noticed two interesting things: one was that the hull had hook-shaped metal fittings bolted to it. In the water, they would project like the tail fins of a swift fish, and the Gage imagined that they might serve to stabilize the craft somehow. When the ice-boat was traveling over land, however, they locked into the chassis that held the runners or the wheels and held the hull there, secure.

The other thing he noticed was that there were scratches through the mud on the undercarriage, into the paint. They were almost deep enough to be called gouges, and they looked fresh. And they were perpendicular to the rail and the keel, not parallel to it as you might expect if the hull had dragged against a bush or stone or something.

The Gage thought about ducking down for a better angle, but if the guards hadn't noticed the marks yet he wasn't going to direct their attention to them. *What did we pick up? And why the hell aren't we doing a better job of hiding it?*

They could try to fight their way out, if they really had to. He and the Dead Man and Nizhvashiti were a formidable group. But they weren't an army, and even if they were, the ice-boats, the cargo, and the passengers were all vulnerable—to the soldiers, to the ballistae, to something as simple as fire. Even if the exhausted oxen could be goaded to crash the improvised gate, they could not drag the mud-caked wagons faster than a shambling walk. The border guards could just drop them with crossbows, or fire flaming bolts into the ice-ships.

The Gage's brass hide itched with vulnerability.

Druja was showing the officer some paperwork, a series of chits, a piece of parchment heavy with ribbons and seals. The officer nodded, then turned and waved the men who had been standing with him forward. They gave each other uneasy glances at approaching the quarantined caravan, but did not linger long enough over them to make their officer take notice. The Gage admired the discipline.

"But I've paid the duties," Druja said. "Here are the affidavits. And you can't enter the ships—they were interdicted and sealed by Himadra's own men!"

"We too are Himadra's own men," the officer said. "And it wouldn't go well with us if we took every traveler's word for their good behavior. I'm sure you understand."

"It's your risk," Druja said. He rolled up his affidavits and his cargo manifest and stuffed them into a leather tube waterproofed with beeswax, then forced the tight lid on.

The Gage kept himself calm and quiet as the men came up on him. They approached warily, but not as if in fear—it was just the reasonable caution of the professional. One stopped a cart length ahead of him and said, "Raise your head, foreigner."

The Gage did, and heard the soldier's gasp as his own face was reflected, distorted, in the Gage's curved metal mirror. "By the Good Daughter!" he cried, stepping back in haste.

"What is it?" the officer called.

"Some kind of automaton!"

Instantly, the officer was at his side. "A Gage."

The Gage nodded.

The officer jerked a thumb toward Druja. "There is no Wizard or sorcerer listed in this man's passenger list."

"There is no Wizard nor sorcerer with the caravan."

"Where is your master, metal man?"

"Buried," the Gage answered truthfully. "In the desert south of Messaline."

"Who do you serve?"

The Gage nodded to Druja. "I am masterless. This man hired me as a caravan guard. That is whom I serve."

The Gage caught a glimpse of muddy red wool and knew the Dead Man was slipping closer.

"We do not wish a fight," Druja said, his tone almost begging. "We wish only to leave. There are sick people here."

"Hey," the second guard said, pointing to the scrapes on the bottom of the lead ice-boat. "What caused these?"

Druja stepped forward, frowning as he moved to examine the gouges. "Well, you see—"

"Exercise," said a woman's voice from above.

They all looked up. Ritu was halfway up the sail-less mast, looking down on them. She clung with one hand and both feet, leaning far out, braced with the edge of her shoes.

"Exercise?" the officer asked.

"Sure." She slid down the mast, landing lightly with bent knees, and walked across the deck to the rail. She hopped up on it without breaking stride—not the display of nimbleness most people would expect from a middle-aged matron, but the Gage had grown accustomed to the acrobats by now. "My family are performers. We need to stay in shape even while traveling. I was using the ice-boat as a scaffolding."

The guards looked at one another, confused.

"The boat has juggling swords in the hold, too," she continued. "Are you going to confiscate those as war materiel?"

The officer bit his lip, looking as if he might argue. But at just that moment, the Godmade gasped theatrically on the far side of the ice-boat and doubled over, one hand on the hull. The black hood fell back, revealing a cavernously gaunt face, a single red-rimmed eye. Nizhvashiti retched, but nothing except a thin stream of stinking bile came up. The Godmade looked exactly like the Gage's idea of someone in the throes of a fatal contagion.

Apparently the picture matched the one in the officer's head as well. All three guards stared horrified for a moment, then scrambled back, the senior one moving fastest. "All right," he said, "Move on, move on. You, men! Get those sawhorses out of the way! And get some bleach on that." He turned back to Druja. "Didn't you hear me? Get rolling, or I'll burn your whole caravan where it sits!"

Druja had already turned to the teamsters and had them chivvying their oxen forward. The animals lowed and balked, but soon responded to their handlers' urgency and leaned into the harnesses. The Dead Man moved to assist the Godmade up a boarding ladder and over the railing. The Gage got behind the lead ice-boat and pushed to get it rolling; then the next team of oxen pulled harder to catch up. Before long, they were creaking and slogging past the border post, heads bowed, not looking back until they were well clear indeed.

The Gage walked in a little group with Ritu and Druja. They were all silent until the guard post was just a smudge against the muddy foothills.

"You owe me one," Ritu murmured to Druja, as soon as the guard post had dwindled behind them. "You risked us all. Who the fuck is that man that he's that important?"

Druja blinked at her. "I'm sure I don't know what you mean."

Ritu nodded. "Of course you don't. The man you waited for, at the last stop. The one who scrambled up under the ice-boat, and then climbed the hull to get inside. The one who's huddling where the bilges would be if we were in the water, and who looks like he lost a wrestling match with a Cho-tse. That man."

Druja set his mouth stubbornly.

Ritu shrugged. "He's going to need food and water soon, you realize. And those wounds cleaned. Smuggling him out of Chandranath isn't going to serve any good purpose if he dies of neglect." She paused, and the Gage could almost see her calculating what she was going to say next. "A curious thing. He almost looks like he was tortured."

Druja turned his head and spat. The ice-boat wheels churned mud over the residue. "He's an assassin," he said.

Then, more quietly, "He's my brother."

8

LATER, WHEN THEY WERE WARM AND DRY IN THE HARBORMASTER'S hut at the top of the cliff, Sayeh cupped a steaming bowl of tea between her scalded hands and inhaled over it—as if the milk and spices and sugar could erase the memory of that terrible stench of rot.

Her son had been sent back to the palace before she even made it up the streaming road. Now they awaited the palanquin's return so that Sayeh could venture home as well, and in the meantime huddled together against the storm—Wizard and rajni and commoners.

She had the only padded chair in the place. Tsering-la stood against the wall, studying his own tea as if he could read the secrets of the future in its lees. The guards were divided—a pair stood one each on either side near the door, with the other two beside the shuttered windows. The harbormaster sat at her desk, working on some documents. And the water-diver was curled before the fire, her head nodding as if she struggled with sleep.

When Sayeh had finished her tea—the harbormaster's husband emerged from the kitchen to offer more, but only Tsering-la and the water-diver accepted—Sayeh straightened her shoulders. She would have stood, but that would have meant the harbormaster and the water-diver both would have needed to leap to their feet as well. And the water-diver was exhausted, and Sayeh happened to know that the harbormaster's back pained her greatly.

So instead she cleared her throat and said, "Honored diver, are you sleeping?"

The girl's head snapped up. She spilled her tea across her fingers, but did not seem to notice the heat. Sayeh saw that her hands too seemed burned.

"No, Your Abundance."

"What is your name?"

The girl glanced around the room as if seeking inspiration or escape. Only a few moments passed, however, before she sighed and said, "I am called Nazia, Rajni."

"Are your family water-divers?"

The harbormaster looked up. She was old, but not yet frail. However, Sayeh knew that she too had once been a water-diver, and when she retired because of a serious injury, Sayeh and her husband Ashar had awarded her this post in thanks for her service.

"I am Nazia Sandhya's daughter," the water-diver clarified. "My mother was of the line of Kamala."

They were traditional water-diver names, with their endings that sounded masculine to Sayeh's ear. She had heard that the water-divers had originated with a different tribe than her own.

In any case, Kamala's was the oldest lineage of water-divers. Or one of the oldest, as there would always be conflicting claims, but Sayeh had always thought that Kamala's daughters' evidence for the antiquity of their ancestor was probably the most well-documented.

"Your mother died this year," Sayeh said. She had attended the funeral, to show respect for a woman killed providing for Sayeh's people. The woman had been honored; she had claimed the right of the first dive, at the beginning of the season. But despite her experience, despite her family tradition, something had gone wrong in the deeps. She had not surfaced again.

Her body had washed up days later—or what was left of it, after the beasts of the sea had had their fill.

Sayeh felt a pang. If she were not what she was, she—a firstborn daughter—would have been trained to make the ritual dive herself. After a fashion, this child's mother had died in Sayeh's place.

The girl nodded. That look of defiance flashed across her face again.

Sayeh glanced at the shuttered window. Rain drummed on the roof like fists. Cisterns all over the city were filling to bursting with clean, pure rain.

From desperation and drought, to this. Her kingdom was a strange place.

"I am sorry for your loss."

"Thank you, Rajni."

"You're angry about her death?"

Nazia looked down.

"She dove in my place," Sayeh said. "Because the Guild protects the profession. Because neither men nor women such as I are permitted to become water-divers."

"Rajni?"

Tsering cleared his throat. "Did someone pay you for what you did tonight?"

It was a perceptive question—and an accurate one, Sayeh saw, from the sidelong glance Nazia gave the Wizard.

The Wizard shared a similar glance with his rajni, then turned back to the girl. "Tell the truth."

"A—there was a man. He said his name was Varjeet. He . . ." she shrugged. "Rajni, he and I agreed about many things. And after talking to him . . . I could not say if it was his idea or mine. But we agreed that you were . . . ill-omened. And that it was fitting that the water that burned my mother . . ."

She twisted her hands together. She was very young.

Sayeh saw what the girl was thinking, but that she was also too much a child to own her prejudices in the face of someone she thought she despised because of what they had been born. Sayeh saw the pretense of ignorance, and despite her gentle temperament, she was not in a mood tonight to be kind. "Say what you are thinking, then. Am I ill-omened because I am shandha? Is that why you polluted the water?"

"Women such as you are not women," the water-diver said viciously, glaring up from her hands, seeming taken aback by her own explosion. "You and your unnatural child have brought a curse upon us. I did not pollute that water: it is as I brought it from the deeps. The Sea itself rises up in revolt against your abomination."

Sayeh glanced at Tsering-la. The Wizard gently shook his head.

You could not permit someone to speak to you so. Not and remain in power long. Especially as a widow. But she could not make a martyr of the girl either. Especially when her mother had been so important, and when her death had been seen as a portent of evil, especially as Sayeh's husband died so soon after.

"If the Guild of the water-divers would permit it, I would have trained. I would have made that dive."

The girl looked up. "You are too old."

"Am I older than your mother?"

That silenced her. At least for a little. Sayeh sighed, and the girl thought. Then the girl shook her head and said, "You could have forced us. The Guild."

"Could I?"

"You are rajni."

Sayeh closed her eyes, opened them, bit her tongue and looked to Tsering-la for support. He smiled a little, but that was all.

"Oh," said Sayeh. "I could. And how would the Guild feel about such an abrogation of its authority? And what would the other divers do to any shandha who joined? How much power would a rajni who spends it so profligately soon have?"

The girl shrugged. She'd obviously never thought much about the limits of power. She was young enough to believe that when one had authority, that meant one could command. Without consideration or repercussions.

Tsering was looking interested, though, so Sayeh continued her catechism, hoping to draw the girl out more. "Power may be made an investment, returning dividends, my child. Or it may be made an expense and a waste. Do you think that power so wasted would not result in the erosion of the foundation of government, in ill-will and revolt? In death for me and thirst, loss, privation, possibly death for my people, as well?"

"I . . ." She glanced about the room. The harbormaster was writing as if she heard nothing. The guards' eyes were stones, staring unfocused into space.

Sayeh shook her head sadly. "There are limits, little girl, on what even a rajni may decree and do."

Tsering-la stepped forward. Sayeh recognized him, and he spoke. "Where did the bitter water come from?"

The girl resisted, but his voice was so reasonable, she did not demur long. "There is a place where it wells high. Higher than ever before, this year. Still deeper than any of the others dive." She shook her head. "I think—I think my mother dove into it by accident."

"So you found this . . . plume. Of bitter water. And decided to use it to create an ill omen."

Miserably, the girl nodded. "I was trying to duplicate my mother's dive. To discover what happened to her. She was heavier than I. I used weights . . . I was fortunate that I only touched the bitter water with my hands. It was warm. They teach us . . . to fear the warm currents. For that reason."

"Some of them are bitter." Tsering's face was very grave. "Sometimes, the springs that arise near burning mountains are so."

"There are no burning mountains here," Sayeh said. "The closest—"

"Is in Tsarepheth," Tsering-la agreed. It was the Wizards' city, place of their fabled Red-and-White Citadel. It was in that place, Sayeh knew, where Tsering-la had learned his Wizardry.

He was looking at the girl with something like interest. Sayeh imagined that a solution to their problems might lie there. She turned her attention back to the girl. *Nazia,* she thought. *If you must condemn her, learn her name.*

She studied the young water-diver's face. Her eyes were downcast. The worried lines of her frown made her seem far older than her years.

"I cannot let your insolence go unremarked," Sayeh said tiredly. "You spoke to me as you did in front of witnesses. And I know you hate me. It is not safe for me to leave people who hate me unchecked."

"I do not hate you!" the girl cried, jerking upright. Her expression crumpled from worry into despair. "I hated . . . I hated the person who hurt my mother."

Tsering-la had known Sayeh for a long time. He cleared his throat, and when she recognized him he said what she was relying upon him to say. "Your Abundance. This girl . . ."

"Continue without fear, Wizard."

"She is clever."

Nazia stared down at her hands. Unaccustomed to praise, Sayeh saw. Too smart, too odd to fit in well with the other water-divers? Clever was not always the way to popularity.

"She is," Sayeh agreed.

"She is fearless." Tsering-la steepled his hands before him. He crossed to stand beside Nazia, seeming to tower over her despite his plumpness and slight stature. "She has the wit and will to"—he paused, one of his small plump hands disengaging from the other to dip sharply, plane, and wobble side to side like a gull adjusting its trim in an updraft—"craft a daring plan, research it, and carry it off."

Sayeh pursed her lips. Stagily, she supposed. But staginess was part of the business of being a rajni as much so as of being a Wizard.

Tsering-la crouched, knees jutting between the panels of his pet-aled coat. He took Nazia's hand and inspected it in the firelight. "These are not so badly burned as I would have expected. Did you use a salve to protect your skin?"

The girl, unable to meet his eyes, nodded. He looked up at Sayeh, and she read it plainly in his expression: *Do not waste this one. This one is worth something.*

Sayeh sighed. "She cannot go back to the water-divers."

"Let her come to me," Tsering-la said, and smiled.

Her eyes went wide. "Would I have to—" She pressed her fists to her middle. Rasan Wizards gained their power through a terrifying surgery, men and women both. They must consent to be neutered before they could wield their magics.

Sayeh herself felt an answering twinge at the idea. She knew a little something about terrifying surgeries, and Tsering-la's delicacy with a knife. And she had had the comfort of knowing that the Good Mother had blessed and ordained her own quest for motherhood, or her propitiations would never have been answered. And that she would surely have died, and her child with her, if she did not submit to having that babe cut from her when there was no natural path for him to be born.

She'd healed fast and clean, under the ministrations of the Good Mother's nuns. And now she had her beautiful heir, her son.

The rajni wondered if Nazia would someday make a similar frightening decision, and if the girl would be blessed to regret it as little.

"That is not a decision you would need to make for many years," Tsering-la said, releasing her hand. "First we must see if you have any aptitude. Not everyone takes to the training. But you have the wit for it: that, I'll warrant. Will you come with me, Nazia?"

The girl murmured something.

"Speak up," Sayeh said.

"Yes," the girl said.

Sayeh bit her lip and twisted her head away. She caught the harbormaster watching her from across the desk in the corner, and smiled so the woman would not look down. She needed the comfort, for the moment, of another grown woman's gaze.

On the choices we make in thoughtless childhood, are the rest of our long lives hung.

Those who got any choice at all.

"Well," she said. "That's settled. May I trouble your husband for more tea, Harbormaster?"

"WELL, THAT'S ONE PROBLEM DEALT WITH," SAYEH MUTTERED, IN THE shelter of the palanquin. The drumming rain wanted to comfort her. She rocked in misery.

There was only Tsering-la to see her. She could allow herself the luxury of distress.

"But not the major one."

"No." Sayeh gathered herself before she continued. "The omen at the beginning of the dry season was bad. The woman died on the first dive. And now the rains have come on so swiftly that the divers and tenders were endangered, and the dead diver's daughter has closed the season by bringing bitter water back. None of it is promising."

Tsering-la sighed. "My training did not prepare me for the interpretation of omens. You need a priest for that."

"The wisest abbess of the Good Mother couldn't pull a positive interpretation out of this."

"Perhaps," Tsering-la said, carefully. As if feeling his way on uncertain footing. "Perhaps what you need now is not a positive interpretation. But an accurate one."

FOREWARNED IS FOREARMED, SAYEH TOLD HERSELF FOR THE THIRD time, and girded her loins to approach the abbess. She did not travel to the cloister in state, but moved in a simple palanquin with a minimum number of guards, and those not in livery. They took her out the palace's postern gate, and spirited her down one of Ansh-Sahal's side streets so quickly that not even the beggars managed to swarm her conveyance.

This was in part to keep her consultation of the abbess a secret, and in part to thwart the Sahali folk who clustered by the palace gates, demanding an audience, demanding that Sayeh take a new husband immediately. Her people could make their own interpretations of the omens, and they had obviously decided that the Good Mother disapproved of a rajni ruling alone—even one ruling as regent for a minor son. They'd stop her if they could, and they would not hesitate at all to tell her so.

But all the same, no one would expect a rajni to make her escape by the ignominious tradesman's gate. And Sayeh took a certain joy in being unpredictable.

Out the back she went.

IN SARATHAI, THE NUNS WOULD HAVE BEEN EASIER TO REACH. THE custom there was to build the palace so that the women's quarters interlocked with the women's quarters of the temple, being separated by grates of sandalwood, ivory, soapstone, or gilt. Nuns and ladies could thus converse, and both were said to benefit by it.

But here in Ansh-Sahal, the palace was at the hill's peak and the temple stood atop the cliffs, overlooking the ocean. So it was that Sayeh must be whisked there, veiled and hidden, for her meeting.

Ironically, stepping out of the plain palanquin into the luxury of the temple's courtyard was like emerging from a nun's cell into paradise. Sayeh, having accepted the assistance of a eunuch doorman to rise from her seat, paused for a moment amid trees that had bloomed heavily, instantly, once the rain reached their roots. A dragoncrystal roof on pillars between the trees kept the monsoon from her head, and diverted more water to their thirsty roots. Its panes, faintly luminescent with their own light, were scattered with heavy gold and purple petals, bruised and folded by the falling droplets. The scent was fermented, cloying, not unpleasant.

Sayeh had a rajni's knowledge of poisons and their uses. And so, despite its source, Sayeh knew the dragoncrystal was supposed to be safe for such purposes. It was poisoned, yes, with the dragon-poison that could cause sores, brittle bones, falling hair—but it was nearly unbreakable, and unlike most things that had absorbed the dragon-poison, the crystal was only dangerous if ingested. Ground to powder and inhaled, or used to store food—then it could kill. Otherwise, the panes were no more dangerous than the lead foil that held them in place.

Sayeh had heard that her cousin Mrithuri, who dwelt in the Al-chemical Emperor's palace, had a throne room entirely skylighted with dragoncrystal mosaic. Sayeh had never seen it, and could barely imagine such beauty—and such expense.

Rain pattered through the leaves and rang on the crystal, chim-ing an improvisational glissando. Sayeh moved forward, leaving her guards behind. This was the house of the Good Mother, and she was safe as any Good Daughter here. And if she did not feel safe, it would be impolitic to show it. Even if she wanted to shriek and storm, she could not have done so.

So much of the courage of rajnis rested in keeping a straight face and a level tone.

As she stepped clear of her entourage, accompanied by the temple eunuch, she saw a group of six women draped in silk, contorted in poses recollecting the wind-bent, sky-reaching trees all around the covered area. Jewels and ropes of gold dripped from them like weep-ing blossoms and bunches of sweet fruit.

Silently, in golden sandals, they began to dance.

There was no music but the music of the storm. They moved in time to the timeless rain, and yet they were perfectly in step with one another. Their feet provided an arrhythmic beat that was the only percussion, and they whirled with slow precision so strong and sure that it seemed the afterimage of a faster gesture. They crossed and wove together as she advanced, guided by the eunuch, and only when she was nearly close enough to touch them did they sweep apart, bent gracefully, their arms waving toward her as if the wind's benediction.

Their heads were bowed. Their bodies made the columns of a

corridor she walked down. There were rituals and secret signs in patterns they held by their hands.

Sayeh went between them, and entered the temple's open door.

Within, all was calm and dim. The abbess waited for Sayeh herself, and Sayeh was surprised to see that the old woman wore no jewels or silks or robes of estate. She had on silver slippers, yes, but they were down at the heels and the strap across the toes was worn at the edges. Her clothes were plain pale wool, a tunic and trousers, and she wore a bright indigo and turquoise knotted shawl wrapped carelessly about her shoulders in defense against the chill.

Her face was creased like a wizened fruit from smiling; wiry strands escaped her pinned-up bun. Her hair was steel-colored, and vermilion laced her part. Two golden rings gleaming in the left side of her nose were her only jewelry.

"Your Abundance," the abbess said to Sayeh, bowing surprisingly low for one with such old bones, on such a wet day.

"Your Wisdom," Sayeh replied, amused as always by the exchange of titles.

"I hope we have some of both for each other today," the abbess said. "Come into my study."

The eunuch was left behind. The two women—one old, one merely matronly—walked down the tiled temple corridor. Oil lamps flickered dimly on plinths, to mark dark intersections. The walls were pierced and filigreed to show internal spaces, but Sayeh did not see any immured nuns in the corridors and cells so revealed. Perhaps they were gathered at prayer, on this first full day of the rains. Perhaps they were sleeping.

They came to a carved rosewood door, inlaid with jet and ivory, that had no door handle. The abbess pulled a ring of keys from her pocket. Bronze and iron, they clattered unmusically. She selected a smallish one and fit it into the lock, then pulled against the key itself.

The door eased open noiselessly. They passed within.

The abbess's study was a small room with uncharacteristically solid walls. Sayeh wondered if there were another room in the entire temple where a woman could have privacy. It was bright within, after the shadowy corridors: bull's-eye windows in the vertical segments of a peaked and folded roof let light stream down despite the continuing rain. The walls were lined with shelves and racks and cubicles for books of all descriptions—scrolls and tablets and panel books and stitched books and fans—except on one where a small hearth smoldered softly, rendering the space both warm and dry. There was a desk with some papers and pens and a vase of catkins in what Sayeh guessed was sacred river water. There was a Song-style oxbow chair with a slung leather seat—old and cracked, but soft-looking—and there was a long couch strewn with cushions that were threadbare, but plump. Several thick knotted rugs were heaped on a tile floor glazed the whited blue of skim milk.

There was someone in the room besides the abbess and Sayeh.

An old woman, and a foreign one. Not large—still slender, even in her age, and dressed in the style of the lands far north and west, beyond the Steles of the Sky and the Great Salt Desert. An Asitaneh, perhaps—except she wore Qersnyk boots, even here indoors, and a shawl with the edges worked in sky-blue knots and Qersnyk bangles. And she was not veiled. She was wearing a cloth wrapped over her hair, but there wasn't even a loose end that could have been drawn over her face if she chose. And yet, as far as Sayeh knew, all the Asitaneh women—and quite a few of the men—covered their faces among strangers.

The abbess locked the door behind them—it also only pulled shut with the key—and turned to face the two women. "Your Abundance Sayeh Rajni," she said, "this is the poetess Ümmühan."

Sayeh put a hand to her mouth like a girl.

She had heard of this old woman. She had been a slave-poetess in the Caliphate, when there was a Caliphate still, and she had been the historian of the court of the Qersnyk Khagan. She was said by some to be the greatest living smith of words in the religion of her strange sky-dwelling Scholar-God, and their God held words as sacredly, as mystically, as Sayeh's Good Mother River held dance.

Sayeh made her hand fall to her side and worked the fingers in their rings until she felt she had herself under control again. She was rajni; she could be charmed, but she could not allow herself to be starstruck or overwhelmed. She extended the hand to the old woman and said, "What a delightful surprise, Poetess. Your reputation precedes you."

She did not ask what brought the poetess to Ansh-Sahal. But perhaps her raised brow and her glance at the abbess gave her away, because before the abbess could speak Ümmühan smiled toothlessly and said, "I have come to witness with my own eyes the famous beauty, the famously kind, Sayeh Rajni."

Sayeh knew flattery when she heard it. You did not get to be a rajni and over forty without a certain well-honed sense of when you were being buttered up. But the poetess Ümmühan managed to deliver her compliment without sounding either oily or self-conscious.

She was a court entertainer. And one who was famously good at her job.

"It is my honor," Sayeh responded. "Word of your own beauty and wisdom, and the beauty of your poetry, has reached even this far land."

Ümmühan grimaced, clowning, and pinched the creased skin of her cheek between a knotted finger and thumb. "Such beauty," she said dryly. Then she grinned her wicked, toothless grin. "But the words are still good, I hope."

Sayeh lowered herself to the couch edge, aware that she was keeping two older women on their feet, because not even the abbess could sit before the rajni did. She waved them into places, and they both sank down as if this were her solar, and not the abbess's own study.

Utterly disarmed, Sayeh thought nevertheless that Ümmühan was wrong. She was beautiful—lovely, with her piercing eyes and her elegantly soft skin. Perhaps nothing that would make a young man's head turn . . . but Sayeh was no young man. She hoped she looked as well in forty years more. And had as sharp a wit.

"You shall have to come to my court and demonstrate them, then," she said. "We are fond of foreign arts, and your reputation precedes you. It is said there are no better poetesses."

"That cannot be true," Ümmühan replied. "There is one poetess of whom there is no equal. She Whom I serve. She is the poet from Whom all words spring, and Ysmat of the Beads is Her pen."

"What does she write upon?" Sayeh asked, genuinely curious.

"Souls," Ümmühan replied, still twinkling wickedly. "And the ink is chance, and fate, and the deeds of men."

Sayeh thought about that—about chance, and fate, and the deeds of men. It seemed to her that these contradicted one another. "Can all three of these things exist at the same time? If there is chance, can there be fate? If we have free will, then how do chance and fate hold sway? What good then are oracles and prophecies?"

Ümmühan looked at the abbess. The abbess had taken a seat in her oxbow chair. She nodded, as if to encourage the poetess—or as if she too might be interested in the answer. Sayeh wondered which it was: were the two old women conversing, or colluding?

"I do not know how it is in your philosophy," the poetess said. "But in mine—in ours—we believe that fate and chance and the will of men are all three strands of the cloth that history and the world are made of. Fate is just another word for the will of the Scholar-God. Chance is that which happens outside of Her will. And the will of men . . . is the will of men."

"And the will of women?" Sayeh said it archly, with a knowing rise.

"That too," Ümmühan answered. "Although I suspect we all know men who would prefer we had no wills with which to thwart them."

"Strands in the cloth, you say." Sayeh leaned forward, elbows on her knees. This had a direct bearing on what she had come here to discover after all. "Like embroidery?"

Ümmühan shook her head. "More like warp and weft and . . . some third thing, as if the cloth existed in three dimensions. Perhaps it is like felt, yes? That you weave with a little hooked needle?" Her fingers beaked and her hand made a picking motion, like the head of a bird. "The threads mesh together and go in all directions, and are woven together so close you could never tug a single one free without severing it, and a dozen others. Some of those threads are fate and some are chance and some are will."

"You've thought about this."

"I am a scholar servant of the Scholar-God," Ümmühan replied. "Thinking about things is my calling."

Sayeh barked laughter. "At that, I guess it is. Your Sahali, by the way, is excellent. Where did you learn?"

"I have always had a gift for languages," the poetess said with the modest air of one drawn to an admission. "Yours I learned in Qeshqer, in the house of the imperial Wizard of the Khaganate. She herself did not speak Sahal or Saratahi—but many people came and went from that place, and most of them of them were scholars."

The porthole windows above were dimming slightly. Heavier rain, or the rising behind the clouds of the veil that would end the bright night. Sayeh recollected why she had come—not for company, even the company of wise and delightful women, and not so she could be feted by sacred dancers in courtyard. She glanced apologetically away from the poetess.

"I need to speak to you of omens," she said to the abbess, with a sideways glance at Ümmühan. "Perhaps in private?"

It was a suggestion, only. Even a rajni did not order the first daughter of the Good Mother around. Except when it came to such small matters as when to sit and when to stand.

The abbess said, "The sour water. The burned water-diver."

Sayeh swallowed, nodded. Reminded herself that she was the rajni. "My people do not wish to be ruled by a rajni, Mother Abbess. They see these mishaps as signs that the Good Mother does not favor my rule."

The abbess steepled her gnarled fingers. "You could take a new husband, Your Abundance."

Sayeh shook her head. "I cared for my husband, Your Grace. I do not wish to remarry. Certainly not so urgently as this."

Ümmühan turned to look at them both, the pale cloth of her headscarf stretching gracefully with the gesture. She spoke carefully, as if to be sure she understood. "And if you remarried, you would be subject to the word of a man. How long were you married before you were widowed, Sayeh Rajni?"

Sayeh counted in her head. "Thirty-three years, Poetess."

Ümmühan's head tilted as she did the math. Sayeh had married at age eleven, because the council had willed it. Her husband had been much older, and he had been her regent until she herself was of age to take the crown. They had ruled together as raja and rajni, and she had, indeed, cared for him very deeply.

And now she very deeply enjoyed being her own woman, and making her own decisions. She just had to cling to, build, and consolidate power enough to survive until she was in a position of strength and stability.

She said, "A new husband would only wish his own children to inherit. This would not protect my son."

She had fought hard for that baby, suffered greatly for him. Far more than most women endured. That the Good Mother had blessed her with a child at all, Sayeh reminded herself, was a mark of divine favor. No one would harm her son. The boy was not merely the raja-in-waiting: his *existence* was a sign that the Good Mother protected him with Her own abundant hand.

Who would risk the wrath to be brought down on anyone who might willfully or by negligence bring to harm a child so sacred?

The old women seemed very much to understand the nuances of the situation. They were sharing glances, and the abbess was shaking her head.

"I do not think your reign is the danger the oracles warn of," the abbess said slowly. "I think there are mortal perils aplenty facing us, but I do not believe that any of them have to do with your proposed unsuitability for the throne."

Sayeh breathed out slowly. Her eyes squeezed shut and she nodded, hating herself for the show of weakness and relief. "Can you tell me more of these perils?"

"We have martial neighbors," the abbess said. "Ambitious ones, as it happens. The Boneless is raising troops, and I imagine he'll either come to us, or south to Sarathai-tia. And then there is the poisoned water from the sea. . . ."

She shook her head again, a tight little shiver, and waved her hand to Ümmühan.

The poetess nodded thoughtfully. "Such things are recorded. In the old city of Ur-Sahal, which once stood not far from here, on the old shore of the Bitter Sea, which some histories refer to as the Sea of Weeping."

Sayeh hadn't heard that before. "Who calls it that? And why?"

"Old documents," Ümmühan said. "Records, in fact, that I came here to study. The Bitter Sea was larger once. It has been shrinking for as long as records have been kept, and growing more salt. And tears—well, Your Abundance. Tears are very bitter."

They endured a pause, while that sank in. Then the abbess cleared her throat and said, "The poetess's research concurs with mine. What is not recorded, to my knowledge, is the manner of disaster these omens presage."

A cold ache of anticipation chilled Sayeh's spine. "But how . . . How is that possible?"

"No one has survived whatever catastrophe befell long enough to record the happenings," the abbess said. "All that is known is that trade stopped, and when it resumed, the city of Ur-Sahal was empty. The buildings stood unmarked, and within were skeletons, undragged by vermin or scavengers, desiccated where they had sat or slept or fallen as they walked about their business."

"Mother," Sayeh swore. She looked at Ümmühan. "You say there are other incidences?"

"At least one. When the Bitter Sea was greater, its eastern reaches swept as far as the Dragon Shore, and the plains of Song. It is said that there was a city there, too—a city that is now gone." Ümmühan shrugged. "It is not far from where the Dragon Road leads to the Singing City, though. It could be—it could even be plausible—that a dragon rose up from under the sea, and the poisoned burning water was some exhalation of the great beast. They are not known to attack cities, except in unproven legend. But it's not as if so mighty a creature is necessarily more careful of human life than I might be of stepping on an anthill."

Sayeh thought of the peaceable cults where members went masked and walked barefoot in order to avoid doing mischief to any living thing. She wondered if dragons had any similar religions. If they did, if she had to meet a dragon, she would prefer it be one of those.

She made herself sit up straighter, despite the weariness of worry. "So it's a terrible augury. What can I do about it?"

"Evacuate," the abbess said plainly. "Move our people west, as fast as possible. As far inland as possible. Away from where the bitter water flows."

"In the rainy season," Sayeh said. Not arguing, not quite. Just confirming that they all understood the foolishness of it all. "When we are all short of food after a long dry season. When the roads are mud, and the wind is cold. With children and the elderly in tow."

"It will not," Ümmühan admitted, "do very much for your popularity. Unless a true calamity *does* come to pass."

"A big unless. Do we have any evidence of times this augury was not followed hard on by a catastrophe?"

"Once," Ümmühan said. "Perhaps twice."

The abbess shook her head. "Scraps of records only," she said. "Undated. They could have been salvaged from Ur-Sahal. Some are even in the ancient Song dialect, and could have been from the city that perished on the eastern shore."

"It's a far shore," Sayeh said. *The pen moves on, and leaves a thought behind.* "I can take my people west, but that is the territory of Himadra, and brings us close to Chandranath. Shall we come as refugees to one who would desire to conquer us?"

Or she could marry that pustule Anuraja, and beg him for safe harbor for her people. And then what if nothing happened? What if the augury was false? He had no fear of the Good Mother or even the terrible Good Daughter. Duty and felicity had no hold upon his conscience.

He would have her put to death and claim her lands as his own. And if her son ever grew to contest Anuraja . . . well, what was the likelihood he would be allowed to do so?

"Good Mother help me," the rajni said, and did not protest when the abbess reached out to take her hand.

ÜMMÜHAN ACCOMPANIED SAYEH BACK TO THE PALACE IN THE OPPOSITE seat of her plain palanquin, with the intent of seeking further information in the palace records. There might be something there that was not recorded in the archives of the nunnery. The old woman weighed next to nothing. She did not discomfit the strong young bearers, even in the pelting rain.

Along the way, she continued to charm Sayeh with her tales of a storied life, told in the rising and falling, nuanced style of an Asitaneh entertainer. She gave her characters voices, and in so doing gave them life.

Sayeh did not doubt that this woman had been a great poet of three separate courts; she would have liked to have offered her a place in her own entourage. But somehow she did not think the poetess had come to Ansh-Sahal with its bitter sea and its terraced hillsides desperate for rain—of all the godsforsaken corners of the earth under all the gods-determined skies—seeking a retirement placement. She was indeed here on research, and perhaps as a gift of the Good Mother. Or her own Scholar-God. If ever two deities were made to be allies . . .

It was full day when they reached Sayeh's palace, and the sky had further darkened behind the rain. Vidhya the guard captain himself helped them out of the palanquin under a protective awning, and if he was surprised to see that the rajni had returned with a guest, his face registered only serenity. "Your son has been asking for you, Rajni," was all he said.

Sayeh looked at Ümmühan. "Would you care to meet the prince?"

Ümmühan's smile showed empty gums, but it lit her face. Sayeh confirmed her impression that this woman had once been a very great beauty. "How old?"

"This will be his third rainy season," Sayeh said. She led the poetess into the palace, stopping briefly to exchange their damp sandals for warm, dry, wooly slippers covered in red and blue embroidery. The servants had provided two pairs, and guessed the visitor's size close to exactly. Sayeh would have to remember to have the chatelaine issue praise to whoever was in charge of the door on this rainy day.

Ümmühan sighed in pleasure as she slid her knobbed feet into warmth. "The small pleasures grow greater as one ages."

Sayeh hid a smile. She was just old enough herself to appreciate how true this might one day become—and how the small pains of life could become all the greater irritants with time as well. Whether it was down to having a son to think forward for, the faint browner spots that had begun resolving on the backs of her hands, or some combination of both, of late she had found herself often pensive of the future and all too aware of what she was leaving behind her, and how soon it might be important. And Ümmühan . . . at a casual guess, Ümmühan was close to twice her own age.

That was both reassuring and unnerving. Reassuring, because there might be so many more years yet to come. Unnerving, because how fast had those years passed by for this poetess? And what would Sayeh leave behind as her legend?

She found that she was greedy for a legacy in a way her younger self could never have imagined.

That made her think of the young rajni Mrithuri, her cousin to the south and west. Mrithuri, who had as yet remained unmarried, maintained her independence, and yet . . . would she one day wish she had chosen differently? There was time yet for the young woman to change her mind. But that meant so much sacrifice, and Sayeh felt the pressures of those sacrifices—demanded of her now again—very keenly of the moment. You could be your own woman; or you could be part of something larger, and leave behind a legacy of your body and your heart as well as your mind.

Men.

Men did not have to make these choices.

If she could offer her cousin advice, Sayeh wondered, what exactly would it be? It was a terrible choice to have to make, autonomy against posterity.

"What are you thinking?" the poetess asked. They had been walking together in silence, but Sayeh's pensiveness must have been written on her face.

Sayeh said, "Do you have children?"

Ümmühan shook her head. "I never lived a life I would have brought a child into, until I had no one to give me children. And then I had someone, but I was too old."

"So it's true what they say, that there are arts of the Asitaneh to prevent conception?"

The poetess's lips bend in a secret smile. "The Scholar-God has many wisdoms. Some are for her daughters alone. So you were thinking of children?"

"And women," Sayeh admitted. "And choices."

"Choices every woman makes, in some fashion."

"Some don't even know there is a choice. It is so expected."

Ümmühan nodded. "And yet you treasure your son."

"He was badly wanted," Sayeh replied. "And his conception was . . . unlikely in the extreme."

"Your Good Mother no doubt saw that you, too, would be the best of mothers."

It was grossest flattery, and when Sayeh glanced at the poetess she saw the sly sideways glance that told her the poetess knew that very well. But it was a conspiratorial glance, inviting her into the game— and it was, as well, the *right* flattery. The correct thing to say, at the perfectly correct moment.

She's good at this, Sayeh thought. As she would be: she was Ümmühan.

The poetess paused to sigh, then continued. "I leave my mark with ink on paper, with stylus in sand. I am the mark I leave, and the mark I leave is me. I am the act of marking. You leave your mark in blood and sinew, and in the history that I shall help to record. That act is you, that act of marking. That act of leaving a mark."

It was a pretty thought, and Sayeh liked it. But honesty compelled her to ask, "What about those who leave no mark? Or whose marks are erased by the vagaries of history? Are they real? Did they live?"

Ümmühan shook her head inside her coif. "On that, my books are silent. Or, perhaps, not silent. Contradictory."

They had come to the nursery door. It was open, though guarded on both sides by Vidhya's chosen men. They inclined their heads faintly to the rajni but did not bow; they would not relax their vigilance so much when they were detailed to protect their underaged king.

Voices came from within. Drupada's piping, piercing tones, and the murmur of his nurse Jagati. And also Tsering's crisp phrasing, sentences rising to questions at the end. It was time for Drupada's catechism.

Sayeh paused for a moment outside, gathered her trailing hems, and swept into the room with every intention of making her son squeal delightedly. She was surprised to see he did not sit alone on his tasseled silken floor cushion. Another, larger and plainer, had been drawn up a little behind his, and Nazia the water-diver sat cross-legged on it, bent over a slate with a wet brush, figuring. The marks would endure for long enough to be examined and then fade into the air, and so keep from wasting valuable ink or paper for exercises that would only be checked and discarded, after all.

Drupada jumped to his feet and yelped, indeed. He would have run to Sayeh, but she looked down at him sternly and said, "What is your duty to your teacher, my love?"

He dragged himself to a halt with obvious effort, while Nazia

184 ★ ELIZABETH BEAR

looked on with a frown. Sayeh was frowning herself, inwardly—
Tsering was taking a risk, adding this possibly treacherous young
woman to the same classroom as Drupada. Although Nazia was
starting off from scratch where the learning from books was considered, and perhaps Tsering-la had judged that a show of trust would
gain her loyalty. And Tsering *was* the Wizard Tsering, which meant
there was very little Nazia could have done to harm the prince with
Tsering in attendance and paying attention.

She worried too much.

Drupada looked back at Tsering. "Teacher, may I go to Mama?"

Tsering struggled to keep a stern mouth. "You may."

He scampered to her so fast that he would have measured his
insignificant length on the rugs if Sayeh hadn't crouched and been
there to catch him. She squeezed him close against her chest and
looked at Tsering and at Nazia.

Tsering-la had that Wizardly way of seeming to know what the
problem is before the words were formed. He said, "Nazia, you are
dismissed for now. Work on the letter-shapes you've learned."

"They're a mess," Nazia said, not deprecatingly but with brutal
self-assessment.

Tsering said, "Once you can make them confidently, I promise
the line will smooth. You're old enough that the fine control will come
more quickly than it does for the prince."

Once the girl was gone, Sayeh lifted her son into her arms—he
was heavier every day—and went to shut the door. "Ümmühan," she
said, "this is my court Wizard Tsering. I think you ought to tell him
what you told me, about the Bitter Sea."

Wizard and poet eyed each other, but both seemed content to
trust the rajni's judgment for now. Ümmühan explained. At first
slowly, but then with increasing trust as Tsering-la asked questions
far more intelligent and knowledgeable than the ones that Sayeh had
brought out. Before long, the two had entirely lost her, and she enter-
tained herself by taking Drupada to the corner of the nursery

classroom and helping him stack bright-painted and gilded wooden blocks so that he could then push them over, trumpeting like an elephant. He'd seen the elephants working only once that she could recall, in the previous dry season. She was startled to discover that he remembered.

He started to explain to her that the elephant was the prince of the animals, and all the other animals had to do what the elephant said. She listened politely, pleased to be the focus of his attention for a little while. It happened less and less often now, as she began to have the feeling that their conversations sometimes intruded on his internal world in ways he rejected or found irritating.

It was not so different from dealing with adults, she supposed— they embraced whatever supported their worldview, and rejected anything that might disrupt it. But it was far more transparent in this young child.

Sayeh was painfully aware that this would only continue. That her relationship with her son was evolving, growing into a chimerical monster with two heads, and those heads, while inextricably linked by a shared body of experiences, might have extremely different ideas of who they were and what they wanted. She had experienced this, after all, with her own mother.

So for now, she just stroked his hair when he swarmed into her lap, and said occasionally, "Is that so?"

"And the tiger is a wicked animal," he said. "So the elephant has to explain that the tiger is bad, and make him stop eating the other animals. And sometimes because the elephant is the biggest he has to sit on the tiger."

"He sits on the tiger."

"He does. He tries not to hurt the tiger too much, though. Because maybe the tiger can get better. And sometimes . . ."

His face screwed up in thought.

"Sometimes?" she prompted, aware that Ümmühan was watching her, while Tsering-la busied himself with a page of notes. Their conversation seemed to have finished for now, though Sayeh had spent enough time around Wizards to know that they were most likely only gathering their strength for another engagement.

"Sometimes the elephant has to get his mother to make the tiger stop being bad."

She gave him a little squeeze. "Does the elephant always do what his mother tells him?"

He shook his head, very serious. "Not always. Because he's the prince and princes can't always listen to their advisors. Sometimes they have to make up their own minds. But she can make the tiger listen. The tiger's a warlord, and he tells all the bandits what to do."

Children, Sayeh thought, understand so much, without understanding it at all. She swallowed. "Isn't it your bedtime, little king?"

"Kings don't have bedtimes." But he said it brightly, without pouting. He had never been a pouting or a whining child. Occasionally stormy and stompy, but Sayeh would rather have that any day.

She gave another thanks to the Good Mother, who had blessed her so uncritically after so long a wait, and answered, "Little ones do. They need their sleep to grow up to be big kings."

Jagati came forward from the corner into which she'd erased herself. Her skill at doing so never stopped amusing the rajni, especially as she was so outspoken when it was just women alone. And Sayeh had always been pleased that Jagati seemed, effortlessly, to consider Sayeh as one of the women.

Sayeh nodded thanks, and they exchanged a few words on the rate of his majesty's toilet training, which the nurse assured her was excellent—his new facility with targeted urination aside. Or perhaps that was a sign of his improving facility with controlling his bladder. Alas.

Sayeh thanked Jagati and kissed her son good night. Once they had vanished into the inner bedroom where both would sleep, Sayeh turned back to the Wizard and the poetess.

Both stared back, formality forgotten for the moment. Hard lines were graven beside Ümmühan's mouth, her usual smile carved into a stern expression. Tsering-la merely scowled.

"Bad news," she said.

Tsering's hands fidgeted as if on their own. He wrapped them in the black petaled skirts of his coat. "What Ümmühan has described to me as the threat . . . what we saw at the sea earlier. I think I know what the omen portends."

Sayeh waited. The Wizard paused for a long time, then just shook his head.

"Tell me," said the rajni.

"You know I was born in the shadow of the Cold Fire. That I lived my apprenticeship and further training in the Red-and-White Citadel."

The Cold Fire was a smoking mountain, the greatest—as far as Sayeh knew—that anyone had ever heard of. The heat of its bowels soaked the narrow valley of the river below it, rendering it habitable year-round despite its position high in the Steles of the Sky, and providing the Rasan Empire with their fortified summer capital, Tsarepheth. The Citadel that was the seat of the learning of the Wizards of Tsarepheth bridged the gap between it and its even larger neighbor, called the Island-in-the-Mists, like a tremendous dam of alabaster stone and crimson tile.

Deep within that Citadel, Sayeh supposed, were Wizards who spent their entire lives studying the science of the Cold Fire. It had erupted twice in living memory—once in her grandfather's lifetime, and again, less significantly, in her father's. The first eruption was generally supposed, at least in Sahal-Sarat, to have been a direct effect of magics thrown irresponsibly about by the embattled sides in the Necromancer's War some decades before Sayeh was even conceived.

She thought of the reek of sulfur, and had a sickening sense she knew what Tsering-la was about to tell her.

"There's a volcano under the water," he said. "And it's active again. That's what's causing the acidic plumes—do you understand what I mean by that?"

She bit her lip. She thought she did. She could almost visualize it. But it was a wise ruler who admitted when they did not know sometimes, so she shook her head. "I'm not sure."

He picked up Drupada's slate, and a wet brush. "Here." With quick, sketching gestures he drew a series of horizontal lines, and then a vertical curve cutting over them. "Hot water rises, you see? So the springs that normally feed the drinkable water into the depths of the Bitter Sea produce cold water, and it stays down there, even though fresh water is usually less dense than salt water and floats upon it. Eventually the fresh water comes up, and dilutes the salt, but by then it's too brackish for us to drink. But this water, now—it's been heated by gas or molten rock, and it's absorbed the gasses of burning brimstone from the volcano's breath. These gasses can become dissolved in water just as salt or sugar can, but instead of making the water bitter or sweet, they convert it into a burning fluid we call the oil of vitriol, or the vitriolic fluid. Which is what burned Nazia's hands and yours, and killed her mother. The mild tremors we've been feeling are a sign of the underwater volcano's reawakening."

"There are earthquakes all the time, in Ansh-Sahal," Sayeh protested. "They're never bad. These haven't even cracked stones."

"They likely will," Tsering-la said gently.

Sayeh's stomach tightened and her throat closed as implications crowded her. "So there will be no water to be had in the next dry season? Only this oil of vitriol?"

"Unless the volcano sleeps again," Tsering said. "And worse could happen. Far worse. The volcano might erupt in truth."

"Walk with me." Sayeh needed to be out of the suddenly stifling confines of the nursery, away from all this closeness and clutter. She swept the poetess and the Wizard into her wake as she turned and headed out the door. The guards closed it quietly behind them.

Sayeh would have strode out confidently, just to hear the decisive patting of her sandals on the floor. But the slippers—hers and Ümmühan's—shushed against the tile, and Tsering-la's bootheels thumped counterpoint.

It struck Sayeh as somehow deliciously ironic. This should have been portentous, epic—a storyteller's scene of decision. Instead, she got slippers.

She held her tongue, contemplating what she should do next. The poetess waited a few polite moments and then filled the silence. "I knew another Tsering-la once."

Tsering's face did something strange, as Sayeh glanced over to chart his reaction. "I'm sure you did."

Ümmühan shrugged lightly and smiled. "It is a common name."

They came to another guarded door—the entrance to the royal apartment. Sayeh waited a moment for the guards to acknowledge and admit her—the one with the key was young and fumbled a little—and led her little party of visitors within. The first room was a sitting room, fit for receiving guests. A long wall of expensive, louvered glass windows looked out upon the courtyard, which was dim now with rain. The palace cisterns kept it watered in the dry season, so Sayeh's Orchid Court did indeed sport its namesake flowers in every season. Now, though, they were beaten down and rain-swept wherever they had peered out from under the sheltering arbors.

Sayeh's pet bird roused itself on its perch as they entered, fanning brilliant wings and raising its trailing crest to flash all the dozen colors there concealed. No lammergeyer for her court, foul carrion beasts that they were. The rajni of Ansh-Sahal kept a phoenix—a *feng*, a gift from a distant relative in Song, and not from the equally spectacular but more common Ctesifon or Kyivvan species.

"His name is Guang Bao." Sayeh could not entirely keep her pride from her voice.

"After the poet?"

Ümmühan was obviously delighted. Tsering, who had seen the bird before—and knew about the volume of his voice and also about his unfortunate tendency to bite, stood well back.

"He was a gift of the prince of Twenty Palaces to my husband, Ashar." She chirruped to the bird and he cocked his head at her and trilled back. "But he liked me better. Didn't you, Guang Bao?"

If you did not take the crest and train into consideration, Guang Bao was the size of a large parrot or conure. He was kept unclipped, for the glory of his intact plumage, and as he spread his wings now and shook out his tail, the room—even in dimness—seemed to blaze with reflected light. His primary colors were orange and teal, and something in the structure of his feathers made the individual strands act like they were strewn with powdered diamonds, or with tiny mirrors. The plumage itself scintillated from the gorgeous blue-green head to the vermilion-copper-malachite eyes on the lyrelike feathers of his tail, which almost brushed the floor though his perch was as tall as Sayeh's chest. He also reflected pinpoints of light everywhere, so they sparkled like tiny glass beads on all the furniture, the walls, the clothing and skin of the gathered people. The leading edge of his wings was also beglittered, and that same richly iridescent blue-green color. The primary and secondary plumage, revealed when he flapped lightly, was shades of flame.

"O great is God," Ümmühan said, pressing one hand to her chest. "I have never before encountered such. I understand why some say they are afire!"

"You should see him in bright light," Sayeh replied. "I think their greatest protection is that they dazzle and sun-blind anything that might care to eat them."

The poetess had paused arm's length from the perch and was examining Guang Bao with elaborate awe. She glanced back at Sayeh and spoke significantly. "For so many of us, it is our only natural defense, to be in some way dazzling."

Sayeh felt an enormous rush of kinship with Ümmühan in that moment. She scratched at the all-but-invisible spots on the back of her hand with her thumbnail, then forced herself to stop. "And to find new ways to dazzle, when the old feathers grow worn."

Ümmühan winked. "Pretty bird," she said to the phoenix. "Who's a pretty bird?"

The phoenix cocked his head at her, alternately smoothing and fluffing his crest in interest. Tsering-la handed her an imported ground-nut roasted in its shell, and the poetess offered it gingerly to the bird on the flat of her hand. She'd spent more time around horses than around parrots, Sayeh decided.

Guang Bao leaned way out to pick it up, stretching his neck to the utmost as he kept his body back, balancing by fanning his tail and wings. He clucked cheerfully to himself as he settled back, moving the nut around in his bill with his thick, black tongue. He lifted one horny taloned foot to grasp it, and nibbled at it experimentally.

Ümmühan watched with the excitement of a small girl as he picked the fibrous shell open and extracted the two nodules inside, one by one. They were crunched up and vanished with little ceremony, and then the bird dropped the shell and looked around for more. "Pretty bird," he said, in a distracted tone. "Pretty."

"Oh," Ümmühan said delightedly. "He talks!"

Guang Bao chose that moment to spread his wings wider, emit a piercing cry that was stunning in its volume, and defecate into the tray of pebbles in which the base of his perch had been strategically placed. Ümmühan surprised Sayeh by laughing out loud in delight. She might be old, but her voice still rose on light, feminine peals. Sayeh knew very well how much practice it took to laugh like a bell, and appreciated the art in it.

"So it is with all beauty," she said cheerfully. "Every glory also shits."

GUANG BAO HAD OBVIOUSLY TAKEN A LIKING TO THE MUSICALITY OF Ümmühan's laughter, and spent the remainder of the afternoon practicing his own version of it. This incited the poetess to more laughter of her own, and bribing the bird with bits of fruit and seeds until he finally consented to step onto her hand. Sayeh had expected the old woman to strain under the weight, but Ümmühan held Guang Bao up easily, and showed no fear of him even after Tsering and Sayeh both warned her that the big bird would bite.

Tsering, watching with slightly envious amusement, shook his head. "She could charm snakes from their dens, that one. I've never seen that bird of yours take to anyone that way."

It was true, even if Guang Bao did seem to despise Tsering-la in particular. Sayeh shrugged. "He's a contrary beast, for certain. But it's also said that the phoenix has a particular love for poets. Maybe he can smell it on her."

"You wanted to talk further," Tsering reminded her.

Sayeh scratched at her cheek. "You would counsel that we evacuate?"

His lips thinned. He looked away from the burgeoning love affair between old woman and gaudy bird and faced her directly before nodding. "I would, yes, so counsel."

"Now? Or after the harvest is in, when we will have some resources to travel on?" Sayeh caught herself picking at her cuticle with an opposite thumbnail, and forced herself to stop.

"It's a hard question," he said. "Every day increases risk. And every day increases the opportunity for Himadra to mass at the borders and stop us from leaving."

She sighed. "You've been talking to Vidhya."

"You should listen to Vidhya," he said. "Your Abundance."

It made her laugh—just a little, but enough. "So we're caught between a sword and a boiling sea. How long would it take to get everyone moving, if we started today?"

"The whole city? The whole nation?" He shook his head. "Some won't. Even if you make of yourself and your court an example."

"I could have the army force them out," she answered. "But every man I detail for that is a man I then won't have to move to the border and block Himadra, if he advances."

"And it won't bring you any love from the people."

"Leaving them there to suffocate or die of thirst or burn won't win me any love from the people either," Sayeh pointed out.

Ümmühan looked up from where she'd been gently scratching Guang Bao at the top of his neck, under the upraised feathers of his crest. "You don't need an army for this."

Sayeh tipped her head to one side, aware even as she did it that it probably made her look a lot like Guang Bao. "What do I need, then, poetess?"

Ümmühan smiled tightly. "You need an augury."

9

DRUJA'S BROTHER WAS NAMED PRASANA, AND WHATEVER STRENGTH
had sustained him through scrambling into the ice-boat had apparently been his last. He had wedged himself well into the ice-boat's
bilges, and then lapsed entirely into unconsciousness from which he
could not be roused. If the thin, ragged sound of his breathing had
not echoed, amplified by the wooden hollow, they might have all
assumed he was dead.

The Gage was strongest, but too large for the confined space. So,
when the caravan was safely beyond sight of the border, the Dead
Man and one of the acrobat Ritu's slender, athletic grown sons clam-
bered down into the bilges to attempt to retrieve him.

The space between the hold and the hull was narrow and stank
of wet wood and mildew, two of the desert-bred Dead Man's least
favorite scents. The spores made him sneeze repeatedly despite the
protection of his veil. The wood was slimy under his hands. The
curve of the hull bent his spine as he slithered through the trapdoor.
When he and Ritu's son, who was named Amruth, finally managed
to get their hands on the well-concealed alleged assassin, they had to
drag him out by his ankles, far less gently than the Dead Man thought

salutary to someone whose moaning and muttering could not quite be dignified with the description "consciousness."

"Like serving a breech birth," Amruth muttered as they maneuvered Prasana's head around an obstruction.

"I was thinking it was like getting a terrified kitten out of a privy hole," the Dead Man admitted.

Amruth laughed easily, leaving the Dead Man comforted, and wary of his own desire to find in this young man a friend.

They were still probably more gentle than the Dead Man, in his irritation, would have preferred if they had been handling a healthy man. But he could be tender to the wounded, despite what those who maligned his profession might think of him, and he in his own turn had spent enough time in hiding and in flight to allow a certain sympathy in leavening of his choler.

So they got the man out, bruising and scraping him and bruising and scraping themselves, and Lady Golbahar insisted on the peculiar extent of charity to offering him her "cabin," as everyone referred to her sheet-delinated emergency boudoir. "We're still flying the plague flags," she insisted. "If they come after us, he'll do for a sick man, don't you suppose?"

The Dead Man grunted and went off to clean himself, leaving the lady and her small entourage contentedly walking beside the wallowing ice-boats. He had glanced at a map that evening, and seen the curve of the Sarathai bending close again. They would, he supposed, be back in the river soon, and picking up pace—as soon as they reached the trade town where Druja meant to sell off the current group of oxen. They were getting too far south for these hairy ones, anyway: even in the intermittent rain, the beasts were suffering visible distress from the heat. Best to offer them up to somebody who would rest them for a week or two and then turn them around for a leg back up into the mountains.

So it was good for Lady Golbahar to walk and stretch her legs as she wished, as long as she could do so. Good for all of them. Men were not meant to be raddled up in wooden coffins and cast adrift down rushing streams. No matter how much quicker it was than riding honest horses, or being drawn by honest oxen.

They could sail downriver. There would be black water-oxen to tow the boats back up, or so Druja had told them. The Dead Man and the Gage did not intend to be with the party returning. Even if Druja decided to risk the brewing war and make a quick return rather than waiting it out, or trading farther south in the Lotus Kingdoms, or east through Song to the Banner Isles, the Dead Man and his partner would leave the caravan in Sarathai-tia and deliver their message.

And then what?

A nameless frustration welled up in the Dead Man. It was composed of equal points loneliness, alienation, and lack of direction, and he did not know what to do with it. Or where to take it. Drifting from place to place was not much of a purpose in life for one who had been raised as he had. But what was there for such as he to give his loyalty to?

And he could not bear to rest still in one place, when he could not call such a resting place his home.

Having cleaned himself and changed to a dry shirt and trousers— not that that would last, in the rain, when even his fine red wool coat dragged at him with steamy dankness—he went to find Druja. The caravan master was in the cabin that had until recently been Lady Golbahar's, staring down at his restless, unconscious brother.

The Dead Man drew up beside him and cleared his throat. Druja didn't turn, but he stood up a little bit straighter, so the Dead Man was sure he'd been seen.

He asked, "Is this man's escape why you chose this course for us, caravan master, instead of an easterly path? We could have gone through Ansh-Sahal."

"What's in Ansh-Sahal that's worth trading for?" Druja replied. "It's even poorer than Chandranath."

That wasn't much of an answer. The Dead Man thought about calling Druja out on the risk he'd placed them all under, but Ritu had already tried that gambit and had garnered only a little information. "There shall be increased traffic on the road soon, now that we've navigated the border."

Druja nodded but said, "We won't be in the lowlands until tomorrow. I'll pull the plague flags down now that we're past the border."

It would save them some explaining coming into the caravanserai if nobody had seen them flying those.

"How much further to Sarathai-tia?"

Druja shrugged. "The roads are better here. And the river is swift with the rains. We'll travel fast once we're in it. Ten days at the most. He glanced over at the Dead Man and smiled. "There will be a bonus for you and your partner if we make it intact."

"Arriving intact is the only way either of us may expect to be paid, as it stands."

Druja looked at him levelly. "We're out of the Boneless's territory. Are we entirely free of his agents?" The caravan master swallowed, likely to steady his nerves. "Are all my guards immune to being bought? I'll sleep better once we're on the river, in any case."

"Yes," the Dead Man answered. "On the river is where I will sleep."

THEY MUST STOP TO REST THE OXEN, IF NOT THEMSELVES. THE DEAD Man thought that was the only reason they didn't roll all day as they did all night. Druja did catch catnaps, as did the Dead Man. Nizhvashiti and the Gage, however, were ever-present and ever-watchful. Even if the Godmade's watchfulness seemed sometimes to consist of standing like a carven figurehead on the crow's-nest of the lead ship, black robes whipping, seemingly impervious to wind or rain.

By benefit of this post, Nizhvashiti was the first to spot their objective. Though the smell hit them all not long after the Godmade called down and raised a pointing finger to mark the column of black smoke spiraling into the sky.

"Shit," Druja said, clambering up to join the Godmade and the Dead Man, who had been the first to answer the priest's urgent shout. The three of them crowded the narrow crossbar of the unrigged mast, and Druja shook his head bitterly. He leaned out, holding a spar, and bellowed down, "Set the brakes! Set the brakes!"

The rumble and sway of the ice-boat's motion stopped so abruptly the Dead Man clutched the mast for balance. He kept his place, at least, which was good news. He was getting too old for broken bones to heal as quickly as they used to.

"Raise the plague flags again?" the Dead Man asked.

Druja's mouth twisted. "Do you think they'll fool anybody? Anybody it would benefit us to have fooled, anyway?"

Moving through silent consensus, Druja, the Gage, the Dead Man, and the Godmade climbed down from the lead boat. They walked forward, up the rocky and scree-strewn slope, the stones turning underfoot crumbly and yellow and very like in texture to the clay of the road surrounding them.

They did not speak as they crested a rise and the ruins of the burnt stockade on the banks of the broad, blind-white river came into view. That the ruins still smoldered despite the rain spoke of a tremendous fire, especially since—by the smell—what was dead in the stockade had been dead for at least a couple of days.

Druja said, "Any sign of an ambush still here?"

The Dead Man craned his neck and strained his eyes. There was a churn of mud leading south, along the riverbank. Many hooves and many boots. "I think they're gone."

"Bandits?" Druja asked.

It was the Godmade's head that shook in disagreement then. "Not enough bodies among the ruins, and not enough of those that are there are the bodies of fighting-age men. They took conscripts. And probably hostages."

No one wondered that the Godmade could see so clearly, so far—not with that featureless golden eye.

"Army," Druja said.

The Dead Man's pulse rose in his throat and accelerated. "They're on land," he said. "The river will be faster."

"And we want to get ahead of them for some reason?" Druja asked.

"Sarathai-tia. It's fortified. It's a royal seat, isn't it?"

Druja nodded. "You want to sign up to sit out a siege?"

By the pen of God, no. Even the thought made the Dead Man's stomach churn. Once had been enough in one lifetime. He remembered the reek of the trapped city, the eyes of the starving populace seeming to enlarge day by day in the sockets of their skulls.

"I'd rather stop the siege before it happens. But that's not the track of a large enough force to lay a big city under siege." He waved at the churned mud as the caravan paused at the top of the switch-backed hill. "It's a raiding party. The Boneless is still putting his army together. This was for supplies and men. They'll make an arc, I warrant, foraging as they go, and bring back whatever they can get to Chandranath. We're getting into farming country here; it's not like the rocks and scruff we're leaving. There's resources here worth stealing."

"So you think they'll bend east and north, away from the Mother River?"

Nizhvashiti said, "It's the logical choice. Why come back along the same route you left by, if your aim is pillage?"

Druja stared at the river below. "You don't think we'll pass them if we continue southwest."

"Downriver," the Dead Man said, trying to put more trust in his own tactics into his voice than he felt, necessarily. "It's our best choice."

"Downriver," Druja muttered. He raised his hand and waved.

HAMMERING HEART AND SEARCHING EYE: VIGILANCE AVAILED THE Dead Man not as they rolled down the hill onto the riverbank. He had been right in the first place: the reavers had moved on. He and the Gage and Nizhvashiti fanned out around the ice-boats as they were fitted for sailing—the rolling frames unbolted, the boats backed into the river by the oxen and floated free, the oxen unharnessed and the frames disassembled and stored. Some of the pieces converted into bits of the ice-boats' rigging; others were lashed to the gunnels, where they took up surprisingly little room.

The dock had been burned, but blessedly the reavers had not done a workmanlike job, and between the rain and the river some planks and all the pilings remained. Crewmen hopped out along those to secure the ice-boats with their hawsers. The Dead Man would have liked to bury the bodies of those who lay among the rubble of the shattered caravanserai, but he thought the passengers—especially Prince Mi Ren, who was pacing and swearing alongside the shore—might stage an actual revolt if he tried to delay them long enough to see to the dignity of the dead. So the Dead Man contented himself with a muttered prayer, read from the tiny book he kept wrapped in oiled silk and pocketed against his bosom, and looked over to see Nizhvashiti also murmuring words and making passes in the air.

Perhaps some saint or God would intercede for them in death, since no such mercy had been forthcoming in this lifetime.

Druja watched the process of converting the wagons to boats like a cat with one kitten, though he tried to constrain his own pacing and swearing to areas where Prince Mi Ren's pacing and swearing was not taking place simultaneously. He scratched the oxen behind the ears as he and the teamsters unharnessed them, and petted one shaggy brown beast on the nose before turning away.

The Dead Man gave him an arch look as Druja came up beside.

"Some farmer will be glad to have them," Druja said, glancing back at the confused, huddled beasts. One lowed forlornly. "Still, I'm sorry to take the loss. But we can't bring them."

He paused and scratched under his scruffy beard. "I'm sure they'll be fine."

"Better than we will, most likely," the Dead Man said kindly. "Better row Mi Ren out to the boat before he explodes, though."

"Bless his little pointed head," Druja replied. "Load up, then. It's a long, slow old river."

✳   ✳   ✳

THAT IT WAS, AND FULL OF PEOPLE. AFTER THE EMPTINESS OF THE mountain roads, the bucolic patchwork of fertile fields, farmhouses, and fishing villages along the riverbanks seemed like crowding. And after the caravan had been so long alone on the water, it seemed now that the river itself seethed with boats—coracles, dinghies, barges, scows. The narrow houseboats, long and low in the water, with their low roofs. The ferries that wore ceaselessly back and forth and back again, roped against the current, tugging their pulleyed tethers as they made their rounds. The ropes were marked with flags of brilliant cloth, and as the ice-boats came upon each, it had to be met with forked poles and lifted smoothly over the dragon prows. They had not rigged the masts and sails—the current alone would suffice to carry them.

The richness of the land in Sarathai-tia was a striking contrast to the barren brown hillsides of Chandranath. The Dead Man found himself thinking that if he were Himadra, he'd want to annex it too. And this was the heart of the old Lotus Empire, wasn't it? There were propaganda reasons behind such a conquest.

And then there was the richness of the river, so white with soil it seemed it ought to taste like milk. Yearly floods would replenish this land, and keep it forever fertile.

The Dead Man turned from the rolling farmland, seeking the glint of starlight off his partner's carapace. He leaped from the prow of the second ice-boat as it crowded the first, landing lightly at the stern of the leader. Not too bad for an old man nearing fifty, even if the landing hurt more than it once would have.

Trotting up alongside the railing, he found the Gage planted stolidly before the helmsman's little house, balanced so that his weight was directly over the keel. Still the ice-boat wallowed: it was overloaded even before the Gage, with a third of the cargo and passengers from the destroyed boat. But Druja's cargo masters knew their business, and the boat maintained its trim.

The Dead Man folded his arms and settled into the same stance as the Gage—braced with legs shoulder height apart. He imagined he looked a little less like an implacable mountain.

"I feel a little better about the oxen," the Gage said.

"Abandoning them?"

Light shimmered on the brass pate as the massive head nodded.

"They'll likely find work," the Dead Man allowed. "Farmers such as these aren't going to inspect a windfall like a dozen trained draft animals too closely."

"Especially in the wake of reavers slaughtering all their cattle, or driving them off for soldiers' steaks." The Gage shrugged. "The mountain oxen won't love this weather, but farmers are probably smart enough to shear them for wool. It is what it is, I suppose."

The age-old lament and acquiescence of the soldier. *It is what it is.*

"You are not capable of softheartedness," the Dead Man said. If they'd been alone, he would have rapped on the Gage's carapace. "There's nothing housed within you but cogs and gearshafts."

The Gage said, "I hate to abrogate a responsibility."

They were silent for a while, watching the river slip by. The Gage at last muttered, "If I were Himadra, I'd want to conquer this too."

"I thought the same thing," the Dead Man answered with a snort. "Are you brooding?"

The Gage mimicked a sigh like a rusted gear breaking loose and reluctantly turning. "What would I have to brood over?"

A murdered love, the Dead Man thought. *Unsatisfactory vengeance.*

But he didn't speak—just paused again, to see if the Gage would fill in the space that followed. When his invitation was met with silence, he at last made a face and spoke himself. "I wish you'd be a little less . . . invested in nurturing your pain. You water it daily. You've had your revenge: it's time to think of new things."

"You think of new things for both of us. Besides, it's not as if you don't brood."

"I don't brood as a lifestyle." The Dead Man rolled his eyes. "Aren't you growing tired of this peripatetic way of being? Aren't you weary?"

"The Gage that stops being restless is the Gage that lies down and rusts." The Gage shrugged. "I only outlived my lover because I had a goal in mind. I only outlived my maker because I still cared about things outside of her. Most of us don't go on like that, you know."

Most of us, in this case, meaning most Wizardly creations. Some had a life beyond their makers. But those were not generally things that were created to be Wizard's servants.

"I need my pain." The light of the Heavenly River glittered off the Gage again as he cocked his head. "It gives me focus. Redeems my ceaseless existence. Reminds me of compassion."

The Dead Man stared at him.

"What?" said the Gage.

"I am memorizing the moment for posterity," the Dead Man said. "In all seriousness? 'I need my pain.' You sound like an adolescent prat with his first broken heart, who's just learned about black cloaks and shocking his parents, and who thinks what he's discovered is a true eternal secret of the universe. 'I need my pain.' The Scholar-God weeps a single inky tear for you, and wipes it into her pen. This may come as a startlement to you, metal man, but pain isn't *good* for anything. Pain is merely suffering. Pain is the proof that sometimes God is too busy thinking about blowjobs to do Her work properly, and in the interstices people get hurt. Pain is just a thing that happens, like a broken toe, and it doesn't teach you anything except to wear boots if you're out kicking stone walls."

The Gage might have been staring right back. How was one to be sure? Light dimmed on the curve of the mirrored skull as the automaton flipped up the hood of his rough-spun robe.

"What?" the Dead Man asked, in turn.

"I never thought I'd hear you blaspheme quite so enthusiastically," the Gage admitted.

The Dead Man's veil hid his smile. "It is the province of true believers above all."

Silently, the Gage crouched, picked up a ballast stone as big as the Dead Man's fist. Effortlessly and without ceremony, he crushed it into powder in his hand. He cast the sand on the Dead Man's boots and said, "It would not be good, for me to forget compassion. Pain reminds me that other creatures suffer."

The Dead Man drew himself up. He paused, considered. Then said, "Your pain does not make you deep or creative or compassionate. It just limits you."

"Maybe so," said the Gage. He dusted sand from his palm, leaving a dusty smear on his homespun. "But a lack of limits would make me a monster, my friend." He put a hand on the Dead Man's shoulder. The touch was light, feather-gentle. Controlled. "Are you sure you're not arguing with yourself, and all you've left behind or had taken from you? I have wondered how deep your own equanimity at your loss lies."

"Equanimity?" the Dead Man said. "What's that? I can't go back. There is no back to go to. My duty is lost, and my love lost with it. If I recollected my honor, I suppose I would lie down and die. So I can't go back, no. But I can go forward, and perhaps make a new life somewhere."

"This is not a life?" The Gage's careful gesture took in the sweep of fields to the horizon, and the star-bright sky beyond.

"This is a passage. Between lives, or into eternity. I do not yet know."

There came no answer.

"Look," the Dead Man said. "It is not a betrayal of your old love to have new relationships. I know you know that, or else we could not be friends."

The Gage shifted injudiciously, twisting to stare at the Dead Man exactly as if he had eyes. The ice-boat rocked. The Gage stabilized himself, and carefully made an incredulous gesture down the length of his own massive brazen body. "Are you telling me to go out and get laid, Dead Man? That seems impossible in every particular. As well as tragically unfortunate for the family of any young man or lady that I might so burden."

The Dead Man felt his face burning behind his veil. He hadn't meant that, not exactly. But even eunuchs had those they loved. The

Dead Man had not been young enough in decades to imagine sex was all that tied two people together.

He didn't get a chance to answer, because the Gage continued. "I think you assign your own desires to me, Dead Man. We have both lost homes, both lost families. That much is true. Both lost our purpose, also true. We move through the world and leave no lasting trace, much as this boat cuts through the river."

"Nobody actually does that," the Dead Man said. "A charismatic loner from some tale is just a man who won't take responsibility for the effect he has on people's lives. He doesn't help pick up the pieces when something shatters. He just leaves them lying around to cut others and create work for them. I do not care to find myself behaving like that . . . that irresponsible jackass. Your metal skin doesn't keep the world out, Gage, and it doesn't keep you out of the world."

The Gage thought about it—the Dead Man had to credit him that. Then he shook his shrouded head and chuckled. "Maybe you're right. Maybe I do want to be a jackass. Maybe I am one."

"Maybe you don't have to be," the Dead Man said. The Gage was all he had left in the world too—a precarious position for both of them. And he—the Dead Man—wasn't getting any younger. Which was hard for the Gage to remember, because the Gage wasn't getting any older.

Hadn't, in decades. Wouldn't, for centuries to come.

"I'm going to have to settle down eventually," the Dead Man reminded him. "Flesh is brittle, old friend."

The Gage gleamed down at him innocently, like some faceless angel of the Scholar-God, some beatific djinn. It was blasphemy to think so, and the Dead Man put the image from him.

The Gage said, "I won't abandon you when you need rest, you know."

"I just don't think it would cause you any hurt to have more friends," the Dead Man answered. "I can't be here forever."

The Gage nodded thoughtfully. "You're worried I won't want to go on alone if I lose my little mascot?"

The Dead Man snorted. "I wouldn't put it in those words exactly."

"You're not that old, Serhan."

"Old enough for a mercenary," the Dead Man answered.

The Gage shook his head. "When are you going to retire that red coat? It looks like somebody boiled it in beet juice a hundred years ago and then dragged it through a midden."

The Dead Man touched his sleeve. It was a fair question, he supposed. And here he was, claiming the Gage was too spiderwebbed into his past, and unable to commit to a future. "When we settle down somewhere," he said finally. "And take up jobs as greengrocers. Failing that, when the sleeves wear through."

"You mean, besides at the elbows?" the Gage said archly.

The Dead Man unfolded and refolded his arms, relieved that they seemed to be friends again. Side by side, they stood and watched the horizon slip by.

THEY CAME INTO SIGHT OF SARATHAI-TIA SEVERAL UNEVENTFUL DAYS later, at nightfall as the sky was brightening. As the city hove into sight over the horizon, the Dead Man thought that this was probably the best of all possible approaches.

The first thundering, ceaseless downpours of the rainy season had given way to daily afternoon showers. The river was high, having spread across its banks to enrich the fields beyond, but had begun receding. Druja still had men in small boats rowing out ahead of the caravan to pole the depth of the channel and seek out snags and hazards, but their work was slowly becoming less critical as the waters calmed and slowed.

They had spent the afternoon drifting past flotillas of lotuses that grew thick at either bank, the milky water rilling at their edges. Now, a tall solitary bluff rose up downriver, and at its peak, something glittered under the light of the revealed Heavenly River.

"Well," Nizhvashiti said from the rail beside the Dead Man, "it's certainly prettier than Chandranath."

That was an understatement. The grim little stockade in the

mountain didn't even seem as if it should be allowed the same noun as this gleaming edifice.

The Dead Man guessed that what he and the Godmade could pick out so clearly from this distance was the palace. He could make out golden stone, so clear in color it seemed almost translucent under the starry light, and tiles in speckled blue and white and green, shrunk with distance until they seemed like the sequined dust of a butterfly's wing.

A castle—a palace—that size must have a teeming community surrounding it. The Dead Man thought they would have to come closer to see any such town above the level of the floodplain.

"You've been here before. What's that glow?" The Dead Man raised a finger to indicate the faint green-blue radiance along the ridgeline of what he took to be the great hall, or whatever the local architectural equivalent might be.

"Probably skylights of dragonglass." Nizhvashiti's voice was mild, unworried. "The stuff shines with its own light, and they use it a lot in palaces."

The Godmade grew ever more skeletal. The golden orb winked in its socket whenever Nizhvashiti glanced around. The dark olive face was drawn up against the bones so tight that it was startling that the Godmade could speak or smile without that leathery complexion cracking. A harsh metallic scent lay on Nizhvashiti's breath.

Still, the Godmade moved with strength, and no apparent weariness or discomfort.

The Dead Man winced. Dragonglass. He'd heard of the stuff but never seen it, and the idea made his skin crawl. Everyone knew that dragon treasures were cursed *and* poisoned, and that anyone who touched them or took them from the lair would die, slowly and horribly.

Nizhvashiti laughed like a bell at his posture, or perhaps whatever they could see of his expression. "It's perfectly safe stuff. As long as you don't crush it and breathe the dust in. I mean, I probably wouldn't sleep on a bed of it, either. But they use a lot of it for windows in this part of the world and I've never heard of anyone sickening from *that.*"

"Look," the Dead Man said, wanting to change the subject to anything but how amusing his fears were. "Is that the top of the city wall?"

It was of the same golden stone, patterned with something gray, like granite. And along the tops, it glittered too, and faintly shimmered. "They've set more dragonglass into the mortar," he realized, then also realized that he'd spoken aloud.

"Shards along the wall-top."

"Well," he said. "That will keep the riffraff out."

Beyond the wall, the tiled roofs of the city were larger speckles and flat sequins of glazed green, blue, white, and occasionally yellow. Flowering trees crowded the base of the palace walls, but had been kept clear of the lower walls of the city, which was set back behind and beneath the castle, away from the river. It was high enough to be above the flood, at least. The Dead Man wondered if it was built on fill to keep its feet dry. That didn't bode well for the walls having deep footings.

He sighed when he realized that he was already making plans about defending it from Himadra. For no good reason at all, except that he disliked a man who would raid a wealthier neighbor, even if he himself was poor.

No, the Dead Man and the Gage would not be traveling on with the caravan. And not just because the Dead Man felt the terrible pang of need in his chest easing as their objective hove into sight. He itched to give their message to the queen, but beyond that, his decisions again felt like his own.

He remembered then that Druja's brother Prasana still rested in the hold, slowly strengthening. And that the injuries Prasana was strengthening from had been incurred as he was escaping the lands and possibly the hands of that same Himadra.

Caravans transported news as well as trade goods and travelers. And they also transported secrets.

The Dead Man felt a shiver of epiphany. Perhaps the caravan would *not* be traveling on past Sarathai-tia. Without his partner, and him.

THEY DRIFTED PAST A HEAVILY GUARDED MOORING SERVICED BY A swept and polished alabaster stair that must have been the water-gate for the palace. This was upstream of the river frontage of bustling Sarathai-tia proper. You wouldn't want your pleasure gardens sprawling beside the outflow sewage of the city.

The river here was so wide and slow it might almost have been a lake, but the shipping and docks of the town were wildly busy. Boats of shallow draft zipped across the placid water in complicated patterns. Stevedores heaved cloth-wrapped bundles and crates marked FRAGILE with recklessness.

The Dead Man's heartbeat accelerated. Soon, he thought, they would be rid of the current task, the precious message. They would be rid of a blood debt to a powerful Wizard, though that was a different story. And he might be rid of the geis that itched under his skin, if a geis it was and not just his own pathologically overdeveloped sense of duty.

And then? he wondered, as the prow of the ice-boat swung heavily toward the pier and the waiting dock crew. Where would they go, what would happen? What fate awaited in the heathen lands, for a Dead Man and a metal one?

He wanted to go home. That was why he had been giving the Gage such a hard time. He wanted to go home. And home was a place that not only didn't remain, but had never existed.

AS THE CARAVAN TIED UP, A SLENDER BOY IN LIVERY BUSTLED BETWEEN bare-chested, sweating stevedores and dockhands until he balanced at the edge of the pier. The boy raised a speaking horn to his mouth with the flourish of a trained herald and called out, "Is there a messenger aboard from Messaline?"

The Dead Man almost failed to register that the question was directed at him. He hadn't expected to be met at the docks by a royal entourage—travel being what it was—but apparently the package the Gage was holding was important enough to the intended recipient that every new arrival in Sarathai-tia was being checked against the need to expedite. Either that, or the rajni had some way of knowing that her answer would come aboard this particular caravan.

He turned and found Druja at the top of a newly affixed gangplank, negotiating duties with a harbormaster. Druja looked up from the sheaves of thick, soft rice paper long enough to say, "Go see about your errand. We won't leave the dock for a couple of days. You can have your pay later. Or . . . sign on for the next leg?"

In which case, Druja would continue to hold the money. The Dead Man would have to talk that over with the Gage. There would be work here for mercenaries. But the Dead Man had fought on enough losing sides for a while. Where by "a while," he meant "a lifetime."

He wanted to stay. He wanted to go. He wondered who Druja—and Prasana—were really working for.

He remembered his first lingering look at the city: the shimmering walls, the golden palace. Reflexively, he imagined it in flames. He'd probably already made his decision, but he wasn't really ready to admit it out loud yet.

Besides, he remembered his suspicion that Druja too might not be moving on particularly quickly. Was this then a gambit to hold the Dead Man in place, as well?

"The Gage must come with me," the Dead Man said.

Druja looked a little unhappy at this, which reassured the Dead Man that he hadn't been planning to skip out without paying them. He'd want the Gage offloaded before he made any attempt to leave behind the Dead Man. "Don't be gone long," Druja said. "I'm still paying you to guard this caravan."

Technically not true, as their contract ended the moment the iceboats made port in Sarathai-tia. But it wasn't currently worth fighting over.

The Gage joined the Dead Man at the base of the gangplank. The

Lotus acrobats were swarming off the boats as well—this was as far as their passage was booked. The Dead Man wondered if he'd ever have a chance to see them actually perform. Ritu waved from across the docks. He waved back to her.

Then he turned and followed the Gage over to the waiting herald. The boy looked even younger up close, with long-lashed eyes as brown and liquid as a heifer's. Perhaps he'd been chosen as much for his beauty as for his carrying tones.

He greeted them effusively, with much low bowing. "Honored guests, this poor herald would ask that you name the one who has sent you, that Her Abundance my mistress may be assured of your authenticity."

That emphasis came through clearly, perhaps intended to assure them that they were not being deceived in turn. The Gage said, "The one who has sent us is Eyeless."

The Dead Man held back, the weight of damp heat sticking his veil to his face, and let the Gage handle the introductions and negotiations. The Dead Man was trying to re-accustom himself to the bustle of a city of this size.

Sarathai-tia had been the imperial capital, when there had been a Lotus Imperium. Now, it was a major trade center for the divided, tangled network of principalities that made up the Lotus Kingdoms, or Sarath-Sahal, or Sahal-Sarat, or any of the various other things that various representatives of the various local populations called it.

It was a peculiar political arrangement, the Dead Man thought. All the little Lotus Kingdoms seemed to take great pride in their former Imperium and the history of the Alchemical Emperor from whom their various royal families were derived by means of his various wives and even more various concubines. But they had as much trouble uniting against outside enemies as any group of principalities, despite their common ancestry and nearly common languages.

One thing the people of these broad and ancient river valleys had in common, though, was a ceaseless hunger for novelty and the exotic.

This city was no Messaline, no Mother of Markets, but it bustled and hummed with strange imported people and strange imported wares. As the herald led the Gage and the Dead Man through the teeming streets, the Dead Man saw such a variety of faces and garbs that he could almost imagine himself back in the City of Jackals from whence he and the Gage had embarked so many months before.

The herald led them through what was obviously an immigrant Song neighborhood, peopled by a fairer folk with narrower eyes. They passed through streets full of veiled women and men with their heads dressed in bright cloth that both reminded the Dead Man of his home and seemed simultaneously more alien than the bulk of the Sarathani populace. Perhaps it was because they should have been so perfectly familiar, and yet the styles were slightly different.

He spotted a temple of the Scholar-God in the central square of that quarter, though, and made himself a promise that before he left this city, he would go there and pray properly. How long had it been since he read the words of supplication under a sky-colored dome? Since the caravan had left Asitaneh.

He thought of all the Sarathani he had met in his travels, and how cosmopolitan they all seemed, how comfortable with and accepting of other cultures. He thought of Nizhvashiti, adopting the self-excoriating religious rites of the far Banner Isles.

These people, in this city, didn't even seem particularly distracted by the existence of a giant metal man walking through their streets accompanied by a comparatively diminutive veiled and red-coated swordsman. The Dead Man could get used to not being notable, he realized. Or at least, to the metropolitan air of worldliness that encouraged people confronted with an unfamiliar sight to act as if they saw such things every day. Even in Messaline, he and the Gage drew a little more interest than this. Maybe ignoring the strange was a form of Tian politeness.

The herald pointed out a few sights, but mostly they walked quickly and without talking. The Gage had adopted the careful gait he used on paved streets, so as not to crush the cobbles into accidental rubble. His footsteps clicked, muffledly. The Dead Man's scuffed in his soft, worn boots, but he was far more comfortable walking now that he'd left behind the mukluks that had kept his toes from freezing in the mountains.

Their winding path through the city took up the better part of an hour, even walking at a brisk pace. No Mother of Markets, no. But Sarathai-tia was a proper imperial capital after all—even deprived as it was now of its Imperium. And when they left behind the markets and the houses built wall to wall, defending interior courts full of fountains and bright birds that the Dead Man glimpsed through guarded, elaborately wrought iron gates, there was still more walking left before them.

The causeway leading to the palace was broad and well-graded, though steep in places. It curved in an inviting arc up the perfectly conical hill upon which the palace rested, resembling the long train of a Kyivvan noblewoman's gown. The palace complex that crowned the hill like some elaborate diadem sprawled even more impressively from this angle—long curved wings jeweled with bright glazed windows reaching out to either side; trees heavy with bloom shedding petals as a maiden strewed confetti when she danced for the blessing of the Scholar-God.

The wind that blew across the hill was sweet and sharp and musty with the scent of the trees and the scent of the river. The Dead Man breathed deeply and thought with slight sadness of the Gage, who had no nose. He had no eyes, and he could see; no mouth, and he could speak—and even taste the rich red wine he liked to imbibe, occasionally. Could he also smell the flowers?

The Dead Man realized that he'd never asked. He knew that the Gage had no sense of touch, no sensation should he stroke the fur of a kitten or crunch a man's bones with his fist. So what else was there?

You couldn't catch the Gage looking at you, but the Dead Man glanced over at the automaton's featureless head anyway, to see his own face distorted and reflected.

"Just a little further," the herald said. "I'll usher you in past the guards. It's quickest that way. Otherwise you'll have to spend half the day dealing with issues of protocol, and Her Abundance made it very clear that she was eager to hear your message."

They passed within with only a little trouble. The guards at the outer gate let them past unmolested. After they navigated a complex labyrinth of corridors and halls and chambers, they came to the ornate doors that controlled entrance to the audience room. The guards in the antechamber to that audience room insisted on relieving the Dead Man of his saber, his powder horn, and his pistol. The Dead Man offered not so much as a token by way of protest. He hadn't expected to be allowed into the royal presence with a gun.

They didn't take any weapons from the Gage, because the Gage did not need or carry any weapons. He was far more dangerous to the royal presence in his own body. But you couldn't very well relieve him of that body, and the rajni had, herself, requested that he be shown in.

The doors were sandalwood and rosewood, redolent of spicy resin, and not gilded. The contrasting colors made tiers, each of which was worked with relief carvings illustrating significant events in the life of the Alchemical Emperor. They were a history lesson in miniature, the bodies of lords and ladies and common soldiers all carved in the round-limbed, idealized Sarathani style. The Dead Man wished he had time to study them more closely.

But those doors were swiftly thrown open—silent on their hinges—and the youthful herald led the messengers within. His black hair was thick and slippery, parted on the side, and by now they had been following it for long enough that the Dead Man thought he would recognize the back of the young man's head anywhere.

Glancing up in the audience chamber, the Dead Man caught his breath at vaulted arches carved to imitate a towering forest of smooth-boled trees. Between the stone limbs, dragonglass panes shimmered, tinting the Heavenly River's pure white shine with unnatural colors.

The Dead Man had seen a great deal of architecture in his life, coming as he did from a caliphate that celebrated construction as one of the sacred arts of Wizardry. What struck him about this place was how light the stone seemed—not as if the hall had been lifted by brute force and science against the pull of gravity, but as if it had lofted itself there on light and living wings.

The floor had been scattered with gold dust, and as the herald walked forward it swirled into the air on either side of him, filling the hall with an ethereal shimmer. The Dead Man had expected an audience hall full of people, a court in swing. Instead, the echoing chamber was all but empty, so all his attention focused on the things at the far end.

The queen—the rajni, the Dead Man supposed he ought to call her—sat at her ease upon a large, boxy chair on a raised dais. Her chair of estate was draped with heavy, glowing silks. A hulked shape of some sort crouched on a heavy pillar beside her. Her chair, despite the dais, was below and to the right of the enormous flowed-wax shape that the Dead Man knew must be the storied Peacock Throne.

The queen might have been almost lost in the dazzle of its jewels, each curl of its footings being paved with tiny diamonds and sparkling, colored stones to imitate the eyes of a peacock's tail feathers, but her calm charisma was sufficient that the massive object served her merely as a backdrop. As they came forward across the gold-scattered tiles, the Dead Man could see now that the thing at her right hand was a heavy perch. Upon it an enormous, rust-red and black bird of prey roosted, its dagged crest upraised half-curiously. He could see now that at the queen's feet lay a beast whose attention made the Dead Man's heart race uncomfortably when it raised its head.

It levered itself to its feet, and as it came casually down the steps toward their little party its size and ferocious aspect caused him to catch his breath. He told himself that what he felt was wonder. The beast was slope-shouldered, round-rumped, bobtailed. Big as a bear, but with sleek short fur brindled with broken copper and black stripes that gleamed over the bulges and hollows of writhing muscles. The head was a mastiff's, with the rose-petal ears of a gazehound folded softly against the massive skull. It probably weighed as much as a big Cho-tse, and it moved like a monster in a dream.

"A bear-dog," the Gage said softly, a little bit in awe.

The Dead Man looked over at him. "Did you learn that from your Wizard, also?"

The Gage shrugged, metal shoulders rolling silently under the rough-spun robe. "They say that the Alchemical Emperor's true-born daughters have a gift with animals. That it's the magic of the royal line as expressed in the women."

The bear-dog paced toward the Dead Man and the Gage. And toward the herald who led them, but other than a slight squaring of the shoulders, the boy seemed to pay it no notice. It circled them, snuffling softly. The Dead Man tried not to glance down as it came up to his flank. When he failed to restrain himself, he tried not to notice the faint tension in its flews, as if it barely mustered the self-possession not to reveal enormous canines in a warning snarl.

He forced himself to look up and away, and study the silent figure who sat below the throne.

She was arrayed so magnificently that he almost missed how slender and young she was beneath the draperies. Her face was concealed, except for the heavily kohled and brooding eyes, by a golden mask wrought in the shape of a snarling leopard's muzzle. Her head was unbowed under a heavy and begauded tower of hair, jewels, dangles, and intricately woven golden diadem. Her hands rested calmly on the arms of her chair, her fingers lost beneath ornate fingerstalls that turned them into a falcon's grasping talons. Her brooches and necklaces shimmered faintly with each breath as her bosom rose and fell.

There seemed to be no one else in the audience chamber, although it was quite possible that the queen had her advisors concealed behind the draperies at the back of her dais. There were not even musicians, but the silence as the Gage and the Dead Man walked forward was more disconcerting than any plucking and drumming might have been.

Ten steps from the dais, the herald bent a knee and lowered his forehead gracefully to the floor. The Dead Man did the same, half a beat behind, and he heard the tiles groan under the Gage's weight as the brass man mimicked them.

"Your Abundance," the herald said. "Messengers from the Eyeless One, in Messaline, as you anticipated."

The Dead Man heard a rustling within the walls. When he glanced up involuntarily, his lifetime of training in protecting his caliph overriding his sense of protocol, he saw that the wall to the left of the throne was actually a series of filigree-carved stone-and-bone screens backed with more heavy silk draperies. One of those had been drawn aside by an elegant dark-fingered hand, as bare and plain as the queen's hands were jeweled. He remembered something about the Lotus religion, that there were nuns who lived cloistered in separate corridors within public buildings, and by their prayers protected the state and the royalty.

Maybe this was such a one.

He averted his eyes out of respect. The Lotus women did not as a rule go veiled, but it was a man's duty to honor a woman's privacy. Especially so the privacy of a holy woman.

When he glanced back at the queen—more comfortable, because her mask concealed her face as well as any veil—she had not moved at all. And yet the Dead Man could not help his distinct impression that she was both worried, and nervously smiling.

She raised one bedecked hand and clicked her clawed fingerstalls in a rippling, beckoning gesture. "Rise," she said. "And approach me. I'd rather not have to shout across half an empty throne room."

Her voice was light, pleasant. She spoke so slowly and clearly that the Dead Man had no difficulty in understanding her Saratahi. The accent was strange, and he was far more accustomed to Druja's dialect and inflections, but the languages were close enough to one another that he thought he would not struggle.

The Gage seemed to learn languages as easily as he wiped water from his metal skin. The Dead Man wasn't worried about him following the conversation.

As one, the two strangers and the herald rose and approached the queen in her chair. As they came up to the dais, the bear-dog paced away from them, turned in a slow circle, and lay down across the feet of her mistress with a heavy sigh.

"You have a message for me," the rajni said. There was eagerness in her voice, and fear. She wanted desperately to know what they had for her, and she was terribly afraid that she would not like the news. The eagle-like bird roused and shook out its wings, perhaps responding to the air of tension that rolled through the room like a heavy perfume.

Gently, the Gage slid open the front of his robe. A tiny hatch that had been invisible in his seamed metal hide popped open and a drawer slid out, smooth and oiled, releasing a scent of frangipani.

The Gage reached a fingertip within.

The queen leaned forward, lifting her chin to keep her heavy headdress centered.

The Gage extracted a tiny packet from the secret drawer and extended it to the queen on the open flat of his dented brass hand. "Your Abundance," he said. "You are Mrithuri Rajni?"

She said, "I am."

"I have been charged to place this into no hands but yours, great queen." Ceremoniously, he offered it.

She took it with hands that trembled, and made her wire-fine glass bangles ring like birdsong on her arms.

10

THE PACKAGE WAS WRAPPED IN EGGSHELL-YELLOW SILK PAPER, THE surface patterned with fibers so fine that they snagged even on Mrithuri's uncallused skin. She balanced it carefully so as not to tear the silk with the hooked points of her fingerstalls.

It was light, balsa-light, dragonfly-light, but it felt rigid nonetheless. She pressed it lightly, and the boxy shape beneath the wrapping did not flex or indent. What could be both so delicate and so strong that it would not have smashed in transit? Or were the inner crevices of the Gage's metal body lined in felted wool against just such an eventuality?

She had sent for armies, war magic, wisdom. Anything that might save her kingdom and her life. She had paid in crimson rubies and the orange sapphires for that help, and when her messenger had not returned with an answer, she had feared that despite her trust, he might have absconded with the treasure; or that he had never made it to Messaline, and to the Uncourt of the Eyeless One who dwelled there.

Half the year later, she cupped what she was terribly afraid would be a completely useless answer between her palms.

She bit her lip, aware that the two foreign messengers were staring at her. Well, one was staring—and, by the lines at the corners of his eyes, above his veil, frowning. The other's head was an impassive oval of metal, so it was hard to rightly say what expression it might have been intended to convey. It reflected her, unsettling, and she refused to look down.

She let her hands rest upturned on her lap. "Do you know what became of my messenger?"

The Dead Man shook his head. "We have a reputation, Your Abundance, for getting where we are going through difficult circumstances. That is why the Eyeless One entrusted us with her reply. We were informed that you had sent a messenger and that he had returned to your court, to tell you to expect a reply once the Eyeless One could construct such a thing for you."

"And this is it."

The Dead Man bowed—impressively low for a man who seemed well past the first flush of youth. "That is what she sent with us. She is not. . . ." The Dead Man glanced over at the Gage, as if seeking support.

"She is not accustomed to explaining herself," the Gage finished.

"And you, automaton," Mrithuri said.

"We prefer to be called Gages, Your Abundance," he replied, in tones so deferential she could not take offense.

"Gage," she corrected herself. "Are you a servant of the Eyeless One? That is the source of your kind, is it not?"

The Gage said, "I was constructed by a Wizard, yes. But the Wizard who constructed me is dead. The Eyeless One is merely . . . well, no one would ever refer to the Eyeless One as *merely* anything." The Gage shrugged, powerful machine shoulders rising and falling almost silently.

"The Eyeless One hired us," the Dead Man explained. "We are merely employees, is what my partner is trying to say." He glanced at the featureless oval of his uncanny partner, as if something went unsaid.

Perhaps they owed the Eyeless One a debt. So many did, these days. Herself among them now, she supposed. If she lived long enough to be collected on.

Mrithuri reminded herself to have a care for her paint, and successfully resisted the desire to lick her lips. She wished she had a serpent near, that Chaeri would come with the sandalwood box and she could lay the fangs against her vein. She could have used that clarity now, that sense of certainty and focus.

Instead, Chaeri was alternately working on gaining entrance to Mahadijia's locked and sealed quarters, and having the vapors, and Mrithuri's head was splitting with lack of the venom. She should send these two away, take her poison, find her strength. It would be better—all this petty business of running the government of her probably doomed kingdom—if she were not hungover and needing the snakebite so very badly now.

The tiny package on her palm nauseated her with hope and worry. What could be in there that would be useful? What could help her win a war, or account for a murdered ambassador, or—well—get out of this alive and unmarried to a man her father's age, who had buried his own weight in wives?

What good could this scrap be? She wished it away, back into anticipation. She couldn't bear to pluck off her fingerstalls and go to work on the ribbons and seal.

She sighed and glanced over her shoulder.

A footstep paused on the tile as her head turned. It was not Chaeri, alas—or perhaps just as well, as Mrithuri was not sure she could have resisted temptation and remained elegant and regal if the opportunity to do otherwise were to abruptly present itself. It was, rather, the spare and elegantly robed figure of Ata Akhimah. The Wizard was looking down, distracted, weighing a chased and decorated but obviously functional pistol across her palm.

The Dead Man stiffened, by which Mrithuri knew the gun was his. Her Wizard glanced around and seemed to come to the same conclusion. "This pistol."

"Yes?" the Dead Man drawled.

"I could make it better," Ata Akhimah replied. "If you will permit me?"

Mrithuri thought the mercenary would choose to argue, but that didn't happen. Instead, his eyes narrowed, but after some consideration he nodded thoughtfully. Perhaps he realized that if Mrithuri wanted him dead, the easiest way to manage it would be to have already spoken to Syama about the issue.

"Better?" the Dead Man asked. He glanced at the tiny package in Mrithuri's hand, frowning. As if he were as avid to find out what it contained as she was.

Ata Akhimah sighted down the barrel. Her bangles slid along her wrists, making a duller sound than Mrithuri's. "Increase the accuracy, range, and rate of fire. There would be small cosmetic differences."

"This is my court Wizard," Mrithuri said, with the feeling of someone wading into the middle of a tense standoff. "Her name is Ata Akhimah. I suppose you already know who these two are, Ata?"

"An Aezin Wizard?" the Gage said.

Ata's face unseamed itself into a smile. "We are supposed to be the best doctors, you know."

"That is your legend." The Gage rumbled when he spoke, a voice that seemed to come up from a great and hollow depth.

The Dead Man's voice was lighter, with a pleasant accent. "The Eyeless One said there was a Wizard here she was acquainted with. Would that be you?"

Mrithuri looked at his hands because she could not see his face. They were callused, the cuticles rough and peeled. He'd hooked a thumb through his sash as if uncomfortable without a sword-hilt to rest it on, but the gesture did not seem threatening.

Ata Akhimah bounced the weapon up and down lightly, not quite tossing it but weighing it across her palm. She looked at the Dead Man and smiled. "We have met."

Mrithuri felt a ridiculous spike of jealousy. She swallowed it and said, "Ata, come and open this message for me."

The lammergeyer stretched his neck out as Ata Akhimah crossed in front of him. At first he meant to solicit petting, but when she ignored him he opened his maul-hooked beak and croaked at her disparagingly. She continued to ignore him, shoved the pistol into her belt, and reached out to lift the tiny yellow package from the rajni's hand.

She weighed it, and might have given it a shake had not the rajni looked at her in warning. She sniffed the red wax seal, and said, thoughtfully, "Frankincense."

"It was frangipani a moment ago," Mrithuri said.

The Gage said, "I have it from the hand of the Eyeless One herself. That, I can attest to you. And none have touched it since."

"How long after my messenger came to Messaline did she entrust it to you?" Perhaps if Mrithuri called Julaba *her messenger* in the cold tones her grandfather would have used, she could keep her eyes from pricking tears at his likely fate. He had trained her in dagger work and bow, and played at the tea ceremony with her when she was so small her cups were flower petals, the tea milky river water.

"Ten days," the Dead Man said. "It is possible he could have been delayed on the road. Injured. Ill. Or some mishap. We made the best time we could, and even our passage was complicated."

"It is possible," Mrithuri agreed. She was a rajni, and her voice would not shake for an old friend missing somewhere in thousands of miles of travel. She felt like a dreadful person for fearing he might have betrayed her—but who could a rajni really trust? If they had come sooner, would Mahadijia be alive? She felt very young, in all the ways a rajni could not afford to be young. She addressed her next remark to Ata Akhimah. "Wizard, what has your mentor sent us? Torture us no more."

The Dead Man glanced quickly at the Wizard. His veil mostly hid his expression, but Mrithuri thought she detected startled respect in the slant of his brows.

"All right," said Ata Akhimah, and began picking the narrow ribbon apart with the tips of her own short fingernails.

Mrithuri almost didn't want her to open it. Her hands trembled as if she herself unknotted and unsealed.

After a few careful moments, the Wizard's nimble fingers picked open and unfolded the precisely creased flaps of a stiffly corrugated paper box. Within was more silk, just vibrantly colored scraps of crepe and chiffon. And, as the Wizard delved inside, a sphere. A sphere of dragonglass, softly radiant, hued in shaded overlapping petals of cobalt and emerald.

It was no bigger than a large marble, and it seemed to be hollow at the center. Something chimed softly within it when Ata Akhimah turned it gently in her hand.

Blown, then, like a miniature fisherman's float.

Could you blow dragonglass? What art would that require, what risks entail? Who could survive it?

But the Messaline Wizards had arts that not even the Wizards of Song or Rasa comprehended, when it came to construction and artificing. Why, look to that metal man standing calmly on the tiles of Mrithuri's very court at this very instant, if you needed more proof than a legend.

Mrithuri realized that the Asitaneh mercenary was watching her avidly. As her eye caught his, he blushed and dropped his gaze at once. Was it attraction, she wondered? Or was he just hoping she'd know what the mysterious gift was for?

And this—this scrap of a thing—this was the answer to her begging the fabled Wizard-Prince of Messaline for assistance from across the half of the world?

The *only* answer?

"Did the Eyeless One send . . . anything else? Any hope of a relief?"

The Gage bowed his shining pate. Mrithuri supposed it was answer enough.

She looked to her Wizard. "Do you know what it is?" she asked in a low tone.

"A dragonglass marble," Ata Akhimah said softly. And before

Mrithuri could take offense, continued, "As Your Abundance can no doubt discern. But I suspect that you are asking me what it is good for, and that . . . well, I have no idea."

"There's something written on the inside of the wrapper," the Dead Man said.

Ata Akhimah set the sphere back into its nest of scraps and lifted the tiny paper box from the wrapping that still lay slack across her hand. She turned her palm and bent close, squinting, to get a better look at letters so spider-fine that Mrithuri could barely make out the color of the ink from where she was sitting. It was a browny red, like . . .

"It's henna," Ata Akhimah said. "It looks like it was scratched on with a pin, it's so delicate. Oh, by the jealousy of the Good Daughter . . ."

"What?"

"It's another damned oracle. May the Eyeless One's own basement flood, come the spring." She laughed, though, and read it over again before reciting, "'A child can come to a maiden; a bride can travel afar. In a stone in a skull lies great wisdom; healing grows strong from a scar. A king ascends from a princess; a harvest arises from war.' Well, I can't say much for the old bat's poetry. But she always did love her riddles. Some days I used to have to solve a riddle to learn the spell I needed to unlock the breakfast cupboards."

"Read it again," Mrithuri said.

"It's terrible doggerel."

"Read it," Mrithuri said, "again."

Ata Akhimah cleared her throat and declaimed in much grander style: "'A child can come to a maiden;

a bride can travel afar.

In a stone in a skull lies great wisdom;

healing grows strong from a scar.

A king ascends from a princess;

a harvest arises from war.'"

"Plain enough," Mrithuri said. "It's just another marriage prophecy, it seems. Even more specific than yours, Ata Akhimah. *This* one
expects me to travel to some other kingdom to marry, and raise my
lord a raja." She glanced over her shoulder and up. The Peacock
Throne glittered with shreds of refracted light. "That's the only way
a king's getting up that thing."

"What about the child?" the Dead Man asked.

Mrithuri sighed and put the back of her hand to her forehead,
successfully avoiding a catastrophic tangle of headdress, fingerstalls,
and forehead jewel only due to years of practice. Her head hurt more
and more. She wanted her serpent. Chaeri had been nearly useless
since she'd killed the ambassador, and Mrithuri knew she ought to
be kinder. But . . .

Ata Akhimah interceded. "It is a custom of the Sarathani kingdoms to send a child with a message of intent to woo."

"And there has been another prophecy of marriage?"

Mrithuri nodded, tight-lipped.

The Gage spoke slowly. "It seems to me that there might be other
interpretations. It's said that maidens have given birth, from time to
time. Although those children are usually plainly the offspring of
gods."

"Great," Mrithuri answered. "I'll start hanging around in temples."

"No heir, great lady?" the Dead Man asked. Not taken aback
at all, which made her very much like him. Even more so than she
had already, and she knew she was taken with his charisma and his
foreign courtliness.

But Mrithuri knew that if she answered the question, she'd start
treating the Dead Man as a friend. And that wouldn't do, for a rajni,
at all—to be taking foreign mercenaries as friends. No matter how
peculiar and engaging they might be.

"I assume you'll wish your reward," she said, instead, to the Gage.
"And then the two of you will be continuing south with the caravan?"

The Dead Man and the Gage traded a look. But neither one managed to speak before Ata Akhimah cleared her throat.

"Nobody's heading south," the Wizard replied archly. "That's what I came to tell you, Your Abundance. The word is in from the southern tiers. The border is sealed."

"Sealed?" said Mrithuri, feeling slow and stupid.

"The armies of your cousin, Anuraja Raja . . . they are moving." Her face said there was more to the message, but she would not say it in front of strangers. Even strangers trusted by the Eyeless One.

Suddenly, Mrithuri couldn't take the disappointment and the frustration anymore. So even the Eyeless One saw no way forward for her except that she marry . . . marry who? Marry Anuraja? And leave, as the prophecy suggested, her home?

Dire, dire oracle. Why had she ever sent Julaba off, if this was all the result? She could not fight a war with a dragonglass marble no one knew the purpose of and a scrap of advice to marry.

And why was this . . . gnomic *horseshit* always in the form of some kind of cryptic poem?

She stood, balancing her headdress, her drapes trailing around her, and waited a moment for Syama to heave herself up and get out of the way. Mrithuri started forward, the bear-dog pacing click-nailed on her right. She stepped down off the dais and began unpinning her diadem.

She looked at the Dead Man as she set the thing on the seat of her chair of estate. It was heavy and had left dents in her forehead. She fingered her serpent torc, but left it where it was. Her snakes were waiting for her, once this audience was done. She'd keep the reminder heavy at her throat for now.

"I have a horrible cousin," Mrithuri answered slowly. "But he's from the wrong side of the family, and mostly seems to wish to marry me, not inherit from my death. So no, no heir exactly. I'd be in better shape politically if I managed one."

"Ah," said the Gage. "And he's the chief contender for your hand."

Mrithuri nodded.

"I can see why you would find the Eyeless One's response un-settling."

Ata Akhimah snorted. "Another gods-damned oracle. Well, let's see what we can prize usefully out of this one."

"It's not exactly troops and siege engines," Mrithuri complained. She hadn't expected either, not really. But she'd hoped. "See what you can find out about the bauble, too. Maybe it throws lightning bolts."

Well, if she had to buy peace for her people with her body . . . she might. Even if she'd never cared to be rajni. She unclasped her mask as well, and set that also on the throne. Yavashuri was going to have a fit about her stripping off her regalia in public. She was too tired to care.

But was it likely that damned Anuraja would even give them that peace? Or would he just starve them with taxes once Mrithuri was his wife, and helpless to oppose his will?

"Peace, Daughter of the Good Mother. That's not all the Eyeless sent us," Ata Akhimah soothed. "She did send us weapons. She sent us these two, after all." She nodded to the Gage and the Dead Man rather than gesturing to them, because her hands were still laden with the scrap of silk and the tiny box with its radiant and apparently useless mystery.

Despite herself, Mrithuri felt a flush of hopeful excitement. She glanced over at the Dead Man and the Gage, and rationed herself a thoughtful frown. "You are weapons fit for the hand," she allowed.

"We are not much against an army," the Gage said.

"Two armies," the Dead Man said, looking down.

"Oh, right," the Gage said.

"Two armies?"

"Your Abundance. Begging your pardon. The caravan came through Chandranath."

"Oh," Mrithuri said. She began plucking her fingerstalls off and setting them beside the diadem. Her hair, disarrayed, was slithering out of its pins. She didn't care. "Himadra too, I take it? Signs of massing?"

"And raiding on your northern borders," the Gage said. "For both conscripts and food. And we saw his troops with some I assume might have been those of Anuraja in the city proper. Himadra, his colors are red and so on?"

"Yes."

"The other man looked like a wine-tun, and his troops wore orange and blue."

Mrithuri rested her forehead against her fingers. Would they come and take her by force, then? Good Mother, she'd prefer Himadra, if it came down to it.

"The wine-tun is probably Anuraja," she confirmed.

"They seem allied."

Mrithuri held her breath until her chest ached. Then, she sighed.

"Well. I suppose it's just flood after rainstorm." Mrithuri could not believe how level, how resigned her own voice sounded. "We'll think of something."

The Dead Man looked at the Gage. The Gage nodded. The Dead Man said, "I might as well starve in a siege as on a road after the troops requisition everything I'm carrying. Or press me into their conquering army."

"You're in?" Ata Akhimah asked them.

The Gage rattled slightly. "I guess we're in."

YAVASHURI, AS PREDICTED, HAD A FIT AT MRITHURI AS SOON AS Mrithuri returned to her dressing room. It was a quiet, contained sort of fit, involving mostly pursed lips and the phrase, "Let me find you a new headdress, Your Abundance." But a fit it was nonetheless, and Mrithuri almost managed to summon the humility to feel a little guilty.

Guilt made her snappy, a character trait of which she was not proud. Today, however, while Yavashuri was pinning her hair back up and fussing with a thankfully much lighter diadem, she lost her temper and snapped, "What is taking Chaeri so long? And when were your agents going to discover that my esteemed cousin is raiding the northern border? Why do I have to rely on caravan guards to bring me this intelligence?"

Yavashuri tugged a lock of Mrithuri's hair into place just sharply enough for it to serve as a correction, without losing the element of deniability. "I learned it when you did, Your Abundance." *Tug.* "I believe your caravan guards managed a faster trip downriver than any of my agents might have. Assuming that any survived the raid and remained unconscripted. We'll know by morning, if they did." *Tug.* "As for Chaeri, she has managed to boss a locksmith and a sorcerer into opening Mahadijia's rooms, and is preserving those rooms until we can inspect them. Apparently the real problem was *locating* the suite. Mahadijia had gotten a Song Wizard to rearrange the world so the door was not findable. Or so that nobody without a key would notice it. Chaeri's description was confused."

"I can imagine," Mrithuri answered dryly. Her head still ached, but the hair dressing, savage though it was, was comforting. Yavashuri had tugged her hair in just this very way when she was a child. "Is it safe to enter?"

"The locksmith believes he's disarmed the booby traps. Also, what do you want me to do with the rest of that caravan? The master is that same Druja who has done some work for us in the past, but they're scheduled to pass on to the Laeish port next, and—"

"Give them shelter," Mrithuri said tiredly. "It's not us that closed the border. And maybe some of them can fight."

"There are acrobats," Yavashuri said. "And a couple of annoying noble types."

"Acrobats sound more pleasing." Mrithuri glanced at her repaired visage in the small mirror Yavashuri held up, and then turned to see her profile in the large one. "Pay them for a performance."

"Your Abundance," Yavashuri said, and bowed low. Exactly as if Mrithuri had a mind of her own, and was not just stamping and sealing decisions Yavashuri had already made for her.

Mrithuri braced her hands on the curved arms of the square, uncomfortable chair. She stood, balancing her headdress carefully. Her drape was creased, but she imagined that overseeing the tossing of a dead man's apartments was likely to get one at least a little untidy, so it didn't matter. She'd just have to change again for the coming meal if she let Yavashuri fuss over her now.

"Acceptable," she said to her mirror. Ignoring her maid of honor's patent but silent disapproval, she added, "Please bring me the Eremite box."

CHAERI STOOD BY THE OPEN DOOR OF MAHADIJIA'S SUITE, TWISTING A corkscrew curl around one slender finger. She had bitten the stain from her lip and nibbled as well at the skin. She started when Mrithuri approached her as if startled from deep worry or consideration.

The rajni walked flanked by Hnarisha on her left and Yavashuri on her right. Ata Akhimah followed, and Mrithuri shortened her steps to make the older women's progress easier. She knew Ata Akhimah and Yavashuri were aware of the politeness, even if there was no way under courtesy that they could acknowledge it.

Chaeri remembered herself and bowed low as Mrithuri approached her.

"You have preserved this place untouched?"

The girl did not raise her head. "I am sorry, Your Abundance—"

Mother River, what now? Mrithuri leveled a voice that wanted to sharpen. Frightening the girl would just drive her into uselessness. "What has happened?"

No blame in her voice, no irritation. Just a dulcet invitation to share information.

Miserably, Chaeri said, "I thought I would please you, Your Abundance, and save you time." She fell silent, and Mrithuri sighed inwardly, but forced herself to wait. Ata Akhimah, who was only sometimes patient, started forward, but Mrithuri restrained her with a raised hand. Chaeri gathered herself and continued, "But I found nothing. I am afraid I might have triggered a trap of some sort, though."

"Are you hurt?" Yavashuri asked.

Chaeri shook her head. "I smelled something . . . burning."

Ata Akhimah muttered something and slipped past Mrithuri into

Mahadijia's vacant room. A moment later, and she cursed briefly in her native tongue, a sound Mrithuri remembered from childhood and so, perversely, found comforting.

The rajni slipped past her head-bowed maid, sweeping Yavashuri and Hnarisha in her wake, pausing only to dismiss the girl. The Aezin Wizard was standing beside Mahadijia's desk. "The document box," she said. "The contents have immolated."

"Magically or mechanically?" Hnarisha asked, stepping forward to inspect the damage. Below Ata Akhimah's hovering hands, a lacquer box sat on the desk. Its finely decorated surface was blistered with the internal heat, and the desk beneath it showed marks of char.

"They're not that different," the Wizard said. "I question how the inside burned with no air to fuel it, though." She drew on a pair of thin leather gloves, then touched and fiddled until the box sprang open. A silver needle with a discolored tip smacked forth from the lockplate, but her hands were well clear of its arc. Gingerly, she pressed the thing back in with the end of a brush until it clicked and vanished into the scrollwork. She pointed the box away from them when she opened it, but nothing dangerous emerged beyond a wisp of smoke and some curls of crisped paper.

Hnarisha bent over to peer inside and said, "Ah."

He held out his own hand and gently cupped it. Something tiny floated from within the box and hovered by his hand—a small, flat disk. "This was the trap," he said. "Looks like a coin, until you arm it by pulling out a film that keeps the two powders within from mingling. Once that happens, it burns hot and fierce within a couple of moments, even underwater. No sign of a triggering mechanism, but it could have been consumed by the fire."

"It's floating," Ata Akhimah observed.

"So it is."

"I had not known you studied Wizardry."

He smiled at her. "I learned a few things from the Cho-tse. This is the most dramatic, and I cannot use it for anything much heavier than a brush or a couple of coins." He shrugged. "The powders in the incendiary—well, I don't know if it means anything, but they're a device manufactured mostly by the Wizards of Tsarepheth. My own people use them occasionally for sabotage, for starting fires, but they have a number of legitimate uses and are not hard to come by."

"Dead end?"

"Maybe." He looked at Yavashuri.

She raised a shoulder as if shrugging a slipping blouse back into place. "Mahadijia cared enough about these papers to make sure they were destroyed after his death."

"Or someone else did." Mrithuri drew herself up. "All right, find me a way to figure out what was in them. Who he was corresponding with. Whatever you can."

MRITHURI FOUND THE DEAD MAN LOOKING AT THE RIVER. THE CALM and the fire of snakebite soothed her mind and burned in her blood. Her wit felt charged with cleverness.

She had changed into a tunic and trousers, bleached cotton hemmed and trimmed with gold but otherwise plain. Only a simple chain and a streak of vermilion weighted the part of her hair, and her fingers were blessedly naked. She stroked the warm metal scales of her necklet and sighed with pleasure.

In the rainy season, unexpected guests were a good excuse for unexpected hospitality. They had a Ctesifoni noblewoman to entertain, after all, and Good Mother help them, the Song prince. Also, the elegantly starveling dark-skinned cleric whose gender was indeterminate enough that Mrithuri had decided to use neuter pronouns and wait to be corrected—one did not, in polite society, question such things.

The afternoon rain was over, and the evening sky was dawning bright and starry. The Dead Man leaned over the golden stone railing, watching the crowds below. He had found a place on a high, broad balcony, above the tiered and stacked plazas of the pleasure garden, far enough from the musicians and the refreshments both that it had remained otherwise uninhabited. At least, until Mrithuri had arrived there.

She found him leaning on the garden wall, elbows among her marigolds. She stood silently not too far behind him, looking down over the terraces and gardens intermingled below. It pleased her that she had slipped up on this warrior without being noticed.

Those gathered on the plaza tiers were mostly her own courtiers, though the great and small both of the caravan had been invited. They moved in unchoreographed swirls of color and conversation that she found she much preferred to all the pomp and ritual of the throne room. Here, she could be—

Well, no. There was nowhere she could be Mrithuri. Just Mrithuri, and not the rajni. She wasn't even sure, she admitted wryly to herself, that she knew who a Mrithuri who was neither rajni nor princess might be.

She observed that the Dead Man was garbed in clean, possibly new shirt and trews, a gauzy indigo wrap studded with spangles, and that his red coat had been brushed. So she was reasonably confident of the answer when she asked him, "Has Hnarisha seen to your purses?"

He jumped, the party scarf turned veil fluttering, and sketched a shaky bow. This was not a man accustomed to or comfortable with being surprised. As he turned away from the railing to do her courtesy, she saw that he had a deep cup of chased silver in his hand. The red wine within lapped the rim, but even startled he balanced it well enough that it did not seep over.

"We are not formal out of court," she told him. "That is entirely too deep a courtesy."

"My lady is most generous," the Dead Man murmured. "And Druja has seen out his debt to us as well, since this is as far as we were contracted."

She studied the backs of her hands. A rajni should never show uncertainty. Perhaps it would be taken for thoughtfulness. Anything, she hoped, but vulnerability. She said, "You look like a man with some military experience."

He chuckled, but his gaze stayed wary. Here he was alone with a foreign noblewoman who might be just about any species of man-eater. And he was Uthman, of some stripe, if you could still use the word, and he wore the veils affected by some men and most women who worshipped the Uthman Scholar-God.

They had had some peculiar ideas about relations between the sexes in the Caliphate, from what Mrithuri had heard.

He glanced down at the serving tables some distance away. "Would Your . . . Your Abundance care for some wine?"

It would only dull the sweet slither of the snakebite along every vein, as if she were a harp wind-strummed. "I am well, thank you. But I would like to talk with you about logistics."

"Logistics?" His relief was palpable in every line of his frame. Mrithuri would have thought the veil would render him inscrutable, but even his fingers were more relaxed on the cup when he raised it and slipped it under the spangles.

"I'd like to know about your history," she said. "Yours and your friend's. The military parts, at least. How do you fight. Where have you fought? Who and what have you commanded? How much experience do you have, the both of you? And what are your weaknesses as well, an honest self-assessment?"

He paused again, head tilted, and she thought he might be bracing himself to attempt just that. You couldn't trust the ones that were too confident, because they were rarely as good as they thought. But the ones who excoriated their own every move were no better—they'd either paralyze themselves with self-recrimination, or they'd react in a panic rather than acting to an improvisation, or a plan.

Below, the music was rising. Mrithuri's people and the guests were drawing back around the central square of the middle terrace. She scanned the crowd, but couldn't see the overdressed Song prince, Mi Ren. Stroke of luck if he'd sulked off, she supposed.

She crossed the few steps and leaned against the railing, far enough from the Dead Man not to be encroaching on his space. He turned, taking her gesture for permission, and leaned again as well. The heavy, herbal scent of the marigolds rose between them.

The acrobats were coming out. Now, there was one small comfort of the soon-to-be-invaders. At least the entertainment was trapped in here with them. Mrithuri leaned against the garden wall calmly and listened while the Dead Man spoke of the fall of the Caliphate, his own survival. His voice took on the rhythms almost of a poem. She heard the words between the lines, the things he did not so much keep secret as keep private.

He, too, had lost what he had in the world.

More so than she, who had still a palace and a kingdom, if she could hold them.

And if she could not, well. She would hardly be the first monarch overthrown for a crown. Or even the first in her own family.

"And the Gage?" she asked, when she realized he hadn't spoken in a while.

"The Gage is a Gage," the Dead Man said, with a swirl of his cup more eloquent than his words. "He's not much of a tactician, but he can level a wall with one punch."

She laughed. And then she waited. The snakebite made it easy, peaceful even, to wait.

"You're young to be a queen," the Dead Man said finally. Conversationally.

And the snakebite made that easy, peaceful, too. Or as easy and as peaceful as it might ever be.

It was strange, she realized, even as the story unspooled from her lips. Strange that she could find this man, this stranger, so peaceable and so easy to talk to. Perhaps it was the sun-scarred skin around his eyes, or the facelessness of the veil—so that speaking to him was safe, like whispering to a nun through the screens of the cloister. Strange that she could tell him things she did not even tell her maids, who cleaned her teeth and hair and body and who tended her secrets and her snakes.

Strange that she could tell him things she found it hard to tell herself. Even when the snakebite slipped softly through her veins.

"My parents are dead," she said. "My grandfather was raja before me."

Already she suspected she would tell him more. It was there inside her, pressing to get out.

He stared out over the festivities below, the acrobats tumbling and tossing one another in ways that should have made Mrithuri's hands tighten on the balustrade. But she was only half-aware of their skill, as they built towers of their bodies and threw their sisters and daughters between those towers, spinning in their bright silks through air. Her attention was on the sights behind her eyes, as she struggled to find the words to explain things she had never said, but merely known.

If the Dead Man had spoken, it might have broken the spell. If she had seen his face, likewise. Even if he had looked at her.

But as she turned to regard him, he kept his eyes trained below, and merely nodded once to show that he was listening.

"My father would have been raja now, and I would have been his heir unless he got a son." She picked a cuticle for a moment, made herself stop by an act of will. Chaeri would cluck over her hands, already. "But he is gone, and my mother also."

The Dead Man listened. That was all.

Below, the tumblers and towers had given way to something else. Men and women came out, arrayed themselves in two rows. Each wore a long curved saber on either hip. As Mrithuri watched, gathering her breath for what she would say next, they drew their swords and faced each other. They raised sabers in salute then posed arms akimbo and blades cocked, like awkward illustrations of sword-dancers.

A child came down the line, dressed in lilac, gilt, and rose. She held a panel of silk, so transparent as to be gossamer. One of the swordswomen came forward to meet her. She held her right-hand blade out parallel to the left-hand one, edges upward. The child stretched the silk over the blades and dropped it.

It passed over the blades and fluttered lightly to the ground, in three pieces. It was not even slowed by its passage across the steel. You couldn't even say that it was sliced; it merely . . . *parted.*

"You could never fight with those edges," the Dead Man said conversationally. "They'd shatter."

The woman returned to her place in line.

Mrithuri expected, perhaps, a passage of arms, some fencing demonstration. What happened instead was that their arms snapped up in unison, they released the blades—and suddenly each pair in the two lines was juggling four whirling swords, so the whole of the line became a flashing tunnel of steel.

"Mother!" Mrithuri said. All her life in Sarath-Sahal, and she had never seen a thing like it. The Dead Man tensed beside her, then slowly, carefully, she felt him force himself to relax. His coat shoulder had brushed hers. She felt a thrill and thought, *Do not even think on it. You could never make him raja.*

He put his hand over hers. "I'm sure they know what they're doing."

"I hope so," she quipped. "We'd never get the blood out of the stones."

He glanced at her. Through his veil, she was not sure if the quirk at the corners of his eyes was amusement, or a question.

If it was the latter, it so happened she had the answer. "In the reign of the Alchemical Emperor's son, when the Imperium was collapsing, there was a massacre in this palace," she explained. "Some of the stains are still there."

Amusement, definitely. "You were telling me about your father and mother."

She had been. And tried to change the subject. Perhaps even now it was not as easy as she had been telling herself, she supposed. Below, a man walked along the line of jugglers with a bundle of swords on his back. With exquisite timing, he added another blade to each fall, so each pair of jugglers was working now with five swords.

He took his place at the end of one line, with no opposite number. And then, at a signal cried out loud, each juggler took a step to the left.

The lines scissored. The additional man caught a flung sword and entered the dance. At the other end of the line, the woman who had been pushed out of sequence stepped to the back. She ran around to take up a surplus position at the head of the other line.

The loud voice cried again—there, it was the big man at the center, the one with gray in his hair—and again the lines scissored.

Mrithuri said, "They died badly. They were poisoned. It took a week and more."

The Dead Man nodded, waited, then said gently, "Not bad food? It happens more often, you know, than an actual poisoning."

"Two weeks after it happened, Anuraja of Sarathai-lae sued my grandfather to make him heir in my place, as I was a girl and a minor."

"Oh," the Dead Man said.

Mrithuri nodded. The fury was there, the sharp irrational pain that made her want to indulge in hasty errors. To whip up an army and ride down the river to crush Anuraja.

Anuraja, with his rich farmlands and thriving seaport. Anuraja, with his wealth and trade and his professional standing army. With his alliance, so it seemed, with her northern mortal enemy.

The snakebite chilled the seething in her blood. She breathed deep to steady herself. "I do not care to be his sixth wife, bedded and buried."

"Nor should you."

More children entered, sprites in their lilac-and-rose garments, sparkling with sequins. They ran down the middle of the flashing tunnel of steel, hands spread out and heads upraised, dark hair flowing. They were barefoot or in sandals. They were laughing, as razor-blades flashed past their faces.

"God preserve them," the Dead Man whispered. He glanced sharply at Mrithuri. "I mean, I know they are well practiced. They will come to no harm."

"It is how we all live our lives," Mrithuri observed, waving languidly to the jugglers. "At least they have the advantage that in their case, someone they trust, who loves them, is throwing the fucking swords."

He snorted, but seemed a little comforted.

"You have children," she said. She felt a spike of disappointment. *He is a heathen and a foreigner,* her head told her body. Her body shivered anyway.

"I had a daughter," he said. "And I had two baby sons." He shook his head and she was grateful for the veil. "That was long ago and in another land."

She was silent for a moment out of respect. Then, "Of course," she said.

The jugglers ended with a flourish, because what could follow the children amid the blades? Mrithuri allowed herself a sigh of relief. They were giving place to the dancers now as the musicians took up again.

"Tell me about the caravan master's invalid brother," she said.

"We picked him up along the road," the Dead Man answered. "I believe he was tortured by Himadra."

She looked at him carefully. "Did you suspect Druja worked for my spymaster?"

He made an amused noise. "I suspected he worked for someone. I will not ask who your spymaster is."

"You *are* a seasoned mercenary." She raised a long arm and pointed beyond them, to the slow pale swell of the earthly river.

"She is our god," Mrithuri said, with a gesture she had practiced to make her black hair ripple over her shoulders as if it too were a sort of river. "She shows the path of existence. Each life, you see, is a droplet that flows into a rivulet, and the rivulet flows into a trickle, and the trickle flows into a runnel, and the runnel flows into a stream. The streams gather into lesser rivers, and eventually those lesser rivers come together into the great river, the Rich-Bosomed One. There are those in what you outsiders call the Lotus Kingdoms who follow another god, another Good Mother. They call their god Sahal, there. They call their dialect something similar." She shrugged. "You outsiders think we are all the same."

"But that river herself flows into the sea, just as does this one."

"So She does," said Mrithuri. She turned over her shoulder. Yavashuri was there—at the far edge of the terrace to give the rajni and the Dead Man privacy, but also to serve as a chaperone. Yavashuri seemed to understand from the glance what Mrithuri wanted and she brought the tools at once.

Mrithuri snipped marigolds, one by one, with the silver scissors, and laid them in the basket. They made a tidy golden heap, and soon they would make an offering.

"And you are right: God meets Her demise in the delta, where the tide flows in as the river flows out, in the heartbeat and pulse of the world."

She laid the scissors beside the blossoms. Their rank, vegetative scent was more medicinal than floral. She continued, "But She also *becomes* the ocean. And She rises again, from its far reaches, to cross the heavens in a shining twine, separate into newly admixed and measured droplets, and rain down again where She began."

"Our god is a woman, too," the Dead Man said. "But we say She is a Scholar."

Mrithuri hummed softly behind her teeth. She wasn't sure if there was anything in response that she should say.

"That's lovely," the Dead Man said, trying again. Possibly because it was, or possibly because he felt a pressure in her silence to say . . . something.

"Is it?" Mrithuri asked.

"You don't think so?"

She turned from her garden and arched her eyebrows at him. Chaeri spent so much time at plucking and blackening them; Mrithuri might as well get some use out of the things.

"Tell me, Dead Man. What happens when I prick my finger—so!" She slid the jeweled pin back into her hair, padparadschas and jacinths shimmering vermilion and madder, reminding her of stars in blacker skies, and walked to the far railing, the one overlooking the bluff and overshading the river. The Dead Man followed her.

Mrithuri held her hand out over the railing. A slow milky red drop appeared, welled, and fell as she pressed the flesh with her thumbnail. Another followed, and another. Each dripped into the milky white water below and vanished, without seeming to offer so much as a splash.

Slowly, consideringly, he offered: "It spreads out—through the rivulets and trickles and whatever else."

"All the way to the ocean," she answered. "And then back to the place where all rivers start. Now. What if I had scattered a drop of poison?"

"Oh," he said. "Eventually . . . it is dissolved in the others? Diluted?"

"Everything leaves a trace once it touches the river. And when the river spreads itself into droplets again, each carries some taint of that poison. Which must somehow be expunged, before the river can be sweet and pure again. If there is too much poison, the river itself might become tainted. Then . . . well. Nothing could drink."

She stared over the railing. She had forgotten herself in her thoughts, and she realized she had forgotten her queenliness too. She straightened her shoulders, but still raised her pricked finger to her lips, and stuck it between them like a child. The sting of her saliva in the tiny wound called her back to herself. She blinked, feeling her mascara brush her cheek. She tried to gather her thoughts before he tired of waiting, and just when he must have decided that this was a calm sort of dismissal and had squared his shoulders to turn away, she managed to clear the lump from her throat and say, "Souls are like the river, Dead Man. Exactly like. So what becomes of a poisoned soul?"

"Is yours poisoned?"

She shrugged. "Is yours?"

He seemed to give it serious consideration. Then he sighed and said, "Honestly? I do not know. Time fixes a lot of things, young woman."

"But it doesn't fix everything," she answered, hiding a grin behind her hand. "Does it, old man?"

PERHAPS THEY WOULD HAVE TALKED MORE, MRITHURI THOUGHT. Perhaps she would even have made the terrible error of bringing the Dead Man back to her rooms. But the tension between them was broken by hasty footsteps and the thump of a fast-moving Gage, and when Mrithuri turned she saw that Ata Akhimah, the Gage, and the gold-eyed priest were hurrying up the steps behind.

Their urgency drew her back up, and from the edge of her vision she saw it send the Dead Man's hand to a sword he was not wearing. She saw them glance at one another—or, at least, she saw Ata Akhimah glance from side to side, and the other two also slow their steps to match those of the Wizard of Aezin.

"Speak, then," Mrithuri commanded when she saw them hesitate. It was not easy to get words out with her heart stopping up against breath, but because she *was* the rajni Mrithuri forced them past the weight, like a stone. "There is news."

Ata Akhimah stopped quite sharply on her soft-soled shoes. She took a quick step closer, tunic swirling at her calves, bangles clink-jangling, and stopped again. "I thought of something."

Her gross discomfort unsettled Mrithuri more than anything Mrithuri could have imagined. This was Ata Akhimah, who could say anything to anyone.

Mrithuri almost laughed at the thought, then, remembering where she had dug down to find her own voice of command, found a strange crumb of compassion and fellow feeling. Ata Akhimah was so much older, so much wiser, so much more worldly and more traveled. She was a Wizard from a foreign land, a teacher, a mentor for whom even a rajni still held some litle awe.

And yet Mrithuri suddenly saw her as human, and as kind.

"You thought of something to help us?" Mrithuri prompted.

Ata Akhimah said. "I have had no luck with the dragonglass marble yet. But. I thought of something that explains the poem. Or the first little bit of the poem, anyway." The Wizard turned and looked at the Gage. "I was talking to the brass man about it, and it occurred to me—so the Eyeless One entrusted this message to you. But she could not be sure you would bring it to Mrithuri and to me. She could not even be sure it would reach us, and so she had to write in this . . . cryptic sort of prophecy."

"A cipher," Mrithuri said.

The Dead Man said, "A code."

Ata Akhimah nodded, rubbing a hand across her close-cropped, blue roan curls. "She knew, however, that if the message did reach us, I would be here."

The Gage adjusted his gorget with two fingers. "This is getting complicated."

"Give her time," the Dead Man said. "I think I know where she's going."

Ata Akhimah opened a limp leather wallet, and from within it drew the scrap with the poem. " 'A child can come to a maiden;

a bride can travel afar.

A king ascends from a princess;

a harvest arises from war.' "

"Red harvest," the Gage muttered darkly.

But Nizhvashiti, who had not yet spoken, shifted softly. "A child can come from a maiden. Yes. Directly, or indirectly, as it happens. Through medical means, or ritual means, or simply because every person and every thing is maiden to begin with, at least for a little while." They wheezed a little on each breath.

Mrithuri licked her lips. "Well, if you mean that when something ceases being virginal, it is not that something is lost but that something is gained. A white dress dipped in crimson dye is still the same white dress, underneath. A river with silt in it is no less a thing of water, though it carries earth as well."

"Your theology is sound," the one Mrithuri had heard the others calling *Godmade* said in hushed tones. The praise made her warm a little, as Ata Akhimah's had when she was young. Ridiculous, but to be told her theology was good by someone blessed by the Good Daughter with the ability to command ice-wyrms and wield the elements was a pleasure she had not experienced before.

"All true." A grin burst through the tautness of Ata Akhimah's expression. "All true. But not what I meant."

"The Carbuncle," the Gage said.

Nizhvashiti's head cocked to one side, the skeletal face scrunched in thought. "Aren't *you* full of surprises?" Nizhvashiti said, pleasantly. "You don't think it's that bauble that came with the poem?"

Ata Akhimah shook out a sigh. "That's a stone all right, but it doesn't fit the description. That's another thing the Eyeless One could have been more clear about. Why send along an object—a tool?— with no instructions? She always was of the opinion that people should be able to figure out more for themselves than I ever found reasonable."

"Beg pardon?" Mrithuri asked. "Back up. What's a Carbuncle?"

Ata Akhimah's head jerked up and down with delight, like a woman in the exuberant first flush of her blossoming. "The Carbuncle. A stone of great power and reputedly poisonous emanations. Said to have been brought to Old Erem by the Dragons of Erem, owned at one point by Sepehr the Carrion King—who used it to get a son on his wife Ysbal, it is recorded, *after she was dead*—and upon his downfall and overthrow by the Mother Dragon, returned with her to the Singing Towers, where it vanished quietly from history."

Mrithuri swallowed with wonder.

The Dead Man shifted beside her. Much more practically, he said, "Do you think it's still *there?*"

"It doesn't matter if it is," Mrithuri said, almost sadly. She remembered this all from her geography lessons, which had been heavy on politics and tactics, suitable for a princess, but which had nonetheless fascinated her. "The Singing Towers are in far-off Song, east of the Steles of the Sky. And they lie in ruins now. And even if they did

246 * ELIZABETH BEAR

not, they were inhabited by dragons for millennia. They are thick with the dragon-poison, and no one could walk there and return. They say strange noises spiral from the ruined towers, and they say also, stranger lights. . . ."

She trailed off, aware that everyone was looking at her. Her voice had taken on a singsong quality, and Ata Akhimah was smirking with one corner of her mouth. She recollected that she was a rajni before she accidentally apologized, and drew herself up. "I am not uneducated."

"No," said the Gage. "You are most evidently not uneducated."

The stark brass sphere of a face and rumbling tone made it impossible to know if the Gage's tone was arch, or admiring. Mrithuri saw her own face reflected in it and looked away.

Ata Akhimah replaced the limp leather wallet, and dug in her capacious pocket again. She came up with a book this time, a small scroll in an ivory case with an ivory wand. She must have left it scrolled to where she wanted it, because she came forward and set it on the railing, pulling it open just about the span of her hand. The characters that marked it swam before Mrithuri's eyes, seeming to twist into the fathomless words that adorned the backs of her serpents, but she knew they were just Song syllables marching in orderly rows down the page.

The Wizard rested her book on the balcony but angled it up, stretched between her hands as she peered at it. "Somebody—ah."

This as the Dead Man discerned the cause of her distress, leaned over neatly, and plucked her half-glasses from her pocket. He slipped the spectacles over her nose and she smiled up at him. "Thank you."

Then she gazed farsightedly down. "This artifact, the Carbuncle. It's said to have power over human fertility, Rajni." She paused, and when she spoke again it was softly but as if each word were pushed out with great force. "It is recorded in this text as a mystical relic. There are . . . well, I would call them case histories. I do not know how a Song doctor would refer to them."

Mrithuri was leaning forward, trying to find her balance. "What are you saying?"

"The Carbuncle is probably, I think, the same jewel described here as the Eye of the River. It was used in the treatment of infertility, Your Abundance. It is said here that it's so potent that it should not be handled by virgins, lest they conceive."

"How does *that* help us?" the Dead Man asked, and Mrithuri was a little grateful to him. Not because she didn't know the answer, but because providing it for him would leave her feeling a little more in control, a little less gobsmacked and silenced.

"If I produced an heir," Mrithuri said. "If I produced an heir. Even unmarried. While provably still virginal. It would be proof that the Good Mother blessed my dynasty. There's a rajni northeast of here who's third-sex, who might have had a very hard time of it after her raja died. There is . . . prejudice. She has no womb, and yet the Good Mother saw fit to bless her with a son. I understand surgery was involved in getting the child out. That kind of miracle—divine favor, an impossible birth—cements even a shaky reign at least for a little."

"It might give even Anuraja and Himadra pause," Ata Akhimah agreed.

"And it seems to be what the Eyeless One is counseling us to do. Or predicting will happen. Or whatever the hell it is that she does other than sit on her throne and rule over Messaline," the Gage said. "The rajni sent for advice; this is the advice she was given."

"A virgin can get a child," the Dead Man said, his lips pursing as he eyed the ladies present. Mrithuri suspected she knew what he was thinking.

"Without cheating," Ata Akhimah replied. "Without putting your seed into her with your hands, or whatever you had in mind."

"*My* seed!"

The Wizard waved his protest away as unimportant. Seeing him flustered behind his veil, Mrithuri loved her teacher a little more than she had mere moments previously.

"But this thing—it has not been seen since the age of Dragons," Nizhvashiti said. "This book confirms that it is in the Singing Towers. It's not too terribly far."

"It's halfway across the world!" the Dead Man protested. He lifted his face. His eyes narrowed as the light fell across them.

Ata Akhimah shook her head. "Close or far, no one can go there."

Nizhvashiti tapped the air above the scroll with one long finger. "Past the Bitter Sea, around the Steles of the Sky. Not far as such things are determined. Closer than whence you came with this message, Dead Man."

He subsided, folding his arms.

The Wizard sighed. "It *is* in a place that was inhabited by dragons. Their sickness *is* there. Anyone who ventured there, who stayed for long . . . they would sicken, terribly, and die. Bones grow brittle; skin peels away. Cataracts blind the eyes. The dragon-sickness is real; their poison destroys as surely as does anything of Erem."

"Well, not entirely."

As the Wizard and priest had moved forward, they had left the Gage behind. Now his voice pushed through the conversation, and everyone turned.

He shrugged. "I could go," said the Gage. "I have no bones to crack nor skin to peel. I have no eyes to be blinded. I do not need rest. I could go today."

"And who will fight the invading army?" the Dead Man asked. "Me and a couple of pages? We need you here, old friend."

The tension stretched. Mrithuri thought it might have broken into something softer but it never had the chance. A hacking sound startled her. When she turned, she saw that the Godmade's sudden thready cough was covered by a clean white rag, hastily produced. Lowered, it showed blood. Mrithuri was shocked, but kept her face impassive. Could not the blessed of the Good Daughter heal such a thing with ease?

She did not know. She was a priestess too, after all. And while she could ease some pains by laying on her hands, see some truths in the eyes of those who spoke them, feel some connection with the minds of animals if she exerted herself past bearing—her gifts were not many, nor strong. Perhaps she was overestimating the power of the Godmade as others overestimated hers.

She turned to look at the river. *Mother,* she thought plaintively, *your daughter is too young to be alone in this world. Too young, too young, too young.*

The river rolled silently on.

THE SONG PRINCE WAS THROWING A FIT. IT WAS AN IMPOSING ENOUGH fit that her general, Madhukasa, had come to tell Mrithuri about it, and Mrithuri knew she ought to care. Mi Ren was a foreign dignitary, a potential ally, somebody whose regard would be of profound assistance to her.

He was also a tremendous pain in the ass who had already tried to order one of her servants tortured for insolence, and she couldn't make herself care very much about an alliance with him. Still, she ought to go deal with it. The increasing weariness in her bones aside.

You can't eat "ought to," Mrithuri told herself—Yavashuri's old advice from when the rajni was a small girl. *You can only eat "did."*

She regarded Madhukasa, knowing her eyes were unreadable above her mask. He stood before the mass of her courtiers, composed and silent, a stout pillar of a man whose shoulders held up her kingdom. He wore an unfashionable beard, grizzled at the sideburns. His hair was slicked back in a wiry tail.

She wished she'd gotten to see her father at this age. She wished, for a moment, that her father were sitting in her chair. Except he would have been on the throne behind her. And Madhukasa hadn't been able to protect him.

Perhaps he would have better luck this time.

She lifted herself from her seat. Her joints ached. The edges of her nails itched. She thought longingly of the snakes, but there wasn't time. She turned to Hnarisha, who stood beside her chair on the side opposite the vulture perch, frowning with concern. Madhukasa, still before her, had spoken in a low voice that would not carry. Her mask had left her face wet with sweat beneath it. She dropped it on her throne and used the same tone to speak to her castellan. "Send for my maid of honor, please."

He bowed. "I shall have her join you along the way. And clear the court."

Madhukasa extended his fist on an arm like a pillar, for Mrithuri to use if she chose while descending the stair. She rested a hand on it, trying to look as if she merely accepted the courtesy, but the fact was she needed the balance and the support. It was like resting her hand on a stone balustrade, and she managed to alight with every outward indication of nimbleness.

He swept her past courtiers and servants, through the filigreed marble halls. Syama rose from her post to pad after, claws clicking.

Mrithuri heard the hush of penitent's slippers, the murmur of their prayers. The plainchant should have soothed her, but it lay as if a weight on her heart. Here were yet more innocents who were hers to defend, who faced any number of untold horrors if she failed them. And here she was: untried, with barely an army, unprepared for a siege at the end of the dry season when food reserves were scarce.

Which was, of course, why her enemies came for her now, to lay a siege she was ill-prepared to resist.

At least water was falling from the sky with the regularity of a water-clock. They would not go thirsty.

The heat and humidity plastered her dressed hair to her skull, beaded sweat atop her cosmetics. The hall was cooler, and the pierced hallways of the palace allowed air to flow through. It did not suffice to relieve the oppression that adhered her silks to her skin. Her bare gilded feet left wet smudges on the tile, distinct toe-prints visible, outlined in golden powder.

She was in a fine mood by the time they reached Mi Ren's chambers—of the best, she saw, that the palace offered for visiting dignitaries. She and Madhukasa had walked over lapis and jade tiles all the way to the wing that perched overlooking the Incorruptible. It was breezy from the height and shady from terraced trees.

Yavashuri waited, hands folded and head bowed in disingenuous servility, beside the Song prince's door.

"Well," Mrithuri said, "I don't see that we can offer him better."

"Turn him out to walk home." Madhukasa huffed into his mustache with stolid gruffness. "You could even loan him a pony if you felt generous."

Yavashuri smiled into her hand. "He's not here."

"Mother River, where's he gone?"

Yavashuri looked at Mrithuri pityingly. "To harass that poor caravan master into taking him to a proper port when he can get a ship home, if I understood the page properly. He was . . . somewhat garbled."

"Oh dear." Madhukasa never swore. He looked at Mrithuri.

She nodded.

They went.

Druja's room, which he shared with his brother, was in a far less imposing portion of the palace. The Ctesifoni bride-in-waiting—Golbahar, a name which Mrithuri almost remembered having been told once Yavashuri whispered the reminder in her ear—was quartered quite close to Mi Ren. Golbahar poked her head through a door open to catch the breezes, holding her veil up with one hand.

"Mi Ren?" Golbahar asked, in a bright, bored tone. Fearlessly, she extended a hand for Syama to sniff. Syama obliged.

Mrithuri had not seen the lady before. The creaseless honey-brown skin around the bright hazel eyes suggested this foreign noblewoman was about her own age. Traveling, she recalled from Yavashuri's briefing, toward an arranged marriage to a lord she'd never met.

Mrithuri never asked how Yavashuri came by her information, but she suspected that many of the caravans that called in Sarathai-tia ferried paid informants as well as goods and news. Nevertheless, she felt a certain kinship with this woman from a far land, sold like a broodmare on account of her bloodline. Could Mrithuri be so clever-spirited in the face of such things, if she had not had the option of resisting them?

She smiled into Lady Golbahar's eyes and said, "I don't suppose you've formed a bond with him in your travels?"

The woman giggled. "The only bond I want to form with him is the link of a blade between hand and belly. Is he in trouble?"

"He *is* trouble," Madhukasa rumbled.

"Oh good," said Golbahar. "I'm bored." She darted through the doorway, securing her veil is some quick tucking gesture that Mrithuri couldn't quite follow. A maid tried to follow her, but the Ctesifoni lady shooed her back. "I can come to no harm with the rajni as chaperone."

Madhukasa reached a hand out to block her path—he wouldn't lay hands on a lady, even a foreign one, unless she attacked the rajni—but Yavashuri shook her head. "Let her come," the old woman said. "She might be useful."

As they walked, Yavashuri acquainted Mrithuri with the fact that Druja shared his room with his injured brother Prasana. It was easy to find—even though they were missing the expertise of Hnarisha, who assigned such things. It was another long walk to get to the quarters reserved for merchants and solicitors visiting the court, and here the walls, though still golden, were not pierced with grilles. The ceilings were lower, without vaults and with only minimal, marginal decoration around the molding line. The air stifled, even in the protective shade of the heavy stone roofs.

Also, they could hear Mi Ren screaming through the panels of the closed door. The Song prince's entourage of servants—five men—lounged about the entry in various poses of embarrassment and amusement, depending on their temperament.

These straightened themselves as the rajni and her own entourage approached.

Yavashuri addressed them, Madhukasa lurking behind her for emphasis. "Go back to your master's apartments."

They traded glances. One seemed about to speak.

Yavashuri cut him off with an imperious lift of her chin. "This is the rajni's house. You exist by her grace here."

This was not entirely true: there were laws governing who the ruler of Sarathai-tia could order executed and when. But these men probably didn't know it, and it seemed Mi Ren's principality back in Song did not subscribe to such modernities as the rule of law. Whatever else you could say about how Mi Ren treated his minions, they were well-cowed before authority. And probably slightly more scared of Mi Ren than they were of Mrithuri, but Mrithuri was the one standing before them.

The apparent ringleader held his ground until Madhukasa took a silent step forward. Once he broke, the rest scuttled after him down the hall. Mrithuri found it in her heart to feel a little bad for them. Servants were not to blame for the poor temperament of their masters.

She moved to the door to eavesdrop. Yavashuri and Madhukasa stepped aside for her. Golbahar hung a foot off her left shoulder like an escorting cloud. The foreign lady smelled of almonds and saffron and something bitter: altogether a pleasant combination. Perhaps she should import a half-dozen Ctesifoni and place them around the court to sweeten the air.

She could hear Mi Ren's tirade through the door, and Druja making occasional placating noises. Yavashuri stiffened in concealed wrath at the abuse, confirming to Mrithuri that Druja was one of the intelligencer's own.

Perhaps Mrithuri should send for her Wizard, or Hnarisha, whose specialized skills came in useful at odd times. But Syama was here, and Madhukasa. There was very little in the way of physical threat that they could not handle between them.

With her own hands, Mrithuri flung wide the door.

It struck the stones with a crash, and rebounded. Madhukasa was there to catch it in an unflinching fist. Mrithuri strode inside, Golbahar and Yavashuri flanking, Syama at her heels.

Mi Ren looked up—he had been glowering down at Druja, who knelt before him in the timeless gesture of placating ranting nobility. Mi Ren had one booted foot upraised as if to kick. It might not have been the first blow. Prasana lay on the bed, propped on his elbows to remonstrate with the prince. The strain showed in his face; apparently his injuries had been severe.

Injuries that had occurred in her service, Mrithuri was now certain. Yavashuri didn't tell her everything, but Mrithuri had gotten good at guessing.

Mi Ren stopped mid-squawk to stare. He was a man of modest size and ascetic build, though his clothing gave the lie to any illusion of austerity. His black hair, twisted into a tight high bun, drew attention to the catlike angle of his cheekbones and eyes snapping with self-righteous fury. He was a handsome man.

What a pity he was such a terrible creature, Mrithuri thought. She had to marry somebody. But it wasn't going to be this thing.

His lip curled in disdain when he turned to her, though she outranked him. She was a ruling rajni: he a mere prince. He sketched the most cursory bow possible without causing a diplomatic incident. "Where are my men?"

Madhukasa growled, "Where are my men, *Your Abundance?*"

Waiting for Mi Ren to correct himself was probably pointless, and would only complicate his existing insolence with more. Mrithuri said, "I dismissed them."

"They're *my* men." The handsome features were spoiled by an expression as obdurate and uncomprehending as that of the proverbial ox receiving instruction in higher mathematics.

"And this is my house. So perhaps you would care to explain the problem to me instead of bellowing at this poor fellow?" Gently, she insinuated herself between Mi Ren and Druja. She pushed into Mi Ren's space to do it, so he took an involuntary step back.

He was bigger than she was, broader and more tall, and he wore shoes that increased the advantage. He tried to loom over her, aided by his broad-shouldered robe that must be beyond stifling in this heat. She stiffened her spine, thinking with all her might that she was rajni, a daughter of the line of the Alchemical Emperor, and that his wit and courage must run in her veins as surely as his blood.

She knew it was nonsense. Anuraja was a scion of the same line, after all. And—well, he had wit and courage. It was simply honor and self-discipline he lacked. But if quality of heart could be inherited, the world would be a very different place. Still, thinking of her grandfather and her great-grandfathers gave her courage, and fool's courage was as effective as the well-founded sort in accomplishing acts of bravery—though the eventual result might be quite different.

Mrithuri stepped forward, crowding Mi Ren. Syama's hackles brushed her fingertips, though the bear-dog made no sound of threat. Silent support, unflinching loyalty. The Song prince was self-aware now, and would not give her more ground, but Druja was taking advantage of her distraction and had withdrawn to crouch beside his brother's bed.

"This weasel," Mi Ren said icily, "refuses to take me on to Sarathai-lae as contracted. I appeal to Your Abundance as the legate of this land to force him to abide by the letter of our agreement."

"I see," Mrithuri said. She curled her fingers in Syama's warm ruff. The bhaluukutta leaned against her hip. "There is a problem, Your Highness. The honest Druja cannot travel to the Laen port, as he arranged with you, because his caravan is under interdict. We are at war with Sarathai-lae. A war that has come upon us unsought, but you see, I cannot allow anyone who might bring news of my court to travel to the enemy."

"This is ridiculous!" Mi Ren didn't quite explode, but he did huff savagely and stomp his foot like a child. "I have business interests at home that suffer in my absence. I am losing money and prestige with every day I remain in—"

Whatever pejorative he was about to level at what Mrithuri considered her own perfectly lovely little kingdom, the jewel in the Mother River's parted hair, Mrithuri had no interest in hearing it. She reached across the gap between herself and Mi Ren and shocked him into silence by laying the very tips of her golden fingerstalls against his cheek.

"Hush," she said.

He hushed.

A thrill rang her. A realization. She had no intention of marrying this man. Of binding her fate and her kingdom to him. But there was no reason at all that she could not make him *think* he had a chance of winning her. In fact, to do so would be statecraft at the highest. Yavashuri and Hnarisha would be pleased with her cleverness, and if she seemed to be courting, some of the pressure to marry might, for a little while, ease.

She might even manage to wrangle an alliance with this odious twit's father or his elder brother, both of whom she had heard were not so bad as this one.

She smiled at him through false, lowered lashes, and purred, "Isn't there any reason, dear prince, that you might wish to stay in my fair kingdom for just slightly longer? I'm sure we can divert you for the duration of such a little war."

11

It wouldn't matter in the long run. The world would wind on; the world would wind down. Kingdoms would rise and sink again. Cities would be founded and cities also would fall. Races of beings would come to prominence and wear away again, like mountains thrust up and then ground to dust. Where there had been djinn would come ghulim. Where there had been ghulim would come dragons. Where there had been dragons would follow men.

The Gage wondered briefly what would follow after men. The Cho-tse? The Bear-Men of the high plateaus? Something he had never heard of? Something like himself?

He, himself, might even possibly be around to see it, having traded living heart and living bone for a carapace of brass and a flawless mirror. He was already feeling the pressure of his age, though, and he had not yet truly outlived one long Wizard's lifetime, though he would be impossibly old by the standards of people who were not Wizards, if he wore his own flesh still.

The Dead Man aged, though. And the Gage himself did not.

It wouldn't matter in the long run.

But it would matter to these people. And he cared about some of these people, and was coming to care about them more.

He knew he should be better. He knew he should care about them for their own sakes. Because they were people. Because they had feelings and were alive.

Perhaps the Gage had known too many people already. Perhaps, not enough. He found he could not care about them very well at all in the abstract. But he could care hard when he thought of a specific face, a way of moving, the fall of someone's hair.

He moved through the rajni's palace in the dark daytime hours when almost everyone was sleeping, and he thought, and considered, and planned. He needed to be two Gages: one for erranding and one for war. Two tasks only he could undertake: enter the dragon's ruined city, and be an army unto himself. Two tasks that were mutually exclusive, as well.

For all his weight and size, a well-oiled Gage could be surprisingly silent when he chose. And he wore on his brass feet an enormous pair of carpet slippers that muffled their clatter and clunk, and served to protect the rajni's mosaic-tiled floor.

The nuns in their cloisters moved through the day-that-would-elsewhere-have-been-nighttime with him. Or not with him, precisely: he never felt followed, or even escorted. But he was aware of the rustle of robes, the curve of draped heads. The soft singsong of prayers.

How would it be, he wondered, to be mewed up like a songbird all one's life? Did they choose it themselves? Was it an escape for some, a refuge? Or was it a dumping ground for unwanted daughters? They had their prayers—did they have books and scholarship and arguments late into the night in places where they were not observed, untouchable, through the pierced and folded palace walls?

They were human, he supposed. They must. They must have their secrets and their arguments and their politics, their love affairs. It was only that the cowled identical heads and robed identical bodies were designed to make you forget that they had identity. Individuality.

With a metal knuckle, the Gage stroked the side of his own perfect mask.

Were they chained, or had they fled there?

What was it like, to live within walls, between grilles, moving in circuits and murmuring. Flowing in a constrained course like a river. Going not where one chose but as one was habituated and directed?

Then he paused, and thought, But isn't that every life? Every existence? Or almost every: some lives burst the banks, as had his own. As had the Dead Man's. But neither of them had chosen that leap across unmarked territory. Both of them had been thrust.

The idea disturbed him so that he had to find the doors and go outside, where he could not watch their owl-like whispered migrations anymore. He told the guards his destination—just a walk around the grounds—and they told him what the landmarks were for stopping before he reached the outer walls. Finally, with their blessing and permission as a guest of the rajni, the Gage was turned loose in the dimness of day.

His footsteps led him out into the palace gardens, and a softly falling rain. The early torrents of the besieging season had mellowed to something gentler over time. And the Gage, in earnest, was glad of the rain. He and the Dead Man had discussed their gratitude more than once between here and the border.

It was hard—damned hard—to move an army in this weather.

Thank the god of your choosing—the Gage was out of gods of his own, as it happened—it was hard to move an army in this weather.

Something vast and pale caught his attention among the dripping violet and orange blossoms of so many wet, weeping trees, and he moved toward it to investigate. He stepped out of the sodden carpet slippers—they dragged and were doing worse to the grass than his feet would, anyway—and picked his way across the garden, avoiding stone borders and hedgerows for the sake of the gardeners.

The great white curve was moving, sliding, reminding the Gage of the breathless silent progress of some foreign moon. He followed it with what silence was in his power, half-expecting to find Nizh-vashiti again, engaged in some species of sorcery.

The gardens were enormous. It probably couldn't have gotten away from him, if he'd been willing to crash through flowerbeds and crush brick paths under running metal feet. But it moved fast enough that in maintaining silence, he stretched himself slightly to close the distance.

And then he came out of the trees and saw two figures standing in the rain-dimmed light. An enormous beast—and beside it, the small, curvy outline of a woman dressed in flowing, sodden trousers and a tunic that was plastered to her body by the rain.

The beast was great, as he had seen, and pale, as he had seen also. Its head was like an enormous knobby boulder with a flapping sail affixed on either side. The snake of its trunk reached out before it, prospecting among the leaves of a hedgerow for something either tasty or interesting. The curve of its back was like the hull of a barge.

"An elephant," said the Gage. But not such an elephant as he knew from the lands south of the mighty desert men called the Abandoned Lands. This one was smaller, with smaller ears, a higher-domed head and steeper back, and it was much lighter in color.

The woman heard his voice and turned. Her curled hair had frizzled tight in the rain, her pointed chin lifting as she peered through the gloom at him.

"Who is it?" she said.

It was Chaeri, the rajni's handmaiden. She reminded him of someone not herself, and he put the thought away.

"It is the Gage," he said, and stepped out of the shadows. His robes draggled with rain, swinging heavily as he raised his hands to show he had no weapons. As if that mattered when he was so much a weapon himself.

She did not seem, however, frightened.

"Is this a private rainstorm," he asked, "or can anyone walk in it?"

"Only the gardens are private," she replied. "And you are, after all, a guest. The rain is anyone's who can catch it."

She tipped her head in a way that seemed like an invitation, so he crossed the open grass to stand before her and her elephant. Or more likely the rajni's elephant, since he did not think that handmaidens often kept them.

"I shouldn't be out in the rain," Chaeri said matter-of-factly. "I'll get ill. But I couldn't resist."

The beast raised its snakelike trunk and sniffed him curiously, then did something with its ears that seemed almost a shrug and made a similar and more thorough investigation of Chaeri. Then it came back and sniffed him again, fogging his mirrors where the brass was cold between beaded raindrops.

The Gage waited until it seemed to have made up its mind. "Does it have a name?"

"Hathi," Chaeri said. "She is a friend of the rajni's." A curious way to put it, but he had to admit, he had never known an elephant well enough to determine how thoughtful an acquaintance one might be.

"So are we all," the Gage said, and was bemused by the curious frown that creased the woman's visage. "Are you tired, Chaeri?"

"I could not sleep." She turned once again to fall into step beside the elephant. "I killed a man the other day. And I've been sick, of course. I slept too much, and then not enough. I did not want to take the poppy today."

She looked at him searchingly. He nodded. He would not ask, but his impassive shell made him an excellent listener. She would elaborate if she wished.

She changed the subject, instead. "Hathi has the run of the gardens; she is very sacred to the river because of her color. And she is very well mannered: it's been ten years or more since she uprooted a tree."

The Gage laughed, even though he could tell she was serious. Serious, but also clever and funny. And brave enough to be out alone in the dark, in the garden, in the rain.

She did, in fact, remind him of someone. Someone of whom he did not usually choose to be reminded.

Someone who had been taken from his life a very, very long time ago.

"I could not sleep either," the Gage admitted, dry and—as always—deadpan.

Chaeri shot him a look, brow wrinkling in another thinking frown, as if to see if his sober tone was mockery. Of course, to glance at his face would teach her nothing but the curve of her own cheek inverted, the rain-taut spiral of her curl.

"Do you sleep often?"

He shook his head. "Not in the better part of a century," he admitted. He was curious about her, and curious about the lightly admitted murder. "Do you want to talk more about what's keeping you up? I haven't so much as a mouth to spill your secrets with."

"Maybe later," she said, after a hesitation. Then: "Hathi likes you."

"How can you tell?"

The woman giggled. It was a sharp, musical sound. "She didn't rub mud on your hair."

The Gage rather wished he could give her an arch look at that moment. He had to settle for turning his mirrored egg inside the puddle of his cowl and angling it at her.

She grinned at him wickedly, pleased with her own cleverness. She reached up herself—standing on tiptoe to do it, as she was not tall—and slid her palm over the rain-glazed brass of his carapace. She flicked her fingers like a cat that has stepped in a puddle and said, "I could do it for her."

Metal hide and metal heart or not, the Gage felt a tremulous shiver. Was she flirting with him?

Was she *flirting* with him?

He wasn't sure. He couldn't remember, exactly, what flirting had been like. People did not *flirt* with an enormous brazen, mirrored man.

It was like his playful banter with the Dead Man, he supposed. But a little sexier. A little more enticing.

Now his body ached with a remembered thrill, and his metal mitts ached with emptiness. Longing; it was longing, this sensation that crowded the empty spaces within him where nerves and muscles would have been had he such things as nerves and muscles.

It was a terrible thing, longing. He wished it away. It made him think of how useless his strength was, how his hands *were* empty, and had uselessly closed on emptiness again, and again. There are so many stories about those who lose almost everything, then sacrifice what remains for revenge. There are so *few* stories about what happens to those people afterward. Their metal shells. Their metal hearts.

How they learned to do something else again. Did they learn to do something else again?

The Gage was glad he had no face.

He would have had to turn it away, otherwise.

They walked in silence a little—woman and monster and beast—and the Gage found himself easing, somewhat, just walking himself and listening to the heavy tread of the elephant and the light step of the girl.

"Where are we going?"

Chaeri splashed through a saturated patch of grass that was not quite yet a puddle, almost decorously, lifting the hems of her trousers with her hands. The Gage noticed she was barefoot, and watched, fascinated, the way the muddy water, with every step, seeped between her toes.

They curled, those toes, reminding him of the delicate fronds of some young fern, the sticky ephemeral pistils of a night-blooming flower. His own feet had no such delicate olive-brown appurtenances, being more after the fashion of hobnailed boots. The Wizard who had built them had harbored no designs to echo anything transitory, natural, or lovely. They had been built to hold him up, he thought.

And yet, did not her little curling feet, bright with rings and anklets, do the same job far more daintily and just as well?

"Is it safe to walk in the rain alone?" he asked.

Chaeri's laugh, this time, was strained. "You mean, for a woman? Is it safe to go out in the dark of day unescorted except for a monstrous beast, almost as large as, say, a giant metal man? Is it safe for her to wander through her own garden without a man to defend her? Is that what you ask?"

She raked a rain-slick curl from her face with small fingers tipped with pointed oval nails. "What is there for a man to make me feel safe from, brass man, except for another man? It is a most excellent piece of flummery your sex has cooked up."

"You do not seem frightened of the dark, or men, to me."

She snorted. "Oh, how can you know what it is like, for a woman?"

The Gage raised his mirrored head, making the rain ping against it with shifting tones. When Chaeri was silent and he had her attention, he said softly, "I was a woman once."

She stopped, stared at him, hands half-upraised and stopped there. "You were a woman."

"Before I was a Gage."

She smiled in bitter triumph. "And instead, you chose to become that . . . thing."

I had my reasons, the Gage could have said. But he held his peace, and wondered now what they had been. Surprising him, eyes steady in his mirror, she reached out once more and stroked the metal of his wrist. Most people flinched away, looked away. Chaeri's touch lingered. He couldn't feel it, not exactly. But it made him shiver anyway.

He said, "Do you rail against the frailty of flesh, then?"

"I have loved frail flesh," she answered. "Frail flesh hasn't always returned the favor in what I would term a gentlemanly fashion."

"Loved," he said, savoring the word. Thinking of someone of whom she reminded him. It came welling up in him—not pain, after so long. Not pain, but not the absence of pain either, exactly. Perhaps it was grief, when grief had burned hollow, consumed everything it could touch. He found himself speaking, and he didn't mean it as a flirtation, now. It came out instead as if it were the hollow truth he had been forged to echo, as the shell is forged to echo the sea.

"You're going to love somebody," said the Gage. "And their fragility is going to break your heart. It's easiest if it's their frailty of courage or of honor. When it is their character that breaks, and the love breaks with it. That hurts, but there's the refuge of betrayal. Righteous anger can see you through almost any sort of winter, Chaeri, if its flame is stoked hot enough."

He could not sigh, but he mimicked the sound of a sigh anyway. Sometimes one performed like an actor, for the sake of communication.

He said, "The worst frailty in a lover, though, is when it's the frailty of the body, through no fault of their own, because then you cannot even be angry for it. There is no one to blame but the world."

"No one else? Not ever?"

"The world. And perhaps whoever brought this harm down upon the beloved."

They paused to watch Hathi browsing. The foliage made ripping sounds like fabric as she pulled it apart. She must keep a platoon of gardeners busy.

Chaeri mused, "What if I love you?"

"Because I am not frail?" The Gage contemplated it, reflections chasing his empty mirrors. At last he replied, "How will you know that you love, if there is no terror of losing? Is it love at all, if there is no risk? If it is safe?"

"Is that why you became what you are?" she asked, with a perspicacity that left him feeling flensed. "The terror of losing?"

"Revenge," he replied. "That is why I became what I am. Because this shape could hope to face a Wizard, and win."

"Did you get him?"

"Him?"

"The Wizard who killed your wife?"

"Husband," the Gage replied, and watched her face rearrange itself cryptically again. "The Wizard stole my husband's soul and locked it away."

"So it wasn't revenge. Not exactly. You had to get your husband's soul free. Didn't you?" She spoke so soothingly, as to a child, startling him. Who saw a metal automaton half again her own height as a fragile thing in need of comforting?

He said, "It was revenge."

She did not step away from him. Her hand was on his arm, so heavy for its size. The white elephant had taken two steps away and was picking through rain-beaded tree leaves with her trunk, every so often selecting and plucking one in particular that seemed identical to all the others, except she popped that leaf over all others into her maw, where she more folded and mouthed it than chewed.

Chaeri was still looking at the Gage. He wished to sigh and said, "And yes, I did. Find him. Put a stop to it. That was how I met the Dead Man. He was looking for the same fellow for similar but not identical reasons."

"His wife?" Chaeri asked. As if on some prearranged cue, they turned shoulder to shoulder once more, and started walking toward the palace again. Hathi ambled after, though no one suggested or required her attendance.

"I never asked," the Gage said. "But I am certain that she died, in the sack of Asitaneh, and his sons and daughter too."

"Dead Men have sons," she said, as if it had never occurred to her before.

"And Dead Men have daughters."

"How'd he survive, then?" Her gaze was avid. "If his family perished?"

The Gage shrugged. "That is his story to tell."

She frowned, but did not press him further. "And you? If you survived after your husband's murderer, what kept you here? Doesn't something like you have a purpose and a limited time of use, customarily?"

"I am a machine," the Gage said. "That does not mean I am without feelings."

"Desire to live, then? Like every other thing?"

The Gage thought about it, and did not know the answer. "I think

I stayed alive on charity." He meant his own, as well as that of others, but he wasn't sure if Chaeri understood him.

Mercurial, though, she straightened up and sparkled at him. "Conveniently, my duties are not always strenuous. It may be that I have the time for charity."

"Really?" he said.

She grinned, flashing creamy teeth in the dimness. "It's completely out of pity," she teased.

He regarded her. He watched her hair move in the rain. When he spoke, it was softly, and as much as to the girl, he spoke to the rain. "I think I would like to experience your charity."

As NIGHTFALL GATHERED WITH A GROWING BRIGHTNESS, THE RAIN tapered off and threadbare clouds began to fray and tear. The Gage helped Chaeri return Hathi to her stall—a pen only by courtesy, he thought, as he could have battered it down almost effortlessly and he could not imagine any different of the elephant. Then he walked her back to the palace, and left her by the entrance to the rajni's rooms. His carapace was still rain-spangled, light collecting and seeming to amplify in the droplets, as if he had been jeweled in cabochon diamonds.

He found the Dead Man, to his surprise, awake, and sprawled elegantly across three steps of the palace's curving grand stair with one leg propped higher than the other.

This put the Dead Man slightly above eye level. At least, to those who had eyes.

"You look louche," the Gage said, pausing at the bottom of the stair.

The Dead Man lifted his head. His eyes were red with lack of sleep, but he did not seem drunk and no reek of alcohol surrounded him. His clothes were rumpled and his shirt half-open, but it was the lack of a blade that made him seem naked. "You look drenched, on the other hand."

"Walking in the rain will cause that."

"Patrolling the boundaries?"

"Walking a lady home," the Gage admitted, though he had a sudden strange desire not to mention it.

"A lady." The Dead Man sat upright, swinging his legs down the stoop, then seemed to come to the conclusion that straightening his spine was too much effort and slumped forward with his elbows on his knees. "I thought your preference ran the other way, old friend."

The Gage demonstrated his dripping robe and his brass armatures with a conjuror's sweep of his hand. "I can't see it mattering much one way or the other to me, when it comes right down to it. But it was just a conversation between strangers who might perhaps become friends."

The Dead Man nodded, and did not caution him against making friends in places they could not stay, which the Gage found . . . slightly curious. Instead he said, "Do you want to stay for the war, then?"

The Gage shrugged. Water slid down his carapace to litter droplets on the floor. "The Eyeless One would certainly owe us a favor, after."

"She does seem enamored of . . . of this little queen."

Ah, the Gage thought, with resignation. "You think we were part of the message?"

The Dead Man sighed and ran his hands across his veil, through the sweaty disarray of his curls. "I do."

In the morning, word of the armies came. The Gage and the Dead Man were drilling troops near the barracks. They were less desperately unseasoned than the Dead Man had feared, though perhaps not quite what the Gage had hoped.

One of the acrobat lads, who were functioning as pages for the time being, came scrambling up with his bare horny feet slapping the practice-yard clay. His sweaty face and wild eyes told the tale before he even got the words out.

"Where are they, lad?" the Dead Man asked, while the Gage was still formulating his questions.

The lad stammered.

The Dead Man rolled his eyes and silenced the boy with a wave. "Well of course you don't know where they are, exactly, this minute. Where were they when the scouts spotted them? Do they have an idea of the terrain? The rate of advance?"

The child shrank a little from being interrogated as if he were a professional field runner. He glanced over his shoulder, looking for a place to bolt, but there was only the wide, noisy, wet clay yard full of shouting, pushing soldiers and the clatter of blunted, weighted practice blades.

"Dead Man," the Gage said, stepping between them gently. His bulk should have been intimidating, but he knew how to make it seem like a protective wall. "You're flustering him."

The Dead Man's sigh puffed his veil. He gave the Gage the eyeroll that translated as, *So you're Sympathetic Mercenary this time, then?* and turned back to the drilling soldiers as if nothing had happened at all.

The Gage led the boy aside. The lad was at least situationally tough and rallied well, pulling himself together fast. The Gage steeled himself against a moment of self-loathing, that he was assessing the suitability of boys to become soldiers yet again.

Maybe it was time for him to find a quiet lonely place to lie down and rust, after all.

But was it better that a boy such as this become a soldier, or that he be left in innocence a little longer that he might then be overrun, conscripted, raped, or some combination of those?

The Gage placed a heavy metal hand on the lad's bony shoulder, careful not to let him feel the full weight. "Now tell me," he said evenly. "Do you know whose soldiers these are? Or if not, who told you to run and see the Dead Man and me?"

Nizhvashiti awaited the Gage at the top of the palace's grand external stairway, as if the Godmade had known from which direction he would approach. The daily rains were blowing in, and the sky was mottled. Black robes whipped in a freshening wind, revealing the cuffs of jet-colored silken trousers. The overall effect was of a raven struggling on storm winds, silhouetted against a knotted sky.

The priest's gold eye glinted as the Gage approached. The skin of the brow above it had split slightly, perhaps due to dehydration. Within, the flesh seemed pale and waxen, as if the juice and vigor were already gone.

"You need to keep your strength up for the war," the Gage said. "Try having a cup of tea with some milk and sugar, and maybe a little less poison in it."

"There is strength and there is strength," the Godmade intoned. It would have been pretentious if it weren't for the little wink—that split the cracked brow further. No blood trickled. The Gage wished, anyway, for thread and a needle.

The stones settled under the Gage's weight as he climbed them. He was careful to step toward the back and keep his bulk forward, so as not to chip the edges of the stairs. They were well-masoned, laid in the earth with a level, sandy foundation. He had not cracked one yet. Not in this palace, anyway.

There were other dwelling places where the stonemasons were less skilled, or less scrupulous.

He paused a step or two below Nizhvashiti, so their heads were level. "Your messenger found us."

"And the Dead Man?"

"We're dividing the duties. He's scaring the troops, and I came to interview you."

The Godmade turned, robe skirts flaring so heavily the Gage wondered if there were weights stitched into them. When it came down to it, everything was theater and theatricality: his own mirror of a mask no different from the Dead Man's veil, the Godmade's swirling cloaks, the rajni's towering headdresses and claw-wrapped fingertips.

He followed up the stairs.

"How bad is it?"

"Ata Akhimah has a map room ready." And would say no more.

THE MAP ROOM WAS A PECULIAR CHAMBER, OVAL IN DESIGN, WITH HIGH piecework windows and heavy chandeliers hanging low enough that the Gage must move with grave caution among them. Their branches were twisted bronze, wrought to look like the stems and leaves of water lotuses, with the illuminated portions standing in for the blossoms. They bore no candles in their sconces, though: these fixtures burned with witch-lanterns in sunlit shades of peach and soft rose, casting a warming light on the faces of those assembled.

The room was full of reluctant generals, and their haggard complexions needed all the flattering such a soft glow could offer. Mrithuri Rajni stood at the head of a long and wide sand table dotted with tiny figures, out of her full court garb and headdress but still formally painted. Beside her was Ata Akhimah. Along the far side of the table were two men the Gage had never seen before, the older one smaller and more scarred than the younger, both in tunics and trews but both with the look of soldiers.

Ata Akhimah quickly introduced them—the general and the lieutenant general, Madhukasa and Pranaj. The Dead Man had spoken to them about drilling the troops, the Gage knew, but this was the first that he, himself, had seen of them. He liked the way Madhukasa both deferred to his queen, and seemed always to be protectively but unobtrusively near. He reminded the Gage of a father walking alongside the pony upon which his child is learning to ride: protective, but careful to stay out of the way.

The queen's maid of honor—Yavashuri was her name—stood behind her and to her left, hands folded and head bowed. She was a sharp-faced woman of medium height, slender of bone but stout of flesh, her hair dressed plainly despite court. As if to make up for it, and her restrained jewelry, she wore a tunic and trousers that were somewhere in color between a ripe orange and a ripe peach, trimmed with bullion and crimson embroidery. Some part of the Gage's mind wondered where, where on the earth, the Sarath-Sahali peoples got these amazing dyes. They were known throughout the world for their colors—but the Gage was starting to believe that the best ones were never exported. This was some Wizardry to make his own construction seem a little plain and everyday.

Behind the women, Syama the bear-dog lolled on coffee-colored tile, the flecks of gold in her eyes picking up radiance from the flecks of gold in the glazing.

The Dead Man was not there, but before the Gage and the Godmade had even settled themselves on the near side of the sand table—both ducking chandeliers the whole way across the room—the door behind them opened one more time and the Dead Man slipped inside. He wore his threadbare red wool again, but the trousers and the shirt beneath it were new and clean and in the Sarathai style, so he'd taken a few moments to tidy himself after the practice field.

The Dead Man nodded to the room in general and to the Gage in particular. Then the Gage watched with a failure of surprise as the Dead Man crossed the entire room to stand beside the queen. That the queen turned her face to the Dead Man and cocked her eyebrows in a silent smile, though—that would have brought a frown to the Gage's face if he had one.

Well, if they were definitely staying, then, he might as well make himself comfortable. He wondered if there was a nice, reinforced, dry cellar somewhere he could set up with a heap of stones to serve as an unbreakable chair.

Mrithuri called their attention to the sand table once the introductions were all finished, and they gathered around it while the Wizard rolled up her sleeves. With a sweep of her hand, she gathered quartz dust and held it loosely, a soft thread filtering and falling between her fingers, its pale straw color warmed by the roseate light.

She said something then, singsong and under her breath so it was barely more than hummed, and when she moved her hand all the sand on the table moved with it. It rose up as if connected to the falling thread like a snake with a hook through its mouth, writhing and sliding, following her gestures and the sweep of that thin trickle. When she was done, the sand had piled itself neatly into what the Gage recognized immediately as a sort of topographical representation of a piece of unfamiliar terrain: a map, but in three dimensions.

The tiny figures—the Gage could see now that they were minuscule representations of men-at-arms, cast in lead and painted in any of several bright and easily distinguishable colors—had neatly sorted and stacked themselves against one edge of the sand table in the process. They were close to him and he would have liked to pick one up, weigh it in his hand and examine it more closely. But lead was soft: it would have dented under his lightest and most delicate touch. He left them be.

Once the map was completed, the Gage expected that either the general or his lieutenant would step forward and begin arranging the little men—some mounted, some afoot, some holding particular weapons or other banners. There were miniature cannons and siege engines too, and more than one tiny figure of an elephant.

He'd seen war elephants in use, and the giant beasts the Kyivvan called indrik-zver. He never cared to witness such again. Far more so for the sake of the beasts, as it happened, than for the inevitable savage carnage they wreaked among the men.

But it wasn't the general. It was the queen's maid of honor, Yavashuri, who stepped forward briskly once Ata Akhimah was done with the table and pulled her long henna-decorated fingers from her sleeves. Working with quick concentration and occasional glances at a list of notes on pale thick paper that was crumpled to softness in her hand, she set up the tiny figures as if she were laying out a board for a game of Rank and Ruin.

Each piece, the Gage knew, would likely represent not a single soldier but a company, a specialized battle group of some sort. Infantry, cavalry, pikemen, archers, musketeers, Wizards, cannon. And that did indeed seem to be how Yavashuri was deploying them. She spread little figures over the miniature hillsides for some time, but when she was finished the Gage felt the tension shift in the room. He leaned his own head to one side and considered the layout.

There were not so many of the enemy as he had feared, though more than he would have been happy to accept as a reasonable minimum to keep things challenging. What this was, though, was not an overwhelming force. Simply one against which the overmatched and inexperienced forces they had at hand could not reasonably hope to hold off without some sort of miracle. The Gage's help in combat, he knew, might prove to be exactly that sort of miracle.

If he'd been hoping for a clear direction to arise from better knowledge of the enemy, it seemed he would have to resign himself to being sadly disappointed.

"How did you come by this information?" Nizhvashiti asked, leaning forward. A long finger hovered over the sand table, but did not touch.

Yavashuri smiled coyly. "A woman has her wiles."

Yes, the Gage thought. And the wiliest woman is the one who is the queen's spymistress and will not admit it. *Prasana*, he guessed. She had been to interview Druja's injured brother. And probably other sources as well. Or possibly she was the face drawn over the true spymaster, who might be elsewhere among the queen's close courtiers.

The generals unselfconsciously asked Yavashuri questions about unit strengths and compositions. She knew rather a number of the answers, and had a good idea of her confidence level in the information, too. Like many of the better professionals that the Gage had known, she did not seem to invent information where she honestly had no clue.

"All right," the Dead Man said. "We know where they are and their relative strengths. That's something. Now what do we do about it?"

The queen, it turned out, was a brilliant tactician. And her handmaiden kept revealing new and intricate depths of knowledge, as did the generals. *Maybe we have a fighting chance after all*, the Gage thought, and tried not to think it again in case some god should overhear him. He was standing right next to a Godmade, after all, and while the Good Daughter might be dutiful, she was also known to be ruthless and to have a terrible sense of humor.

The Gage was almost equally impressed with the sand-table map. Ata Akhimah could animate the little figures and the terrain, make it simulate weather and troop condition, have them fight their miniature battles again and again with minor—or major—variations in tactics and conditions.

It was at first fascinating—the tiny figurines scaling sandy rises under withering hails of arrows, being crushed under death-or-glory charges, vanishing into trapped approaches and never emerging again—and became rapidly stultifying. Even for a metal man, there were only so many iterations of the same set of starting conditions through various possibilities that a mind could bear.

Or perhaps it was just that the Gage was not, and never had been, a particularly military-minded creature. When he had been human, she had been a potter, making useful and beautiful objects with the stroke of a fingertip and the turn of a wheel. He could fight—of course he could fight—but that was more a function of his monstrous metal armature than any skill or training.

Everybody else in the room seemed fascinated.

The generals and the Dead Man were head-bent over the eastern corner of the map, discussing the uses, dangers, and nuances of some bit of rough terrain. Nizhvashiti, the Wizard, the queen, and the spymistress were at the other corner, talking about chains of supply and if they could prevent, somehow, the Boneless's men from foraging.

"Not that there's much to forage from, there," Ata Akhimah said with some grim satisfaction. She had something small in her hand and was rolling it like a worry-stone: that damned dragonglass marble. "It's why the border at that point is so poorly defended. Rough terrain and not many people."

Mrithuri shook her head. Her brow folded between the eyes in thought; the Gage could already tell that in five or ten years, that would be the site of her first line. Her face was so smooth now that it seemed out of place with her wit.

She said, "That just means that he'll have to move faster. We need to be moving troops within a day and a night."

The Gage did not have to turn his head to see that the Dead Man was regarding her with fond respect. The Gage felt a welling of grief and protectiveness, some of it for his foolish-hearted partner, but more—most—for women of tender ages everywhere. *He can't have her, and his wanting her is only going to get all of us killed. Women like that marry princes; they don't do more than dally with mercenaries.*

Not if they know what's good for them.

The general looked like he was only constrained from spitting by respect for the inlaid floors. "Who starts a war in the rainy season?"

"A genius." The Dead Man shrugged when everybody looked at him. "Either that, or an imbecile."

The spymistress disguised as a handmaiden found some point in that she wanted to argue, and the Gage sighed inwardly and drifted away to look at the rain, which had begun once more falling. The windows of the map room overlooked the river, and he watched raindrops planish the milky surface and did not turn even when he heard Chaeri's voice behind him. The maid of the bedchamber was bringing in refreshments—strong sweet tea and spicy vegetables wrapped in thin, crackling pancakes—for those whose strength depended on rations. His own urge to speak with her would be transparent if he made some excuse to go over. Besides, he didn't need eyes on the back of his head to see her as she moved around the room, light-footed and full of energy.

So he stood and observed the rain and the river, and a single fishing boat sliding between those two things, and after a short time she came over to him.

They stood side by side, not so much shoulder to shoulder as shoulder to elbow, because he topped her by a third of his height.

Her breathing was slow and relaxed. Her hands smelled of cardamom and curry, strongly enough that the Gage reflected on how his
altered senses had become natural to him over the decades. Once he
would have remarked on how the scent, like his vision, seemed carried on the air around him, saturating, rather than focused at a point
or cluster in a nose he did not have. Now, he realized, he was remark-
ing on the absence of that nexus of sensing—something he had
also, generally speaking, ceased to do tens of years before.

Proximity to this odd little creature with the tousled curls was
making him aware of the limitations of his carapace in ways he had
not experienced since he first became it.

"What is a Gage?" Chaeri asked. Her skin moved against his metal
every time she breathed, where her shoulder brushed his arm.

"That is a complicated question," he replied. "In what sense do
you mean?"

"You were a woman with a woman's heart, a woman's hand. What
is this thing that you have become, that you chose to become? I want
to understand."

Who hurt you? The Gage thought. He did not think to wonder at
the how or the why. Women were all different, but each of them was
wounded in the same way by the world. The details of that wounding didn't signify much in the long run. They were, eventually, only
a matter of discussion for purposes of bonding and comparison.

He decided that he would answer her question literally, truthfully,
and see where it led them.

"A Gage is a pledge or a troth," he said. "Specifically one given in
battle—a security, guarantee, or parole in the sense of one's word-
of-honor. The word may also be used to mean something given as
security on a loan—a pawned object, basically. A gage is also an object used to take a measurement.

"And last but not least, it's an object thrown on the ground in
knightly challenge, such as a cap or gauntlet."

"So it's a pun," she said promptly.

He paused to consider. "When you put it that way, yes, I suppose it is. The Gage is one who is *engaged*—sworn—to the Wizard, and is also the Wizard's defender, and has also given themselves—their physical body—as a sort of security against the loan of strength, and Wizards being Wizards I'm sure there's a joke in there about 'taking the measure' of somebody, and also of challenging them. Or being the object by which another is challenged."

She said, "Also, it seems from what you are explaining that the Gage is owned, more or less, by the Wizard, so there's that."

"Yes," he simply said.

They stood and watched the rain a little. He thought she might be considering his words, working through the implications. At last the unease within him grew so great that he had to speak it.

He made sure his tone was low, intimate. He held out one brass hand between the girl and the window, and said, "What do you think I can do for you, exactly?"

"Everything," she said, and made a rude gesture. "But that." She looked at him speculatively. "Though you do appear to have hands...."

The Gage shifted restlessly, glad that mirrors could not flame with embarrassment. The imperviousness of his carapace was a blessing yet again.

"And with no risk of pregnancy," she pronounced, with a sly smile. Then she looked him up and down, speculatively. "Unless..."

"Unless?" he whispered, too aware of the men and women and the Godmade discussing tactics around the sand table. The Gage could see them all clearly, though his back was turned, and they appeared to be paying him and Chaeri no mind.

She rapped lightly on his upper arm. "What's under that skin? Is there still a person sealed in there?"

"I..." He paused and thought about the process of replacement, how one bit of his body at a time had been converted from fragile meat and bone to eternal metal and gears. Until at last in the final outcome, the armor was the Gage; the Gage was the armor. The Wizard's cat's-paw; the glove thrown down in challenge, unworn by any hand.

"I am the skin," he said.

"There's nothing underneath?"

He slowly shook his mirrored head, sending watery sparkles flashing around the room. Now the strategists glanced up, but seeing nothing amiss, quickly turned their attention back to war.

"No heart?" she asked. "No brain?"

"Nothing you could touch, and feel that you were touching me," the Gage replied. "Metal is what I am."

"And can metal feel?"

That, he knew the answer to. "Metal is alive," he said. "It bends to pressure; it stretches under blows. Work hardens it, and if you place it under too much stress it shatters. Yes. Metal can feel."

Feel too much, in fact. Feel so much more than it should.

She reached out with her soft, fragile hand and squeezed his unyielding fingers then.

12

SAYEH AWOKE TO THE SENSATION OF HER BED FALLING OUT FROM under her, and the baby's sudden baffled howl. Muffled by intervening walls, still Drupada's cry carried.

She struck the bed hard enough that it knocked the air out of her lungs and her jaw snapped together. It seemed to smack into her, shoving her upward, and then dropped again.

By the time she was trying to struggle into a sitting position upright in the bed, sheets tangling her legs like heavy, wet tentacles, the wooden platform buckled and pitched beneath her batten mattress like the deck of a ship. The baby's screaming was now echoed by the startled shrieks and yelps of adults, both in Sayeh's bedchamber and outside.

A tremor, it's just a tremor, she told herself. She rolled to the edge of the bed, trying to find her balance and get her feet under her. She wore only a plain, short shift—the rajni had decided years before that she had nothing to prove in her own bedchamber, and comfort for sleeping was preferable to ostentation—but when she tried to swing her legs away from the clutch of the sheets and get them under her, the bed pitched so violently against the floor that attempting to bridge the gap between them with her body seemed sure to get her crushed, battered, or slammed between.

The room was dark, dim daylight seeping in at the edges of the blackout drapes, and there were no lanterns. Tsering-la had made some undying witch-lanterns with which to illuminate the royal chamber. But they were shrouded and thus did Sayeh no good if neither she nor any of her maids couldn't manage to stand up to un-hood one, let alone find it in the pitching dark.

She heard heavy creaking in the dark and imagined the heavy canopy poles that held mosquito netting crashing down upon her body. She couldn't stand—she couldn't even sit or kneel without being pitched over again immediately. The initial hard bucking and rolling was dropping off now—how long had it been? Minutes? Merely moments? She could not guess—the world had always been shaking.

Finally, with a last residual shudder like the hide of a horse flinch-ing from a fly, the trembling stopped. Sayeh dragged herself to her feet, coughing. The air was thick with dust. Someone appeared beside her in the dark, a white-clad reverse shadow, and threw something warm over her shoulders. "Rajni"—a woman's voice—"we must leave the palace, Rajni. There may be another tremor."

"Drupada," Sayeh said. She could not hear the baby crying any-more. "Take me to the nursery at once."

"Rajni!"

Sayeh would hear no protests, and her people would not lay hands on her to stop her, which is what would have been required. She pushed through them, found one of the shrouded witch-lanterns on its side on the floor, and picked it up. Shards of glass spilled from the frame as she lifted it, cutting her fingers somewhat. The cloth slipped away and light poured out, revealing billows of pale dust in the air: powdered mortar or stone. Sayeh hoped that the dragonglass in some of the palace windows had not cracked. If there was dust from that mixed in, and she or her people breathed it, it would poi-son them as surely as would tea of aconite.

One of her women handed Sayeh a scarf, which the rajni wrapped

over her face. Her breath still came in chalky, and even more restricted, and her eyes clogged with grit the tears that streaked her
powdery face could not wash free. They were all coughing and wiping their faces, and suddenly Captain Vidhya was with them, choking and struggling, clutching a piece of muslin to his face.

"Rajni," he said urgently. "We must get out of the palace at once.
There will be aftershocks."

"Drupada!" she insisted, pushing past him toward the nursery.
He could have stopped her easily, but Sayeh was certain that he would
never lay hands on her either.

Nor did he, whether out of habit or out of respect.

Sayeh charged down the hallway toward the nursery. The dust was
thicker here, her eyes now streaming so hard she could barely blink
them clear enough to see even vague shapes, despite the caged witch-
lantern she thrust out before her. Something wet slid down her arm
and dripped from her elbow as she raised the lantern. Blood, from
where she had cut herself on the shattered glass.

At least it wasn't dragonglass, she thought, then put the thought
away. Because ahead of her she saw the cracked doorframe and twisted
door of the nursery, the arch slumping over it, the keystone cracked
clean in two. The halves had slid, and the weight of the wall above
and the second story of the palace now rested entirely on the wooden
uprights of the door. They had splintered and bent but not quite
buckled, and the door was sprung in its hinges.

A knife of ice had slipped into Sayeh's chest. Her heart felt as if it
slashed itself with every beat, as if the insides of her ribs had become
a cage of knives. "Drupada," she whispered. "Jagati." She tried to
shout the nurse's name: it came out a breathless moan, as when she
tried to scream in a nightmare.

She went to the door. The gap was slight—a thin woman's width
and no more. Splinters of wood and jagged blocks of stone rendered
it sharp-edged and unstable to entry.

More blood dripped as Sayeh studied it, sickly sticky streaks
through the white dust on her skin. She wanted to hurl herself at the

narrow passage, to tear at the kindling and stone chips, but that would be her own death as well as Drupada's. And perhaps—she could see within, a narrow slice of floor. There was rubble and dust, but no great boulders or heavy lengths of beam strewn on the tile.

The earth pitched beneath Sayeh then. She heard her women shriek, Vidhya swear. The doorway groaned. Her captain reached to take her arm and draw her back. He got as far as laying his finger-tips on her shift before his courage failed him—but when the rajni would not be moved, he desisted. She would have fought with every-thing she had if he had tried to move her now.

For within the nursery, she had heard a small, terrified whimper, a young animal's fearful cry.

Her women were plump, middle-aged. Vidhya was a broad-shouldered, deep-chested, barrel-stomached man past his first youth—and his second youth, too, if Sayeh was honest about it. There was one person here who could go into the room, and Sayeh knew if she gave them the slightest indication of what she intended, they would do anything—even commit the treason of laying rough, re-straining hands on her person—to stop her.

"Captain," she said to Vidhya, struggling to keep her voice calm. "Where are your men?"

"Overseeing the evacuation," he answered promptly. "I came for you myself."

She nodded. "Have you seen Tsering-la? Or his new apprentice Nazia, the little slight strong one?"

"Tsering was shoring up the main gates when I left him."

"Send one of my women for his apprentice," Sayeh said, with a little gesture to the door.

Vidhya stepped back away from her, and as he turned to speak to the closest maid of the bedchamber, Sayeh darted forward, turning sideways and slipping like a dancer between the splintered upright and the edge of the cracked door. She was within with her caged witch-lantern before Vidhya could even respond to her woman's startled cry.

And once inside, she froze.

The real damage in the room had not been visible through the angle of the door crevice, in that restricted light. Now that she was inside, the witch-lantern and the shafts of dim daylight filtering through the rents in the ceiling revealed the terrible truth.

The ceiling had not collapsed, not totally, but thick beams had slipped from their divots in the wall tops and leaned crazily together, supported by one solitary undamaged crossbeam. That beam bowed crazily under the load. And in the corner of the room farthest from the exterior wall, a beam had come all the way down, and blocks of stone and all the stuff of construction that Sayeh had not the engineering skills to name were scattered on the floor by Drupada's crib.

There was a hue outside, Vidhya and the women yelling after her, but Sayeh could not consider it now. She could barely even hear it over the roar of panic in her ears.

Good Mother, Sayeh thought. *Save my child, and I will make you any sacrifice you ask with glad heart, up to and including that heart's own blood.*

She stepped forward. There was blood, red and sticky, and more horrible things than that scattered on the floor. She caught her breath and made herself take another step and another, until she was close enough to the crib to raise the witch-lantern and take a better look.

She hated herself that her small cry was as much relief as despair.

There was a body sprawled across the crib, blood still spilling from a savage head wound, though more slowly than it must at first have done. But it was not Drupada; it was his nurse Jagati, and under the arch of her corpse—it could not be other than a corpse, not with a wound like that and the blood already slowing—the boy huddled, seemingly safe and terrified. Jagati had covered her charge with her own body, and she had died for her pains.

Good Mother, preserve her. And preserve her children, too, as she sacrificed herself for mine. Sayeh would have to find them, and make sure they were raised well and provided for. It was the least a rajni could do in such a circumstance.

Sayeh looked at her child, and not at Jagati. She could not bear to regard the dead woman, even out of the corner of her eye. So she stared at Drupada through the settling masonry dust, glad of the grit that obscured her vision and blurred her eyes. Drupada's eyes were huge, his hair slicked to his head with blood Sayeh told herself was not his own, could not be his own. Surely, Jagati in her great courage had taken on the hurt for both of them. Surely she had.

Sayeh walked toward the crib slowly, hand extended, and waited until he seemed to notice her. He was huddled small, his arms wrapped around himself, ducked down like a cub in a den. He flinched when he saw her, then opened his mouth and closed it again. The only sound that came out of him was a thin, high whine.

"Little king?" Sayeh asked him, when he finally seemed to recognize her and settle back into himself, so it seemed less like his spirit haunted an unrelated body and more like her little boy looked at her out of wide, frightened eyes.

"Mama?" he said.

She looked at the creaking beams, the crib, the dust sifting from the cracked stones overhead. *Go if you're going,* she told herself.

She walked forward quickly, confidently, reaching out with both hands to pick Drupada up. His tiny hands were knotted in Jagati's bloody tunic. Sayeh had to tuck the boy under her arm and pry them loose with the other hand, talking soothingly all the while. He squirmed and kicked. She kept one eye on the canted beams overhead and when she had him free turned back at once.

Voices were calling her from the corridor again. She wasn't sure if they had paused, or if she had merely ceased to hear them for a time. She stepped quickly, remembering now that her feet were bare when splinters and broken stone chips pressed into them. Where she stepped, she left patches of blood behind. Drupada was heavy in her arms, face buried sticky with tears and blood against her throat where he'd burrowed through the scarf wrapping her face to get to skin. The witch-lantern was at least cold, though she still had to keep its jagged shards away from his tender flesh, and in the process she cut herself on them again.

Scratches stung on her bare arms and thighs. She almost sobbed as she saw lights moving beyond the door. All she had to do was pass Drupada through, into Vidhya's arms, and squeeze there herself. All she had to do.

The floor pitched under her. Kicked up against her bare bloody soles and then dropped so far that she was left kicking in midair. She fell, clutching at Drupada reflexively, curling her body around his so when she landed badly on a sideways foot, she rolled and tumbled to the floor and could not break her fall. She grunted as the wind was knocked out of her, and then the air kept going in a rush. Her lungs cramped; she could not get a breath. The pain was stunning.

She clutched her boy as the witch-lantern tumbled away into the rubble, its dim light made dimmer by suspended dust. She could not see the door.

Sharp fragments lacerated her skin. She curled tight around Drupada as the ceiling hissed and settled overhead. Wood cracked; stone shattered. She felt herself begin to scream, and thought, *A rajni would not do such a thing*. It didn't matter: she had no breath for more than a thin keening. A huge, breathless rumble shuddered through the room, a sound so low and deep she felt it through her bones and not her hearing. It jarred something loose in her belly, and suddenly she could get a breath. She gasped for air desperately, then coughed, retched, as the dust filled her lungs.

The earth rolled under her, huge unsettling waves as if she were tossed on a ship. She gagged, tried to push herself up. Drupada clung around her neck, choking her, screaming between his own desperate hacking coughs. She got an arm straight and pushed herself to her knees.

There came a tremendous, splintering thunder. A cascade of brown water dashed down on Sayeh's hair. The pressure of the air in the room changed like a blow. She saw the suspended ceiling move, the great bowed crossbeam splintering, and hunched herself over her son. Nothing but her own frail soft bleeding body—

It fell with a landslide thunder. She cringed instinctively, awaiting the blow, without even time to wonder if she would feel anything.

She did not. For a long, timeless instant . . . no blow fell.

She was tucked, cramped into the protective position. It took long moments, two dozen racing heartbeats or more, before the calls of voices penetrated her stupor. Someone shouted her name, shouted urgently, "Rajni! Hurry! *Hurry!*"

She lifted her chin. Looked up. Saw a mauve light suffusing the room, or what remained of the room. Saw, through the swirling dust, the enormous blocks of stone and splintered tree trunks suspended a hand's-breath above her, embedded in light. Saw the mass of it pulse like a breath.

She looked up, then, and saw the broken door hauled wide. Figures, silhouetted beyond it. Moving lights. A figure in a skirted swirl of black with violet flames licking his hands. A girl with a shaved head, slight to starving, running crouched into the nursery. Nazia, who grasped Sayeh's wrist in her burned hands as if there were no difference in rank between them, and hauled the rajni up, supporting half her weight and the weight of her son, so they could slither and scramble under the heaving rubble to the door.

They were barely in the corridor, bloodied and dust-choked, when Tsering-la gave a great pained sigh like an ox heaving a plow through knotty turf, and let fall his light-wrapped hands.

Behind the wall, there was a terrible thunder, and more dust rolled forth through the shattered door. Sayeh hugged her son to her and crooned his name over and over while he clutched her and whimpered his wet-nurse's name.

Sayeh met Nazia's eyes over her child's dark hair. They were wide and wild and deep as the Bitter Sea. This was the girl who had tried to bring down her reign through ill portents. This was the girl who might have succeeded.

This was the girl who had saved her life, and the life of her only child.

They stared at one another.

"I won't forget that," Sayeh said. She turned to Vidhya. "We need to get everyone out of the palace, out of every stone building, now."

✳   ✳   ✳

THE RAIN FELL THICK AND STEADILY OUTSIDE AS SAYEH STAGGERED INTO the dark day, supported by Tsering at one elbow and Vidhya at the other. She clutched Drupada to her chest. The child was no longer howling, not even sniveling, and his silence scared her more than any noise could.

At least the rain was warm. At least it washed the blood and masonry dust from her face and limbs. Her feet hurt, now: Sayeh could not so much feel each individual cut or slice—except when the wet flagstones happened to sting in one of them—so much as just a scalded sensation over the entire surface of the soles. She limped; she still left blood behind, she was sure. One of her women tried to relieve her of Drupada, but she clutched him tighter to her, reassured when he suddenly gave a little squeak of protest.

The rain felt good. She turned her face up to it, letting it run unfettered through her hair and down the front of her nightdress. She knew it plastered the thin cloth to her and revealed her body without any art or artifice to cover her, and this once she did not care. She was alive, and her son was alive, and it might so easily have been otherwise.

"Feel the rain, little king?" she asked him. Relief and joy fizzed in her veins like alcohol. "That rain is the Good Mother's benediction on us this day."

She heard Vidhya ask Tsering how long until the veil set and the rain might taper off, how long until the night sky would brighten their prospect enough to search for survivors.

"I'll make light," Tsering replied. "If there are survivors, they cannot wait until sunset to be found."

Sayeh sobered. She must be a rajni now—a mother to all her people—and not merely a mother to her son. She must see to it that such help as was possible came to those in the palace and to those as well in the city beyond as might need it.

She gritted her teeth and handed Drupada to her closest lady. "Find something woolen to wrap him in. And someplace to get him out of the rain."

"Rajni," the woman said, and vanished with one of Tsering-la's witch-lanterns burning on her shoulder to light her way, and one of Vidhya's guards at her elbow.

"What do we need?" Sayeh asked.

"Troops," Tsering said. "Anyone who can listen for the voices of the trapped. Anyone who can dig to free them."

"There may be more aftershocks." The voice came from behind Sayeh. Momentarily, she startled, then flushed warm with relief to realize that the words came from the slight elderly frame of the poetess Ümmühan. "We must be careful about digging, yet, or allowing anyone to go within."

Even more warmth filled Sayeh when she saw what the poetess held in her arms. A bundle of cloth, richly figured—Sayeh recognized a tapestry from the throne room—and emerging from it the bedraggled, broken-feathered head of a very sleepy, very sullen phoenix.

"Well, I couldn't very well leave him," Ümmühan said irritably, seeing the direction of Sayeh's gaze.

Sayeh realized the poetess was fully dressed, with sandals on her feet. "You were awake?"

"I am old. The old don't sleep much. I was wandering." The brusqueness of the poetess's voice was belied by the gentleness of her hand as she stroked the head of the unhappy phoenix.

Around them, the courtyard was filling up with a reassuring number of survivors. They clustered together, some who had thought to grab bedclothes or warm wraps sharing them with others. Somebody brought Sayeh a shawl of softest woven goathair, dyed with shades of blue in a coiling, teardrop pattern. It stank of wet goat, but she accepted it gratefully and pulled a corner up over her head to protect her from the continued downpour.

Tsering glanced at the poetess with what Sayeh recognized as respect. "Do you have recommendations, grandmother? Have you seen this sort of thing before?"

"I was there when Asitaneh burned," she said. "But that was a different sort of disaster."

"Different?" Sayeh asked.

Nazia had taken Vidhya aside. Their heads were bent together—over what, Sayeh currently had not the energy to wonder.

The poetess grimaced, folds rearranging in the topography of her weathered face as if she, too, underwent some sort of internal tremor. Sayeh could not tell how many of the droplets coursing through the creases of the old woman's skin were tears, if in fact any were. Ümmühan said, "In that case, it was an act of war. There was a djinn."

"Ah," said Tsering, as if he had heard of such . . . weapons? Such creatures?

Sayeh gave him a curious look.

"A sort of spirit," he said. "A spirit of fire."

Ümmühan nodded. "One of the most powerful of the djinn, it was." She shook her head as if shaking off water, or the memory. "This was not like that."

"No," Tsering agreed. "I think this was another sign that the volcano under the Bitter Sea is coming to life again. I think that we need to evacuate, to flee west into the hills. High ground, and quickly."

Sayeh's first reaction was to storm and swear, to insist she would never abandon Ansh-Sahal and flee. That not fire nor flood could move her.

She glanced after her woman, bearing Drupada away, but the mauve light had faded into distance. She hoped they had found someplace warm and dry that was not in immediate danger of collapsing. She might stay here in danger herself, as rajni of this place, knowing that if she surrendered the seat of the throne she placed the throne itself in danger. But she could not so risk her son, and right now, nor could she bear to be parted from him.

"All right," she said. "We'll make plans for evacuation. We can retreat into the foothills and find shelter there. Someone needs to find Jagati's family and see that they are provided for, and given means to escape."

"The whole city will have to take to their heels," Ümmühan said. "If Tsering is right—"

"Anyone who stays is doomed," Sayeh agreed. "I am abandoning my throne and my palace. I can give no stronger recommendation than that that they accompany me."

SLOWLY, VIDHYA ORGANIZED HIS MEN, AND WITH HELP FROM NAZIA as a messenger—that must have been what they were talking over—he had search-and-rescue teams in place before the rain tapered off and the brightness of nightfall began to dust the horizon. At first they quickly brought out the dead—not too many of those, thank the Good Daughter and her Mother—and those who had been too injured to extricate themselves but who were not pinned or crushed or otherwise trapped within the collapsed portions of the structure.

Then the harder work began. Tsering-la was unrelentingly busy when it came to locating and extricating the victims of collapse. But so, it turned out, was Ümmühan, who had some surprising knowledge of architecture and engineering. Apparently she had in one place or another spent considerable time with an Aezin Wizard who was also an architect. And Nazia proved indispensable worming her way into confined spaces with little air or room to maneuver. She was fearless, and even when her acid-burned hands broke their blisters and bled through the bandages she did not hesitate or complain.

Sayeh tried to emulate her. Tsering had picked the broken shards from her soles. And someone had found her a pair of slippers—too large, but she wrapped her feet in rags and they stayed on—but it was all she could do to sit in a chair under a hastily erected fabric awning and try to direct her men and women in a series of fraught, exhausting, dangerous tasks for which she had no skill and little knowledge of how to proceed. Guang Bao roosted on the back of the chair, his feathers fluffing a little now that they were under shelter, offering an occasional low stream of nonsensical commentary that at least cheered Sayeh, if it accomplished nothing else. He preened her hair, too, and once bit her quite hard on the neck in jealousy when Vidhya leaned down too close.

And then the refugees from the city below began to trickle in.

With them came reports of protests and disarray, and Vidhya, his face troubled, came and knelt at Sayeh's feet and told her that the city watch had declared martial law without consulting her. She bit her lip: depending on the motivation, it was a vote of no-confidence in her abilities as rajni that was tantamount to treason. But deniable—if she had the strength to confront them on it, they could claim that messages had not gone through, and that they had done the best they could in the absence of instruction. In the meantime, Vidhya informed her, they were enforcing a curfew, and returning people to their damaged homes.

"There could be another tremor," said Ümmühan, who happened to have returned to Sayeh's side for a consultation. "There *will* be another tremor."

Sayeh nodded, the knowledge cold in her throat, stark around her breast like a cooper's bands. That was good, she thought—such bands bound the barrel staves tightly into a barrel, and at the moment she felt that she might fly apart at any provocation. So the pain served a purpose. It held her together.

"Do you or Tsering-la have any idea how long?"

The poetess shrugged. "Could be a heartbeat. Could be days." She rubbed her forehead with the heel of her hand, pressed her eyes. For a moment, her lids closed, the light of cleverness and courage went out of her face, and all Sayeh could see was how tired Ümmühan was.

How brutally tired.

She looked like that herself, she was sure. Perhaps there was tea to be had somewhere in the ruin of the palace. She should call for some, for both of them. No, she should make sure that there was a kitchen running under a tarpaulin somewhere, and hot tea and rice gruel—at the very least—for everyone.

She cupped her hand to summon one of the young recruits that Captain Vidhya had loaned her as pages, especially as she herself could move no faster than a hobble on her bandaged feet. But a hubbub from that quarter drew her attention, and she caught the swirl of some bright-colored commotion that she could not, quite, turn her head far enough to see. She pushed at the arms of her chair, and suddenly Ümmühan was there to support her—a strange role reversal, the old woman steadying the younger—while Sayeh struggled to her feet.

Those recruits—there were three of them, unarmed and clad only in tunics—were giving way quite sensibly before a rank, a wedge, of armed and mounted men. Hooves clopped on the flagstones, heads bobbed under still-damp plumes.

The horse's caparisons were richly colored in shades of red, brown, and gold. Most striking among them was a mare gray as silver, her hide strewn with dapples like the marks where the mastersmith's hammer had dimpled the thing he forged. On her back, with the grace of a master horseman, sat a crumpled figure with elegantly dressed black ringlets and a brow that made you imagine that grave and stately thoughts must exist behind it.

Himadra the Boneless, the prince of Chandranath. It could be no other.

Sayeh hastily resumed her chair. She would not stand to meet this foreign lord in her own courtyard, even if he came uninvited and found her bloodied, wounded, terrorized, and dressed more like a pauper than a rajni.

She still had a gilded chair and a phoenix to perch on the back of it, though—and a poetess to stand at her right hand. Sayeh glanced at Ümmühan and found the old woman regarding her steadily.

"The neighbors?" she said softly, in a savvy tone.

Sayeh nodded, the crisp nod of a rajni in public now. She did not deign to notice the armed men.

"Seems a little far to get here overnight. They must have been on their way already."

"There is probably an army beyond the Razorback Mountains," Sayeh replied through stiff lips—behind her hand because she did not have a fan. "I've been expecting this, or something like it. Where's Vidhya? Tsering-la?"

Ümmühan shook her head. But she strode forward with a high

head and the bearing of one entrusted to a great and ceremonious office. She called out. As she was facing away from Sayeh, and she did have somewhat of an accent, her words were unintelligible to the rajni. But her voice was like a lash.

The cutting tones of a court poet long trained to declaim in vast, crowded, echoing spaces clove the bright night, and had as much effect on the mounted men as if they had run into a wall.

From her chair, resolutely sitting with her spine untwisted and her hands relaxed in her lap, Sayeh could only see from the corner of her eye. But that glimpse was enough.

She did not think the men had *chosen* to stop at Ümmühan's challenge. But they were mounted, and the moment of hesitation and uncertainty they had felt when she stood up to them boldly and in challenge had been sensed by their horses, which now pawed and stepped in place. The gray mare alone seemed more watchful than restive. She was a war horse, Sayeh now understood, and it was her place to be calm and certain when all around her shuddered with their fear of what was coming.

Having broken the advance, Ümmühan made her own now. And such was her charisma that she swept the disarrayed recruits into her wake. They found their courage, that this woman as old as their great-grandmothers stepped up and raised the flat of her hand to two dozen mounted warriors.

"Who approaches the rajni's seat?" Ümmühan asked. Now Sayeh heard her clearly, for she need not compete with the clatter of hooves.

Sayeh allowed herself to turn her head when the answer was slow in coming. She made sure it was imperious—a lifted chin and a glance down the nose beneath lashes—and because of that she witnessed a hasty consultation between the man she knew as Himadra and the man who rode at his left.

The man—tall and well-formed, with a warrior's red rectangular wrap trimmed in wolf fur thrown carelessly around his shoulders—seemed to be arguing with his lord, though softly. His horse sidled with his vehemence, and his hand gestures were sharp and abbreviated. His saddlecloth was a tiger skin. Himadra sat and listened peaceably enough. But then he shook his head. The other man seemed inclined to argue. Himadra pinned him with a glance as imperturbable as that of his mare, and that was the end of it.

Sayeh felt a moment of spiking envy for that power of command. She was as good a leader as any man: she knew it. She gave more and cared more about her people and was better at juggling logistics, tactics, strategies.

But she did not have that charisma, that effortless force of command. And right now, she sorely coveted it.

Himadra raised a hand, gesturing his men back. And they stayed, to a one, as he reined his gray forward without any gesture so gross it would be visible to her across the courtyard. She took two gliding steps and hesitated again, then made a little bow at some command Sayeh could not discern. "I am Himadra," he said in a clear and cultivated voice. "Raja of Chandranath. I wish leave to approach the rajni and with her share a word in confidence."

"You alone," Ümmühan said, with a glance at Sayeh to see what she wanted.

Himadra touched his bright felt cap. He gestured to his body, shrunken and strange. "Will you deny a cripple his gentle mare? I assure you, my Velvet will do no harm to anyone."

Not unless you command it, Sayeh thought, but allowed Ümmühan a slight nod. If Himadra wished to kill her now, no geriatric poetess was going to prevent him, no matter how otherworldly the force of the woman's personality.

"You may go forward mounted, then," Ümmühan agreed, without the slightest hint that she in any particular disagreed with Sayeh's decision. "You, Your Competence, and you alone."

He smiled—quite dazzling, really. For all his formidable reputation of brilliance as a war leader, Sayeh realized—or remembered—Himadra was only a little more than half her own age.

The mare glided around in a soft circle, her pale hooves barely clicking as she set them down on the still-wet cobblestones. Himadra stopped her before Sayeh's chair, some dozen steps respectfully back, and doffed his own cap while he made the mare perform an even deeper and more elaborate bow.

"Sayeh Rajni," he said, when the mare had straightened herself up once more with a lash of her bannery tail. "Royal cousin. I am sorry my visit comes at such an inconvenient time."

Sayeh did her best to forget her disarray, her frizzed and knotted hair, her haphazard clothing. She smiled and said, "Perhaps if we had received proper notice of a state visit, we would have waited to remodel the palace until we had offered you proper hospitality."

He smiled, and with his crooked thumb indicated the man with the wolf-trimmed cloak. "My ally Ravana and I come to offer assistance, royal cousin. I witnessed the earthquake from the hill road. Understanding that your people must be suffering, I took the fastest of my vanguard, leaving all the rest behind, and rode hard through the day and most of the night to reach Ansh-Sahal. Tell us how we can be of help? My men are hardy, hardened warriors, and will not scruple to sleep on the earth or labor hard to rescue such subjects of yours as may be trapped in the rubble of their homes."

That, translated, meant that an army was at his heels, as she had suspected. And that there was very little way she could refuse his assistance, thereby becoming beholden to him. A debt, no doubt, that could be discharged by a marriage or some other dynastic concession.

He laid his cap across his saddlebow. Looking up at him was giving her a pain in the neck, but she would not offer him the smallest hint of it.

Especially not when he, having waited a few seconds to see if she might speak, took another breath and continued, "Your heir, royal cousin. My young cousin Prince Drupada. I hope he is well?"

If he wasn't, that was one more reason, after all, for her to marry. She did not think the Good Mother would bless her again: to carry a child to term was rare enough for one such as her. To give birth and live, even rarer. She had Tsering-la's skill to thank for that.

And if she allowed herself to be coerced into marrying Himadra . . .

well, it was said that the Boneless was impotent. And even if he were not, could he father a child that lived? That mattered little, however, as he had several brothers, some much younger. Perhaps he had her in mind for one of them.

She did not imagine an heir of her body with no connection to Himadra's blood would long survive any dynastic marriage she might offer to the house of Chandranath. All those brothers . . . Himadra must be eager indeed to secure an extra kingdom or two to divide up and pass on to them, or to their sons.

How ironic that it was the scion of the Alchemical Emperor's line with the poorest patrimony that had borne the most abundant fruit.

"My son is well, Cousin," she said lightly. "Thank you for your concern. We were lucky: the palace withstood the first shock, and most successfully evacuated before the second began to bring the roof down. And even that damage was only in places. My household and men-at-arms are intact. I assure you."

"Very intact," said a welcome voice from nearby. Sayeh's focus had narrowed so completely onto her charming enemy that she had not even noticed Vidhya's return, or that he came along with Tsering-la and ten mounted men-at-arms. One of those dissolving recruits had apparently managed to think on his feet after all and send for help without Sayeh noticing.

Sayeh heaved one soft sigh, and allowed herself to relax back against the cushions slightly, though she kept her posture queenly. Guang Bao spread his wings to shade her, framing her tumbled hair in such glory as no crown could emulate. If Himadra had managed to bring his entire army to her broken gates, then nothing they did could have stopped him. But he had only two dozen men. And she had, albeit wounded, a city entire.

Tsering-la had allowed a bit of witchlight to creep out of the crevices between his fingers. Just enough that though it was not very bright and that soft shade of mauve, it made the stained and tattered fabric of his Wizard's coat seem unfathomably black. Vidhya stretched his wrists casually, showing as if by accident scarred bracers.

Himadra glanced at his men. One touched his nose with a fingertip. It might have been a signal, or perhaps it was just an itch. Whatever the case, Himadra looked back at Sayeh and nodded. "Madam," he said, "my men have ridden a day and a night to come here. We and our horses are tired. May we camp beyond your walls, and begin assisting in shifts with the rescue?"

There was no gracious way to refuse.

TSERING-LA BROUGHT THE NEWS THAT THE GUARD WHO HAD BEEN with Drupada and the temporary nurse had been found dead in the pavilion erected as a makeshift nursery a little before nightfall of the next day, when all was darkest and most cold. Sayeh, who had not slept, but who at least had managed to bathe in cold water and who had been found some plain but suitable clothing, stared at him as he stammered and explained that the nurse—and the boy—were missing.

"Himadra," she snarled, rising to her feet. She ignored the shock of pain from swollen flesh. Despite Tsering-la's arts, there were infections. Due to Tsering-la and Ümmühan, however, those infections were unlikely to kill her. Or even lose her feet for her.

"His camp—" Ümmühan started. She stopped. She looked to Tsering-la for support.

Sayeh snarled wordless rage. If she were queenly then, she did not know it. She felt a mother's fury, sharp and hard.

"Where is my son?" she cried. "Where is Drupada?"

"The camp is empty," Tsering-la said. "They deserted tents, cookfires, and even a few horses—enough to make it look inhabited at a distant glance. Himadra and all his men are gone."

SHE WAS RAJNI, AND NO ONE COULD RESTRAIN HER. TSERING-LA MIGHT even have endured her blows, but when she seemed ready to turn her fists on Ümmühan, or anyone who would come close to her, he wrapped everyone around her in a bubble of soft light that did not let her come close. At last, it was Nazia—Nazia, already condemned—who calmed her by throwing a bucket of cold salt water on her.

Plain water, as it happened. Not the burning, bitter sort.

Her rage spent, she gave chase to her son's kidnappers herself. She would not be prevented. Vidhya tried to keep her from the saddle, and she looked at him and said, "If I were his father, would you try to stop me?"

The captain of her guard, the companion of her youth, met her gaze without flinching before he stepped aside.

He held the reins himself while she mounted.

She could not take too many men. They were needed in the palace. They were needed in the city. She took Vidhya and a handpicked few of his soldiers—five in all, shamefully little to bring against twenty-odd warriors. She took Nazia, because Nazia was not afraid of her, even in this mood, and anyway she was now an apprentice Wizard and fit to any use. She took Tsering-la because he was her Wizard, and she took Ümmühan for advice.

And she took Guang Bao, too, because there was nowhere to leave him. And because he comforted her.

They took remounts, at least, because there was no reason to leave behind horses that were not draft animals, broken to harness and trained to pull. Some of the remounts were those Himadra himself had left behind, an irony that gave Sayeh a small, bitter pleasure.

They rode as if the rising river itself, wrathful and swollen, were at their heels. They rode as if the moon were burning, as if the Heavenly River were cascading down upon their heads. They rode to reach Drupada and his kidnappers before those kidnappers reached Himadra's army, because at that moment he would be lost to them forever, and that, every one of them knew.

They rode, and every one of them pretended not to be searching the verge of the highway for a tiny, shattered corpse with every stride.

That they found no such object was a comfort and a torment both. A comfort, because it meant there was a chance that Drupada was still alive. If Himadra had merely wanted him dead, he could have killed him with the guard instead of snatching him up nurse and all. A torment, because so long as they found no body, they must ride.

The stirrups—a technology borrowed from the tribesmen beyond the Steles of the Sky within Sayeh's lifetime—goaded her lacerated feet.

Vidhya, following the tracks of their dozens of horses in the muddied road, said that Sayeh's smaller group on their fresh horses were gaining. But slowly, too slowly. Whether they caught the invaders or not had a great deal to do with where, exactly, the army was.

Sayeh took Guang Bao up from his perch on the saddlebow and whispered in the phoenix's ear: fly low, be safe. Beware of archers. But fly ahead and see how far we have yet to ride.

When he had been gone for a tenth part of the day, she began to fret anew—that he had flown off, that she had sent him to his death. He was a clever bird. But he was a bird, and not clever as humans are clever.

Finally he returned as it began to rain again, bedraggled with wet but unharmed. "Found prince," he croaked in his cracked old voice. "Came back."

"Did you see the army?"

"Not yet," the bird said. "No army."

The phoenix flew much faster than a horse could gallop. Sayeh tried some calculations in her head, sighed, and gave it up. Tsering said, "They are a dozen li ahead or more."

Sayeh cursed and punched herself in the thigh hard enough to make her mare sidle. "How do they ride so fast?"

"They had a head start," Vidhya said. "Let us change saddles to our remounts and ride on."

THEY RODE ON. THEY WERE CLIMBING THE FOOTHILLS NOW, THE Razorbacks rising in heavy tiers of ridges before them. The hills deserved their name. They were sharp-topped and angled, steeper on one side than the other, so in profile they resembled enormous sand dunes.

Thankfully, they were not, however, sandy. Instead they were made of heavy bands of clay in shades of ochre, white, and dusky violet. The spiky plants that grew on their more gentle slopes were unusually verdant now, with the help of the rains. And the clay of the rising and falling roadbed was thick and slick, slippery and treacherous.

It slowed the horses greatly; they struggled and slid in the slop, and a fall could have meant skidding down the precipitous slope between the knife-sharp broken faces of flint boulders that jutted from the banks of the clay.

They had come so far from the Bitter Sea that they could not smell it, though gulls still circled and keened on the wind.

There were other scents. Some were the smells of the rain, of the broken resinous twigs of the scrub near the road. Some were unsettling ones, so rank that even though their presence was faint they still tainted the air. Brimstone and char, so that Sayeh thought of gunpowder. The thought made her rein her horse aside and retch, though her stomach was empty. Nazia urged her to drink some broth, some rice gruel. Merely holding the cup before her mouth sufficed to make her gag.

They pushed on to exhaustion and beyond. None of them had been at their best to begin with. And now, Sayeh grudged dismounting the horses even to answer a call of nature.

Half asleep, dozing in the saddle despite being too anxious to rest more than that, Sayeh wondered how long it would be before Tseringla and Vidhya revolted and forced a stop. They were drenched, worn out. Chafed from wet clothes rubbing between legs and saddles. Injured in various small ways. And yet, she could not admit defeat. She could not stop.

As her gelding's hooves splashed muddy water up her calves, she thought that if he bore her up to the ring of the army encampment itself and Drupada was not yet in her arms, she would ride right through it and surrender herself to Himadra. If she was his prisoner, as his royal cousin, she could expect to be treated gently. And allowed to see her son.

And all it would cost was her kingdom and her freedom. A price that at the moment seemed like no price at all.

The blow that struck her came so long before the sound of the explosion that she almost did not hear the massive thundering that followed. The narrow red ribbon of the wet road, clay slick in the rain, seemed to jump up beneath her gelding's hooves and twist him off, as if it were suddenly animated into an angry snake. He fell, and Sayeh shrieked, clutched his mane, and fell with him.

The impact knocked the breath from her body, and she heard her scream cut short. Around her, a confusion of slipping horses and shouting women and men. The heavy beat of Guang Bao's gilded wings as he broke his own fall above her: he must have instinctively released his grip on the saddlebow.

The earth heaved again. That was when the sound came, so vast that it was more a physical object that she found herself in the center of. Pain now, loose and quick in the leg that was pinned under her mount. The horse tried to heave himself up, failed, panicked and began to thrash and scream—horrible noises attenuated through the sudden dullness in her ears. Sayeh found herself sliding with him toward the dropoff at the outer edge of the road. Her head dangled over the edge. She could not breathe; she could not shriek for help. Her leg beneath the gelding felt as if it were being pulled in two.

Someone was there, grabbing her, holding her shoulders and head. No, it was light, mauve and dusty rose, Tsering's magic keeping her from falling. The horse gave one last terrible heave and fell silent, limp. Sayeh caught a glimpse of Vidhya standing from a crouch beside its head with his dagger streaming red.

Poor Star, she thought. Everything seemed far away, even the shouting, even the pain. Tsering was beside her for real now, holding her with his own hands. Someone was lifting the poor gelding's body and she screamed again, she thought, as she was drawn free.

In a just world, she would have fainted. If the Good Daughter were more merciful than dutiful, she might have spiraled away into darkness and relief. Instead, as they lifted her, she opened her eyes.

She saw a plume of ash and dust, a horrid roil of steam. The whole horizon was gray and white with it, the distant sea lost behind its veil. It was a wall as tall and broad as the vault of sky above, billowing and glittering and faintly translucent in the light of the heavens.

The whole of the Bitter Sea had exploded from beneath. Ansh-Sahal, like the historical kingdoms of Tsering-la's memory, was no more.

"Good Mother," Sayeh whispered. "What have you done?"

THEY COULD NOT HAVE OUTRUN THE WALL OF SMOKE AND STEAM, so it might have been for the best that it faded out and flowed apart before it reached the lowest of the hills east of and below them. Might have been for the best, though in her heart Sayeh wished it would roll over her, melt her flesh from her bones, end this incredible pain in her breast and belly that made the pain of her broken leg seem like a minor irritation at best.

Tsering-la glanced that way over and over again, frowning, though Sayeh could tell he struggled to keep his attention on her, suddenly transformed as she was from his rajni to his patient. Once it became evident that they were not all about to die immediately, Vidhya took command again. Sayeh was somewhat surprised to discover that Nazia was still with them. Her manner was brittle and distant, but she stayed.

They found a place off the road, level enough to raise a tarpaulin and call it a pavilion, though nobody bothered, just now, with walls. Ümmühan built a fire, smoky from lack of dry wood, and started preparations for tea. Meanwhile, with the help of two of the largest men-at-arms, Tsering-la and Vidhya set Sayeh's snapped bone.

She screamed for that, all right. Screamed, but still didn't faint.

She hadn't fainted either when Tsering cut Drupada from her belly. Now she wished she were weaker of spirit, so she could fall into a dreamless place and be untroubled instead of sending her nails savagely into Nazia's callused hands.

She had a hazy recollection that she had first ordered, and then begged and pleaded with her men to go on without her, to follow Himadra and do whatever it took to retrieve Drupada. They had ignored her, and eventually she had found her dignity, silenced herself, and let them work.

When her leg was splinted, though, it was another matter. Now, she asked Vidhya to complete a task she could not order him to: to turn her over to Himadra as a hostage so she could be near her son.

"I have no kingdom to return him to, even if we could catch up to them." Which she would not believe was impossible.

Vidhya shrugged. "We are alive, Rajni. Where there is breath, hope also lies. The evacuations you ordered had commenced: some of your people will have escaped. The Good Mother will see your loyalty, and perhaps she will aid you."

It was a useless argument, trying to send them away. But she made it, over and over, with variations. Ümmühan poured tea, and food was passed around, and the rain stopped—and Sayeh was *still* repeating her argument when a rising sound interrupted her. Vidhya jumped to his feet, turning, a hand cupped to his ear until the rumble resolved into the steady thunder of hundreds of hoofbeats drumming across the hillsides, reverberating with layered echoes rolling from the sharp escarpments of the neighboring hills.

"Where is it coming from?" Ümmühan asked.

Vidhya said, "I can't tell. I can't read the echoes. There are too many."

"But that's an army," Nazia said.

"Yes," Tsering said. "I think we found them."

SAYEH HITCHED HERSELF HIGHER ON THE DANK LINENS OF THE PALLET her people had made. She looked at them—Tsering, Vidhya, Nazia, the men-at-arms. Ümmühan, who was not hers, precisely, but who was under her authority and protection nonetheless.

They were staring, one and the other, each trying to decide if it was his or her decision to make. But Sayeh knew it was not any of theirs. It was her own.

"You have to flee," she said to Vidhya.

Her captain started to argue. She straightened her arms, pushing herself as upright as she could get, and stared him in the eye. "Silence, Captain."

He stammered to a halt.

She said, "You, Tsering, the men-at-arms. You will flee. Take Ümmühan. Himadra will not harm me: I am too useful to him for politics. All of you, he would kill. And there are too many of them even for a Wizard of Messaline to handle. Nazia—" She looked at the girl. "I won't order you to stay with me. But I will ask you. They will not forbid me a maid, and I should be able to protect you." She tapped her splinted leg. "I will need hands and feet that I can trust."

Nazia blinked, her expression startled. Perhaps pleased. By that word, "trust"? Sayeh hoped so. One who was flattered by trust would strive to be worthy of trust.

"I will not leave you, Rajni," she said in the formal inflections of an oath.

"Sayeh," Tsering said sternly, abandoning her title for what she thought was the first time. "If this is just to save our lives, while you get close, again, to Drupada—"

Irritation rose up in Sayeh, a sharp hot burst that they thought so little of her tactical sense as that. She hoped she kept it from her tone: she wanted them working with her because they were convinced her plan was a good one, not because she had commanded it.

"Mrithuri," she said. "Go to my cousin. Seek her help, offer her our men. Her lands are between those of Himadra and Anuraja. And it is she who holds the Peacock Throne, even if she cannot sit on it. Do you think for an instant that my bastard cousin thinks taking Drupada is anything except a prelude to an assault on her sovereignty? Go to her; help her. Take Guang Bao as proof of your service to her family, and ransom or rescue me when you can."

"Rajni—"

"I cannot *ride*, Vidhya!" she snapped. "You cannot get away if I am with you. So go; go now. And live to fight another day. Ümmühan—"

"Oh, no, Rajni," said the poetess with great dignity. "I am too old for such wild riding." (A patent lie, given how she had kept up on the chase.) "Besides that, I am a historian. Where else would I go but beside you?"

Sayeh imagined they made a strange picture to the soldiers riding up on them. Three women—one in the last dry season of old age, one in the first bare flush of youth, and the other a middle-aged shandha propped under an improvised awning—waiting beside a muddy road. She almost wished she could see herself and her companions through the eyes of those men.

She felt a swell of unease looking at them, though. Because they did not wear the mountain russets of Himadra's soldiers, but the blue and the orange ochre of her older cousin Anuraja, from the south. Two armies. There were two armies in her land. Or what had been her land, once upon a time not so very long ago. Was Anuraja allied with Himadra, then? For a moment, Sayeh wished she had her men back, to give them this bit of information as well. Mrithuri would need to know it.

Nazia had used her diver's hook knife to razor the saddle off the cinch that bound it to the dead gelding. She'd set it up across a small boulder and helped Sayeh onto it sideways, as a sort of throne. Sayeh stretched her broken leg out before her and loosely held a crooked crutch Nazia had also cut for her as if it were a scepter, though the end remained a bit higher than her head even with the butt resting on the ground.

Her broken leg was a constant, heavy presence, like an angry spouse. The pain clouded her thoughts. Tsering had left her poppy oil, and she had touched a little under her tongue—but enough poppy to do more than slightly dull the agony would do much more than slightly dull her wits. It was a cobra's bargain—suffer the venom, or be swallowed alive.

So she watched the vanguard of the army ride up to her, and she tried not to let the fear or the pain show on her features. A rajni was serene.

The men paused, seeming confused by the odd tableau of woman seated on a rock under a tarpaulin, dead horse, and attendant maiden and crone.

"Good afternoon," Sayeh said. "I am Sayeh Rajni of Ansh-Sahal. I have broken my leg in a fall from my gelding. Please bring my cousin, Himadra Raja, to me, that he and I may parley now."

AFTER SOME CONFUSION, THEY BROUGHT HER A LITTER. BEING LOADED into it hurt, quite fiercely as it happened. Sayeh was a rajni. She did not cry out.

They bore her along with them, Ümmühan riding with her and Nazia walking alongside. The girl trotted to keep up. They covered quite a distance, too—not just into the depths of the traveling column, but with it, and overland by crooked ways that Sayeh, drawing the curtains aside, was sure were leading them south. When she asked, the man who guarded her litter—who had a thick Sarathani accent and was difficult for her to decipher even when he spoke slowly and clearly—shook his head so his braid bobbed against his shoulders and said, "We're taking you to the raja, Rajni. I am sure he would not have it any other way."

So she was forced to be satisfied with that.

When they carried her and Ümmühan—and led Nazia—into the camp, it was obvious to Sayeh's experienced eye that it had been there for a while. Still, she saw very little sign of the russet livery she expected. A man here, a man there, scattered through the crowd wearing the uniform of Anuraja. How much of this army was his, after all? Where were all of Himadra's men? Where were even the men he had brought into Ansh-Sahal?

And how had he known that Ansh-Sahal was in such dire danger? Had it been but an accident of timing? Or had either Himadra or Anuraja, through some sorcery, had something to do with the eruption?

Himadra had saved her son, whatever the incitement, whether it was intentional or accident. He had saved Drupada, and he had—quite incidentally—saved the life of Sayeh herself as well because she had pursued him. Did she owe him a debt?

Perhaps she owed him several, both for good and ill. But she did not think they cancelled one another out. Not until Drupada was safely returned to her own care.

When the men set her litter down, it was in a frame. She tried to arrange herself to make it easy for them to help her stand—whatever dignity she could salvage would only help her, though she was not above also relying on pity for her injuries—but they only drew the curtains back. It turned out that the entire top section of the litter, in fact, slid up and into itself like a curved wood-and-fabric fan, and when they had pulled it back Sayeh simply sat in a cushioned chair on a wooden and bamboo framework, exposed to the Cauled Sun which for once in the rainy season was plainly visible against the day-veiled stars and the Heavenly River above her.

Who moves armies in the rainy season? she thought yet again, and then forced herself to focus on what was before her.

Sayeh had heard Himadra could not walk on his own due to the brittleness of his limbs, which explained the existence and construction of both the palanquin that had brought her here and the framework upon which it rested. But it was not Himadra that she faced now, either in a litter or on the back of his satiny gray mare.

It was the thickset, gloriously raimented figure of Anuraja, her cousin from the south. His barrel-like body seemed the more stocky and impressive for his jeweled and bullion-embroidered robes. Like Sayeh, he clutched a walking stick. Unlike hers, his was clad in hammered gold and set with red stones too dark to be rubies: spinels or garnets, perhaps.

He was standing, and he came toward her, but he limped on his left leg and scowled with each step as if it pained him. Faintly, over the bright herbal stink of poultices, Sayeh could pick out the fetor of his abscessed leg.

She felt a sympathy for him that she had never quite managed before.

Still, she drew herself up to be as queenly as possibly when she could not stand. "Have you taken me prisoner, Cousin?"

Anuraja smiled. "You are my honored guest, royal cousin." He stressed the word *royal*, perhaps to emphasize that she herself had omitted it. "Perhaps I had fantasized that you had come to pay me court in hopes of winning my hand."

Sayeh had been a rajni for decades. She did not roll her eyes. How many queens had this fool buried now? "I am an old widow," she told him. "And beyond bearing. I have only one heir and that is all I shall ever have."

A test. He knew those facts: she was giving nothing away. Still she was sure she saw a flash of cupidity across his face at the thought of the single, defenselessly young heir of her body.

Good Daughter, dutiful and terrible, was Drupada here somewhere in this camp? Or had they already ... dispensed with him? The spike of cold in her chest hurt more than the coals burning her leg.

She said, "Where is Himadra? I need to speak to him about my son."

Anuraja sneered. "Ridden off west with his army, *Rajni*. You are with *my* army now." His face enlivened as he considered what she had said. "Where *is* your son? Not in Ansh-Sahal, then? Not"—he waved a hand airily so that jewels glittered—"perished?"

She cursed herself. She could have kept her secrets so much better, for purposes of bargaining. The poppy, the pain, her own exhaustion and lack of information—all worked against her.

Nazia was still beside her, she realized. Nazia reached out and up and squeezed her fingers softly. Ümmühan did nothing so obvious, but Sayeh felt the comfort of the old woman's presence nonetheless.

No respect for the rajni's personal autonomy, Sayeh thought, even as she was grateful for the gesture. Anuraja might think the girl was her lover, to touch her unsolicited. Well, fine then. Let him think what he liked.

"Perhaps if you would consent to ally your house to mine, royal cousin, we could work together to protect your son." He eyed her avariciously. If Sayeh has been standing, she would have stepped back. As it was, she felt herself edging into the cushions.

Anuraja leaned forward. He rested his hands on his knees, the richly embroidered fabric of his trousers smooth and unwrinkled under relaxed fingers. He smiled. "Give yourself to me. Or I shall forge your destruction—and your son's destruction—upon the anvil of the world."

SHE HELD HERSELF TOGETHER UNTIL THE MEN SET HER PALANQUIN DOWN within the walls of the tent that had been assigned to her. Until they left, and she saw their shadows against the canvas walls. She sent Üm-mühan out to fetch water or wine, if they would give her either, and sat without moving on the silks, staring.

How could she have made such a terrible mistake? How could she have miscalculated so badly, given herself to the wrong army entirely? She should have fought, should have hidden—

She was only being cruel to herself. She had had no choice, with her broken leg. She had done what she could. And perhaps her people would be able to find help and rescue him, even rescue her. Surely the Good Mother would not abandon a child who she had created by means of an outright miracle!

But where was Drupada? Where, where was her son? How could she protect him when she was captive of another raja entirely?

Nazia came to offer Sayeh her crutch, and a hand. Sayeh could not lift her own hand to accept either. She stared at them as if they were meaningless. She felt her lips move, the breath move through them. She did not form words with any intent, but she heard what her body, without her own volition, said to Nazia. "Get out. Get out. Get out."

Her voice rose to a wail. "Get out! Go to hell! Get away from me!"

An older woman, a more experienced woman, might have stayed. Might have sat beside Sayeh, and even if she were too decorous to touch her rajni without an invitation, might have positioned herself so that if the rajni curled forward or on her side, she would fall into supporting arms.

Nazia was young. The girl backed away. She wouldn't flee the tent, not with the alien men-at-arms waiting beyond. Not when her only protection was the rajni with whom she had chosen to allow herself to be taken prisoner, and Ümmühan already outside. But she backed into a corner of the canvas structure and pulled a rug up to conceal herself, hunched knees and hunched shoulders, leaving exposed only a corner of short regrowth of hair and two stark eyes.

Sayeh, for her part, curled on her side, as best she could manage with a splinted leg, and wailed as if she were an abandoned child and not a rajni at all.

Sayeh lay on her pallet and felt the shudders creep up her body from her tailbone to her ears. They ran up her spine as chilly shivers before detonating somewhere in the vicinity of her shoulderblades. Each time she gasped, clutched her coverlet in both fists, and hoped it was the last. Each time, in a few seconds she found herself spasming again.

Ümmühan returned with wine and flat, buttered bread on a tray. She seemed to assess the situation at a glance, and set it down on a rack nearby before crossing to the palanquin. Sayeh ignored the old woman; the old woman said nothing. She simply sat down, and did not move at all except in the rising and falling of her breath.

Nazia lay beside the door, asleep or pretending, curled on her side. It was a comfortable captivity at least: even if they had not been trusted with a brazier—too much like a weapon—they were well-stocked with blankets.

Every time Sayeh closed her eyes, she heard her own voice in memory say, *"You'll be as old as Old Parrah before I go away."*

She had meant every word of it when she had said it. How was she to know it would turn out to be a lie?

Under her breath, Ümmühan began softly to hum.

Sayeh wished she had the strength of will to command the old woman to be silent. But that would require speech, and speech was a thing women did, not animals blind with grief and pain.

She thought of the story of the elephant prince and the tiger and sent a prayer to the Good Mother that she was doing the right thing, and a prayer to the Good Daughter that Drupada would be dutiful, and that she and Tsering-la had taught him enough to lay a foundation of love and trust. That Himadra could not suborn him in some way before she returned for him. Surely, no one could replace a mother's love?

"I'll come back for you," she whispered under her breath. "I shall. I *will*."

The shudders came again, worse this time, and worse again, until she was curled sobbing and her gasps for air woke Nazia. Nazia came to her, but Ümmühan stayed her with a hand. From somewhere, the old woman produced a thumb harp, an instrument Sayeh had always hated. But as Ümmühan played and softly began to sing, Sayeh found she did not hate the sound so much. First her sobbing eased, and then her breathing. She did not think she ever slept, quite, but at last she slipped into a sort of haze and half-dreamed.

She was not sure how much time passed, then.

"You have to eat, Rajni. Rajni, you have to take food. A little wine, at least, Rajni."

The smell of the food, the wine, sickened her. She turned her face away.

I want to die. I want to die. I want to die, I want to die, I want to die.

But Sayeh could not die. Though she could feel the emptiness in her gut, worse than when Tsering-la had cut Drupada from her belly. Though she could feel her heart like a hot stone in her chest that still somehow beat and beat again. She could not rest. She could not even flee the pain.

Not for herself.

But for her son.

I want to die. I want to die.

Sayeh opened her eyes. The lashes gummed, sticky. She blinked them, but a hand was there with a cool cloth, wet and warm. She recognized Nazia's tendons and tidy nails. Another hand cupped her head, lifting it.

"Rajni?" Nazia said.

"Wine," Sayeh agreed.

The cup came to her lips. Smooth horn, light, easy to drink from. From somewhere nearby rose the plink of the thumb harp and the soft, cracked sound of an old woman's perfect voice.

I want to die. The wine was watered, barely wine at all. The scent made her want to gag, even so. Her stomach twisted with acid and despair.

She was Sayeh Rajni, daughter of Ajeet Raja. Widow of Ashar. Mother of Drupada. Rajni of Ansh-Sahal, whatever remained. She took a mouthful of the watered wine and waited while the gentle hand took the cup away.

She could not swallow it. It did not taste to her like anything that might sustain life, but like . . . dry tar. A mouthful of feathers. She held it behind her tongue and thought of something else, listened to the lullaby an old woman sang in a foreign language, until her throat relaxed and it slowly, slowly trickled down.

I will not die.

She gasped for air but did not cough, and did not resist the hands that supported her. She breathed deep, got some air inside her. "More, please, sweet Nazia," she asked, and marveled at the gentleness of Nazia's scarred hands.

I will not die.

I will make them burn.

13

THE DEAD MAN AND THE GAGE WERE SEATED ON ONE OF THE TERRACES overlooking the wall when Ata Akhimah found them. She carried a tray of tea on her palms, which made the Dead Man realize that he had never seen a Wizard so burdened before. And yet this one took on the labor of servants as if it were as much her due as the silken robes and embroidered slippers she wore.

She set the tray on the railing. It held a curious carafe that, to the Dead Man, resembled the sort of alchemical glassware the Hasitaneh used. It consisted of two large bubbles, one inside the other, joined at the top. The external one was transparent, and the light of the Heavenly River gilded it with a satiny sheen. The interior one was a swirl of teals and blues. Both bubbles stretched into nested teardrop shapes at the top, forming the neck, and there was a spout where they merged. Three fluted, gold-rimmed porcelain bowls sat beside it.

"I didn't know if you took sustenance from tea," the Wizard said to the Gage. "So I brought you a bowl just to be sure."

"I would enjoy some tea." The Gage held out his enormous brass paw, already curved to hold the cup. He held his fingers still and let

Ata Akhimah balance the fragile thing between them. They did not shift at all once it was settled in.

The Dead Man hid a smile behind his veil. He'd seen this before, though more usually with wine. The Gage would merely touch the outside of the cup. He would never lift it to his shining visage. And yet, in a little while, the contents of the vessel would be gone as if they had evaporated, but leaving no residue.

He too accepted a cup. The porcelain felt smooth and hot in his fingers, a strange combination of fragility and hardness, or delicacy—for the cup was so fine the light shone through it—and strength. The tea was a yellowy green, like a peridot. It smelled of drying grass at the end of summertime.

He passed his free hand under his veil, lifting it away from his face so that the cup could pass behind it cleanly. He'd worn the veil for so long, and in so many situations, that he normally performed this action without thinking. Now, though, he found himself self-conscious.

Ata Akhimah was watching him. Not salaciously, but with the focused curiosity of a child bent over an interesting bug crawling up some stem.

Wizards, the Dead Man thought resignedly, and tilted up the cup of tea.

"Any luck with the marble?" the Gage asked.

The Wizard sighed and shook her head. "I have something for the Dead Man, though." She, having sipped from her cup—or perhaps only sniffed it appreciatively—set it down again. Her face creased elaborately to frame a smile. "Here."

She held a little teakwood box out to the Dead Man. It was heavy. When he opened it, he found his pistol. His pistol, the one he had given her just a few days before, and a second one that matched it almost perfectly. The chasing on the butt and barrel were slightly different: a design with a more Sarathani flavor. And something about—

The hammer had been modified, and the powder pan for the

primer was gone. Instead, the tip of the hammer rested forward, against . . . there was no striking rasp. Nothing to make a spark. Just a smooth little nub like the head of a pin.

He lifted one of the pistols. He did not cock it, nor aim it anywhere except at the terrace at his feet. The Dead Man had enough experience with Wizards to be sure that just because he couldn't immediately see how the damned thing worked, didn't mean it didn't.

"No pan?" he asked, inspecting it.

She held out her hand, fingers pinched like the beak of a bird. He put his own palm under it, and when she opened the fingers, a shiny metal pebble fell into it.

He felt the Gage watching him. He lifted the thing and examined it under bright starlight. It was a little concave disk, fat, like a tiny dumpling somebody had poked a tinier finger into from one side only. He could see immediately that it would fit over the little peg the hammer rested against.

"What is this?"

"When you fit it over the peg," she said, "assuming the gun is loaded, then the pistol is armed. It's like . . . a portable firing pan. Once that does not have to be filled each time the weapon is used. You simply load the pistol as you normally would—you do carry premeasured loads?"

He nodded.

"Then you place the portable primer over the pin and cock the hammer. When you pull the trigger—the weapon fires."

"And you've tested this?"

She smiled. "Extensively. And you don't have to keep the pan primed—just prime it for firing—so the danger of it going off when you won't want it to is actually reduced. And the firing time reduced as well."

The Dead Man carefully aimed the pistol at nothing in particular—out in the middle of the white swell of the river—and sighted down the barrel. The balance was the same as it had been.

He tried the second one. It was functionally indistinguishable. "How do I get more primers?"

She fumbled in her pocket and produced a bag as big as the Gage's fist, that clinked as if it were full of tiny stones. "There are a few thousand in here. And here's a schematic on how to make them. Any Wizard who can work with black powder should be able to make you more—or a good gunsmith, for that matter."

The Gage watched, unmoving. Or perhaps he simply stood stolidly, far away in his thoughts.

The Dead Man said, "There are two pistols here."

The Wizard grinned wider. Her teeth were very broad and very white, unusually so given the cheerful attention she was providing to her tea. "They're often effective to carry in pairs. Or so I've read.

"Which reminds me, Dead Man. There is quite a library here. And many books in your native language, some of which have not been translated. You could make yourself useful."

The Dead Man rather thought he was already making himself more than useful, what with the drilling of soldiers and the reviewing of defenses. But he also supposed, now that he thought about it, that a Wizard's standards would be different.

He said, "If I stay—*if*—I stay—I believe they expect me to fight the war, not scribble out books."

She leaned her head to one side, a gesture that would have been coyly fetching in a young girl and was now, in her middle age, soft and charming. He wouldn't have expected such an unselfconsciously feminine gesture from such a pragmatic creature, and it softened him toward her. Always these reminders that people were layered and complex and had a thousand unexplored crannies. Every man, every woman, was like a vast system of caverns that stretched unimaginably in secret places underground. You could explore somebody for years—decades—and yet you might not even know there was a passage in a particular place, let alone where it led or what it revealed.

And when you found something unexpected, it might lead you to a place where you could get dismembered or killed.

No wonder so many people never strayed from the smooth-floored, brightly lit chambers well-worn by their presence, in themselves as well as in their knowledge of another person. But for a moment, just for a moment, the Dead Man felt the itch to get to know this woman better. It reminded him of his feelings for the Gage. No matter how hard you looked, there was always something else hidden down there.

Ata Akhimah was looking at the Gage as well. She pursed her lips and said, "Does that armor still suit you?"

The Gage looked down at his gauntlet, carefully cradling the diminished cup of tea. "It is what it is," he said. "Do you propose to repair and improve my carapace as well as the Dead Man's guns?"

Ata Akhimah laughed, appealingly musical. She said. "I could do that, certainly. Or possibly I could take you out of that shell, Gage. Give you back the person you were."

The Gage said, "They take one bit at a time, entire. And leave it until the new bit becomes a part of the person who is becoming a Wizard's servitor. Once the transfer of identity is complete, they take another bit, and another. Until finally the whole thing has been replaced—head, breath, heart, and will—and what remains is a Gage."

"A Gage that remembers being a man."

"But without a single original part remaining. Unless you count the will that animates it."

The Wizard leaned back against the railing, careful of the tray— no one on the terraces below would thank them for a shower of hot tea, glass, and porcelain—and folded her long fingers into the crooks of her elbows as she crossed her arms. "My tradition teaches that every body is replaced, bit by bit, in just the same way. Except what is put in place of the old is meat, rather than metal. You can see this process in a broken bone, say, or in the skin of a man's face when he is old. It isn't the same skin he had as a child. But it's still *him*."

The Gage glanced down at a shiny metal arm. "Is that possible?"

"What one Wizard can make, dear automaton, another can break." She shrugged. "It would hurt. Probably rather a lot. And you wouldn't look like you did."

"Thank you. I find this shape is suited." The Gage bowed a little, an inclination of his head that made the pate sparkle.

"If you change your mind," Ata Akhimah said, "let me know. By the way, Dead Man, the rajni said she'd like to see you at your convenience. And before you get all Asitaneh about timeliness, she really does mean at your convenience. Not 'conveniently half a day ago.'"

She winked. She left the tea. They watched her go. The Dead Man picked up the carafe and examined it. The tea within still steamed and he poured another cup. He refilled the Gage's cup as well, since that had gone bone-dry.

The Gage wished to sigh.

The Dead Man did sigh. "I don't know why you can't have conceived of a tenderness for her," he said crossly, "and not that doe-eyed chambermaid."

THE DEAD MAN FOUND THE QUEEN ALONE.

Her maids ushered him into her presence, then closed the door behind him. He thought the older one—Yavashuri—gave him a warning glance as she took his new and newly returned pistols from him before she stepped aside. He had never broken the politeness of refraining from staring at the uncovered faces of women, though, and so he was not sure exactly what her expression held.

He heard the rustle of armor as a guard took up a post beyond. He wouldn't be leaving, he supposed, if Her Abundance was not pleased.

The room surprised him. It was small, snug, not stately at all. The windows were covered in layers of sheer gauze—silk, he thought, from the sheen and drape—in peacock shades of teal, violet, copper, green. Light fell through them, stained in soft colors, but they rendered the world beyond into an appealing haze.

The floor was wooden, wide springy boards with patterned rugs of knotted wool and woven hemp laid over them. These colors too were jeweled, and something was twisted in with the wool in some of the knotted rugs that glistened in the light. Cushions abounded, great tufted things for sprawling on, and they were peacock-shaded too. The queen's enormous bear-dog, her constant companion, lay among a pile of them against the far wall, watchful and calm.

Above it all hung a great brass chandelier, its candles—or lamps, the Dead Man could not tell which from below—casting their satiny glow through cut-crystal prisms.

The light was being put to good use. The queen reclined in a nest of the cushions, her feet tucked under a woven shawl. Beside her was a black enamel tray picked out in copper that had been set up on a stand to serve as a tea table. Fruit, small sweets, cups, and a pot of tea on a warmer littered it. All around her was a scatter of papers and maps and books of various designs left open here or there for quick repeated reference. Some of the bound variety, with leaves, had been weighted down at one page or another with small pretty objects such as those that also decorated little shelves here and there on the walls—a jade elephant, a cinnabar box, an antique key, a strange little nubbin of a statuette or game piece that showed a heavily bearded man on horseback, wearing the clothes of the traders who came from the far north. How on earth had that gotten here?

There were too many tiny art objects in the room for them to all be Mrithuri's. And they came from too many foreign places, in the styles of too many centuries. This was a repository, then, of the sorts of things that had been presented as gifts to various emperors of Sarath-Sahal in the past. This was the stuff they had liked enough to keep, to put someplace where they could fondle it once in a while and be reminded of the reach of empire.

It was a royal retiring room. And in the process, it had become an accidental museum.

For a moment, the Dead Man thought sadly that the Gage would love this room, all the little arty pieces of various gifts presented to Mrithuri's family—but that he could never step inside. He'd go right through those wonderful wide floorboards.

The queen was looking at the Dead Man, so he looked back. Not at her face or form—she was clad in a loose winter robe and trousers, and her heavy dark hair was dressed in a simple braid—but politely past her. Still, even from the corner of his vision, he could not stop himself from noticing the great dark eyes made wider by a light touch of kohl, the way her heavy hair framed and shadowed the bones of her cheeks, the thoughtful pursing of her lips. He stared at the wall behind her so he would not stare at the softness of the ivory wool that clung to the curve of her hip like a caress.

She had no such compunctions and gazed upon him plainly. The boldness—which should have seemed like rudeness—made him uncomfortable, but not in the way he expected. Instead of embarrassment, he felt a sharp erotic chill.

She was so comfortable, so at her ease, so ungilded and unbejeweled, so unpainted and unpinned, that she seemed like a different woman to him entirely. He knew it was an honor that she had let him see her so.

One of the books she seemed to be using was a scroll, rolled open along most of the left-hand wall, various spots along its length marked out with still more pretty knickknacks. She'd also cleared out a space in the middle of the floor by rolling up a gold and purple rug into a bolster, and she had used various dust collectors to set up ranks like a child playing at armies. He dragged his gaze away from her and turned aside, grateful for the excuse.

"Tired of the sand table, Your Abundance?"

She laughed at him. "Tired of the squabbles in the war room, Sir Dead Man," she said, with a quirk of her brows. "I wanted to talk to you about tactics and also perhaps strategy in a quieter environment than we have had. We have to assume that this feint is the prelude to a longer and larger war."

He glanced over at the scroll. It was a series of battle maps—the evolution of a fight from many years ago that had taken place in the same terrain that Himadra and Anuraja's men now occupied.

"This is a good thought," he said, gesturing at the scroll. "But this battle seems to predate cannon."

She rose. The ivory wool spilled between her breasts and across her belly, showing every surprising small curve that rich clothes usually concealed on her narrow form. There was a term for that, when they cut the garment so the fabric clung. It was expensive, he remembered, because it wasted cloth.

She was lovely. So lovely. So like home.

It had been decades since he lost his Zillah, but for a moment the Dead Man felt a stunning pain in his bosom. He missed his darling with an intensity so great it seemed for long seconds as if the grief were new. As if he were watching her die, unable even to go to her and hold her in his arms, and knowing that he was alone in the world now and would never feel her warmth against his back in the cool of night again.

He blinked hard, glad of his veil. How did people bear it, walking around with their whole souls and faces naked to the world all the while, letting anyone see their pain and fear?

At that moment, he realized what surprised him most about this snug little room. It was silent. Not utterly silent—there were sounds from elsewhere in the palace, the twitter of small drab birds made glorious by song in the courtyard, among the weeping cascades of lavender and white that were the flowering trees. But there were no— he looked.

There were no nuns in the filigreed passages between the walls. No shuffling cloistered footsteps. No murmur of hummed prayer and song.

The queen really *was* alone. Not just presenting him with the appearance of intimacy. She had made herself utterly and completely alone.

Except for the Dead Man.

It was unprecedented. The Dead Man's experience of royalty was extensive, and stretched over dozens of cities and half the wide, long world. He had never seen a duchess, much less a queen, alone in a room before.

She looked at him with concern. Standing, she was even a little taller than he: she was stately, and he was not tall.

He didn't mind.

It was an expression of trust that took his breath away. He felt something in his breast that had hung loose since he became a wolf's-head, a masterless man, swing into place and lock tight like the clasp of the box that was his heart. He was her animal now, and as he felt it he rejoiced in it. Service had won him back, and while he knew there would be doubts and discomfort later, for now there was only poignant comfort.

He was home.

"I just understood something," he said. It was all he could make himself admit right now. He gestured to the space. "The walls aren't pierced with passages."

"This room lets me think." She smiled. "Everyone needs some kind of sanctuary."

She sank down again on the cushions and patted one near her. "There," she said. "I am seated, Dead Man. You may be seated, too. Would you care for tea?"

He sank down—not in the place right beside her that she had touched, because being in the place where her hand had stroked seemed at that moment unbearably intimate. But lower down on the heap of cushions, so that his head was closer in level to the queen's shoulder. His knees were even with her feet.

"Yes," he said, "I would like some tea."

The patterned shawl had fallen away from her feet, which were bare. Her toes seemed to him remarkable, and not just because the nails had been painted the color of mother-of-pearl. Where did one get such lacquer? he wondered. What Wizard's art was involved? Was it costly?

Of course it was costly if it adorned a queen. Like the clinging fabric. Like whatever oil scented her hair, intoxicating and redolent of nutmeg. He stretched out his legs and leaned back, on the theory that if he pretended to be more comfortable than he was he might trick himself into feeling more comfortable than he was.

She said, "You have traveled far."

He nodded.

"Is there someone at home?"

"There is no home," he answered, surprised by his own honesty. "When there was . . . my home was as much someone as it was someplace." He had been looking at her hands, which were shapely and strong, unencumbered by rings or fingerstalls. Her only jewelry was the snake torc around her neck and the simple gold rings in her pierced nose and ears.

She said, "The blade is an icy finger beneath the ribcage, groping for the heart."

He recognized it: the translation of a famous line of poetry, by a poetess of his own people from several generations before. The poem was about history, and heartbreak, and how they were not that different.

"Tell me what you have decided about the battle," he said at last, for something to say. A topic that did not feel like a knife edge. And what she had said she brought him here for, after all.

She leaned forward. She lifted a wand—a long piece of cane—from the landslide of upholstery and used it to tap a blown-glass stallion gently on the withers. "So this was Kithara Raja's light horse, which he managed to station uphill of the battle by dint of having possession of the ground before the enemy arrived."

"An advantageous position."

A lock of hair had gotten loose from her braid. She smiled behind it, glancing at him sideways. "One would think. And the raja did. And so did his generals, and the generals of his enemy."

"Who was the defender?"

"Kithara Raja," she said, her tone suggesting she was slightly astonished he did not know.

"Your history is as obscure to me as mine is to you," he told her gently. "I can discourse for hours on the First, Second, and Fourth Battles of Aheera. Have you heard of them?"

Her brow knitted. "What happened to the Third one?"

He shrugged. "No record survives."

That made her laugh aloud—a quick delighted sound very unlike her queenly chuckle. She seemed so young without her paint and performances. He swallowed the unsettling realization that if his daughter had lived, his daughter would be older than this queen.

"Must have been quite the battle."

He nodded. "Not a complete massacre on both sides, but none of the officers survived. Or if they did survive, they deserted, and never after admitted having been there. But you were telling me something unexpected about Kithara Raja's light horse. What was the name of his attacker?"

"He was a foreign prince," she said dismissively. "A reaver from one of the horse clans."

Her voice held nothing but scorn for the barbarian. The Dead Man felt his lips twitch. How easily he recognized his own youthful opinions on her lips. Even as he knew her provincialism for naiveté, it filled him with a sense of kinship to her.

"So how did he defeat Kithara Raja, when Kithara Raja had the advantage of terrain?"

She smiled. "He used an illusionist to conjure up the appearance of reinforcing troops, and he arrayed the phantasms among his own men so that one could not tell that they left no footstep and raised no dust. Of course, Anuraja knows the history as well as I do—"

She was brilliant and beautiful and soft, and another lock of hair was sliding from her braid even now. She turned away and said, "Syama, go to sleep now."

The bear-dog lowered her watchful head to her paws and sighed.

The Dead Man unhooked a brooch and dropped the veil from across his face. And while she was staring at him in wonder, considering his features as intently as if she had never seen a nose or lips before—he moved to kiss her.

Softly, as was appropriate for a first kiss. No passionate clinch that she would have to struggle to escape, but just the fingertips of one hand resting on her shoulder to steady them both. He looked her in the eye as he bent close, noticing for the first time the flecks of amber and green catching light in their coffee depths.

She leaned toward him.

Their lips brushed.

Her breath came in sharply. Not a gasp, and not a sound, precisely. She didn't pull away, though, and when he laid his other hand against her cheek she nestled into the touch like a stroked cat. After a moment, she leaned in and began to kiss him back.

It was a dance, and they took turns leading. Her breath grew ragged, but no more ragged than his. Now she made a sound—a little, eager moan.

He raised his hand and cupped the outside curve of her breast, so small and so heavy through the softness of the woolen drape. She pushed against him, and he ran his hand down the length of her waist to her hip. Only now, as she leaned into him, did he allow himself to curve his fingers into the softness of her flesh under the softness of her garment, and pull her closer still.

She placed her hands against his chest and pushed him back quite suddenly.

He did not resist. He went where she willed, even if it was away. "Mrithuri," he said, daring greatly to speak her name. More greatly, he thought, than when he had kissed her.

Her eyes were dilated, the lashes damp. She drew a flustered breath.

"I cannot," Mrithuri said. "I—I can be rajni in my own right only because I am a virgin. We would be found out. This is a palace. And I cannot—I *cannot*—get with child."

"Oh dear girl," the Dead Man said. "Who told you that all there was to love was that? Let me show you how we worship where I'm from."

He waited. She shivered, her cheek satiny against his fingertips that were roughened by cold and swordplay. Her life hadn't been any easier than his, however. He could sense the steel in her, work-hardened and also brittle.

"I was nine when my father was assassinated," she said. She met his eyes, her own seeming transparent despite the darkness of them. "Nine years old when I became my grandfather's heir. For a decade I was nothing but, and now for half that time I have played the role of raja and rajni both. I was raised to this. Honed to it. I do not know how to be anything but a rajni."

"Then decide as a rajni," he said.

She pondered that for a long-enough time to seem an eternity to his passion-addled senses, though it was probably only moments. Then her lips curved and she lifted her chin.

"Attend me," she commanded.

He kissed her neck, and the soft skin behind her ear that smelled spicy, woody, resinous, heavily sweet. Her hair was dressed in some oil scented with dragon's-blood resin and vanilla, he deduced. It made the inside of his nose itch slightly, but the intake of her breath and the way she arched her neck to give him more of her skin made him stay, and nuzzle, and nip. He nibbled the lobe of her ear, flirted it with the tip of his tongue, a little promise of his intentions if she had been sophisticated enough to read it. She responded with an artless gasp and a shudder that made him swell in anticipation. He made an appreciative noise of his own when she took advantage of his pause for breath to reciprocate, hesitantly, kissing the line behind the hinge of his jaw where his beard faded into naked skin. She was cautious but not clumsy, and he smiled as he thought of the future.

She let him open the soft wool robe. It slipped away from her torso, draping back from the sleeves and leaving bare her body. She was skinny, her ribs a strangeness against the palm of his hand as he smoothed her garment aside. Her small breasts were sandy brown, and nipples soft as silk and dark as saddle leather tensed against the hollow of his palm. All along her left side ran rows of tiny, paired marks—a few scabbed sores, some concave and shiny and pink, the vast majority white starbursts like tiny pinpricks in her skin. Scars, obviously: some recent, some old.

He brushed the tip of her nearer breast with a closed mouth. When she arched, he murmured, "So many hurts," and kissed one of those. He let her feel his breath. She stiffened in a way that made him wonder if it had been a mistake, and put her hands into his hair.

"Shall I stop?"

But her fingertips curled against his scalp, and she exerted her un-trained strength to hold him where he was. So he remained, and let her press his face into the ridged striations of scarred velvet skin stretched over her ribs.

He breathed and let her hold him. At length, she spoke.

"It is the snakebite. They're a thing of Ancient Erem. But not poi-sonous. Or rather—poisonous. But not very. And in small doses, the poison clears your mind. Makes your thoughts fly like quarrels from the crossbow, swift and straight." Her tapered fingertips touched the white stars that stippled the sugar-brown outer edge of her breast, her ribs.

She set him back with her fingertips and he went at the gentlest pressure. But though his heart ached with loss for a moment, he re-alized quickly that she did not seem to be refusing him. She hooked her thumbs, instead, into the waistband of the white wool trousers and skinned them down. He caught a glimpse of the hollow of her inner thigh, the tight dark curls of her delta as she drew up her knees, kicked the trousers off her feet with one mermaid gesture.

She half-turned, showing the angle of hip bone, the outer shape of her hip and thigh. She was so thin it didn't curve, exactly. More pale paired dots outlined her hip, her thigh. She had left the dip of waist, which would be left uncovered by a blouse and drape, unscarred.

She said, "I started using the snakebite when I was made heir. It made my mind more . . . adult."

The scars were like flour dotted on the brown surface of a bun, like the speckles on the flank of a sun-warmed lizard. He passed his hand over them, imagining that if his own skin were not so rough with care and work and war and itinerancy he might feel them as tiny dimples, or as rough spots that might catch.

"I wish things had been different for you," he said.

She startled, eyes widening, then sighed and smiled. Whatever she had been about to say—by her half-raised hand, a similar gentle wish for impossible clemency from the dead past—failed in her mouth. She swallowed it and said, instead, "We can't go back there. We can only go forward. Picking scabs only makes the scab bleed, and scar more heavily in the end."

She was right. Such wisdom from a young queen. But her rightness only served to fan the spark of melancholy that flared in him.

Well, if nothing else, perhaps he could extinguish it in her body.

"Lie back, my queen," he murmured. "If you will."

She caught his eye and frowned, but did so, reclining on the cushions in the embrace of her open robe. She seemed unselfconscious in her nakedness—royalty were accustomed to having people around them in every state of undress, after all. But when he paused for a moment to appreciate her, a tiny line drew itself between her eyebrows. She said, "Is something wrong?"

"No, my queen," he answered. "You are lovely."

He leaned over her and kissed her mouth again, a gesture she returned hungrily. The faintest taste of honey lingered on her tongue from some sweetmeat she had consumed before he entered the room. When he broke the kiss, she quested after him, and he let her catch him for a moment before leaning back.

He divested himself of the discommoded veil, of the old red coat—he stroked it as he laid it aside—of his shirt, and his boots, and his socks, and his trousers. He knew she was watching, and took his time so her eyes could linger.

His body was worn, and marked with combat and privation. He trusted her to accept him for who he was, if he was who she wanted, and to see the kinship in the scars each of them bore. When he'd laid his clothes aside he came back to her—she had come up on her elbows to watch him—and kissed her again while she leaned up and ran one soft hand over him, tracing and exploring.

"You're like wire," she said. "Like those statues they make of twisted wire, every fiber like a muscle. You should eat more."

The last, with childlike sincerity, made him laugh out loud and stroke her spine, like a string of cut jewels under her skin. "*You* should eat more. I have been hiking through the mountains for more than a season."

She let her hand drop lower, and rested her fingertips against his shaft. Though he had roused already, he felt himself stir more, and watched her eyes widen. "Like silk," she said.

He stroked a wayward lock of her hair. "This is not like silk," he said. "It is coarse and shining, like the glossy mane of a strong mare."

Her hand closed around his shaft—still hesitant. He smiled at her. "A man doesn't mind a firm grip," he said. She gave him a little, exploratory squeeze. "As long as it's not too firm. Gentle with the jewels, though."

She laughed. "I know that one."

He ran a hand down her belly and cupped his fingers and palm against her sex. She was warm, but closed tight as a flower-bud, and though sweat from the hot damp wet her body, only a little slickness wet his fingertips.

That was fine. If this was to be his only opportunity to touch her, he thought he might enjoy taking as much time as she seemed to want. He pressed gently, dipped his head, and applied his tongue in arcs and swirls along her collarbone, down her breast, to her nipple. He suckled lightly, and when she seemed to want more pressure, he offered it. She gasped and arched up to him, her thighs parting, and he felt the first yielding of her sex.

He pressed the heel of his hand against her mound, letting her feel his teeth but only just. She whimpered, teeth stretching her lip, eyelashes fluttering. He slid his other hand beneath her ass to support and lift her while he made slow firm circles against her with the first. Her hands were fists now, her forearms pressing down against the cushions and the robe that trapped her shoulders as she lifted herself to him. Her breath, too, was coming faster. He watched the tendons in her throat tense as she turned her head to the side.

When she opened, slick and soft at last, he waited still. Waited until she pushed herself insistently against his touch, hips jerking sharply to create friction. Waited until he could slip one finger gently between her petals and feel the wetness flow. He touched her entrance lightly, but did not press against it. She was so wet now that his finger might have eased inside without effort, and he was determined to obey her taboos.

Instead, he slid his hand up until he found the long bud at the heart of her flower, and stroked it softly.

She gasped and almost cried out. He squeezed her behind reassuringly and grinned at her. "Don't scream," he whispered. "There's a guard outside the door. I'd hate to be run through before you were finished."

"Finished?" she asked.

So he showed her.

Slowly at first, as she roused, and then faster and stronger he stroked her. He felt the moment when her own tiny phallus drew down and away into her body, heard her gasps come swift and sharp. Her sweat-damp legs wrapped around him, hot and moist. He watched her face, once he had her rhythm, and thrilled to see her press her fist to her mouth hard, eyes crushed closed fiercely, sobbing as she fought for silence.

Then, suddenly, she arched up in the throes of a sweet convulsion. Both her hands flew to cover his, and she clutched him to her, hard. Her heels kicked at the cushions; her head stretched back and bared her throat, which worked as if she wanted, in truth, to scream—but she mewled, only.

He wanted to weep with her beauty, her abandon. "Goddess," he whispered, and spoke a prayer to his own Scholar-God, as was appropriate in times such as this.

She held him hard for long moments before she melted. She fell against the cushions and lay panting, undone, her limbs all strewn in sweet abandon. He lay beside her, head pillowed on her belly, and sighed.

He held her until her breathing slowed a little, and so it was some time before he stirred. He raised his head, though, to find her watching him down the length of her body. He kissed beside her navel and said, "Yes, sweet?"

"Is . . ." She pressed her lips together, and he saw her draw her dignity on for the courage it loaned. ". . . is there . . . more? That *we* could do? Without . . ."

"A little," he said.

"Will you show me?"

"I would adore to, my queen."

Her belly was soft under his lips, a carpet of silk so much finer than the woven carpet of silk beneath his knees. He turned his face to rub his cheek above the beard against her, touched the inside of her thigh with the back of his wrist, where his own skin was still soft and sensitive. She sighed, settled, then roused again. He found her little bud, soft now and relaxed, and blew a tender stream of air across it until she pushed toward him, seeking.

She heated so quickly that it seemed he barely had time to savor her changing scents, the aroma of the sea's edge thickening to honey. The sound she made when he brushed his lips against her petals was a guttural cry of need, a salty animal sound without logic or reason, only longing. His hardness had slacked; now again it tightened.

When at last he ceased to tease and instead licked and nibbled, she pulled a pillow across her face and cried into it as if her heart were breaking, cried out through clenched teeth until she wept, but she did not beg him to stop. And so he kept on until she knotted her fingers near his scalp and pulled him away, drew him up beside her, kissed his salty beard and stroked his hair back from his temples while she panted and leaned close.

She shrugged out of her robe to be closer to him, and he drew it over them like a quilt. He held her, and felt the simple pleasure of her warmth and her sweat and something beyond words. In the sensation of her skin against his skin, her body beside his, lay an ineffable connection with the godhead.

The Dead Man became, for a few moments, human again. It happened easily and it felt safe. He knew it was not safe.

The feeling frightened him.

Their breathing calmed. He stroked her hair. They must have dozed a little, because when he noticed that they were breathing in rhythm with one another it was raining again, and he could not have said when it started.

Perhaps his awakening wakened her. Perhaps she had not, herself, drifted. She looked up at him, twisting her neck around as she lay in his embrace. She looked away. She looked down at her hands, cuddled against her breasts in her half-curled position. She shrugged her shoulders back against him, warm and suddenly confident in his presence, his attention.

She said, "Is there something I can do for *you*?"

THEY WERE DRESSED AGAIN, DRINKING COOLED TEA AND STUDYING Mrithuri's dust-collector tactical maps, when the door suddenly rattled with the guard's pounding. A cry carried through the wood, muffled but clear: "Rajni! Rajni! The enemy is on the move!"

The Dead Man reached without thinking to draw his veil across his face. Mrithuri stayed his hand and kissed his cheek, then released him as she hurried to the door. She opened it with her own hands, revealing a guard—not the same one the Dead Man had come in past, so the first one must have been relieved at some point— Lieutenant General Pranaj, the handmaiden Chaeri, the Gage, and the Wizard Akhimah.

The Dead Man had combed the queen's hair for her, and braided it as well, so she looked tidy and calm and not in the least dissipated or gorgeously disarrayed, as she had been so little time before. He kept that memory to himself, tucked up into a warm corner of his heart, and knew that if he smiled inappropriately to the circumstances, the veil would keep anyone from seeing it.

The queen stood aside to allow her staff into the room. They filed in except for the Gage, who looked dubiously at the wooden floor.

"I believe I will wait in the hallway, Your Abundance," he said in resonant, courteous tones.

She laughed. The Dead Man wondered if anyone else would notice how merry she seemed, or the sidelong glances she offered him now and again. The Gage would, probably. But he had long ago given up worrying about what the Gage knew or did not know.

Chaeri, though—she gave him a knowing smirk through lowered lashes as she came into the room. She carried an inlaid box with both hands. Something slid heavily inside it, and through the filigree sides the Dead Man could see a scaled and muscled curve.

"Your pets," Chaeri said to the queen. "I brought them."

The queen looked stark, but nodded. "I have not slept," she admitted. She rubbed her arm as if it troubled her. "Will you aid me?"

While Chaeri opened the box—cautiously, judiciously, wearing a heavy pair of gloves—the lieutenant general and Ata Akhimah began to fill the queen and the Dead Man in on events they had missed.

A series of scouts and sentries who had gone on ahead of the armies of Sarathai-tia had vanished. Then the disappearances had ceased, and the most recent wave of reconnaissance had revealed that Anuraja's army was gone. Just gone: not at all where they were supposed to be. They had left the sort of wide, churned trail an army leaves, and that too had simply stopped, dead-ending.

"As if a rukh carried them off," the Dead Man said.

"I thought those were mythical," Pranaj said, tilting his head.

The Dead Man sighed hard enough that his veil puffed.

"Somebody would have noticed a bird the size of a whale,"

Mrithuri said. "We have to find Anuraja's men. We can't just have an army wandering around unescorted."

Yavashuri glanced significantly at the Dead Man.

"You may be plain," said the rajni. The Dead Man appreciated the trust, though he would have counseled her against it—she could not know he could be trusted, and making it look like a foreigner was her favorite would poison the politics of her court.

Yavashuri's frown told him she knew all these things as well. "At least we know where Himadra's men are. They're in Ansh-Sahal."

Her tone indicated that there was worse to come. She didn't hesitate.

"Himadra's men may have captured Sayeh and her son."

"The prince is captive? We're not sure?"

Yavashuri shrugged. Her shoulders were mutinous. She didn't trust the Dead Man, even if the queen did.

Chaeri, both hands in the piercework box, seemed about to say something, but looked down again as if she thought better of it.

"The royal bearded vultures," Pranaj said.

Mrithuri nodded. If she were about to say anything, it was interrupted by Chaeri, who approached her now with a thick-bodied serpent as long and broad as the Dead Man's arm gripped tightly in her two hands. She grasped it behind the head, disarming the terrible fangs that it gaped to show. Its heavy body wound in loops around her forearm, writhing slowly. It seemed to the Dead Man that she struggled slightly under the weight.

The viper was sandy-colored, with a blunt, jowly, triangular head. Pale irregular pits ran in rows along its upper lip. The Dead Man thought the black patterns on its back scales looked like some foreign calligraphy, but if they were words, they unsettled him to gaze upon.

Mrithuri glanced around the room, and seemed to come to a decision. She brushed the collar of her robe aside, baring the speckled skin, and lifted her braid to allow Chaeri to apply the viper below her collarbone. The snake, seeming to sense prey, lunged against Chaeri's grasp as she brought it close, but Chaeri had the skill of experience, and controlled it until she could herself, gently, press the fangs into Mrithuri's skin.

Mrithuri closed her eyes. She let her head fall back and shuddered in a way he found, suddenly, unnervingly familiar.

The Dead Man looked away, wincing. He found himself staring into the Gage's mirror and had to look away from that, as well: even with his expression veiled, he found he could not bear his own reflection.

He looked back as Chaeri was returning the serpent to its box, and Mrithuri was accepting a clean square of cotton from Pranaj. She pressed it over the slightly bleeding wounds on her chest and held it there with some pressure, though the crimson dots that soaked it did not grow beyond their first blossoming. She blinked, shaking her head until her eyes seemed to focus, and said, "Well, I suppose we should move this to the map room. Chaeri, would you have the austringers ready my birds?"

"What can the bearded vultures do?" the Gage asked, his voice so low that the Dead Man knew it was meant for his ears only.

The Dead Man shrugged. "We'll find out before long."

Chaeri—the box of serpents in her hands—was already stepping around the Gage on her way out. The Dead Man did not miss the way she let her shoulder brush the metal man as she edged past him. Then she was gone, her small feet a gentle patter down the hall.

"Gage," Mrithuri said. "Teacher. Lieutenant General Pranaj. Would you go on ahead to the map room? I have a private word for this mercenary, and then I will join you."

They exited, leaving the queen standing beside him beside the door, ankle-deep in jewel-colored carpets. The red tones had dropped out of her complexion, leaving her face waxy and faintly sheened with sweat. Her eyes glittered, the pupils tight. She floated in an air of suppressed energy. *Can this be good for her?*

But it didn't seem to make her slow or impede her thoughts.

Mrithuri rested her fingertips on his arm. Her hands were chill. She met his gaze. She said in a low tone. "Forgive me for asking—"

"You may ask me anything, my queen."

Her head tipped to the side. "Do you have a name?"

Oh, that. Yes, he realized. He probably should have told her. "My caliph named me Serhan," he said formally. "All things a Dead Man has and is come from the caliph. If I had another name before that, before I was orphaned and adopted into the caliph's service—that, I do not know."

She looked up at him. "Serhan," she said, tasting it. Then, "Would you mind if I used that name? Sometimes? In privacy?"

His mouth dried so it was hard to speak, but somehow he managed to say, "I think I would like that very much."

THE COUNCIL OF WAR WAS OVER VERY QUICKLY, BECAUSE THEY HAD SO little information. Mostly, the time was spent assigning roles. The one distraction was the bearded vultures, of which—it turned out—there were a dozen or so. The Dead Man had known about the one in the throne room. Now he realized that there was a whole family of the gargantuan things, stained red with ochre and hungry for bones.

After the council broke up, he stayed with the queen while she walked the line of them, perched on the gauntleted fists of her austringers, and fed each one a piece of bone from her own hand, that she had dotted with her own blood. He didn't ask the meaning of the ritual: it was plain some royal magic was in play. He simply watched, and waited.

When the queen was done, she dismissed him. With a smile, but unmistakably. "There are things I must attend to in private," she said.

And so he went to find the Gage.

The Gage was, again, on the palace wall. The sturdiest bit of it, standing very still so he could admire the view without cracking the footings. The river coiled smooth and milk-white below, and after the Dead Man came up on him they stood in silence for a little while together.

When the time felt right to talk, though—well, they had killed enough men together by now that the Dead Man did not bother with preamble.

"Have you seen Nizhvashiti recently?"

The Gage tilted his shining egg of a head. "The priest is missing?"

"Maybe," the Dead Man said. "The priest is not immediately obvious, in any case. And has not been for some time. No sign of them at the meeting, though I know Mrithuri sent."

"Run off to the enemy?"

"Do you think so?"

"You do," the Gage said, which wasn't precisely true and also wasn't an answer.

The Dead Man didn't *think* the Godmade was a traitor. It was more that the Dead Man worried what would happen *if* the Godmade was a traitor.

Something like an entire army vanishing, for example? Perhaps that sort of thing?

The Dead Man said, "What are we doing here anyway?"

The Gage shrugged. "You like the rajni."

"Enough to die for?"

"So it would appear."

It was the Dead Man's turn to shrug. "You like the maid of the chamber."

"The maid of the chamber likes me," the Gage said. "I have not yet decided."

He had, though. And the Dead Man knew it. The Gage was a metal man who weighed as much as the rajni's white elephant. Whatever existed between him and Chaeri might not be romance as the Dead Man understood it, but there was a fashion by which all love of a woman served as worship of the Scholar-God. And while love might still be too strong a term, he thought his partner was feeling . . . stirrings . . . of affection and connection.

He sighed and said, "The years pass. Pride fails. You learn to take what is offered."

The Gage turned his head—so the Dead Man would know the Gage regarded him, the Dead Man supposed.

"The years go by," the Gage agreed. "And that pride was gilded ash when you bought it. All we have lost if we walk away now is a little money, and a chivalrous fantasy."

"And a good story."

"Sure," the Gage said. "If we live long enough to tell it."

The Dead Man jerked his chin to the horizon. "You see—sense—anything out there yet?"

"For once it's not raining." The Gage gave that little wobble of his head that meant he was snickering. "You know we're missing something."

"We're always missing something." The Dead Man shrugged. "We're not the heroes of the story. Of any story. We're those guys who wander in during the third act to pick up the dirty work."

"That narrative thing that you call 'the Scholar-God's pen,' you mean."

The Dead Man smiled at a jolt of startled joy. "You have been paying attention after all. But there is another reason to stay here."

"More pressing than nubile queenlings?"

"Yes," said the Dead Man. "I'd stay for her anyway, I think. Though if you left it would be a hard deciding. But remember, old friend: we were sent here by a prophetic Wizard."

The Gage made his gesture of sardonic laughter again. "We could have headed west instead of taking this job." He sounded resigned. It had never been a possibility.

"West. Across the Poison Sea."

"So there's drawbacks." The broad metal shoulders moved on a shrug beneath the rough-spun robes. They were clean. New, the Dead Man noticed. Either the Gage had purchased clothing, or drawn livery from the royal stores, or someone in Mrithuri's household had taken pity on him. The Dead Man had an idea whose hand might be in it. "I don't mind your little queen, you know."

"You're not a jealous Gage, at heart."

"Pain is boring," the Gage said. "And the most boring part about it is that you can't even just decide to do something else instead." He leaned gingerly on the thick stone castellation, folding his enormous cabled arms. "You've mourned your family since I've known you."

"That doesn't stop," the Dead Man said.

"No," the Gage said. "I know. But they wouldn't think less of you, I imagine, for not making the mourning of them your whole life."

The Dead Man snorted with laughter. He leaned beside his friend and said, "You never met my wife."

"I know," the Gage said. "And from the few times you have spoken of her, I think that saddens me."

The skin on the Dead Man's neck shuddered like the flank of a horse twitching off a fly. "We never would have met if she had lived."

"This is true. Because she only could have lived if history had been different. It wasn't your doing, what happened to Zillah."

The Dead Man realized he was holding his breath. He picked at a loose thread in his coat's embroidery and forced himself to stop. The damned thing was threadbare enough already.

He had been silent for a while, contemplating his cuffs, when the Gage said absently, "So we're staying, then."

The Dead Man nodded. "I suppose we are."

THEY STAYED TO WATCH THE SUNSET, THE LOWERING OF THE CAULED Sun beneath the horizon and the lifting of the veil across the Heavenly River, and went inside finally only when Mrithuri Rajni sent for them. She didn't send just anyone, either: it was Ata Akhimah who came out to fetch them.

And the first thing she said, after relaying her summons, was, "Have you seen the Godmade?"

The Dead Man glanced at the Gage, who had in turn inclined his shining ovoid down at the Dead Man. To one who knew him, the metal man's body language gave the distinct impression of a frown. The Dead Man wasn't honestly sure which of them, at that moment, was saying, "I told you so."

"No," the Gage said. "Not in several days."

Ata Akhimah nodded. "We'll look later. For now . . . the rajni wants all of us present for the Ritual of the Red-Stained Wings."

The Dead Man almost asked. But the Gage didn't, and he felt awkward exposing himself as ignorant when nobody else seemed to be, so he held his peace and followed.

The throne room looked as it had before, except it was all but empty of courtiers and there were now a dozen massive perches, their crossbars padded in quilted red leather, set in a pair of offset arcs before the queen's chair of estate. She sat in it cross-legged, still in her plain ivory trousers and robe. Her hands rested on her knees, and her eyes were closed.

Someone had opened vents in the dragonglass vault overhead, long casements between the branches of the stone trees whose boughs made the ribs of the vault. When they were all assembled—the Gage stepping lightly in a gargantuan pair of padded shearling slippers to protect the tiles of the floor—the ropy-armed middle-aged man who seemed to be the head austringer took up the first of the birds, brought it to the center of the throne room, and unhooded it. He stroked its head with a feather, ruffling its roused crest, and held it in place while it settled itself and looked about curiously.

The bird was enormous. Its head, from the hooked tip of the beak to the crested occiput, was as long as the Dead Man's own from top of skull to point of jaw, though considerably narrower. It was shaped like the business end of a hatchet, a heavy bone-splitting thing, and a little tuft of black feathers made a goatee under its chin. The head was crimson—the Dead Man had heard that the birds stained themselves with ochre—with a sharp black stripe across the eye. The breast and legs were also colored like blood, and the feathers of the long wings and tail—the pinions—were charcoal at the edges and crimson near the shaft.

The vulture on the man's gauntlet stood taller than his head. He tilted his arm a little and it fanned wings with a span greater than the Gage's height—and this bird wasn't even the largest of those arrayed on the perches.

The austringer handed the jeweled hood off to one of his journeymen, and supported the elbow of the arm that bore the bird with his other hand. The bird seemed disquieted, fanning its wings and moving its head with a snakelike sway. It lifted a talon as large as a woman's hand and placed it down again, edging along the man's arm until brought up short by the jesses.

The austringer brought the vulture to the queen, walking up to the edge of the dais and levering the bird up to her. It fanned again and began to bate, but even as the wings made their first heavy downstroke, Mrithuri leaned forward without moving her hands or opening her eyes, and seemed to whisper in its ear. And the bird—enormous, with a beak that looked as if it could sever a finger—quieted. In fact, it cocked its head, and seemed to listen.

The Dead Man watched with that odd sensation one gets when discovering something completely unexpected about a new and adored lover. Mrithuri, her eyes still closed, reached down into a pot that rested in her lap and dipped something up on to her fingertips. She offered it to the bird and the Dead Man's pulse quickened: the bird could have snapped her fingers off at the joint.

Instead, the big head dipped ceremoniously. The bearded vulture accepted whatever she offered with surprising gentleness, then began to preen the substance through its feathers, leaving behind fresh streaks of a brighter red. Ochre, yes. And perhaps blood?

The Dead Man was unsurprised when the austringer turned from Mrithuri, lowered his arm, and jerked it up again heavily, releasing the jesses and tossing the bearded vulture into the air.

The bird beat hard to climb, its wings sweeping storms of gold dust from the tiles. Eddies and currents flowed around its feathers, little swirls of precious, shimmering metal flooding from its wingtips. The pinions brushed the Dead Man's arm, and he could imagine the force with which it could strike if it cared to.

Then it was higher, over the heads of the assembled, and folding itself tight to arrow through the open casement.

The process was repeated with each vulture. The Dead Man watched with growing concern as Mrithuri seemed to tire with every word she whispered to each of them. She swayed heavily by the time the fourth bird was launched, and after the austringer brought her the fifth one, there was a pause while Chaeri was sent for the Eremite serpents.

While she waited, the Dead Man took it upon himself to approach her with a cup of wine. She accepted gratefully, sipped it, and said, "It would be easier if I could use the throne."

Her gesture indicated the molten-looking mountain of gold behind her.

The Dead Man realized that from where he stood, he could hear quiet conversations from the others in the room. He glanced up at the arches overhead: a whispering vault, that brought sound to this focal point. So the monarch could stay informed. He glanced up at the Peacock Throne, a massive, invasive presence behind them. The *real* focal point was probably up there. The spot this chair of estate stood upon was likely intended for a queen, or a trusted counselor.

Well, a queen sat here now. With more on her hands than merely advising a raja and bearing his heirs.

Such things as the vault were common in Asitaneh architecture: it was one of the tricks of his own people's Wizards. He'd never before seen it in a realm that stood outside the influence of the Scholar-God. These Sarath-Sahali were not, in fact, barbarians, no matter how heathen their gods.

"It helps you talk to vultures?" the Dead Man asked.

"Among other things," she said. She gave him back the empty cup.

He frowned, remembering her bones so close beneath the skin. "When was the last time you ate?"

She waved a hand. "I'm not hungry."

Not with the snakebite in your veins. But he swallowed his sigh and persisted. "A sweetmeat or two during our discussion of tactics? And what since then?"

She didn't answer, just frowned. But then she said, "All right," and sent Hnarisha for a plate of food. The little castellan gave the Dead Man half a grateful smile before he went.

"Where are your guards?" he asked next.

She sighed. "Readying the city for siege, Dead Man."

"It comforts me not."

"You will have to be my guardian, then."

It was meant to mollify him, and she made her eyes twinkle when she said it. But he nodded, accepting the charge most seriously. So he would, be her guardian, then.

THE FOOD ARRIVED BEFORE CHAERI DID, AND THE DEAD MAN AND Hnarisha between them managed to coddle her into eating almost half of it.

Chaeri seemed to take a long time. The queen grew irritated. Then the snakes were there, and Mrithuri again set her will to charming vultures. She needed the snakebite one more time before she was done.

The Dead Man did what he could for her and tried to ignore the way each successive bite spread wider red patches on the bandage she pressed to her chest. He carried water to her. Sometimes the humble act of carrying water is the finest service one can do.

And there was worship in that, too: he carried water for the queen, and for his lover, and for the Scholar-God herself. All in the same person of this stubborn young heathen whom he was growing to so admire.

At last, all the vultures were launched. Mrithuri sagged against the jewel-set back of her uncomfortable-looking rectangular chair of estate, her spine curved so her belly looked sharply hollow. Her complexion had gone not just waxy, but greenish. She still attempted to wave away the cup of broth Hnarisha and Yavashuri brought to her, but the Aezin Wizard insisted as well, with an appeal to Mrithuri's responsibility to her subjects.

Through his worry, he found himself admiring Akhimah's skill at wrangling royalty. There was an art to it, one that the Dead Man had excelled at in his day. Remind, suggest, make them think it was their own responsibility or their own idea. Ata Akhimah was a pretty good politician.

When she stepped away, the empty cup that had held broth in her hands, the Dead Man went to her. He lowered his voice to a murmur that would not carry, even under the whispering vault overhead, and said in her ear, "Are we done?"

She shook her head. "That was only the beginning."

He wished he could say, "But she's not strong enough for this!" and have it mean anything. The truth was, he had no claim on her—she had offered none. And the truth was, he admitted, that he did not know what she was strong enough to do or not do, and he had no place making that decision for her.

He withdrew to stand beside the Gage, who was waiting as quietly as a statue so as not to damage the infrastructure. They stood side by side, arms folded and legs braced in a nearly identical posture. The Dead Man breathed. The Gage did not.

Mrithuri pulled herself up and laid her hands on her knees once more. She squared her shoulders and settled herself with the air of one pulling on a cloak of determination. She heaved a breath and closed her eyes.

The generals drew close. Madhukasa actually crept up on the dais, though he crouched beside the queen so his head never overtopped hers. Pranaj stood at the foot, a stylus ready. Ata Akhimah and Hnarisha brought in armloads of maps and laid them on a table that had been made ready as the perches were being cleared away. The apprentice and journeyman austringers were gone: only the master remained.

Mrithuri spoke. Her voice was not the strained rasp that the Dead Man expected, but low, detached, dreamy. Like someone in an opium trance, almost—as if she were speaking from far away, relaying back experiences that were happening to someone else, somewhere else.

"We go high," she said. "Above bowshot. We will be safe from arrows."

And from pistols, the Dead Man thought. He put a hand on the butt of one of his own brace, which had been returned to him. They were not so accurate when shooting upward, as his experience with the ice-wyrm had reminded him. Though there was no true safety: somebody could always get lucky, even at extreme range.

"The wind is from the west," she said. "But as we climb, it sheers northward. The world is bright and the sky is high. Some of us ride the wind. Some of us fight it. We climb. We part. We spin.

"We see no soldiers, none but our own men. Our people flee: there are boats on the river, so many carts and walkers on the roads. All come this way, running before the army from the west and the north. The south is peaceful.

"We can see the trail, what an army might have left. But it ends. It just ends. As if they had vanished in their own furrows and ruts. We see the trail end near Star Cross, where the roads are paved. Could they have split up along the roads?

"We see—now that is strange."

The Dead Man held his breath. He wanted to interrupt, to leap forward and demand the next words. He slipped a hand inside his coat and pinched the skin of his arm.

"Horses," Mrithuri said. "Horses, running fast. They are tired, and covered in the dust of red clay mud. They have riders. Not all of them, but some. They are coming hard for the city. I see them, two men and a woman. The woman is old, too old to ride so hard. One of the men wears a Rasan Wizard's coat."

Then her voice went strange and hard, dreamy no longer but precise, razorlike, with inflections the Dead Man recognized immediately. She said, "There is a skull. A stone within it."

No one in the room moved, or spoke. Or perhaps even breathed, except for the young queen, who caught her breath on a terrible gasp and arched as if in spasm before shouting. "Where is the stone in the skull? Why have you not listened to my warning? You cannot prevail without it!"

The Dead Man, his heart seizing in his breast, glanced frantically over at Ata Akhimah. The Wizard was looking at him and the Gage. She nodded: she heard the inflection as well. It was the Eyeless One, the Wizard so powerful she had become the de facto ruler of the Mother of Markets, the greatest city in the world, mighty Messaline. The Eyeless One, who was sometime teacher to Akhimah and sometime patron to the Gage and the Dead Man, was speaking through the queen.

Mrithuri managed one more breath and then collapsed forward, her forehead bending until it pressed her folded shins. She shuddered, long and hard and repeatedly, then seemed for a moment to relax. The Dead Man started forward, not caring if everyone in the room noticed his concern. So did the Wizard.

They reached the queen at the same moment. She was slack, her flesh chill when the Dead Man, greatly daring, touched her. But she roused to his caress and blinked dark, wet eyes that were wholly human and unconfused at him and Akhimah.

"Drink this," Akhimah said. Hnarisha had placed a mug of sugary spiced tea thick with creamy milk in her hand. She pushed it under Mrithuri's nose. Mrithuri turned her face away, but Akhimah was insistent, and though she was green and bloodless with fatigue and nausea, she eventually accepted it and drank.

A little color came back into her face.

"Those people are important," she said. "The ones on the horses. We must find them and bring them in."

Lieutenant General Pranaj was already moving toward the doors.

"The Godmade," she said. "Have you—I saw them." She shook her head. "In the gardens. Where is everyone? I need my maidens! Have them attend me, now!"

"What did you see?" the Gage asked, from his place beside the wall. "About the Godmade?"

"A stone," Mrithuri said. "A stone in the skull." She shook her head again, as if aware that she was making little sense, as if trying to shake all her thoughts into their proper channels so they would run smooth. "We must search the gardens," she said. "The Godmade is out there. Very ill. Perhaps it is not too late."

She started up from her chair of estate. She staggered and would have fallen hard down the tiled steps if the Dead Man had not steadied her.

She leaned heavily on him until he had helped her down. He glanced nervously at Syama, half-expecting the bear-dog to rise from her place when he laid hands on her mistress, but the animal regarded him with preternaturally intelligent eyes.

Mrithuri set herself back from him. With a visible effort of will she made herself stand on her own.

"My queen," the Dead Man said. "Perhaps you should rest now."

Tiredly, she shook her head.

Hnarisha walked up the steps. "Your Abundance," he said. "You must take a loan of my strength."

He held out a hand. She took it, and the Dead Man thought she was trying not to seem eager, or was both eager and ashamed. Hnarisha lifted his chin, gazing into Mrithuri's eyes, and for a moment a current flowed between them. The Dead Man might have identified it as attraction, except at the end of it Hnarisha sagged to sit on the steps and Mrithuri stood taller.

"What strange verse is this?" the Dead Man asked.

"The Sun Within gives us strength," said the odd little man. When he looked up at the Dead Man, his eyes shimmered as if with tears.

Mrithuri, in any case, descended the steps more easily.

Chaeri and Yavashuri had come in, either in response to Mrithuri's called summons or to someone running out to fetch them. There was a hurried consultation as Mrithuri ordered them to have the gardens searched, and Yavashuri went to make sure it happened. Then she turned to General Madhukasa. "I know it is not your duty," she told the general formally. "But will you tell my chief of staff to make refreshments for guests available as quickly as possible? Those riders will be at the gate by the time Pranaj gets there. Ata Akhimah, go down as well. There is a Wizard with them, and perhaps despite your different traditions he will find your presence collegial. Gage, Dead Man, I would ask you to join those in the gardens, in case there is an enemy or some other such trouble there."

General Madhukasa bowed, more formal and stern than most of Mrithuri's court. He was an older man, and the Dead Man judged he might be a holdover from her grandfather's day, when he would have been one of the young radicals, no doubt.

"Chaeri," Mrithuri said. "Bring me my serpents once more."

"Your Abundance—" the Dead Man said, Ata Akhimah in chorus with him.

The queen straightened herself. The Dead Man pretended he did not feel how hard she leaned on his arm, despite whatever help Hnarisha had offered her. It had apparently been his best effort, as he was crouched, head in hands, like a man who had drunk so much the room was spinning. Mrithuri had burned through reserves he could not easily replenish.

"I am the Good Daughter," Mrithuri said. "I will do my duty to my people, even though it be terrible. Even though it be hard. I will rest when there is time to rest, my good guardians." She said the last in a lowered tone, as if to soften the blow. "For now, see to it that my word is done."

She turned away at once to issue new commands.

THE DEAD MAN WOULD HAVE MOVED FASTER THROUGH THE GARDENS than the Gage. Faster too than the small army of servants behind them. But the Gage seemed to have a sixth sense—or perhaps, in the Gage's case, it would be more accurate to call it his twenty-sixth sense. And so it was the Dead Man following the metal man's ponderous tread through rain-softened flower beds.

"Do you hear the Godmade breathing?" the Dead Man asked once.

The Gage, sunk to his ankles in rich black mud, shook his head. The Heavenly River shone above them, a winding light that crowned the Gage's gleaming with a brilliant diadem.

"It's more like a . . . like a smell," he said.

They proceeded more quickly. Spots of river-light filtered through leaves and blossoms, flickered over them like intangible fireflies. Under the shade of a weeping tree whose cascade of scarlet-orange blooms called to mind some firefall of a candelabra, they found a crumpled shape.

The Godmade had grown so thin that at first the Dead Man could not see the shape within the robe, and thought he was looking at a length of black cloth dropped carelessly, crumpled and sodden with the rain. He was still moving when the Gage stopped short, and he ran right into the metal man's immovable arm. The Gage did not rock or tremble: it was as if the blow had not fallen at all.

The Dead Man realized what he was looking at as his eyes resolved wet, dark olive skin from wet, black cloth. The Godmade's hand was a curved claw beside the knife-edge of skin drawn tight over the bone of the jaw. The lips were pulled back from a rictus grin. The gold orb of the artificial eye gleamed richly, as did an array of jewels that the Dead Man had never seen before. Golden rings were set with garnets and emeralds. A diadem of twisted ruddy gold that glittered with diamonds and more emeralds pressed into the shaved skin of the head. A spill of heavy chains slumped about the twiglike neck. A clatter of faceted bangles on the visible wrist, gold and glass intermingled like the ones Mrithuri wore.

The Dead Man made the sign of the pen, not even realizing what he had been doing until his hand returned, slack, to his side.

"Go look," the Gage said quietly, holding out his massive, powerful, useless hands. "See if there is breath within."

The Dead Man gathered himself and stepped forward, the wet grass dragging at his feet. Though it hadn't rained in quite some time (by the standards of the wet season), the ground was still sodden, especially beneath the tree. And the Godmade was sodden too. The body—if it was a body—had lain here since before the storm.

The Dead Man crouched, reaching out before he could think about it too much, and touched the Godmade's wrist.

It was like touching chilled leather. The only moisture was from the rain, which had beaded as if on wax. There was no pulse. There was not even any sense of flesh or vein between the hide and bone.

The Dead Man shook his head. He picked up a slender crystalline vial that seemed to have fallen with its stopper from the Godmade's fingers. It smelled of something medicinal, resinous, acrid. It made his eyes tear up even through the veil, and he hastily put both pieces down again and scrubbed his fingers on the grass. "It's been too late for a while."

"Shit," said the Gage.

"Where in the word of God do you suppose all this jewelry came from? Has Nizhvashiti been carrying it with them all along?"

"They told Druja they had gold."

Others were finding them. Members of Mrithuri's household were drawing up at the edge of the tree's canopy, a little behind the invisible frontier between life and death, observer and participant, marked by the Gage's bulk.

The Dead Man reached to adjust the Godmade's robe, thinking to draw an edge across the frozen face and offer the cadaver some courteous illusion of privacy.

The cadaver raised its jeweled head.

The Dead Man scrambled back so fast that he wasn't even sure how he came to be crouched beside the Gage, a pistol in one hand, the other plunged deep into wet grass and earth, holding on as if the world were trying to buck him off and he had clenched his fingers in its mane. Later, he would be unable to remember his flight except in the nightmares that sometimes attended him, where he was dragging himself with terrible slowness through cloying air and clinging grass. But by the time he was stationary and focused again, the Godmade was sitting upright. Just sitting: not gathered, not seeming ready to lunge.

The Dead Man held his ground and his fire. His racing heart was steadying, his own pulse becoming something he could hear around.

The Godmade's dead eye swerved, rolled wildly, then fixed on the Gage and the Dead Man. Its teeth flashed through dry lips in a permanent smile. Its movements were alien, sticklike, as if operated by an unskilled puppeteer.

"I have been beyond and seen the true world," it whispered, a voice without breath, without resonance. "Seek the Carbuncle. Seek the Mother of Exiles, blind and in her singing catacomb. Time is short, and more is at stake than kingdoms. Something stirs. Something vast and cruel stirs, to the east, beneath the sea. Your destiny lies with the Origin of Storms."

THE GODMADE NEEDED ASSISTANCE TO STAND, AND THE GAGE DID NOT trust himself to be delicate enough to handle it. So the Dead Man holstered his pistol and stepped forward again. He shuddered, skin crawling, but he held out his hand. What sort of Dead Man couldn't handle a dead saint, after all?

The thing was light as a husk: the rain-sodden robes weighed more, as did the jewelry. He wondered why the regalia was important, but he could not find the courage to ask.

Once it was upright, though, the Godmade—the Dead Man did not think he could bring himself to call the revenant Nizhvashiti anymore—walked easily enough, if haltingly. It was coltish in learning to use its body again, as if the limbs were new but the instinct was there. Once inside, there was a hurried consultation, as nobody was exactly willing to release the thing on its own recognizance to return to its rooms for dry clothes. The Gage agreed to go with it, which the Dead Man thought safest—if any creature in the palace were fit to handle a revenant cleric, it was either the Gage or Ata Akhimah—while the Dead Man returned to the queen to bring her the news.

Staring and whispers followed the revenant away, and the Dead Man noticed people leaned away from him as well, as if he carried some contagion from his contact with the Godmade now.

Mrithuri was on her chair of estate again, breathing easier, it seemed, and now dressed regally again, though the courtiers had not been re-admitted. Someone had brought her a glass of wine, and she turned it with surprising dexterity between fingers elongated monstrously with filigree fingerstalls. She sipped with the air of one downing medicine because they know it will make a loved one happy. Syama raised her head, ears pricked in a friendly fashion, as he came toward the queen's chair. The aroma that reached the Dead Man as he approached the queen was spicy and enticing.

His stomach growled, and she grinned at him wearily. The mask that would have covered the bottom part of her face with a vixen's snarl was lowered on relaxed strings to rest over her bosom. "When was the last time you ate something?"

He tried to remember. It took him long enough that she had already waved Hnarisha over and seen him provided with a wine cup of his own, less elaborate than the fluted crystal of hers. But easier to hold, and of larger capacity.

The wine was redolent of apricots, and the first sip told him it was strong. It had the velvet texture and soft heat of something that had once been sweet, and was now rich in alcohol. The Dead Man drank cautiously, but it still heated his empty belly and went to his head.

The color was amber in the transparent crystal. The bouquet, as he warmed it in his mouth, developed notes of nutmeg and lemon peel. The body was full and the aroma complex. He had heard of the stone-fruit wines of the Lotus Kingdoms but never tasted one before, as they were fragile and did not survive shipment either through the wild and sea-monster infested passages of the Arid Sea, or through the equally wild and still more wintry passage that the Dead Man himself had just endured. A frozen wine pleased no one.

This one pleased him greatly. It steadied him, and he could see concentric ripples lapping the walls of the glass, where the wine clung and left syrupy traces. But he paused after a single savoring sip to give Mrithuri his report on the fate of the Godmade. He reported, too, about the cryptic prophecy: the Godmade's mention of the Carbuncle, the Mother of Exiles, and something stirring beneath the sea to the east.

The queen accepted the news of the Godmade's resurrection with lifted brows. The placid expression above her mask led him to remark, "This event gives you no pause?"

Mrithuri frowned thoughtfully. "It is a miracle of duty," she said finally. "The Godmade's service is stronger than the lure of the afterlife, and so they remain. The Good Daughter does what must be done to help her family."

"Even if it is terrible?"

"Especially if it is terrible," Mrithuri said. "That's what makes her the Good Daughter. She serves her duty above all. She is . . . she is the actions she takes, the marks she leaves behind. She exists in the results of her acts. I would think you'd understand."

He did. Duty above anything else. And then the lifetime regret for choices untaken. "The Gage told me there's a word like that, in the Dragon-tongue. Which is not quite the killing speech of Erem."

"I was told that it is truer to think of one's self as a verb, rather than a noun."

He sighed and looked at his hands. "It's best if one's duty lies where one's heart does also."

"This is so." She smiled, and added archly, "And think: how ironic that a Dead Man should fear the dead."

He laughed and admitted it was true, and felt . . . not lighter, precisely. But more settled.

She drank more wine—it seemed to steady her, to take the edge off the nervy intelligence loaned her by the snakebite—and frowned. "The Bitter Sea?" she asked. "Or the Sea of Storms?"

"The revenant did not say," the Dead Man admitted. "But it did mention the 'Origin of Storms.'"

Mrithuri held out her glass for more wine. It didn't seem to be addling her wits. "Well, whatever it has become, unless it rampages through the castle tearing out throats, it's a problem for a different day. We should bring our wits to bear on the issues at hand: the riders at the gates, and the disappearing army."

Hnarisha leaned in and said, "I've had a page from Ata Akhimah and General Pranaj, Your Abundance. The riders at the gates have been received. They are the court Wizard of your cousin Sayeh Rajni, her captain of the guard, and an Asitaneh poetess who is quite elderly, I am told, and unwell with hard riding."

Mrithuri's relaxed demeanor tightened slightly, though she did not shift in her chair. Rapidly, she drank the rest of the wine, and handed the glass to Hnarisha. "Send me my maid."

A woman came in. It was not Chaeri, the one who was pursuing the Gage, but the older and steadier-seeming one, Yavashuri. She helped the queen with her mask, which would have been impossible for the queen alone to negotiate without first removing all of her fingerstalls. It changed her face in ways the Dead Man found disturbing—the bright curves of a young woman's jaw and chin lost behind the face of a snarling vixen—and he looked away. Nobody had ever said that being the lover of a ruler was going to be easy.

He drew aside, but kept the wine.

Still no courtiers. There was no one present except the queen, her personal secretary-slash-castellan, the Dead Man, the maid, and the bear-dog. The long hall rang empty with his footsteps as he stepped to the side, a guard's position near the dais. He still had his pistols, though, and he knew that General Madhukasa and Ata Akhimah would be coming in with the visitors. Perhaps with some of the palace guards as well, if they were all lucky.

The Dead Man realized that he didn't have a lot of trust in any of Mrithuri's multitude of cousins. Even this one. Although if she was sending messengers of such dignity, the news must be vital indeed.

The tall doors cracked, and the visitors came into the throne room in a swirl of trail dust as much as gold dust. They were indeed flanked by the general, and by Ata Akhimah. The foreign Wizard's black petaled coat flared about his thighs as he strode forward briskly. The ripple of the skirts showed themselves frayed and in places torn with hard travel, but he was holding himself proudly. Two of Mrithuri's guards carried the elderly woman, her clothes also tattered and worn. The foreign guard captain limped, his whiskers bristling from inattention, but kept up with the others.

When they reached the spot before the throne, the two men knelt—the guard captain somewhat painfully. Mrithuri gazed down at them, her expression disguised behind the vixen's snarl. She did not waste time demanding further obeisance, and directed Hnarisha to bring the old woman a chair. Madhukasa crossed without being told to take up a place on the opposite side of the chair of estate from the Dead Man, giving him an approving eye-flicker as he did so.

The bear-dog stirred behind the throne, but did not rise. While that was happening, Ata Akhimah said, "Rajni, Tsering-la, Wizard; Vidhya, captain of the guard of Ansh-Sahal; and Ümmühan, a poetess"—the Wizard glanced at the poetess as if to be sure she was getting the information right—"formerly of Asitaneh, now an itinerant."

The poetess smiled toothlessly and dipped her chin in acknowledgment. If she was not strong enough to walk after a hard ride of—apparently—many days, she was at least apparently more than strong enough to sit proudly upright. Strictly speaking, introducing the guests would have been Hnarisha's job, but under the current chaotic conditions it was probably better not to stand on ceremony.

Syama raised her massive, heavily striped head and stared fixedly at the poetess.

"Your Abundance," the Wizard said. "We come as emissaries from your royal cousin Sayeh Rajni of Ansh-Sahal, on the shores of the Bitter Sea. She asks us to beg your indulgence. There has been a tremendous tragedy in Ansh-Sahal: a terrible shaking of the earth, and a poisonous fumarole has erupted beneath the sea. We need your help, Great Rajni, as the guardian of the Peacock Throne."

Syama levered herself to her feet, a play in muscularity. She stepped down the dais risers with such fluidity that it seemed she poured herself. Mrithuri, in the middle of a word, stopped herself and watched as the bear-dog padded past the Rasan Wizard and the captain of the guard. They both seemed too stunned to react. The bear-dog advanced on the poetess. Ümmühan flinched back in her chair, but did not seem capable of rising.

The bear-dog opened her enormous maw and closed it over the poetess's upper arm in a motion that was both controlled—if not gentle—and so fast that the Dead Man's battle-trained eye almost did not see it happen. The animal growled.

He rested his fingers on the stock of his pistol, but did not draw. All his courage was turned to restraining himself, stopping the reflexive clutch of his hand. This was not his decision to make, any more than it had been—

Any more than it had been in Asitaneh. If he admitted it to himself.

What was worse than being culpable for destruction? He knew the answer to that, and that answer was: being helpless before it. Being robbed of even having a choice. He'd seen grown men and women destroy comfortable lives because they felt trapped.

He himself, he thought, had never had such choices in his youth. And never really wanted one. And yet here he was making them. Again and again and again.

"Syama," Mrithuri said past his shoulder. "Release her."

Slowly, Syama opened her jaws. She stepped back—just a single pace—and did not sit down, but regarded her new enemy with a chary eye.

"Poetess," the queen said, with a show of elaborate gestures indicating remorse, "please accept our profound apologies for the behavior of our subject."

Syama curled a lip.

Mrithuri said, "Syama, down."

The bear-dog gave the queen a dubious look. The queen tilted her head and stared at the animal over the top of her mask. The dog lay down.

The poetess put a hand on the arm of her chair and began to lever herself shakily to her feet. She stepped forward, trembling.

The bear-dog watched her unhappily. Bereft that her judgment had been questioned.

Choices, the Dead Man thought. *They make asses of the best of us.*

"Your Abundance," the old woman said, in a voice that carried with the power of a trained bard despite her years and her obvious infirmity. "I am not one of your people. I am not Sahal. I am not Sarath. But I come in concert with one of your people, and with another alien who serves your royal cousin"—she gestured to the kneeling two, who had not budged—"to beg your assistance for her shattered people. Tell me only, Mrithuri Rajni—your cousin Sayeh Rajni would ask only—is it possible?"

Mrithuri seemed to deliberate. Her eyes grew creases behind the mask as if she frowned. She said, "I and my kingdom will do whatever we can to be of aid to her and her kingdom in their time of need. What is most important now? Shelter, food?"

Ümmühan—and the Dead Man could barely believe that this was the legendary poetess, that she was even still alive, no matter that he was in her presence—stepped to the base of the dais. She bowed over her knees again and said, "My rajni, that lies in the future." The Dead Man was already moving as she straightened, aware that something terrible was wrong. Moving—moving, too slow, not fast enough—

As the old woman leveled her pistol at Mrithuri and cried out, "Tonight, the queen dies!" the Dead Man threw himself between the firearm and the woman. He strained as if in a dream—

There was a terrible noise. He would have expected the shattering of windows, but the vaults above were dragonglass, and they did not rain shards on everyone. All to the best, given that dragonglass had poison in it. It was all he had time to expect, because something struck him on the chest with the force of a mule's kick, and when he next knew where he was, he was slumped on the steps of the dais with Madhukasa sprawled across his legs and a ringing in his ears.

The acrid scent of powder filled the air. He tried to drag himself upright, levering himself out from under the dead weight pinning his shins and feet, and the stab of pain made his senses contract to a tunnel and gray. An indeterminate time passed—not too long, because when he regained his thoughts again he could still hear Syama snarling over her prey. He didn't think the poetess would be firing a weapon again.

He looked down and saw his red coat stained, in patches, redder.

When his head stopped spinning this time, he saw the shaved head of the Godmade bent over him. No jewelry now: just a black tunic and simple black trousers and bony, horny bare feet loosely harbored in knotted-twine sandals. There was a faint scent of decay, and a stronger one of incense.

He recoiled from the revenant instinctively, then braced himself with the memory of Mrithuri's words. *How ironic . . .*

"Hold still," the Godmade said. "You're alive because the ball passed through Madhukasa before it got to you, but it still cracked your sternum."

"The general?"

The Godmade shook its head. "A great loss to the nation."

The Dead Man struggled to see the throne room. Yavashuri had come into the room, and was vainly trying to set the general's corpse in order. What the bear-dog had done to the poetess didn't bear description, except the body she was standing over, snarling, didn't look like that of an eighty-year-old woman any more. She mantled the remains of a lean man, young probably, though it was hard to be more accurate with his face and his throat both torn away.

It was also only one of two bodies in the audience chamber, the other being that of the noble general. This seemed wrong to the Dead Man, though he could not say exactly why. He struggled to sit farther upright, and the icy hand of a revenant on his shoulder restrained him.

"Wait," the terrible thing said. "A moment more."

"Where are the foreigners?" the Dead Man asked. And then, as if someone might not know who he meant, said, "The Wizard and the guard captain?"

"Vanished," Hnarisha said from beside him. "When Syama murdered the poetess."

"It was an illusion," Ata Akhimah said. She crouched beside the body. She lifted what looked like an amulet in her hand, then the drape of a length of cloth in deepest indigo. "What we saw wasn't real. Only one of those people even existed, and he wasn't a famous poet and historian. Someone gave the young man this amulet, with a spell of deception on it."

"How in all the hells did that get past you?" Hnarisha snarled, starting forward. The Godmade restrained him with an upraised hand, though—not touching, just barring—and he stopped short and did not challenge it. The Dead Man didn't blame the confidential secretary for that decision.

Akhimah stood up again, looking lost. "I don't know," she said. "How did it get past you? And while we're at it, how does an entire army disappear out of its footsteps?"

Hnarisha crumpled. "This is a phantasm. A delusion."

Mrithuri stood beside her chair, her arms wrapped across her chest. The flimsy fabric of her drape bunched and snagged between her fingerstalls. But her voice was steady, even chill. "The illusions of a sorcerer."

The Godmade, seeming contented with the Dead Man's progress, floated effortlessly erect on legs thinner than stilts. The Dead Man probed the wound over his breastbone with a finger and felt nothing there but new, sore skin and some bruising. He sat up as the Godmade stalked toward Ata Akhimah. Any shakiness, any coltishness was gone; now the revenant moved like some enormous wading bird with iridescent ebony feathers.

It reached out—like a wading bird—and with thick, horny, over-long fingernails plucked something from the sleeve of Akhimah's coat. The hand moved back, pulling, and something near-invisible stretched between sleeve and pinch. "Here's your problem," it said.

They all leaned in and looked. It was a thread. No, a hair. Gray and long, slightly wavy. An old person's hair. "Sewn into the cuff," the Godmade said. "To make even you, Wizard, see what you were intended to see. I would guess it was the woman this hair was plucked from."

"Someone is holding the real Ümmühan captive?" the Dead Man said, stunned. It was a blasphemy he could hardly imagine, to so constrain a poetess.

The Godmade shrugged bony shoulders. "That is one theory, yes."

Yavashuri said, quietly, "Someone prepared the way for the assassin."

"Someone," Hnarisha said, face thunderous, "stitched that into the Wizard's seam unobserved."

"Someone within the household," Mrithuri said calmly, before the Dead Man could make the accusation.

"Some such person, aye."

Mrithuri asked, "Do you think the news they imparted was the truth?"

"Something evil under the eastern sea," Ata Akhimah said.

The Dead Man forced himself to stop poking his finger into the hole in his shirt, and the new hole in his red coat. Servants arrived to carry the general's body out on a stretcher. He still could not look at the uncanny form of the Godmade without a shudder, but gratitude leavened the horror of the undead priest a little. "If the assassin's purpose was to get close to you, Rajni, then would they have risked a lie we might have known for such? They can't know what information you had."

The silence stretched.

"Poor Sayeh," Mrithuri said.

They might have stared at each other all night, the Dead Man thought, but a sudden thudding in the hallway roused them all—all the living, anyway, and those of the dead that were mobile. Including himself, rubbing at the sore spot beneath the new hole in his coat with his left hand.

The Godmade dropped a warm object into his hand. He glanced down, and found the lead ball that had been dug from his now-vanished wound seconds before. He dropped it into his pocket to contemplate later.

Syama roused and hackled. But the Dead Man didn't bother drawing one of his own pistols. Though the even thudding sounded like the blows of the Scholar-God's own pile driver, the Dead Man knew what it was, and felt bad for the floor.

Instants later, the Gage appeared in the doorway, thundering to a halt. "Gunfire," he said.

"Resolved," the Dead Man replied. He gestured to the silvery thread that the Godmade still dangled aloft. "In favor of a more complicated problem."

The Godmade turned to the Gage in obvious disapproval—or as obvious as an emotion could be, when mounted upon the frozen features of a mummified cadaver.

"You were to go," it said.

Which was when the Dead Man realized that the Godmade had returned to the throne room without the Gage.

"I heard gunfire," the Gage replied.

"Wait," said the Dead Man. "Where were you going?"

The Gage looked guiltily at the Godmade. Then, not at the Dead Man, but at Mrithuri. "To the Singing Towers, Your Abundance. As we had discussed."

The queen snapped her elongating fingerstalls off her hands in disgust. They scattered to the dais, pealing like tiny bells, for they were true silver. She dragged the fox muzzle off her face and tore a half-dozen combs from her elaborate coiffure while pulling the straps clear. She cast that down too, though Hnarisha caught it where she tossed it and set it down more gently. She appeared not to notice. "I thought that was my decision," she said dryly.

The Gage stepped forward into the audience chamber, walking softly. Bits of cracked tile from the corridor scattered from his feet anyway. He said, "One too many prophecies."

The Dead Man felt his face curling into a snarl. "You were going without me?"

The Gage rocked back slightly—a flinch, and a significant one. "The war. One of us has to stay. And you can't go where I need to go, to find the Carbuncle. Dragon-poison is nothing to me, little friend."

He shrugged, like a mountain shrugging.

"Rajni," the Dead Man said in appeal. He was proud of himself that he remembered not to use her name in public. Even when his heart felt it was swollen with some unclean life within, something that was slitting it open with razored claws merely to escape. "You must not permit—"

She silenced him with a gesture of her naked hand. It wasn't a cruel gesture, and she caught his eye as she made it, but it was final.

She was not the first queen who had broken his heart.

She looked down from her chair of estate and said, "So we're sending him to the land of the dragons."

"Long-dead dragons," the Dead Man argued. "Alone?"

"One of my vultures will accompany him. So we will be able to reach him."

He started to protest again.

She shushed him with a raised finger. "The thing you must understand is that there are no nouns in the language of dragons. There are only verbs. *Things* do not exist. Only forces. Only actions."

This time, her pause seemed to indicate that she wanted an answer. But nothing could ever be plain. The Dead Man pursed his lips and said, "Is that true?"

She shrugged. "It sounds pretty. Prettiness is a kind of truth. But

I must be a *force* now, you see? And not a person. There will be time afterwards, if we survive, for simply *being*. Ruthlessness is not so much an option as a means of survival now."

He did see.

He looked away.

His attention was drawn by a heavy scraping. He turned almost slowly enough to make it seem that it was that sound that had made him drop his gaze.

Chaeri, cursing mildly, was somewhat ineffectually dragging the chair the false Ümmühan had sat upon over to a bemused Gage. She was a little clumsy, perhaps with the poppy she'd been taking to sleep since she killed Mahadijia.

"I could help you with that," said the Gage.

She snorted and set it down beside him. A lock of her hair had escaped. She pushed it away with the back of her hand and then laid that hand upon the Gage's arm to steady herself. He did not move as she hopped nimbly onto the chair. She stood on tiptoe, and planted a firm, generous kiss upon the polished ovoid of his head.

She left the perfect smudge of her mouth on his flawless mirror.

The Dead Man did not think the Gage minded it there. He tilted his head and seemed to be looking at her, more directly than anything the Dead Man was used to seeing. Whatever he might have said, though, was silenced by a loud, sizzling hiss and a streak of light across the sky behind the glass vault overhead. And then another, and another, until all the starry river of the night seemed to rain fire down on them.

For all their brilliance, for all that some of them left weird billows of smoke behind them, not one touched the ground.

"Falling stars," the Dead Man whispered, awed.

"A portent," the Godmade replied. It glanced from Ata Akhimah to the queen. "The Heavenly River is raining. The Good Daughter speaks to us. A warning."

"The army," Mrithuri said. Not a shocked cry, but a weary statement of infinite resignation.

Everyone looked at her. She had one hand knuckled against her eyes. The other fingers curled sharply into the arm of the chair of estate. The Dead Man longed to go and take those hands and cradle them between his own.

"How the hell did they get here so fast?" Mrithuri asked, her voice not so much afraid as offended. "And without anyone noticing?"

"Phantasm," Hnarisha said, tiredly. "Illusion."

Ata Akhimah nodded. "That is extremely powerful sorcery."

"What?" Chaeri squeaked, face blank and eyes wide. "Rajni. Your birds?"

"We see clearly," Mrithuri answered. She lowered that hand and opened her eyes. "The enemy is here. At the gate, very nearly. Fortunately we already sent the guards and soldiers to man the defenses. They will not merely walk in."

She looked at Ata Akhimah. The Dead Man saw epiphany on her face before she spoke it. "The dragonglass jewel," she said. "You have it?"

"Preserve us," Ata Akhimah murmured. She produced the thing from her pocket, unwrapped the silk that bound it. It rested on her hand, shimmering, reflecting the streaking light of the showering stars above.

Mrithuri straightened until her height, assisted by the dais, dominated the room. "The Stone in the Skull."

Ata Akhimah's face went slack, then she smiled suddenly, brilliantly. "Of course," she said. "And I call myself a Wizard. Of *course!*"

She held the dragonglass sphere out to the Godmade.

The Godmade cocked its head from one to the other, curiously. "Oh yes," it said. "I see."

Mummified claws plucked the stone up and held it aloft. A light kindled within, a dim green glow. The Dead Man watched, fascinated, expecting the Godmade to reach into its socket and prise out the false golden orb.

But the left hand rose up, and with a swift and savage movement, the Godmade insinuated its claws into the socket of its remaining eye and tore the wet orb free. The Dead Man recoiled from a pop like a cork coming loose from a bottle. Around him, others did the same—even the queen turned her face aside, she who was trained to never give away the slightest facet of her thoughts.

The Godmade dropped the squashed-looking thing into Ata Akhimah's still-outstretched palm with surprising accuracy for a creature that should have just blinded itself, and pressed the dragon-glass orb into the empty socket with an equally sickening sound. It stretched the lids, seeming to settle the foreign object into place, and stood for a moment blinking while the dim light flared and flared, dazzling, pouring from eye socket and nostrils, before fading back to a striking glow.

The Godmade blinked like a shutter over the sun. Something thick and dark, not blood, trickled over the desiccated cheek.

It spoke with satisfaction. "Yes. I believe that *will* be helpful. Let their sorcerer bring illusions before me now!"

Ata Akhimah, unable to look away from the terrible thing in her palm, gulped. "I suppose I'll just go burn this then."

Chaeri, watching stricken from atop her perch on the chair, fainted without further ado. The Gage caught her and lowered her to the tiles very gently.

"Holy writ," the Dead Man breathed.

Mrithuri made no time for prayer. She stood. "Gage," she said, "it is time for you to leave us now. The postern gate, before it is sealed. On your errand, quickly. The rest of us, make ready for war. We will not surrender."

"We know they have a sorcerer," Ata Akhimah said. "Perhaps several. Powerful ones."

The queen smiled starkly. "We know a few tricks of our own. Now to arms, my loves." She made a sweeping gesture.

The Dead Man reached for his gun.

Acknowledgments

Thank you to my agent, Jenn Jackson, her assistant, Michael Curry, and my editor, Beth Meacham, without each of whom this book would not exist. Thank you as well to the entire production team at Tor Books, from my copyeditor, Deanna Hoak, to all the production managers and proofreaders and designers and artists and everybody else involved, and to the publicity team that gets the word out.

Thank you to Shveta Thakrar, Nazia Khatun, Ritu Chaudry, and Asha Srinivasan Shipman, who helped vet the manuscript and provide cultural context.

Additionally, thank you to my Patreon patrons, especially those contributing at a Help Feed The Dog level: Alexis Elder, Graeme Wiliams, Clare Gmur, Brad Roberts, S. P., Hisham El-Far, Noah Richards, Cathy B Lannom, Brooks Moses, Kelly Brennan, Emily Gladstone Cole, Jason Teakle, Dave Pooser, Mary Kay Kare, D Franklin, RiverVox, Heather K, Besha Grey, Jordan Colby, Tiff, Jen Warren, Jenna Kass, Jack Gulick, Sigrid Ellis, and Mur Lafferty.

Thank you to my family, who put up with me.

And thank you to my beloved Scott, who makes it worthwhile.

Massachusetts, August 2016